# The Last Stand Down

**The Last series, Volume 1**

Philip J Bradbury

Published by Philip J Bradbury, 2019.

# The Last Stand Down

When dreams and nightmares collide

[First book in the *The Last* trilogy]

## Philip J Bradbury

Published by: The Write Site, Brisbane, Australia

ISBN- 978-0-6453145-4-0

This book has been recorded as a podcast at:

thelaststanddownpodcast.com

The recording was done by Brisbane Podcasting Centre at:

brisbanepodcastingcentre.com.au

eee ggg

I loved reading it, the polite Englishman getting acquainted with the kiwi tribe in London! And the way of using a novel form to explore some important secrets regarding free energy and the world grid and so on. Very enjoyable read, thank you!

Cornelius van Dorp, author of *Crystal Mission*

A compelling read, becoming fast paced and action packed as the plot thickens. I particularly liked the natural and easy way in which ideas from *A Course In Miracles* popped up in conversations between the characters. Riana Avis, Life Coach, London

Your story is well written. I'm hooked early and see you have a lot more in store for us. I look forward to you writing more.

Craig Bandalin, author of *Just Out Of Sight*

As a publisher in New Zealand, I had the pleasure to meet with Bruce Cathie at his Auckland home. He eventually decided to continue self-publishing his books, rather than have my company do it. He did, however, introduce me to his colleague, Robert Adams, in Whakatane, NZ. There is more about Bruce Cathie at the end of this book.

Robert Adams was former Chairman of the Institute of Electrical & Electronics Engineers, Inc., U.S.A., (N.Z. Section). The article about his *Adams Switched Reluctance Pulsed DC Permanent Magnet Motor Generator* (a machine that created 37% more energy than it used) was published in *Nexus* magazine in January 1993.

Because of Robert's experiences (related here in this book) he was naturally suspicious of me. I would not have seen him without Bruce's introduction. Robert eventually dropped his guard, demonstrated his free-energy machine, running his domestic refrigerator, and asked that I publish the manuscript he had nearly finished writing. Several months later I had not heard from Robert, as he'd promised and, after inquiries, I discovered that he'd died and the whereabouts of his manuscript remains a mystery to this day. The nature of his death in 2006 is a mystery as well.

I have a degree in accounting and economics and studied E F Schumacher and his ideas on intermediate technology, some of which have permeated this book.

I have been a student of *A Course in Miracles* since 2005 and it has transformed my life. That, too, has permeated this book for fear and its weak offspring - anger, bitterness, war and so on - foster nothing but further weakness. Only Love has strength.

Anna and I came to Britain in 2008, ten days after we were married (a long honeymoon, really) and, among other jobs, I was a corporate trainer for a development bank, training senior government officials from developing countries, mainly from Africa.

My daily trek – by foot, tram, train and tube – from our house at Tunstall Road, Croydon, to London, each day, inspired the start of this story. Coming from the beautiful expanses of New Zealand to the drab, daily monotony of England's commuters was a shock I will never forget. Most of them, I suspect, feel they have no choice but to put up with such an existence. I was lucky - I saw choices and took them.

*P. J Bradbury.*

# Arise From The Red Earth

*July 15th, 2014, 5.00 am, Uluru, Australia*

The pale Englishman unfurled from his desert tent, the shy morning sun glowed orange on the horizon and on his slightly balding pate.

"We've done it, Joan! By jove, we've done it!" he exclaimed, stretching his arms to the naked sky.

"Mmm," murmured the body in the sleeping bag as it turned over.

"Right," he said to the spiders doing their morning constitutional over the red sand.

"G'day mate!"

He spun round and too fast, wobbling uncertainly, his sleep-weakened senses still warming up. Strong arms grabbed him. Stood him upright.

"Struth! You okay, mate?" asked the paunchy, Akubra-hatted fellow from one of the other six tents scattered among the spinifex grass.

"Aah, yes, I think so," stammered Arthur Bayly, adjusting his spectacles. He still hadn't become used to people greeting him without being properly introduced.

"You a long way from home, by the looks."

Unsure if that was a question or a statement, he decided to blunder into conversation like others seemed to do.

"Yes, a long story, I'm afraid," he said as his legs finally took charge of themselves and he smiled weakly.

"Plenty of time for stories out here. Plenty of time for everything." The man swiped at flies on his bare legs and Arthur surmised his long trousers were out of place here.

"Look," he said, his mind finally making itself up. "I just need a little time to sit and think. And to write."

"Wow, you a writer?"

"Not yet but who knows," he said with an unaccustomed chuckle.

"Righto. See you at breakfast over tea and damper, mate." As the man strode off, Arthur wondered what damper was. In this dry heat, nothing was damp. Oh well, I'll ask later, he thought as he chose a log beside last night's dampened fire and sat. It felt like he could see the shadows of the grass moving as the sun gained confidence and quickly took charge of the cloudless sky. He took out a pen and notebook and started to write:

*The map of Arthur Bayly's life was a narrow one and, like a child in a cot of steel, can only dream of another life. He awoke from his fitful sleep with his usual sense of foreboding and wondered, again, how it was ever possible to feel elated about the day, about life. Apparently, some people did ...*

# Yet Another Day ... Perhaps

*Monday, 5<sup>th</sup> March 2012, 6.30 am, Croydon, England*

The map of Arthur Bayly's life was a narrow one and, like a child in a cot of steel, can only dream of another life. He awoke from his fitful sleep with his usual sense of foreboding and wondered, again, how it was ever possible to feel elated about the day, about life. Apparently, some people did. Quite unaware that his world was to become a little wider, a little wilder, he lay there for a few minutes, pretending that he didn't really have to get up, endure another day and look happy and successful while feeling lost and lonely. He shrugged a little, as if to brace himself, once again, for more of all he'd ever known. His wife stirred slightly and snuggled deeper into the duvet, accentuating his lack of choices.

As he munched his nutrition-free Wharton's bread and chemically-enhanced marmalade, he wondered what agent 007 would be having for breakfast; probably something with long names like Eggs Benedict with Spanish tomatoes and French toast, sparingly dusted with cinnamon and Sargasso sea salt and a touch of Tabasco sauce, followed by a 1966 Darjeeling tea. Like Arthur, Mr Bond would probably be breakfasting alone. The difference, Arthur told himself, was that Mr Bond had probably left, upstairs, an exotic, tanned and lissom young lady asleep, still in dreamy post-orgasmic bliss.

He read a few chapters of his latest book – a Lee Child book with that enigmatic giant, Jack Reacher, who lived beyond life's rules and expectations and battled for lost causes – then rinsed his dishes, cleaned his teeth, packed the lunch he'd made the night before, checked that he had his keys, oyster card, cell phone, glasses and wallet, checked himself once more in the mirror, kissed his wife as she shuffled into the dining room in her favourite pink dressing gown and left the house. It never ceased to amaze him that, though he never looked at his watch during this routine, it was always exactly 7.15 a.m. as he closed the little, black iron gate. He allowed himself a small smile about that, as usual. Then it was a four-and-a-half-minute walk up the street, past the all-too-familiar grubby brick terrace houses, wait a minute for the tram which got him to the East Croydon station at 7.26 a.m.

As he hopped as jauntily as he could into the tram, he saw, yet again, the Russian spy with the suitably battered brown trilby hat, seated and facing Arthur, pretending not to notice him. He had heavy jowls and pig-eyes and had been keeping tabs on Arthur. So Arthur did what any MI5 agent would do, which was to adopt a devil-doesn't-care-a-toss attitude by looking at the flaccid neck of the woman wobbling near him as the tram bumped along. He was determined the Russian would never detect his fear and uncover his secret.

With his mind on some distant planet, wondering what 007 would be doing today, his body's automatic system took him off the tram, into the station to wait two minutes for the 7.34 to Victoria station.

While he was aware, in some part of his mind, that he was doing this routine with hundreds of others on the tram, thousands of others on the train and the two million others who poured into London every day, it never occurred to him that they might also be feeling that sense of quiet panic. In his thirty years of working life, he had never conversed with or smiled at anyone. Never tried to, even. He was jostled a little. He had to walk around people. He had to stop and wait for people. There was no denying that others were there, in their multitudes, but a different coping part of his mind just didn't register that they were like him – humans with two legs, two arms a head and mixed feelings about life and work. He knew they were there but his mind couldn't acknowledge them.

On the train he noticed the Russian spy had again taken up a strategic position, facing him on his seat, pretending not to notice Arthur by reading today's free *Metro* newspaper. Again, Arthur adopted the MI5 attitude by looking at the ear of the man swaying in front of him. Arthur grimaced inwardly as the fetid smell of nicotine and cheap deodorant washed over him.

As the train approached Victoria station, he braced himself for the larger struggle ahead. With nineteen platforms disgorging their human payload, the herd became an avalanche of people, all going the same way, approximately. One just had to keep the feet going, the body vaguely erect, and make it through the next half hour of tedious jostling. Then, waiting for the Victoria Line underground train, with his back to the wall, he was roughly in the sixth row back from the edge. As each tube train arrived and left, he could feel himself oozing forward. Eventually, as if by osmosis or some natural phenomenon, he found himself at the edge of the platform ready to be squeezed into the next tube.

The man had disappeared but Arthur knew he was still under surveillance, somehow.

Though the train's machinery screeched, rattled and whooshed, and thousands of feet on concrete clattered, there was no other human sound. The odd cough, perhaps, but no talking. Just silent people in their own silent bubble. For many years Arthur had felt this silence as an eerie and malignant curse – as if the commuters had had their tongues removed, unable to give vent to their crying souls. Over the years, though, he'd become immune to his own silent cry and nothing was left of those feelings now.

He knew the statistics of the London tube system: eleven lines, 270 stations and a ridership of 1.34 billion people a year. But he neither knew nor talked to any of them.

Clinging desperately to something in the tube train – a rail, a hanging strap but never another person, heaven forbid – he stood amid the other black suits and sombre faces, looking through people as if they weren't there. After five minutes and three stops, he found himself near the door and then out on the crowded Warren Street platform.

As he walked from the turnstiles, he noticed the man with the battered trilby hat walk off in the opposite direction, a standard KGB trick. Arthur knew the Russian would soon turn, when Arthur's guard was down, and tail him, taking prodigious notes in Russian for his report to the Kremlin that evening. Arthur sauntered off with his devil-doesn't-care-a-toss attitude, tripped on a dropped purse, bumped heads with the owner as they both bent to pick it up, said an embarrassed *sorry* several times and sauntered out to the fresh air above ground, to find that he had come out the wrong exit. This was, he quickly decided, his clever trick to lose the Russian and he knew he would now arrive at work three minutes later than usual.

As he walked the three blocks to the office, he realised that he hadn't needed his umbrella for ages. Of course he'd read about places like Australia and Africa where it didn't rain for years but it seemed unreal somehow – just mere pictures in a book. Perhaps an artist's fantasy, perhaps not. Perhaps his own fantasy. Perhaps not.

The herd of commuters surged around him and he wondered why he suddenly thought of sunshine and blue skies. Maybe it was last night's news of bush fires near Melbourne. Maybe it was Joan mentioning their neighbour's trip to New Zealand. Instead of feeling the usual dread of the day, the Gclamp of routine, pressing on his brain, as a building labelled *Allied Insurance Limited* glared down at him, his mind went quiet. He reached his destination and the words *Allied Insurance Limited* didn't seem threatening at all. The glass doors opened for him and then he fitted himself into the lift, discretely positioning himself for minimal contact with others.

Instead of his usual thoughts of the papers and programs he needed to start work with, his mind kept jumping back to dry dirt, brown grass, a huge rock, an orange sun and an apricot moon at night. As he emerged from the lift, he felt as if he was smiling ever so slightly, something one didn't usually indulge in. He tried to repress the smile but it just wouldn't go.

"Good morning, Sir. How was your weekend?" the receptionist asked as he passed.

He stopped, momentarily stunned that a stranger should inquire into his weekend. "Ah, yes, er, nice thank you," he said, fiddling with his coat button, not knowing quite what to do next.

"That's great, Sir, you have a lovely day."

"Ah, yes, ah, thank you young lady," he stammered, making a quick and graceless exit.

It wasn't until he reached his desk that he realised that she had a strangely Antipodean accent – Australian, he presumed. Forgetting his usual routine of hanging up his overcoat, turning on his computer, getting files onto his desk, he simply sat there feeling a little limp, while a wan smile crept across his face. *Dashed perplexing*, he thought as he realised that his hands were shaking a little.

It was as if some distant part of him knew something was about to happen but his brain didn't. As if there was some cosmic timetable that told of the next train coming but none of it could he read. He looked around and nothing seemed to be happening so he got up and hung his overcoat up, just to have something to do. This simple thing he could manage but little else.

*Gosh*, he thought, *it's not as if I've been made redundant or there's been a takeover or an earthquake. Just an unexpectedly incessant thought of change in the air, perpetual sunshine and then a new receptionist bids me a cherry good morning in an Australian accent. Scant significance in the events of mice and men, so why is it affecting me so much? Dashed nuisance, really.* He needed to move but his palpitating body, floundering through the main office, could embarrass him. He eventually rose, braced himself and then made a concerted effort to walk brusquely past the receptionist. Thankfully, she was talking animatedly on the phone. He pushed open the double doors into the main office which contained thirty or so people at their desks behind their half-walled enclosures; looking studiously busy and/or gossiping with each other. He imagined a curtain of silence falling as he entered.

In the staff room, habit had him reaching for the tea bags but he knew he needed something stronger, something different. Fumbling around in the cupboard for coffee, a gangly young man – suit too big, collar large enough for two of his necks and tie askew – came in.

"Ah, excuse me, Sir," he said deferentially, "but if you want coffee, you can get it directly from the machine. This button here, Sir."

*How did he know I wanted coffee?* he asked himself, back in the glass cell they called his office. He smelled the coffee and surmised it would be better with milk. Turning sideways in his swivel chair he looked out at the ancient buildings that he loved, at the modern buildings he didn't and at the swarming human ants seven floors below him. Staring through these familiar images, his mind went oddly blank while a sort of relaxation settled in. Time sat still. Like him.

"Interesting view?"

Arthur spun and sprang from his chair, shocked out of his reverie. "Oh, ah, yes ..."

"Oops, sorry, Arthur. I didn't mean to startle you," said Mary Collins, the Assistant Director, smiling apologetically. "How are you going with the Atkinson file – is the inventory list complete?"

"Oh, um, ah, yes ... no, not quite," he said, returning to the real world with a bump and wondering what to do with the clean desk. Strangely, Mary seemed quite unconcerned about it.

"That's alright, Arthur. I know it's a confusing case and the burglary may not be all there is to it. I'm not really here about that, anyway," said Mary, settling in the other chair in his office.

"There's several things I'm still working on," he said, a little too quickly. "I've got most of the reports and claims but some of them don't quite tie up ..."

"Arthur, Arthur, Arthur! It's alright, really it is," said Mary, trying to reassure him. "You're jumpy today. Is everything okay with you?"

"Oh, it's just my womenopause," he said, attempting a little humour.

"Your what?"

"My womenopause. You know, menopause, womenopause ..." he said. He sensed her mind glazing over, missing the joke. "Yes, I'm fine, just planning my day, you know, thinking ahead," he said, trying to recover a little dignity.

"Right. Right. Good. Now, why was I here?" asked Mary, leaning back, crossing her legs and adjusting her designer glasses. "Ah, yes, yes, could you come up to Mr Black's office – we'd like to have a wee chat with you."

'Oh, shit!' was what he nearly said, hearing *wee chat* and the *Mr Black* in the same sentence. Mr. Sam Black. A worm turned in his stomach. Thankfully, there was an infinitesimal space between thinking and speaking and he actually said, "Yes, no problem. What time, Mary?"

"Oh, how about ten – we'll all need a coffee by then!" she said, trying to lighten the atmosphere, with little success.

"Yes, that's fine, I'll see you both then."

As she strode out, her solid figure and business suit created a small wind, rustling the leaves of his peace lily. He slumped back into his chair and felt anything but peaceful. A royal edict and attendance with the master executioner – what could it all mean? Redundancy? There'd been enough of them in this place and he was proud that he had hung in there, though precariously. Demotion? He wasn't sure how a fifty two-year-old should feel with all those youngsters flying up the ranks – probably worse than redundancy, he thought. Promotion? Not likely. Transfer? He knew his wife wouldn't leave the street she was born in. A reprimand? No, Sam Black left the petty stuff to his subordinates, like Mary.

His only real conclusion was redundancy ... it was the not knowing that scared him most.

My God, an hour to fret over it! Okay, old chap, remain calm, act busy and professional, smile, breathe, think, be logical. Oh God, redundancy! How humiliating, after all the years of service. People walked past his office looking in, smiling. What did they know? Probably deciding who would get his office this afternoon; smirking that it wasn't them.

He turned his computer on, retrieved a few random files from his filing cabinet, tried to look busy and tried not to imagine the awful things Mary and Sam had probably said about him, were saying about him right now. He felt so little, so out of control, so sad that it had all come to this, that none of his dreams had eventuated, that he had retired, been retired and, well, just faded into the woodwork – unseen, without achievement, without purpose, without acclaim or even acknowledgement. Arthur ... Arthur who?

His hands busied themselves as his mind went berserk, driving him deeper into a chasm by the minute. Why couldn't they get it over now? Still forty minutes to go and on and on his thoughts stumbled, conjuring up the embarrassment of the "wee chat", the humility of leaving in front of everyone else in the office, of explaining to Joan, his wife. He could imagine her hands running through her thick, greying hair, standing there looking stunned for a minute. And then there'd be the accusing looks he knew so well. And the studied judgement she was so good at, so practised at. Never shouting or getting agitated, she'd give her measured opinion – his blandness, his lack of ambition, his lack of anything approaching exciting or passionate, his nothingness destined for nothing but nothingness. And on and on she'd go. As usual, he'd not have the words or the power to reply which would prick her ire even more and her flow of words would quicken and rise in volume, imperceptibly. Eventually, when she'd repeated herself often enough, she'd turn and walk out, head high, and commiserate with her mother, six houses up the street.

Then he'd have to tell his son, Martin, if his wife didn't first. Martin was always pleasant, polite and respectful with his father but Arthur knew there was disappointment, even shame, there. Martin was a partner in the law firm, Shaftsbury Burton, and could never understand his father sticking with the boring insurance job, with no hope or ambition for promotion. The unsaid disappointment of his father's redundancy – let's be honest, his father's sacking – would be harder to bear than the studied wrath from his wife. At least there was something to argue against, with her, if he'd ever have the gall to do it.

Oh dear, five minutes to go! He quickly tidied his desk a little, trying to keep his trembling hands busy. With a deep breath he mentally girded his loins, stood up and purposefully strode from his office, slipping on a pen that Mary must have dropped. He lurched into the door frame. Nothing hurt except his pride. He looked left and right in acute embarrassment, composed himself as best he could and strode up the corridor towards the lift with a little more caution. Thankfully, in the lift, he had a sweet moment when no one was looking and he was safe. At the twelfth floor the doors opened and he emerged into the corridor which exuded the smell and feel of power and opulence, somehow. He walked the long walk to the receptionist's desk. A young girl looked up and he announced himself. She put down her nail polish, asked him to take a seat and said she wouldn't be a minute. She spoke into her intercom machine and then disappeared through double doors. She returned, seven and a half minutes later, and asked him to go in as Mr Black was expecting him.

He stood up, adjusted tie, suit, brushed shoes on legs, sighed, breathed and marched off through the large doors that proved to be heavier than he expected. A trifle embarrassed in front of a slip of a girl, he heaved again and burst into the spacious office, looking around quickly for falling guillotines.

◇ *Philip J Bradbury*

# Stood Down

*Monday, 5th March 2012, 10.07 a.m.*

Arthur faltered, trying to reconcile the rich expanse of the room it with his glass box five floors below.

"Yes, come on in, old chap," said Sam, easing his ample frame a little out of his upholstered leather, behind his expansive and clean desk. "By jove, we aren't going to eat you, you know. Take a seat here, Arthur." Sam had never used his name before – a bit disconcerting, really. Sam wore a dark, pin-stripe suit, white and blue checked shirt and white, black and red striped tie, an eye-straining combination that some fondly think of as good fashion sense.

Arthur moved uncertainly over the deep carpet, determined not to trip up, and sat in the chair indicated. His head was now below Sam's and he felt intimidated by the big desk, big chair and big man before him. Mary sat in a similar chair to his and he felt a little comforted. Not much but a little.

"Now, would you like a coffee or a tea?" Sam asked, smiling.

"Oh, is there time? I mean, ah, yes please," said Arthur, expecting a handshake, a few words and a 'goodbye'.

"Which one old chap – coffee or tea?" asked Sam, chuckling.

"Oh, just a tea, thanks Sir."

"Chinese, Japanese, Indian or good old English Breakfast tea, Arthur?" "Oh, gosh, ah, Chinese thanks, Sir," said Arthur.

"A man after my own taste." said Sam, "And your usual, Mary?"

"You know me well, Sir," she said, attempting to mix friendliness with deference.

Sam spoke into his desk: "Two Chinese and Mary's coffee, thanks Tanya." Then he turned back to Arthur. "So, old chap, I suppose you're wondering why you're here, yeah?" asked Sam, leaning forward over his mahogany desk, probably unaware that he looked more threatening than reassuring.

'Actually, no, I come here every day, you stupid irk,' his brain cried, while his mouth said, "Well, yes Sir, I am."

"Right, just so ... er ... Arthur," said Sam, obviously keen to repeat Arthur's name for some reason. "Now, you've been here some time and Mary has been keeping an eye on you ..."

'SOME TIME!' his head screamed, 'thirty monotonous years and no one's ever noticed me! Not once!'

"... and now we need to review things," he said, obviously expecting applause.

"Review, Sir?" asked Arthur.

"Okay, Mary, you tell ... er ... Arthur," said Sam, waving his hand at Mary, as if passing a theatrical cue.

Tanya interrupted with a tray of cups and silence ensued while sugar, milk and stirring were administered. Sam leaned back, sipping his tea with obvious delight while Arthur held his cup and saucer gingerly on his knee, desperate not to spill any.

"Pop your cup on the desk here," said Sam. Now Arthur's cup was a shoulder height and more difficult to get at. Should he be rude and forget it or should he attempt to drink it? His cogitations were interrupted by Sam.

"Now, where were we? Ah, yes, Mary ..."

"Oh, thank you Sam ... Sir," said Mary, uncrossing her legs, brushing her skirt and turning to look directly at Arthur. "Now, Arthur, you've been here a long time ..."

'I want NEW information and I want it NOW!' screamed his brain.

"... You're a brick, Arthur, a brick. So reliable. Others have come and gone and you've always been here," said Mary, leaving a deliberate opening for him.

"Oh," said Arthur as more words failed him.

"As you know, however, nothing stays the same. The recent credit crunch has taken its toll and so have the new financial rules. We're being watched more closely now," said Mary.

"Have I done something wrong?" asked Arthur.

"No Arthur, not at all. Of course not," said Mary, smiling bravely. "It's just that some of our connections, some people we know, are coming under greater scrutiny. Now, I'm not quite sure how to say this without alarming you." "Oh?" Arthur said, alarmed.

"Yes, I'll come out and say it bluntly, Arthur," said Mary, fiddling with her black, cropped hair.

"You're working on the Atkinson case, right?"

"Aah, yes, yes I am," said Arthur, wondering if it was a trick question.

"And, well ..." said Mary, unusually reticent to speak. "Okay, I'll say it – there is a small security matter ..."

"But I've kept everything quite confidential ..." said Arthur, feeling an accusation sneaking up on him.

"Yes, yes, of course you have, Arthur," said Mary, smiling. "The security situation has come from outside and ... and, well, we feel it's best ... oh gosh, it's best you're not in your office, not actually in the building for a time."

"Oh," said Arthur as the ground began to dissolve beneath him.

"Would you like to work from home?" asked Mary.

"From home?" asked Arthur. "Would that make things safer?" Not sacking. Not redundancy. Not demotion. Nothing that he'd expected. He felt disoriented. His mind went out the back door and all went quiet. Eerily quiet.

"Safer? Aah, yes safer, much safer," said Mary, looking hopeful and a little relieved.

"How would my home be safer than this building?" asked Arthur. "We have no alarms and things at home." The sense of being tied to a pole at the cliff edge enveloped him. Secure but not.

"No you don't, Arthur," said Sam, leaning forward, over his desk. "But the security risk would be gone when you're ... aah, not here," said Sam, starting to lose his air of mastery.

"So I work from home and everyone's safe?" asked Arthur while finding it difficult to make things add up. The cliff edge started to crumble before him.

"Exactly!" said Sam, sitting back, smiling. Arthur felt none of Sam's evident satisfaction.

"Look, Arthur, we're not able to go into details at the moment and it's a big decision," said Mary, letting out a big breath. "Would you like to go home, discuss it with your wife and come back to us on it?"

"And if we feel I can't do that?" asked Arthur, plucking up courage.

"We hope you don't come to that conclusion," said Sam, smiling awkwardly.

"Oh," said Arthur, feeling the word *redundancy* hovering somewhere close by. "And how long would this be for – days, weeks ...?"

"Look Arthur, we wish we could tell you more but we just can't, at this time," said Mary, looking at Sam as if for support.

"Right, yes, aah, I should go and talk about this to my wife, then?" suggested Arthur as his mind went in and out of focus. He knew he should do something here like stand up, shake hands and walk out but his body wasn't well connected to his thinking and wouldn't budge.

"Yes, that's an excellent idea, Arthur," said Sam, looking relieved. "Go and talk about it with your wife."

"Right, yes, I can do that," said Arthur, feeling as if he'd failed somehow.

"Great!" said Sam, standing and extending his hand. "Nice to chat, what!"

Arthur's body finally responded and got him shakily to his feet. His hand disappeared into Sam's corpulent fist and was thoroughly shaken and stirred – like his brain, really. "Right, Sir, of course," said Arthur, following Mary briskly out of the office and back down to his own desk. He expected Mary to go somewhere else but she plumped herself down on his slightly tatty vinyl swivel chair, while he seated himself behind his desk, feeling less secure by the minute. He looked around and wondered if the Russian spy was not in his imagination but real after all.

"Look, Arthur, I know there's a lot to absorb," said Mary. "Why don't we just find all the parts of this Atkinson file you're working on and you take the rest of the day off. Go home. There's no need to tackle anything else after we've seen to the Atkinson file."

Arthur showed her where all the Atkinson papers and computer files were. Mary shook his hand awkwardly and disappeared up the corridor.

Thirty years in the same, safe job and, suddenly, it's all over. Or was it? His worst fear were realised but, then, were they? And what was this security thing? So many unanswered questions. So many walls and all made of sand. Nothing solid to lean on.

He sat. Even his brain was silent, for a change. 'Right, I said I'd just go,' said his brain, weakly, after an interminable silence. 'Perhaps I'd better just do it. Just go.' No bodily response. Several people looked in as they passed. Oddly, Arthur didn't care what they thought, for the first time in his life. However, he did have to pick himself up, tidy his office, remember all his things and take them and himself from the building in a proper and dignified way. Not too much to ask, one would have thought. So he sat for another minute and planned all he was going to do – turn off computer, put files away, put pens and calculator away, stand up, put coat on, ensure he had everything with him and then just go, which he did, as quietly as he'd entered.

Then, he was outside his office, on the street, at eleven thirty in the morning and he had never been here at that time before. He turned towards the underground station and started for home, as he had on at least eight thousand other occasions. He was about to enter the grimy, brick station but looked down the concrete steps and found he couldn't move.

*What am I doing?* his brain asked his mind. *I have the rest of the day off and nothing to do.* He decided on a whim – a slightly frightening whim – to just wander a little, to just go where he hadn't been before. As he was thinking these thoughts, he discovered his feet had already taken him beyond where he'd ever been before. It was little different from the small part of London he'd previously frequented (or scurried past) and he started to enjoy the pointless amble, the not-going-somewhere-forthe-point-of-it that he'd always done. He was reminded that other people frequented coffee bars and decided, on the spot, to do that ... if, indeed, one can frequent a café just once.

The particular aroma drew him in and, as he sat at the tiny table, with a coffee and pastry before him, in the comfort of this strange café, his worst fears and his lack of safety suddenly washed over him. He dropped his head in his hands and felt like crying. It took all the force of his will to stop the tears. He now wished he had been made redundant as there would, at least, have been some certainty, some safety.

He surveyed the passing parade of humanity. He'd never actually looked at people before and had just assumed that, unlike him, they were all happy and coping with their lives. However, from behind his watery eyes, he fancied he saw the same fear, uncertainty and lostness he felt. Despite the tears, a wry smile persisted. *Have I got it so wrong all this time? Am I not the only one who feels lost and alone? Do others feel like me?* he wondered.

The pastry was adequate but the coffee was actually delicious – the first he had ever had. With a smile, he remembered that he'd made, and not drunk, his first coffee this morning and it was probably still sitting somewhere in his office, a testament to unfinished business ... or, he thought giddily, a testament to starting new business, maybe. About to finish his food and drink, he heard a chair scraping. A lanky blonde chap was sitting there, looking at him nervously.

"I ... I'm sorry," the chap said, standing up again, looking embarrassed. "I just ... I just wanted, aah, I saw you before and something about you just ... I don't know, you know, kept me thinking ..." Arthur was stunned by this unexpected development.

"Oh hell, I'm sorry," he said, looking around wildly. He stepped back, bumped the next table and spilled the two coffees there. He then bumped Arthur's remaining coffee. The men at the next table started chuckling, amid his myriad apologies.

"Sir, please sit down," said Arthur, concerned more disasters were to follow.

The chap looked around as chuckling spread through the café.

"You really do know how to make a scene don't you, Greg Cousins!" said a waitress as she appeared at the table. "I didn't recognise the clothes but I sure know your tricks. Blondes might have more fun but they sure make a mess doing it! Get your arse on the seat and I'll get you all new coffees." She patted his bottom and he sat. She took orders, winked, and marched off giggling along with the rest of her customers.

"A friend of yours?" asked Arthur.

"Uh, oh, yeah, I guess so," he said, turning to watch her departing. "She cleans up after me a bit, I guess."

"Maybe she likes you more than you realise."

"Uh, you think?"

"I'm not sure. Looks like it though," Arthur said, following his eyes. "So, aah, why did you come over here?" Arthur wondered who was speaking and realised it was himself. He'd never conversed with strangers before.

"Oh hell, you're gonna' think I'm weird ..."

"You maybe clumsy but let me decide about weird after you explain." Maybe the morning's disorientation had upset his balance, his psyche, but he felt strangely comfortable chatting with this chap.

"Okay, I'll tell you," he said, taking a big breath. "I saw you across the café about twenty minutes ago. I don't know ... I just wanted to come over and say hello. Dunno'. Just wanted to do that for no other reason ... boy, that sounds stupid or weird or something, doesn't it."

"It's certainly unusual but it seems to be quite brave," Arthur said, smiling. "Maybe we all see people we feel a connection with but few of us venture out of our shell and take the plunge." This other person speaking through his mouth seemed like a calm one. It was just so odd, feeling comfortable with a new person.

"Sounds better when you put it that way," he said, exhaling heavily. "Now, I'm Greg, Greg Cousins, and I'm Britain's last sacked person and the cops seem to be after me. Can I ask who you are?"

"Of course you can," he said, with a small laugh. "I'm Arthur, Arthur Bayly, and I'm Britain's second to last sort-of sacked person and the authorities – not sure which ones – seem to be after me!" "You've just been sacked?" he asked, looking shocked.

"Well, not quite sacked," Arthur said, looking away, feeling close to tears. He turned back, shaking his head a little. "Just stood down, indefinitely, I think. There's some security concern, it seems." He had never confided anything to anyone before and now he was. He chuckled to himself.

"I suppose you've been there a long time, wherever it is ..."

"Allied Insurance Limited."

"And they can't afford to sack you?"

"Oh, I hadn't thought of that," he said. "I am British, you know. And you're not. You're Australian. You're expendable."

"I'm a New Zealander but that's okay."

"Oh, dear, I'm sorry," said Arthur, embarrassed.

"No problem, mate. It's just an error, not a sin," said Greg, smiling broadly. "I'm expendable?"

"You're a foreigner and expendable," he said, looking him in the eye for the first time. "We tend to look after our own."

"Right."

"And who do you ... did you work for, Greg?"

"Empire Aid Bank."

"EAB?" Arthur asked as his eyes nearly flew out of their sockets. "Oh gosh!" "Oh gosh what? You know something, Arthur?" Greg asked, looking awkward.

"Long story, young man, but there's a connection with a case I've just been working on. You have any dealings with the Egyptians?"

"Nearly did," said Greg, laughing. "Seems like my contacting them could have started World War III. Well, seems to be the reason I'm here, smashing Suzie's café about and not over there teaching Africans about finance." The waitress turned up with their two coffees and seemed to be very familiar with Greg.

"Is it safe to approach now, sir?" asked a young man, suddenly appearing at our table.

"It'll be safe if you stop that stupid *sir* thing," said Greg, slapping the young man's arm and bumping Arthur's coffee again. Then Arthur looked around to see three policemen at their table. He was shocked to think they'd crept upon him, unawares, and also because he was already in enough trouble with authorities. They started asking Greg pointed questions and Arthur waited a moment and quietly slipped out, wondering how 007 would have handled it. Arthur was sure Mr Bond would not have been shaking as much as he was at that moment.

# The Accidental Hero

As he stepped from the café and crossed the street, he had the sensation that his feet weren't touching the ground. He kept his head down, like a child, thinking that if he couldn't see anyone, the authorities could not see him.

"Hello Sir, it's nice to get outside for a while, isn't it?" wafted a vaguely familiar Australian accent. He turned and recognised the new receptionist.

"Yes, yes, it is, young lady, very nice," he said, smiling. "Now please excuse me for asking, but can you tell me – are you from Australia?"

"Very close, Sir, I'm from New Zealand," she said brightly.

"Ah, my apologies."

"No problem, Sir. And the Australians would be flattered," she said, chuckling at her joke.

He knew it was a joke but didn't understand. "Yes, yes ..." he said, finding her enthusiasm infectious. She was slightly shorter than him – probably about five foot four inches – with light brown hair and a fringe, making her look pixie-like. She seemed to have more energy than all the plodders and striders about him, put together.

"Anyway, my name's Halee," she said, offering her hand. "Busy place, this London town, isn't it?"

"Yes, I suppose it is," he said, shaking her hand uncertainly. "Oh, ah, my name's Arthur."

"Yes, I know, Sir, though I have to call you Sir – it's the rules here, apparently."

"Mmm, lots of new rules, I dare say," he said, finding this simple conversation in the street quite exhilarating and remarkably easy.

"So where are you off to Sir – some secret mission?" she asked, chuckling again.

"Oh, no, actually I'm just ... aah, on my way home," he said, feeling a huge burden falling from his shoulders from the disclosure.

"Oh hell, are you okay?" she said, looking concerned.

"Yes, I expect so," he said, "I'm not altogether sure, actually. It's all been a bit sudden."

"You look like ... can I call you Arthur?"

"Ah, yes, of course."

"You look like you need a big hug, Arthur," she said, throwing her arms around him. Her sudden embrace stunned him, though it felt quite reassuring as his eyes misted over and he wondered when he was last hugged.

"Look Sir, you seem shaken," she said, standing back and looking in his eyes. "Do you want to go over there and have a coffee?"

"Actually, I've just had one, thanks," he said, disappointed the hug was over, despite it feeling uneasy in a busy street.

"Well, I meant, do you want to talk about it?" she asked. He could feel her warm breath on his face and realised she was still holding his limp arms.

"That's very kind, Halee, very kind indeed," he said, feeling the tears welling up in his eyes and an odd sense of closeness with someone he had never really met before, someone from the other side of the world, someone who listened. "However, I really should go," he said, feeling conflicted between the warm feeling of a caring human and the awkwardness of hugging and talking to a young lady.

"Okay Arthur, if you're sure, I won't intrude," she said, looking at him with concern. "But you know where I live, so to speak, so you just tell me if you want to bend my taringa."

"Your what?"

"My taringa, ears – if you want to talk. It's a great medicine," she said, letting his arms go. "And remember, this too shall pass." She turned and walked off, her bright red top and iridescent blue skirt contrasting sharply with the black masses she disappeared into. He tried to remember where he had been going then turned about and headed for the underground station with a warm glow and a melancholy heart. As he turned into the all-too-familiar station, the customary dread returned, the tears stopped, his jaw tightened and his eyes became those of everyone else here – looking through and not at anything in particular.

On the way home he saw empty seats and realised it was the first time he had ever sat in the train at midday – very different without the rush-hour crowds. Outside East Croydon station, he realised he needed time to prepare himself before meeting his wife with the news. He turned away from home, crossed the dual carriageway, turned left over Lord Atkinson Street and headed for the park he'd seen so many times in passing on his way to the library, of a weekend.

He walked down the steps to the sunken garden. As he sat on the park bench he noticed the three other people in the park – an older chap reading his newspaper with his dog beside him and a young woman with her little girl, both eating ice creams. His bench was some distance from the others and he felt comfort in his aloneness, as well as a vague sense of shared ownership of this soothing green paradise. He looked around at the mown lawns, interspersed with gardens and trees, with ivy growing up the walls to the road, interrupted only by the steps down which he had come and, at the other end, a tiled tunnel that, presumably, went under the road to some other part of town.

He sat and smiled as tears threatened to well up and burst out again. The mask of commuter isolation began to melt away and he looked at the three other people. Really looked. They all smiled back, one by one, and the warm glow and melancholy returned together.

He looked up and realised, with mild surprise, that England does, indeed, have blue skies, at times. As his mind soared up into the open blue skies, delighting in the freedom and simplicity, the beautiful nothingness, he realised what a busy place it was up there. There was never a moment when there wasn't a plane marking the blue blackboard with its white, chalk-line vapour trail. He supposed he had heard them before but never actually listened or looked. Quite obvious, really, considering he was sitting somewhere between Heathrow and Gatwick airports! He had spent his life beneath the flying humans and, as he tried to calculate how many used the skies each year, he wondered where they all might be going. And then there was Gatwick, Stansted and hundreds – maybe thousands – of other airports around the world and there could be millions in the air on any day, all going somewhere. So many people, so many places to go and, with a jolt, he saw his own life as a complete nothingness, a grey unmoving speck amid the colourful movement all about him. He'd done nothing but go to work every day, tend his small garden, read books of others' adventures and watch others' dramas on television. Where were his adventures, his dramas, his life?

He couldn't stop the tears as they began to ease out and he knew he couldn't hide them. And nor did he care. He sat, allowing the disappointment and bitterness leak from his soul, the sobs of pain to shake his body. Just a useless little man in a useless little job in a stupid useless world. He was powerless to live a bigger life, he was powerless to make a visible and lasting contribution and he was powerless to stop his body reacting to it all. For once, he didn't care what anyone else thought.

"Chloe! Chloe! Come back!" yelled the mother from across the park, jolting him back. He looked over to see the little girl – in her blue boiler suit and with blond curls bobbing – trotting over to him with her half-eaten ice cream extended in front of her.

"Are you sad?" she asked, standing in front of him, her large blue eyes full of concern.

"Yes I am," he said, trying to smile as he leaned forward, wiping his eyes.

"Would you like my ice cream, make you feel better?" "Th ... thank you so much, dear," he said, as the tears stopped.

"Here," she said, with her dribbling ice cream nearly in his face.

"Oh, no, that's very kind but you have it all," he said, gingerly sitting back a little. "I'll feel fine by and by."

"But you're sad, Mister."

"Yes I am, Sweetie, but you finish it. It looks yummy."

"Chloe, dear, don't bother the man," said the mother. Arthur was unaware that she had walked over to them and had her hand on her daughter's shoulder. "I'm really sorry, Sir." "That's no trouble, Madam, she's a very kind little girl," he said.

Suddenly he heard the sound of footsteps in the tunnel to his left – many, loud footsteps – coming his way. As he started to register and analyse these sounds, a thin, dark, wild-haired man rushed out of the tunnel towards them, looking back frequently, fearfully. Arthur had no idea how he did it but, in the moment, the instinctive and protective father within him reached out and scooped the two females off the path and, a little untidily, onto the bench beside him, just as the runner, looking back yet again, dashed towards them unsteadily.

No sooner had he reacted to this, than he saw a second runner, dark skinned, short curly hair, tattooed and solid, come racing toward the first man. The front-runner faltered, unsure what to do as the large brick wall loomed before him, quite unaware he was about to run into Arthur and his two charges. He looked back, momentarily, saw the three on the park bench and went to swerve away, had Arthur's instincts not cut in again. Someone – it certainly wasn't his own conscious thoughts – shot his foot out and tripped the man, sending him sprawling. The larger runner behind took immediate advantage and tossed himself headlong through the air, crashing on top of the smaller one.

"Oomph," came from both of them. The smaller one lay still, perhaps unconscious, while the larger one on top rose to his knees and started rifling through the other's pockets with reckless disregard for the apparently lifeless form he was frisking. He quickly found what he was looking for after tearing the man's denim jacket open, popping a brass button off and yanking out two small plastic bags with what looked like, to Arthur, washing powder, inside. The black man leapt up and went to make off with his prize when he stopped. He turned to Arthur, panting, with a huge smile. Arthur's fearless instincts vanished and he was back in very conscious fear. He drew the stunned mother and girl closer for protection.

"Cher bro', you're the man!" said the muscular, tattooed man in an accent Arthur hadn't heard before. The man extended his hand and instinct shot Arthur's hand out, to be engulfed in a brown paw that shook his vigorously. "That was choice, bro'. Kia ora Matua!"

The man turned and – whether it was some trick of the light or a malfunction in Arthur's brain – just disappeared … just, well, wasn't there. Still staring into the space where the brown man had been, he realised more, many more, footsteps were racing up the tunnel towards them. As the panic gripped him again, he leapt up, stumbled and fell over the still-prone man who was beginning to moan and move. Arthur looked back from ground level, fearing the worst and saw several police rushing towards him.

Uncertain about what to do, he rolled off the man and lay there, as before, staring at the sky with body and mind in neutral.

"Grab that man!" yelled one of the police and Arthur winced in anticipation of being grabbed. Nothing happened and then he saw two policemen pounce on the now-reviving body beside him.

"Oomph!" the man said again as two policemen pinned him down. Arthur heard a definite *crack* and a yell.

Still unable to move or think, a face suddenly loomed into his, a blue peaked hat slightly askew.

"Are you okay, Sir?" asked a still-panting but kind voice.

"Uh, yes, I think so," said Arthur, suddenly wondering where his glasses were. Hands grasped his and he was gently hauled up to a sitting position.

"Are these yours, Sir?" asked the same kind voice as his glasses came into view.

"Uh, yes, I think so," said Arthur, again. He put his glasses on and the wider world came into view again. He looked around a little giddily and saw that the previously-prone man had been handcuffed, rolled over and eased into a sitting position.

"You weazley little bastard!" said the handcuffed man, less than an arm's length away. Arthur's panic returned and he tried to leap up, failing miserably as he wobbled and fell like a newborn foal.

"That's enough of that!" yelled the previously-kind voice, now in authoritative tone. "Hold him right there, Constable, till we get these people safely away."

"Yes, Sergeant," answered the constable who pushed rather vigorously down on the wretched man's shoulders, pinning him back to the ground while the other two police stood menacingly by.

"Now, Sir, let's see if you're okay to stand," said the sergeant. "Take it easy, Sir. You're a hero but a very shaky one!" he said.

Arthur managed a weak smile.

"Are you okay to stand, Sir?" asked the sergeant.

"Uh, yes, I think so," said Arthur. The sergeant's comforting arms were under his shoulders, easing him up. He stood, still in the security of those uniformed arms and realised the mother and girl were still on the park bench, both rigid.

"Come over and sit down here," said the sergeant, easing him back to his former seat. As he plumped down, a little giddiness returned and he nearly fell forward and off. "Oops, just sit back a little, Sir," said the sergeant.

"Uh, yes, I think so," said Arthur, yet again.

The sergeant moved over to the mother and girl, where the female constable was tending them.

"Now, how are you two, okay?"

"Alright, I think," said the mother, arm around her daughter while wiping ice cream from her face.

"Right, just stay here for a minute, please, while we take this man away to be processed." He said, indicating the dark, hand-cuffed man who was being marched off, with a definite limp.

"You've got quite a hero here, haven't you?" said the sergeant, looking over at Arthur. "Saved you from a trampling and then tackles a thief." It took Arthur a moment to realise he was the subject of this praise.

He looked over at the young woman and her child. They both looked like dolls – stunned dolls – with blonde hair, pale skin and pale blue eyes. The female constable was crouched in front of them, getting details and reassuring them they were safe. The woman looked over at Arthur and smiled a grateful smile. Embarrassment caught at his throat and he had no words but nodded and smiled back. He felt he should offer support or something but his body was in no mood for action. He looked away and wondered what a normal man would do.

"Now, if you're feeling better, we'd like you to come to the station," said the sergeant.

"Pardon?" said Arthur, not quite comprehending the request.

"Just to get a statement from you," said the sergeant, "if you're okay to come with us now …"

"Look, I'm very sorry, Sir, but I've had rather a bad day," pleaded Arthur. "Could I do this another day? It's all been a bit much, really."

"I understand, Sir, this incident has shaken you badly," said the sergeant, "but we do need to know what happened."

"This incident, I'm afraid, was nothing at all," said Arthur, trying to explain. "It was this morning that was unsettling, quite unsettling."

"Excuse me, Sir, perhaps you'd like me to look after this man while you take these ladies to the station and see to the prisoner," came a female voice behind the sergeant.

"Oh, well, if you're sure, I'd be much obliged, constable," said the sergeant leading the woman and her little girl away. The constable sat down next to him.

"You said you'd had a bad morning," she said, "Do you want to tell me about it?"

"Ah, um, yes, I suppose I could, thank you," said Arthur, wondering where to begin and why she might be interested.

"I'm Constable Broughton – Amanda Broughton," she said. "Call me Amanda if you like."

"Ah, yes, Amanda. Hmm, I'm Arthur Bayly – that little I do know!" said Arthur, his confidence growing.

"Well, you haven't lost your sense of humour yet. That's a good start," said the constable, smiling at him. "And your morning was pretty bad, was it?"

"Yes it was, my dear ... Amanda," said Arthur. "I've been working for the firm for thirty years – all my life – and, today, I've been, well, sent home for security reasons I don't quite understand." "Oh!" said Amanda.

"Yes, *oh* is about all I can think of at the moment," said Arthur, smiling sheepishly.

"And this security situation – do you need protection of some sort?" said Amanda.

"I'm really not sure," said Arthur, not wanting to face the question that had been stalking him since his wee *chat* with *Mr Black*.

"Okay," said Amanda, becoming more animated, "I know you're probably in shock but I suspect you need to ask your employer what the problem actually is."

"You're right, aah, Amanda, but I had the impression they weren't quite sure," said Arthur.

"Or didn't want to say."

"Perhaps you're right," he mused, feeling a small sense of progress with someone who seemed to understand him, to be on his side.

"And, secondly, I may be able to help in another way," said Amanda. "I was made redundant, three years ago, quite suddenly. Would you like to hear a little of my story – it might help."

"Why, yes, Amanda, if you have the time," said Arthur. "I'm sure you're very busy."

"Arthur, I am very busy but, you know what? This is one of my favourite jobs, helping people through what I've been through. It's not really police work but I'd like to help in any way I can," said Amanda.

"Looks like my day's improving!" said Arthur, forcing a smile as the heaviness in his stomach lifted a little.

"Right," said Amanda, "I get off work at one o'clock, in ten minutes. How about I go back to the station, sign out and come back and we can go and have a coffee together?"

"Gosh, that's the second invitation I've had from a nice young lady today," said Arthur, feeling his humour returning a little. "That sounds like a lovely idea, thanks."

"I'll bring my paperwork back and tell the sarge I'm taking your statement. That'll save you having to come in," she said, getting up. "I'll only be a mo'."

He could have felt uneasy, after all that had happened, but he just couldn't be bothered feeling much at all. Besides, he told himself logically, it's unlikely another scuffle would happen right here, again. Then the sun came out from behind a huge cloudbank and he smiled. With absolutely nothing else to do, right then, he wondered what he'd he really love to do that would stir his passions and raise his spirits? Sadly, he had trouble thinking of anything much – all his mind could come up with were unlikely things like writing a book and climbing Ayers Rock. He wondered where those strange thoughts came from. They weren't likely, in the next little while so he tried again. Nothing else presented itself and he began to wonder if his wife was right in labelling him a man without passion and ambition. He also began to wonder, for the first time ever, what he could do that would stir his blood.

# Victim or Graduate

*Monday, 5<sup>th</sup> March 2012, 1.04 p.m.*

She plonked herself on the seat, beside him, with a sigh and a smile, and he wondered how she'd got there without him noticing.

"Now, Sir," she said, looking directly into his eyes, which he found a little disconcerting, "how are you feeling? A little less shaky?"

"Ah, yes, a little steadier, thank you Constable," he said, examining his shoes.

"Amanda, please call me Amanda. Now, I just need to tell my sergeant what I'm doing here, interviewing you, as he wasn't at the station just now." She called her sergeant and told him just that, clicked her phone off and tossed into the bottom of her bag. "Now, a question that might seem a little strange," she said, in an accent that was not English but was one he'd heard before, quite recently.

"Why do you think you attracted this series of upsetting events to you?" "I beg your pardon?" he asked, nonplussed.

"I thought you'd find it strange. While you're pondering that, why don't we pop over to my favourite café and we'll reflect on life," she said, "and I'll take your statement."

"Well, yes, of course."

"Unless you have a favourite café?" she asked.

"Well, actually, I've never been inside a café till this morning."

"What, you haven't? Your education is sadly lacking, Arthur. Let me treat you!" she said, bounding up and taking his hand to help him rise.

"Gosh, how very gallant of you," he said, bowing, "how can I refuse such an offer!"

She tripped along, her golden curls bouncing in the sunlight and he had trouble keeping up. She ordered their coffees and they sat at a bench, looking through the window onto the street.

"Good. Now, as I said, I was made redundant three years ago," said Amanda. "I'd worked for them, the shipping firm, since I left university – ten years I was there. I was shocked, I was depressed and I lost it."

"Lost it?" asked Arthur.

"Yes, lost it," said Amanda. "The shipping business was in a downturn and they had to put people off – I was one of the lucky ones!"

"But it wasn't your fault, Amanda," said Arthur. "My situation's different – it's definitely personal and they see me as a problem, I think, though the problem's not my fault, they said. I'm just not sure
…"

"Arthur, whether it's your fault or not, it still feels like your fault," said Amanda. "Besides, whether it's your fault or not, it doesn't matter. The fact is, you're out of a job, sort of, and you feel like crap … oh, sorry, you feel horrible."

Arthur laughed. "Yes, I do feel like crap, though I dare say I've never used that word before."

"Ok, crap it is," said Amanda chuckling. "And that crap immobilized me. I suppose I became depressed, though depression's what you do, not what you are." "What you do?" asked Arthur, confused.

"Yes, depression's what you do and I'll explain that in a minute," said Amanda, talking faster and faster as if she had so many words to get out in a limited time. "I just became unable to function. I couldn't bring myself to look for another job, to apply for an unemployment benefit, to see my friends, to tell my family … sometimes I just couldn't get myself out of bed for days, except to eat and pee. At times I wanted it all to end but I couldn't be bothered doing anything to end my life … I couldn't even do that properly!"

"Goodness, that's … terrible," said Arthur.

"Yes, it was terrible, oppressing and debilitating." said Amanda quietly. "It was also the best thing that ever happened to me."

"The best …"

"Yep, the best thing ever," said Amanda, brightening again. "You see, Arthur, as I lay in my bed or lounged in my flat that was getting grubbier and grubbier, I saw myself as totally useless, no point to being here and I cried and cried and yelled at God, the world and everything else. I fumed, I bellowed, I cried and I went down screaming, sobbing. Eventually I stopped fighting. I was just too exhausted.

That was when I wanted it to end."

"You mean … suicide?" asked Arthur, shocked.

"Suicide, earthquake, bombing … I didn't care how it ended, I just wanted it to," said Amanda fiercely. "Of course, with no income, I'd used up all my savings and I *had* to do something – my parents lived nearby, in New Zealand, but I couldn't ask them for help. I couldn't tell them or anyone

else about how useless I was. I was so ashamed …"

"You poor thing, Amanda."

"You might say that! I thought it – 'you poor thing, Amanda' – and, after six months of all this pity for poor Amanda, I finally gave up. I gave in. I said to whoever was listening – God, the universe, Buddha, Mother Mary, Jesus, anyone – *Enough, I've had enough!* I was just sick of it all and desperately wanted something to change … anything to change. I cried so hard my skin hurt … all over. Then, *pffttt*, it was all over!" "*Pffttt*?" asked Arthur, bemused.

"Yes, *pffttt*," said Amanda, giggling at the thought. "*Pffttt*, it was all over. Like a small ray of sunshine piercing the clouds, I woke from my bad dream and didn't want the misery any more."

"But you didn't want misery anyway!" said Arthur, feeling the abyss of confusion drawing him down again.

"No, I wouldn't have thought so at the time," said Amanda, wiping her eyes. "But the reality is that I was sad, miserable, crying and every other stupid thing because I wanted to be. It suited some silly need in me to wallow in self-pity. So I wallowed and then, when the pain was too much or I was bored with it, I'd had enough. *Pffttt*!"

"Oh! Oh dear, I hadn't thought of it like that," said Arthur, seeing his own sunlight through a cloudy mind.

"And when I'd had my *pffttt* moment, when I said "*Enough*!" to the universe, my mind changed from one of pity to one of recovery – how can I get out of this?" said Amanda. "Then Brian turned up. Amazing timing, really. But, as I learned, there's no such thing as a coincidence – there's just you and me and everybody else asking for what we want and then, *pffttt*, getting it!"

"Oh dear," said Arthur, seeing his ray of sunshine lighting a piece of reality. "So you're saying I actually asked to be sent out … I actually wanted this to happen … and the accident with that criminal

…"

"You probably won't want to hear this but yep!" said Amanda. "Maybe your job's not exciting enough any more, for whatever reason, and you're looking for some adventure, some excitement, something exotic …"

"Well, I do seem to be thinking of Australia … or is it New Zealand, I'm not sure," said Arthur, feeling strangely uncomfortable, in a world that didn't quite fit any more.

"And so you bump into a Kiwi – me!"

"A Kiwi?"

"A New Zealander, Arthur, we call ourselves Kiwis," said Amanda.

"Oh I see," said Arthur, absorbing yet another new fact. "Actually, you're the second New … Kiwi I've met today. Two lovely young ladies and both caring!"

"Aah, caring," said Amanda, savouring the word and clapping her hands gleefully. "You see, the universe really does want you to realise that it cares, that help is there. Just ask."

"Just ask?" said Arthur. "Ask who?"

"Ask the universe, silly," said Amanda punching his arm playfully. "In your head, out loud, in prayer. It doesn't matter, just ask. You've already got two helpful Kiwis without consciously asking so think what you'll get if you *do* ask."

"Oh, ah, yes," said Arthur, feeling as if the swamp through which he had been trudging his whole life was, finally, starting to release his feet.

"So what did you do next?" asked Arthur, concerned, while remembering that the person telling this dreadful story was a fully functioning policewoman now.

"Well, actually Arthur, I did nothing at all – I just said *Enough* with a passion I'd never felt before and the universe took over," said Amanda, smiling at the memory. "The universe?" asked Arthur, starting to feel lost.

"Universe, God, Buddha, spirit guides, Aunty Mavis ... whatever you like to call whatever you believe in ... whatever you feel that it is that's bigger than any of us," said Amanda, trying to slow down for a concerned-looking Arthur. "I don't know how it happened, really, but it did."

"What did, Amanda?"

"The magic, Arthur, the magic," said Amanda.

"The magic?" asked Arthur, feeling totally lost and wondering if this girl wasn't a bit insane.

"Sounds a bit insane, doesn't it?" asked Amanda. All Arthur could manage was a silly smile. "You see, Arthur, I called for help, with passion, and it turned up," said Amanda. "I yelled, in my head, in my bed, so no one could hear: *Enough. Enough. I've had enough!* And things started to happen." "Things?" asked Arthur, feeling things returning to normal a little.

"Yes, things," said Amanda. "The next morning I received a letter from Her Majesty's very kind Tax Department, suggesting that, as I had been made redundant, I might be in for a refund. You have no idea how something that simple can lift a person's spirits – especially someone who has lost all faith in everything. Suddenly, without effort on my part, I was being offered help." "Did you get the refund?" asked Arthur, feeling some hope for himself.

"Ever-practical Arthur," said Amanda, laughing. "I didn't have the energy, at the time, to do anything about it. I just felt a little better, a little supported. That was all that mattered then. And, yes, I did eventually get the refund I badly needed!"

"Mmm, that's good," said Arthur with his hope supported a little.

"And that's not all!" said Amanda. "That afternoon I received a call from one of my co-workers, Brian, to see how I was. I hadn't spoken to any of them since I'd left – I felt too embarrassed to do so. Anyway, it turned out that Brian, made redundant like me, had also being going through similar stress as me, for about three months and had recently found a new job, moved to a new flat and had met this amazing new girlfriend. Life was on the up and up for him. And, of course, I wanted what he had." "But he helped you somehow?" asked Arthur.

"Yes. He got bossy, told me he was coming around to take me out for a coffee and a chat," said Amanda, chuckling at the memory. "I was too embarrassed to be seen like I was but he insisted he'd be round in half an hour. A girl's vanity is a great motivator, you know! I was off the couch, in the shower, dressed in my least creased and dirty clothes, vaguely made up and at my front door minutes

before he arrived. I sure as hell wasn't going to let him see the state of my flat!"

"And you went for a coffee?" asked Arthur, checking that he was still with the story.

"Well, the coffee was an excuse to get me out and talking," said Amanda. "And, once I started, he couldn't stop me! Anyway, he listened to my moans and groans until I exhausted myself – I think he reordered coffee some way through my diatribe."

"You eventually stopped – was he sympathetic?" asked Arthur, feeling sympathetic.

"Sympathetic? Hell no!" said Amanda. "I expected him to show *some* sympathy or compassion or caring but no! When I stopped raving, he asked, 'so, what are you going to do about it now?'" "Gosh, that was a little harsh," said Arthur.

"Yes, that's what I thought at the time. I just started crying," said Amanda, a tear of remembrance slipping down her cheek.

"You cried ... in front of him?"

"You betcha I did. I couldn't stop it!" said Amanda. "His reaction was such a shock. So he just asked me again, so coolly, what did I want to do about it. I guess I got a little angry and shouted at him to 'shut up, I've just had enough, I just want this to be over!'"

"That must have been particularly upsetting," said Arthur, feeling very sorry for her.

"Upsetting. Hell, he just started laughing," said Amanda, chuckling at the memory. "I was so shocked I stopped blubbing and just stared at him. He said he was so thrilled I'd got angry as that was the start of the uphill run." "The uphill run?"

"Yes, the way he explained it was that depression and anger had the same cause - they're both from unmet expectations," said Amanda, "The difference is in the behaviour to that disappointment. In depression we go inside and cut off from the world. We can't function. Then, when we change our behaviour to anger, we go out, lash out in some way. When we get to that stage, we're ready to actually *do* something about our situation – we're ready to fight back. I must say, I did feel quite empowered when I had my angry outburst. The best I'd felt in months!"

"Ah, I hadn't thought of it that way," said Arthur, quietly. "I suppose I thought anger was particularly antisocial."

"Well, yes, it is if it's misdirected against people and things," said Amanda, brightening up. "However, it's just energy and, used constructively, can be positively powerful. After all, Greenpeace, Amnesty International and CORSO were all started by anger – by a sense of injustice – directed constructively."

"I suppose you're right," said Arthur, trying to take in all these new ideas. "So how did he help you?"

"Well, he tried to explain something to me that I didn't get at the time," said Amanda, smiling crookedly. "You might not get it right now, but I'd like to try and explain it to you ..."

"Yes?" said Arthur, on the edge of his seat, quite oblivious to the people in the café and passing by on the street.

"Okay, well, here goes," said Amanda. "Let's use the word *universe* instead of *God* or whatever. It's just a word for something I don't quite know how to explain."

"Yes?"

"So, let's pretend you have a particular life path to walk," said Amanda. "I know this sounds a bit spooky, but it feels right to me. Do you understand?"

"No, not really," said Arthur as a warm feeling rose up his spine. Though the idea was new and a little peculiar, it had a feeling of rightness about it.

"Okay, as I said, let's pretend that you have a particular life path. Certain things you need to do in this life," said Amanda, obviously choosing her words carefully. "Now, we don't necessarily know what that path is or even that it exists. You with me?"

"I'm not sure. I might be if you keep going."

"So we have certain things to do or achieve and, somehow, someone, something keeps us on the path," said Amanda. "Some people are able to feel that guidance, so to speak, and they stick to the path. Most of us, however, don't feel these things and, though the universe speaks to us in a multitude of ways we don't hear it. We plough on blindly ignorant."

"Mmm."

"So, if we're here for a particular purpose but don't know what it is, don't even know that it exists, how the heck are we supposed to carry out our sacred mission?" asked Amanda. "How do we get connected, how do we plug into the universe to get the right job done?"

"Mmm, a conundrum."

"Absolutely! It's such an illogical system, we might think – being given a job we don't know about and don't have any tools for," said Amanda. "We're all floundering in the dark."

"Sounds very confusing ..."

"It sounds like that but it's not," said Amanda, smiling. "It's actually very logical and very simple, really."

"Oh, is it?" said Arthur, surprised.

"Yep, it sure is," she said, chirpily. "We get out of our own way and we let the universe talk." "Pardon?" said Arthur, returning to the edge of confusion's abyss.

"Exactly!" said Amanda, laughing. "You see, we all get so busy doing what we think we ought to be doing – we get oughtism – listening to the ideas and commands of others, the constant desire to look good, that we forget to feel good. Obeying the clamour of the world that clashes with our own spiritual calling, we live lives of desperate futility, bitter and frustrated."

"You mean that others feel like that ... not just me?" asked Arthur, with clouds of doubt dispersing again, albeit slowly, while he felt a strange sense of connection with this stranger who described his life so accurately.

"Very few people live life happily, peacefully and in accord with their true calling," said Amanda, her enthusiasm never waning. "And yet we all hold the key but choose not to unlock the door of our self-constructed prison. Silly, really!"

"So how do we get out of this prison, then?" asked Arthur, sensing light beginning to dawn.

"You've started the process already, though you don't know it, just like I didn't till Brian turned up," she said. "Now that you've said *Enough!* and I've turned up. Stay open and the rest will unfold itself."

"Unfold?"

"Things will start to happen," she said, "unusual, unexpected things ..."

"Like unusual scary things, unexpected criminals?" asked Arthur, smiling grimly. "All things will pass,"

"Somebody else told me that today!"

"You see – unusual and unexpected!" said Amanda. "Seemingly unrelated things will start to fit together. All I can say is stay open and remember that all this will definitely pass – nothing actually matters. Now, can I get your statement for my report, please?" Arthur dutifully gave her his statement, while anxious to know more.

"Now, I really must go," said Amanda, looking at her watch, "but here's my mobile number if you want to know where to deliver the Maserati to." She scribbled her number on a serviette and handed it to him.

"The Maserati?" asked Arthur, trying to catch up with her.

"My consulting fee! Just joking, ninny," said Amanda, patting his shoulder. "If you want to know more or just want a chat, call and invite me round. Bye!"

'My gosh, invite me round,' thought Arthur as Amanda skipped out of the café, 'these Kiwis are very forward.' That thought was quickly squashed out of his brain as more pressing matters crowded in.

He would normally feel self-conscious, sitting in a café with an empty cup, no paper to pretend to read and nothing to do. This time he didn't. Despite all he had to think about, his mind went blank, quite empty, and he sat staring happily out the window at everything and nothing.

Blissfully unaware of the time, his mind slowly woke as a cat stretching after a nap. He looked around and was surprised the world hadn't changed during his absence. He picked himself up and wafted out the door with an inane smile on his face, quite unaware of what was waiting for him.

# A Second Death

*Monday, 5<sup>th</sup> March 2012, 1.45 p.m.*

With a light and bouncy heart, he set off for home, preferring the ten-minute walk to being squished in a tram – a far cry from the previous dread he'd felt about meeting his wife with the upsetting news. In fact, he wanted to skip like a child but, of course, that just wasn't done. Not for an adult. Not for Arthur Bayly. Not in his suit today. That didn't stop his mind skipping along inside a body that carried a battered leather brief case with proper business-like decorum. He couldn't get the silly smile off his face and he worried that other pedestrians might think him mad or, worse, being silly. However, in true London style, no one looked or even pretended to notice.

The short walk seemed shorter this time and, as he turned the corner into Tunstall Road, he stopped abruptly. A small crowd and an ambulance, with flashing light, was such a contrast to his light mood. He tried to take the unexpected scene into his mind. As he tried to imagine what could be happening, he realised the ambulance men were carrying a stretcher out of his mother-in-law's house. The covered body on it looked chillingly still. His mind froze. His body froze. It was as if he knew, subconsciously, what was happening, thought his logical mind struggled to put the pieces together. He inched forward, searching the crowd and, soon, his wife came out of the house, ashen-faced.

Then it happened. The massive and persistent hand of God – as he would later describe it – was at his back, pushing him forward. With no choice but to obey, he covered the thirty yards in no time imaginable and had enveloped his wife in an uncharacteristically warm and loving embrace. She resisted, at first, the sudden hug from a stranger but, for the first time ever, he did not yield to her attempt to break free. He stood his ground strongly, lovingly and she quietly gave into his embrace, such was her need.

He was, of course, surprised at his decisive action and the warmth he felt inside. He was vaguely aware of other people fussing about him but he felt no concern for them. His only thoughts were for the woman in his arms – the woman, he realised, who needed his love and nothing else in this moment. He surprised himself as these old feelings of affection arose as Joan, usually the forceful one, melted into his arms and nothing needed to be said. As their envelope of silent togetherness wrapped them in, the outside world disappeared and they knew each other better than they ever had before. It was as if all the millions of words over the years had – instead of explaining and uniting them – confused and separated them. Reluctantly they separated, looking at each other, knowing they must allow the rest of the world to intrude.

"Oh, Arthur ..." said Joan softly, wanting to express what could not be put into words.

"It's okay, love, I'm here," said Arthur, knowing this was more important than anything – his job, his future, their future. This moment. He knew he must savour it, cherish it, remember it.

"Ah, excuse me, Mrs Bayly," said an ambulance driver, coming as close as their envelope of silence would allow, "we'll take the, er, your mother now, ma'am. We will need you to come and complete the paper-work for us – today, if possible."

"Yes, yes," Joan said, unable to keep the crack out of her voice and the tears from flowing.

"Thank you young man," said Arthur, with unaccustomed authority, "I'll bring my wife down to the hospital ..."

"No Sir, the funeral parlour, in Orchard Road," said the ambulance driver. "Do you know where it is?"

"Oh, ah, yes, of course, the funeral parlour, as soon as we can," said Arthur with his arm still around Joan's shoulders and a grip of fear around his gut with the mention of the word *funeral*. "We both need a little time to ourselves and then we'll walk down."

"Thank you, Sir," said the young man, "just when you can make it. There's no hurry, none at all." "Thank you so much," said Arthur, thinking with remarkable clarity. "Now, dear, I'll lock your mother's house and we'll pop home for a cup of tea and a sit."

"Mmm, yes," said Joan quietly, apparently happy to hand over control for a change.

As they settled in their favourite lounge chairs, Joan suddenly looked up at Arthur who was placing a cup of tea and a plate of biscuits on her side-table. "Arthur, I've just realised ... what are you doing here, now?" she asked. "I got Dottie, our neighbour, to ring your office but that was only half an hour ago."

"Yes dear, it's been quite a day hasn't it? Quite a day," said Arthur, sitting down with his cup of tea and wondering where to start and how much to say right now. "I, er, left work early today. I would have been on my way here when she rang, I suppose."

"But, Arthur, you've never left early before. Is something wrong?" asked Joan, realising she may not be the only one with problems.

"Well, yes, I'm afraid there is, my dear," said Arthur, still struggling with what details to reveal. "I was asked to leave, to not work at the office. Something about security ..." He waited for her attack.

"Oh dear, oh dear," said Joan, looking confused.

"It's okay, love, we can talk about it later," said Arthur, aware that she was unable to absorb much else at the moment. He was, also, quite relieved to have said the worst of it and avoided the terrible scene he had played out in his mind, several hours earlier at work. He was relieved, too, not to have to continue further explanations and tempt fate.

As he thought of his previous dread of this moment, it all seemed so far away – commuting, work, the interview, the shock – and it seemed to matter so little that he wondered how it could have mattered before at all.

"Do you want to tell me what happened?" asked Arthur.

"Oh, ah, well, I just went up there to see how she was – she hadn't called me," said Joan as her tears started again.

"Leave it for now if you like, love," said Arthur tenderly.

"No, I want you to know ... there's not much to tell, really," said Joan, wiping her eyes, determined to go on. "I knocked and there was no answer. That was unusual. I heard nothing inside, absolutely nothing. I had this horrible feeling in my stomach, that something was wrong ..." she said as another sob interrupted her story. Her crying subsided; she wiped her eyes and sat upright. "I've just got to tell you now, love. There's not much to say but it doesn't seem real, somehow. You know ..."

"Yes dear, I do know," said Arthur, smiling a little as he recalled his own unreal experience that morning.

"Mmm, I think you do," said Joan with unaccustomed insight into her husband's thoughts. She blew her nose, sat up and started again. "I used my key, got in and found her on the floor of her lounge, beside her card table. You know, I always thought I'd scream or run away or do something dramatic when that happened. I always knew it would happen sometime, obviously ... it just, I just stood there and looked and looked. I knew a big part of me was lost, gone forever. I felt sort-of empty, dead, but ... but complete somehow, too. I can't explain it."

"Gosh," said Arthur, wanting to say something but not sure what. Some people just had the knack of saying the right things but he had never acquired it, he mused.

"But, you know, love," said Joan, dabbing her eyes, "it's not nice finding your mother, well, like that. Not nice at all but, well, yes, I was shocked and empty, somehow, but also ... I can't quite explain it ... I just felt fully complete, yes fully complete. That's all I can say. Strange really."

"Quite, yes, fully complete," said Arthur, savouring the phrase as if it was a new food he was tasting. Perhaps that's how he felt after his news at work today – shocked, frightened, maybe even angry. A little bit angry. And, yes, if he had to admit it, a sense of completeness, even peace, seemed to pervade. It certainly wasn't logical but it was undeniable – completeness and peace – there were no other words for it.

"Arthur dear, why are you smiling?" asked Joan.

"Oh, I'm sorry dear," said Arthur, feeling a trifle embarrassed to be smiling at such an inopportune time. "I'm not quite sure but you said you felt a sense of completeness. It is so very illogical, at a time like this bit it does seem oddly right. I'm not sure how, but it does. I'm certainly not smiling at you dear."

"I know you're not, darling. I know that," said Joan as a smile sneaked onto her face. "I know I'm supposed to be sad and that I should be gnashing and wailing and making a scene but I don't feel like that. I do feel sad and shocked – it was unexpected – but I can't deny the completeness thing inside. I feel a weeny bit guilty for it. Maybe I'll feel the full impact later, when it all sinks in."

"Mmm, maybe you will; maybe we both will," said Arthur, feeling empathy with his wife's explanation. "These things are supposed to make us feel the worst, have us behaving the worst but there is this odd sense of rightness to it all. You agree?"

"Absolutely, my love, absolutely!" said Joan feeling less lonely in her unaccustomed feelings. "Oh, Arthur, can I have a hug please?"

"Oh, ah, yes Dear," said Arthur, wondering when he'd last heard those words – maybe during their honeymoon. As they stood and hugged, Arthur could feel the sense of completeness grow imperceptibly. He also felt something else grow a little – a nice but slightly embarrassing movement below his belt. But there were things to be attended to.

"So, what about you, you poor thing?" asked Joan. "Did you say you lost your job?"

"Well, not really. They want me to consider working at home," said Arthur. "A security risk and I witnessed a police scuffle ..." He just couldn't get the words to form logical patterns for her to understand.

"Security risk? Police scuffle?" asked Joan, wide-eyed.

"Well, I did mention my job but we were busy with your mother. I thought I should let it wait till later," said Arthur with a sigh.

"And a police scuffle?" asked Joan, repeating herself.

"Oh yes, I hadn't got round to mentioning it," said Arthur as the memory of it – so recent but so quickly gone from his mind – returned. "I think he was a New Zealander, a brown man. Would that be a Māori?"

"Ah yes, I suppose so ... who?" asked Joan, now totally confused.

"Ah, the man they caught ... and the other one who thanked me and it was all so quick ..." said Arthur as his mind went the speed of light and his mouth was stuck at thirty miles per hour.

"Arthur, Arthur, please stop there," said Joan, patting his hand. "Stop. Take a breath – a deep breath – and then tell me all about it. It's obviously not only me who's had a harrowing day!" So Arthur told her about it – everything he could remember.

"So that's it?" asked Joan, enthralled at the events surrounding her husband.

"I'm afraid so, Joan," said Arthur, relieved that he'd got it all out in the open. "Why don't we get the official stuff done and then we can relax."

As they sat down with a late afternoon cup of tea, after returning from the funeral parlour, there was a thump at the front door. Arthur leapt up and returned with the evening paper. At the bottom of the front page was a photo of the woman and her child. He read the story out and it was mainly the woman's point of view. He was surprised that she considered him a hero and wanted to thank him, if she could contact him to do so. He felt uncomfortable. Joan reached over and took the paper from him.

"So this is you ... my hero husband?" asked Joan, her eyes wide.

"Not a hero quite," said Arthur, embarrassed. "I just happened to be there and the chap tripped over my foot and I got knocked down and was then helped up by a very helpful police woman – Amanda. Just like I told you."

"Mmm, sounds like you were more involved than that, according to the paper," said Joan looking at Arthur with obvious admiration.

The phone stabbed through their peace, shrill and jarring. Arthur was momentarily stunned and then reluctantly moved to pick it up.

"Where have you been? I've been trying to call you time and again," said Martin, obviously in a mood. "And why don't you get yourselves an answer phone? You really must get up to date and it's so rude not to let people contact you or leave messages. I don't know how many times I've told you about this, why don't you get one ..."

"Martin," Arthur said wearily, wondering who was father and who was son for an instant, his quietness stopping the tirade in mid-stream. "Martin, we don't have one because we don't want one."

"But I've told you, it's so rude and so damned annoying when people really want to contact you and you don't even have mobile phones like you should and it's like you're in the last century and you really need ..."

"Martin," said Arthur, quietly, "I've had quite enough of this. Now, what is it that you want?"

"Well, yes, it's still so rude and backward not to have an answer phone or a mobile, everyone else has them ..."

"Martin," said Arthur quietly, again. "I'm going to say this one thing and then I'm going to hang up. Okay?"

"Uh, oh, okay!" said Martin, surprised by this unaccustomed shortness from his father.

"Now, you haven't told us what you want so I'll tell you where we've been," said Arthur in measured tones. "We've recently got back from the funeral parlour because your grandmother died today. I've was also sent home from my job. The funeral is on Thursday and we really hope you and

Ruth and the children can all be there. Good night."

As Arthur sat down, under the admiring gaze of his wife, the phone screamed again.

"Ah, I'm, ah, I didn't know, Dad," said Martin, coming the closest he ever had to an apology. "I just didn't know ..."

"Well, now you do, Martin, and we did leave a message on your home answer phone and I left a message with your secretary. I hope you can all be there to support your mother and I. Now, what was it you wanted us so urgently for?"

"Ah, oh, well, I wanted to know if you could look after the kids for two days," said Martin. "It's a teacher-only day or a half-term break or something ... ah hell, I didn't know, I'm really sorry about you and Grandma."

"Yes, so are we, Martin," said Arthur in a more conciliatory tone. "So, when would you like us to look after the children?"

"Well, I had hoped I could drop them off first thing in the morning ..." said Martin, trailing off.

"Look Martin, it's been a big day so let me have a talk to Mum and we'll call you back within half an hour. Is that okay?"

"Of course, Dad. That's fine. I'm really so sorry ..."

Later, after Arthur's and Joan's minds had cleared a little, they discussed having the children and decided a pleasant diversion from their current concerns was just what they needed. They rang Martin to tell him and he surprised them with two things – an apology and gratitude.

# Slipping Off His Map

*Tuesday 6th March 2012, 6.30 a.m.*

After the deepest sleep he could remember, his body woke him up with a jolt at his habitual time of 6.30 am. He struggled out of bed, feeling his usual oppression and sense of futility at a life less lived. As he went to pick up the day's clothes from the chair, he stopped, embarrassed, uncertainly, smiling childishly to himself. His overwhelming sense of duty to march off to work, grim and stolid, evaporated as a shaft of gentle light penetrated his usual cloud of doom. He plumped down on the edge of the bed.

On any previous day, he would have obeyed the soldier's call, reluctantly. He would have wearily saluted that insanely barking sergeant-major - red-faced with swelling veins - in his head, and gone to war against an enemy that was not his own ... supposedly to vanquish an invisible enemy for the sake of work and family.

Only now, work had changed and family expected no pound of flesh at all ... never had, actually. That monstrous and grotesque parade ground screamer slowly shrank before his mind's eye and became a silly little man, mouthing senseless nothings. Such strange thoughts had never entered his mind before and he wondered where his inner poet had turned up from.

As he pondered a lifetime of obedience and fear to such insane demands – illusory demands – he saw the silly side of his own drivenness, his own blindness and his plodding forever onward on a mission that could never be accomplished. He saw the whole futility of generations of dumb cattle being herded to the milking shed every day, rain or shine, in sickness or in health, for richer or for poorer, till death do us part. Chewing on their meagre cud, the doe-eyed cows knew that no amount of milk would ever be enough to satisfy the appetites of those who had more than they needed. As these bizarre thoughts zipped round his mind, he realised – without knowing how he knew this as he'd never tasted power or affluence – that the more he had, the more he had to fear ... and that fear fuelled the desperate need for more power, money and toys. With surprising clarity he realised just how lucky he was, never having risen to such a position of fear – all he had to lose was the odd night's sleep.

He had reunited with Joan, a person and a reason that felt more real than anything else he had known. As he felt himself plugging back into his marriage, that huge welded plug into his work began to melt and drop away. He sat on the corner of their bed, not sure whether to laugh or cry and he found himself humming an old tune:

*Ringa ringa rosy, a pocketful of posy Atishoo, atishoo, we all fall down ...*

"Darling, you're singing!" said Joan, from under the bedclothes.

"Oh, I didn't know you were awake!" he said swinging around, startled out of his reverie.

"Oh, I've been watching you for some time," she said. "What's going through that busy head of yours?"

"Mmm," he said, not quite knowing where to start. "We just seem to go round and round and have nothing more to show for it than a pocketful of posies ... then we all fall down ... whatever that means!" He smiled at her and at his own nonsense.

"Gosh, that's deep for this early!" Joan said. "You're not going to work are you?"

"No, no, I just realised that I don't have to today and feeling a trifle odd about that," he said. "I know I don't have to but I seem to be a bit guilty about it all. My duty, you know." "Your duty?"

"Well, yes, I was just thinking that there are so many duties one is raised to honour," Arthur said hesitantly, "and I realised, for the first time, you are my first duty ... my first concern and work just doesn't have the hold it had before. I'm not sure what's happened."

"So what is your momentous decision, dear?" she asked, "to flee or not to flee?"

"Not to flee it is," he said smiling, "although, if it wasn't today, the decision would have been different – I'd be off to work, unquestionably but, somehow, I'm unplugging from that ... not sure what's happened."

"Well, why don't you plug yourself back into bed, here, and I'll bring the master up some breakfast," said Joan, pulling back the bedclothes on his side.

"But, I ... I ... should, we should ..."

"We should be getting ready for the funeral on Thursday and doing all sorts of other things but it's not even seven o'clock," said Joan firmly, "so get into this maiden's bed and we could perhaps plug into each other, somehow ..."

"Oh, ah," said Arthur, feeling a tingle rising within. "Gosh yes, well, if you insist!" He gingerly crept back into bed feeling as if he was slightly to the side of himself, watching a strange little play he didn't know the script for ... yet he was also the writer, happily unsure of what to write next. As they snuggled together he had a deep and warm feeling of coming home.

"This, my dear ... why didn't we do this more often?" he asked, brushing a stray hair back from her face. "It's ... it's just, well, so comfortable."

"Comfortable? Comfortable!" said Joan in mock horror. "So you think I'm fat?"

"No, no dear, not at all," said Arthur trying to recover lost ground. "I didn't mean physical comfortable. It just feels, well, comfortable like, oh, I don't know. All I can say is it's like coming home. It just feels right, so right."

"Yes Arthur Bayly, I know what you mean," said Joan quietly as her free hand moved down his body.

As they lay back in each other's arms, feeling hazy and sweet, Arthur felt that familiar, urgent and unpleasant call to arms. He moved as if to leap out of bed and caught himself quickly – today was different – pleasantly, oddly different.

"You're jumpy dear," said Joan dreamily, "are you off to work now that you've had your wicked way with me?"

"Hmm, I nearly was, actually," said Arthur smiling as he settled back into the warmth of her embrace. "It's hard to shake off years of training at the front. I feel like a soldier who'd volunteered to sacrifice himself for some dratted cause I knew nothing about and, now, I've gone AWOL and feel guilty about that."

"Well you can always go back but today you're being ordered by Colonel Joan to stay right here while you are served breakfast!" said Joan. "After that, we can discuss what to do with your work."

"Yes Sir ... Ma'am," he said as she slipped out of the bed and down stairs. 'So this is what it's like not to work,' he thought, 'a bit unnerving, really.'

After a hearty English breakfast of fried sausages, bacon, eggs and baked beans, soldier Arthur was ready to tackle the work, which he did at a leisurely pace. At nine o'clock he reported for duty by phoning his work, just as his son reported for duty with his two children. The latter were hushed and hustled into the lounge while Arthur made contact.

"Good morning, AIL Insurance, Halee speaking."

"Ah, good morning Halee, it's Arthur Bayly here." "Oh, sir, are you okay?" asked Halee, concerned.

"Oh! Ah, I suppose I am," said Arthur, savouring the question. "Actually, I'm strangely peaceful, despite my reason for not being at work today."

"So you've slipped through a crack?"

"Slipped through a crack?"

"Slipped through a crack in the map," explained Halee, "You've slipped through a crack in your map, the way you had life planned. You might slip back. You might not."

"Golly, what an interesting thought," said Arthur, then quickly remembering that he had a reason to call. "I won't be in today or for the next few days as my mother-in-law has just died."

"Oh, I'm so sorry about that, Sir."

"Yes, thank you Halee, but Joan and I feel oddly happy about what's happened," said Arthur, surprised that he found himself explaining this to a girl he hardly knew.

"Well, sir, good luck on your journey," said Halee. "I guess we won't see you back here then." "Oh dear no, I will probably be back next week," Arthur protested.

"Sorry, sir, but you may not be," said Halee firmly. "When you slip through a crack in the map and are feeling right about it, despite any circumstances, you don't usually want to come back. You might try but the old map's never the same again with that rip in it." "Gosh," said Arthur, at a loss for words.

"Oh Sir, I'm so sorry, I shouldn't be telling you what to do..."

"Oh, that's perfectly okay," said Arthur, smiling. "In fact, what you say sounds quite logical. How do you know this?"

"Because I slipped through a crack in my map," said Halee. "I had to get away from New Zealand and here I am in London and enjoying every bit of it."

"Oh, oh, do you think I'll have to move ... you know, to another country?" asked Arthur.

"You may not need to but if you do, it will be much easier than would have been before," said Halee. Arthur smiled that he should be asking questions about his life from a mere slip of a girl.

"Hmm, well thank you Halee," said Arthur, not quite knowing what to say next and reluctant to hang up the phone. "I suppose we shall speak later in the week?"

"Of course, Sir, and don't forget to listen to your heart."

"What? Do you think I might have a heart attack?" asked Arthur, suddenly alarmed.

"No, no, no Sir!" said Halee, chuckling, "No, nothing like that. I just meant to listen to your heart for guidance, for decisions. Hear that quiet voice of peace."

"Peace?"

"Yes. If you're stewing over a decision, make the choice that brings you that deep sense of peace," explained Halee, "any other decision can be rejected."

"Oh, gosh, I'd never heard of that before," said Arthur, wondering how a young lass could propound so much wisdom. "You're quite a wise young thing, aren't you?"

"I'm your angel for today Sir," said Halee brightly, "and you'll be someone else's angel for today. We all get a turn every day. Cool, aye?"

"Well, yes, quite," said Arthur, wondering how such a mundane phone call could become philosophical so easily. "So you'll tell Mary that I am indisposed and I'll ring her later in the week?"

"Absolutely, sir, and you take care of yourself."

As Arthur hung up the phone, he felt quite at peace. He sat a while and Joan eventually came in and put her arms around him.

"Apparently, dear, I've slipped through the map," he said smiling into her hair.

"Hmm, maybe it's been more active than that," said Joan. "Maybe you leaped off the edge of your map. You played your part in this, you know."

"Hmm," said Arthur, vaguely wondering what any of it meant.

"Now, Arthur, you didn't tell me what a hero you were," said Joan leaning back, looking into his eyes.

"Hero?"

"Yes, Martin's bought this morning's paper and there's more of your story. It appears you tackled a local drug dealer, quite a vicious man, apparently. And you saved a woman and her child and the police have been after him for six months and you did it single handed!" said Joan with tears spilling out with the words. "Someone took a photo. It's definitely you!"

"Yes, yes, I told you about it and I'm not sure it happened quite the way they say," said Arthur, feeling that his memory had slipped through some crack or other. "But I do remember they seemed quite pleased to have him caught. But perhaps we'd better let Martin get off to his work now."

As he and Joan entered the lounge he was surprised that his frenetic son and lively grandchildren were peacefully playing on the floor – something he'd never seen before. Arthur found himself easing down with them and, instead of the usual flurry and screaming, the children quietly sidled sideways into his arms.

"Hello Granddad, you look sad and happy at the same time," said Timothy, looking into Arthur's eyes.

"Well, Timothy, you could well be right," said Arthur, hugging him. "And how are you, my young man?"

"I'm staying here with you and Nana," said Timothy, his big smile answering the question.

"And how are you, young lady?" asked Arthur.

"Hmm, I like hugging you, Grandad," said Katie, snuggling in closer.

Arthur looked across at Martin, who looked up from the child's puzzle he was doing with red round his eyes.

"Are you alright, Martin? I thought you wanted to rush off to a conference somewhere?" asked Arthur.

"Yes, I was Dad," said Martin quietly. "Look, I know this is an awful time for you and Mum with Grandie dying and everything. I've got some news too. It's all happening at once, isn't it?"

"Is it bad news, Martin?"

"I'm afraid so, Dad."

"Look everyone, perhaps I'll go and make a pot of tea for all of us," said Joan quickly. "Come on Timothy and Katie, you can help Nana with the biscuits."

"The English remedy for any problem under the sun - a good old cup of tea!" said Martin, smiling sadly.

"Yes, a cup of tea and a chat might be what we all need," said Joan taking the children's little hands in her own. "Isn't that right Doctor Katie and Doctor Timothy?"

"Yes, Nana, we'll make some medicine to make everyone better," said Katie as the three skipped out to the kitchen.

"So Martin, your news?" asked Arthur.

"Oh, Dad, you've got enough of your own stuff going on," said Martin, uncharacteristically avoiding discussion about himself.

"Martin," said Arthur sternly, "I want to know what's happening for you. There's plenty of time for our things."

"Well, Dad, Ruth says she's … she's met someone." "Met who?" asked Arthur, not comprehending.

"A man…"

"A man to do with work? Could this be a promotion?" asked Arthur, knowing Martin's sole topic of conversation.

"No, no, no, Dad. A man," said Martin, smiling through the tears that had started down his cheeks. He wiped his hand over his face quickly. "It's a man, a bloody man."

"Oh, Martin, there's no need to swear…"

"I'm sorry Dad, but she says she's fallen in love with him. She wants to leave me," said Martin quickly. "There, I've said it. I was too scared to think it, now I've said it!"

"Oh, Martin, golly …" said Arthur, feeling out of his depth. "Oh, son, oh, gosh."

"Yes, gosh and bugger and damn!" said Martin. "It's all a bit … bloody much. Sorry Dad, I just want to use every swear word I know. What else can I say?"

"Yes, yes, I suppose these times are what swear words are for," said Arthur, seeing the pain on his son's face and the need for comic relief. He felt he should comfort Martin, somehow, but wasn't sure what to do. "Can I help?"

"Well, actually Dad, right now, I'd like a great big hug!" Arthur nodded dumbly and both men stood and hugged each other for the first time in twenty years. Arthur could feel Martin's sobs shaking his body. He patted Martin's back, feeling decidedly awkward but not wanting to pull away.

"Oh, hell Dad, this is such a mess," said Martin through is tears, "and I'm supposed to be here to support you two."

"Look, Martin," said Arthur standing back with his hands on Martin's shoulders. "We've had four deaths here in the last twenty four hours …"

"Four deaths?"

"Yes, four. My job's become unsafe, somehow. I think I ended some criminal's career. Your grandmother has died and now your, ah, situation," said Arthur, finding clarity through the confusion. "None of us quite knows what to do about any of it. And, as they say, if you're at the crossroads and don't know what to do, do nothing," he said wondering who *they* were and where he'd heard that before ... maybe he just made it up.

"You've lost your job, Dad?" asked Martin, picking up on one piece of Arthur's speech. "Ah, yes, you said something last night."

"Yes, well, not lost it but they've asked me not to work at the office, whatever that means," said Arthur. "Actually, I've been dreaming of change but not quite this one! I was thinking of sunny skies and deserts, really. And, now that it's happened – whatever that is – I'm not sure I want to go back."

"Hell, gosh, Dad, I thought you'd never leave that place," said Martin, probably relieved to be talking about someone else's problem.

"Mmm, nor did I!" said Arthur. "I don't know quite what to do, actually. But, being the wise old man that I am, I'm doing nothing. Just cogitating at the moment."

"Hmm, maybe that's what I need to do right now," said Martin, plumping himself down on the sofa.

"Just stop trying to fix everything, just get through the day."

"Very wise," said Arthur, stepping aside as cups of tea and a plate of biscuits were brought in.

"Thank you children, now you can bring your glasses of juice in, if you like," said Joan, sitting beside Martin.

"But they might spill juice on the carpet. Ee can't have that," said Martin, reverting to his usual control-self.

"Darling, with what's happened, do you think spilled juice is a big concern right now?" asked Joan, handing him his cup of tea.

"No, I don't suppose so," Martin said, sitting back and smiling.

"Now, dear, weren't you off to a conference somewhere?" asked Joan.

"Oh, yes I was, a conference in Geneva for two days but I'm not going now. I've cancelled out," said Martin. "Seems like there's enough going on here at the moment!" "Ruth has left Martin, dear," whispered Arthur to Joan.

"Oh Martin!" said Joan, looking shocked.

"And do the children know?" asked Arthur, quietly, as they left to get their drinks.

"Oh, sort of. They think Mummy wants a holiday for a while," said Martin, sighing. "I just can't bring myself to tell them ... or even what to say. I don't think I'm dealing with it very well."

"What did Ruth tell the children?" asked Joan. "She must have said something to them."

"I don't think she said anything," said Martin. "She just turned up last evening, a bit late, acted normal with them, put them to bed, told me her news, stayed the night and left this morning. I don't even know when she's coming back to get her stuff or what's going on. All I know is that he's an Australian and she met him through work, somehow."

"Oh, Martin, you poor thing, you must be feeling so confused," said Joan, putting her arm around his shoulder.

Uncharacteristically, Martin leaned into her as the children returned. "Are you crying, Daddy," asked Timothy.

"Oh, no, not really," said Martin, wiping his face quickly. "Just feeling a bit tired, Timmy. Now, did you know that Grandad is a hero – he caught a criminal for the police yesterday?" "Grandad did?" asked Katie, wide-eyed.

"You did?" asked Timothy, wide-eyed.

"Well, it wasn't quite like that," said Arthur, embarrassed. "I just happened to be there and he sort of stumbled over me." Martin picked up his paper and read the article out – an article that was remarkably accurate considering no reporters were there, thought Arthur. And it did, he thought, make him sound very heroic. As Martin showed everyone the photo, Arthur wondered who took it – it showed him talking to the mother and child on the park seat and identified them as the people he had saved from this dangerous criminal.

The rest of the day was spent with funeral arrangements and Arthur was surprised at how many friends his mother-in-law had. He'd thought she had spent all her life inside her house and realised she must have had a life while he was at work, each day. He was also surprised at Joan's quietness and her

... softness ... yes, softness was the word. She seemed happy with whatever he did and suggested and seemed happy to let him lead and make decisions. It was a little unnerving, really. But quite nice too.

The grandchildren were no trouble at all. In fact, they were very helpful, doing little tasks that Arthur set them and he found he was able to relax around them, for the first time.

# The Blonde Tracker

*Thursday 8th March 2012, 2.30 p.m.*

The funeral was simple and surprising – many people spoke of Joan's mother and Arthur realised how little he knew of her. Afterwards, they took a taxi to Dottie's where tea and cakes were served for anyone attending. Martin and the children didn't stay long and Arthur and Joan left as soon as they respectfully could.

Walking home from Dottie's, Joan turned to Arthur, "You know, this might sound a bit strange, callous even, but I'm still not sad like I'm supposed to be." "But you were crying in the church," said Arthur.

"Yes I was Arthur, I had a good old weep, didn't I?" said Joan, smiling. "And I've had a few tears over the last few days too, as you know."

"So you must be sad," suggested Arthur, confused.

"Crying doesn't mean we're sad," said Joan. "You see, she had an uneventful life but it became a serene one. Things weren't always good with her and Dad. In fact, he was downright abusive at times. However, through all her trials, she learned to forgive herself and everyone she knew."

"Forgive herself?" asked Arthur, confused again as he stepped back to let others to pass on the pavement.

"Yes, forgive herself – that's the only thing we have to do," said Joan, patiently as he caught up to her again. "When we forgive ourselves our defects, our errors, we can forgive everyone else and the world."

"Right," said Arthur, uncertainly.

"She'd learned to accept herself and, with that acceptance, came a serenity that everyone noticed," said Joan. "You heard what everyone said about her at the service, didn't you?"

"Yes I did and I was quite moved," said Arthur as a warm feeling arose in his chest. "I had no idea she had so many friends – that she'd touched so many people. And she didn't go anywhere." "She didn't have to; they came to her," said Joan.

"So you're sad because she's gone?" asked Arthur, trying to put the pieces of the puzzle together.

"No love, we're never sad for what we've lost; we're sad for what could have been," said Joan quietly as she stopped and turned to Arthur. "I think I was crying for relief – relief that she's come home to herself, to accepting and loving herself. Maybe the relief is that it's possible and I can have that too. I hope so."

"Crying for relief that you could also have her serenity?" asked Arthur, trying to keep himself up with the conversation. "So you're sure you're not sad to have lost her?"

"Yes, I am sure of that, Arthur," said Joan, smiling up at her confused looking husband. "Look, I loved my mother – you know that."

"Yes ..."

"And yes, you and I had our differences but she was a rock when things weren't going well for us," she said quietly. "You know, she never judged or criticised either of us – just listened and smiled. Offered me cups of tea and biscuits and smiled and listened. I guess she knew that I knew my own answers, even when I didn't think I did. Do you understand?"

"I think so," said Arthur, gingerly, "and she never said anything about me?"

"Nope! Not ever!" said Joan firmly. "And nothing bad about me either. She'd just smile and ask, 'So, what can you do about that, dear?'"

"And did you know what to do?" asked Arthur, seeing another side of his mother-in-law.

"Not usually!" said Joan, smiling at the memories. "I had no idea and felt really trapped and so would go on about my troubles, over and over, and she'd just smile, offer another cup of tea and say, 'Well dear, you know what to do about that, don't you?' Of course I didn't know what to do. Or, I didn't think I knew."

"So, if you didn't know what to do, what did you do?" asked Arthur, with some of the pieces of his puzzle missing.

"Not sure. Maybe we don't have to fix everything," said Joan, musing. "Maybe knowing that someone believed in me, accepted me, was all the fixing I needed. And now I have you for that." "Me?" asked Arthur as he dropped the puzzle board in his mind and the pieces scattered.

"Look, Arthur, we all need a human pillow, a friend who will accept who we are, dark and light bits alike," said Joan patiently. "Mum was my pillow. I could fall into her and I was always safe. Now it feels like you've returned and I can fall into you."

"Like a changing of the guard!" said Arthur, trying to laugh away the rising feeling inside.

"I guess so," said Joan, smiling. "And I want to be that for you, your human pillow, a safe place to fall into."

"Oh, sorry!" said Arthur as a pedestrian bumped him.

"Sorry mate," said an Australian voice as a tall, blonde man sauntered past. "Hey, Arthur, it *is* you!" "Pardon?" asked Arthur, his brain registering a likeness but not a name.

"Greg. Greg Cousins! We met in the *Has Beens* café yesterday."

"Are you following me?" Arthur's stomach was flip flopping uncomfortably.

"Hardly, I'm on the run and I can't stop! But we need to talk, Arthur." Greg ran off and Arthur definitely didn't want to talk with Greg Cousins. It was the last thing he wanted to do. Arthur wondered who he might be running from and then pushed the thought from his mind, determined to return to more domestic concerns.

"Arthur, who is that young man?"

"I'm not sure and I don't want to think about him at the moment, if you don't mind." "Are you sure, Arthur?" asked Joan, looking at him quizzically.

"Look dear, I want to hear about your mother," said Arthur, "but don't you think we should move on? Get inside?"

"Yes, you're right."

"And I'll make you a cup of tea and you'll know what to do next!" said Arthur, trying to hide a sneaky smile.

"Arthur Bayly, you *do* have a sense of humour," said Joan as she took his arm and strode off up the street. "You know, Arthur," she said, stopping suddenly, "maybe we've been hiding our full selves from each other, do you think?"

"Absolutely dear," said Arthur, smiling, "and I never realised, before, that you can't talk and walk at the same time."

"Arthur!" said Joan, cuffing him gently on the arm. "Okay, I won't stop again! It's just ... I don't know, it's just that we've started communicating again and I have so much to say to you. So much time seems to have been lost and I want to make it all up right now!"

"You impatient thing, you," said Arthur, smiling and pulling his wife to him. "But we can make it all up here we can do it in the comfort of our home ..."

"Oh, you practical thing, you!" she said as they moved off again.

Joan unlocked the door as Arthur stood there, unable to move. He couldn't stop thinking uneasy thoughts about that Greg Cousins. And who might be chasing him.

"Come in, love," said Joan. "You can tell me what you've been up to when you're safe inside." "But ... but ..." said Arthur, struggling to find more useful words.

"Arthur, inside!" commanded Joan, taking his hand firmly.

"But ... but ..." said Arthur, like a cracked record.

Joan led him to his chair in the sitting room and he obediently sat.

"I'll get us a cup of tea, love," said Joan, looking concerned. "I'll be right back."

As she put the cups down on the small table, Arthur shook his head as if waking from a dream ... or a nightmare.

"So, my dear, what do you make of it all?" asked Joan. "Your job turns shaky, you become a local hero and my mother dies on Monday. Martin's marriage seems over, we have my mother's funeral and a young man bumps into you, and you go all silent ... suspicious."

"Oh yes, it *was* the same man wasn't it – the Australian!" said Arthur, as if a light suddenly went on in his brain.

"What Australian? The one in the café?" asked Joan. "What have you been up to? There's got to be more than you've told me."

"Oh, I don't know love," said Arthur, wiping his forehead. "I keep thinking there's something I've missed ... something I saw that I've forgotten ... something ..."

"Arthur, Arthur, stop, stop," said Joan, holding his hand. "Stop thinking and you'll remember. And have your tea."

"Oh yes, I'd quite forgotten!" he said, smiling wanly. "Stop thinking to remember ..." He found this mildly amusing, somehow.

"And, as far as you know, you don't know that young man, that Australian?" asked Joan, trying to put the jigsaw of Arthur's week together. "You haven't been investigating an insurance case he's in or something?"

"No, but he said *us*, as if there's a group," said Arthur as the lump in his stomach returned.

"Yes, it did sound a bit threatening," said Joan. "Now, why don't we call that police officer, that Amanda, and talk to her about it?"

"Oh Joan, what a good idea!" said Arthur, feeling less vulnerable, suddenly. "She gave me her mobile number. I hope she doesn't mind."

"If she does, she can say so," said Joan lifting the phone.

Amanda was around at their place in fifteen minutes, in civilian clothes. Arthur and Joan had another cup of tea and Amanda cradled an instant coffee, without enthusiasm. She listened to their story.

"Have your coffee before it gets cold," said Joan.

"Oh, ah, yes, I don't usually drink instant," said Amanda, looking embarrassed. She sipped at her coffee with little obvious relish.

Joan went into the dining room and returned with Monday evening's newspaper and showed Arthur the photo of the scene he had witnessed.

"Who's that behind the woman in the photo, Arthur?" asked Joan.

"No one ... oh, gosh, it's blurry but it could be that young man, the one who gave me my keys," said Arthur, wondering if it was really such fun being 007.

"Who took your keys from you in the first place," said Joan firmly.

"Yes, maybe he did ..." said Arthur.

"Look, it's not a good photo but it's something to go on," said Amanda, standing to leave. "I'll get another paper and start some inquiries."

"But we've got you from your home – why don't you stay for tea?" asked Joan.

"What, and deprive me of my reheated, malnourished, microwaved chicken and spud?" said Amanda, laughing as she ran her hands through her golden curls. "That would be lovely, thanks."

As they sat down to dinner, some time later, Joan insisted on saying grace.

"Okay, help yourself, Amanda," said Joan, pushing bowls of steaming food towards Amanda. "We don't usually say grace but I just wanted to thank my mother for her help. Maybe she can help us more from where she is now."

"Yes, the three days are up now," said Amanda.

"Three days?" asked Joan.

"Well, most indigenous people think that it takes three days after death for spirit to assert itself," said Amanda.

"Assert itself?" asked Arthur, wondering how a perfectly ordinary English supper had so quickly turned into a ... a, um, talk on death and other odd stuff.

"Yes, sort of get itself together," said Amanda. "Most of them believe that when we die, our spirit is given three days to decide whether it wants to stay in spirit or to return to earth. A study in America found that twenty five percent of bodies in morgues came back to life within three days."

"Oh my God, do they really?" asked Arthur, unable to continue spooning out peas from the bowl.

"Yes, it seems there's a sort of waiting period while we're given a choice about coming back or not and we can do so within those three days, even defying medical science," said Amanda.

"What a lovely subject for supper," said Joan, chuckling.

"Oh sorry," said Amanda, blushing.

"Oh, no, go on, this is fascinating," said Joan. "I want to know what happens."

"Well, I don't know. I don't think anybody really does," said Amanda, warming to her subject. "But this three-day wake up thing is why most traditions wait at least three days and why they have the body at home in an open casket – it allows the body to wake up and get up. Hiding a body in a drawer in a mortuary goes against all that."

"Oh, my gosh, I hadn't thought of that!" said Joan, gravy jug poised in mid-air. "Do you think we should have had have my mother at home with us, Arthur?"

"Oomph," said Arthur, surprised at such a question while his mouth was full of mashed potato.

"Look, I wasn't actually suggesting anything like that," said Amanda, smiling at Joan and probably wondering how long the gravy jug would remain suspended above Joan's food. "Did you want some gravy?"

"Oh, yes, sorry!" said Joan, pouring her gravy and passing it to Amanda.

"All I was suggesting, based on the indigenous people I've worked with, is that you may get stronger help from her now that the three days have passed."

"Looks like we're not on our own, dear," said Arthur, smiling crookedly.

"On our own ... I don't think we're ever on our own, Arthur," said Joan, smiling. A worrying little spider began crawling about in Arthur's tummy – the conversation seemed to have turned itself back to the dark and shadowy places he did not want to venture into.

"You're right," said Amanda and Arthur studied his steak rather intently, hoping not to be noticed ... hoping it would all go away if he pretended he couldn't hear. "Even in my darkest of times, there was always help when I asked. I just had to want to listen."

"You mean you've had spirit speak to you, do things for you?" asked Joan with peas and steak on fork, aloft.

"I don't know if I'd call it spirit as I don't know what *it* was," said Amanda, trying to explain the unexplainable. "But I do know that when I've been in an impossible position, when I've needed help or answers, when I've stopped to listen, the impossible seemed to happen."

"What, like miracles?" asked Joan who realised her fork had not yet reached her mouth, then swallowed said peas and steak.

"Like I said, I can't put labels to these things – like spirit or miracle – but things just seem to happen, people seem to turn up unexpectedly, and I'm set back on the path again," said Amanda. "Hey, this is the best meal I've had for ages, thanks, and these squishy peas are yummy!" She tucked in enthusiastically.

"Squishy peas? Oh you mean the mushy peas!" said Arthur, chuckling and relieved to be on solid ground again. "That's an English delicacy. We're very proud of our mushy peas. Without them we wouldn't have conquered the world, created the Empire or won the war ..."

"Arthur, you're being quite silly. I don't know what's got into you!" said Joan, smiling while shaking more salt over her potatoes and brussell sprouts. "But I want to know about all this help Amanda's talking about. Go on."

Arthur settled back to his dinner a little mollified to think that things like spirits and miracles had not been dispensed with yet. Like a gazelle at the water hole, he remained alert.

"Well, after my really dark time, when I started to come out of it ... did Arthur tell you?" asked Amanda.

"Yes, he told me a little of it," said Joan.

"So, I decided I needed a job but not one that was too taxing – my mind was a bit, you know, fragile," said Amanda. "So I ended up going for an interview at a government department, doing office work."

"And, by a miracle, you ended up here!" said Joan laughing.

"Well, sort of, but it took several interventions, shall we say," said Amanda. "I went to the interview and the office at that address was shut and so I went next door to the police station to ask where they'd moved to, met up with a friend I hadn't seen for ten years, had lunch with her and ended up joining the police!"

"So you ended up working for a government department!" said Arthur, deciding it was safe to join in again.

"Huh! I'd never thought of that!" said Amanda, helping herself to more mashed potato from the bowl. "Then, two years later ... I suppose you want to hear the end of this boring story?"

"It's not boring at all, Amanda," said Joan. "Go on!"

"I usually do – go on that is!" said Amanda. "So, after two years I found out about this exchange programme with Britain. I had always wanted to travel and, because I'd helped in a smuggling case, with links to England and Scotland and it had seemed to have something to do with insurance scams – I'd worked in insurance before ..."

"You worked in insurance?" asked Arthur. "That's where I've always worked!"

"Who do you work for?" asked Amanda, about to scoop up some potato and stopping suddenly.

"I work for AIL," said Arthur, "up in London."

"AIL? Oh my God!" exclaimed Amanda, going quite red.

"Well, as I told you earlier, my work there has changed, as of Monday," said Arthur, hoping to stop that creeping spider in his stomach from starting up again. Amanda's reaction did not help.

"Of course, of course, changes upon changes!" said Amanda in a vain attempt to act flippant.

"Is AIL involved in any of this?" asked Joan, asking the question Arthur wanted to but couldn't.

"Oh hell!" said Amanda, looking down, sighing. She put down her knife and fork and looked directly at Joan, then at Arthur. The silence was palpable. "Look, I'm really sorry. I've overstepped the mark. I shouldn't have said what I'm working on. I just felt so comfortable with you two – the first two really friendly people I've met in the six months I've been here. I'm so sorry, I just should not have said anything ..."

"Amanda dear, Amanda," said Joan, patting her hand, "it's okay, it really is. We're not police informants, we're not secret agents, we're not going to tell anyone. It's okay dear."

"Oh Joan, Arthur, you're such lovely people and you've had a horrible, shocking week and I go and blab my mouth off!" said Amanda, wiping tears from her face.

"Well, perhaps this is another of those miraculous moments you keep having!" said Arthur, trying to lighten the mood, while wondering how such words found their way into his brain and out his mouth – perhaps he was going mad too. Amanda looked into his eyes and smiled and sighed. Arthur felt quite tearful himself.

"By gosh, Arthur, you're probably right!" exclaimed Joan. "Maybe we're meant to know about this for some reason. It might explain that young Australian man or something ..."

"Yes, maybe you're right, Arthur," said Amanda, wiping the last of her tears as she sat up purposefully. "Okay, I can't take back what I've told you and I can't give you any more details. I'd be out of the police force quick smart and no goodbyes! But what you do know is what you saw on Monday, in the middle of Croydon and that, yes AIL is part of our investigation. But please, please, please don't tell anyone I said any of this. NO ONE. PLEASE!"

"Amanda, of course we won't," said Joan patting her arm. "And we'll be fine with my mother's protection now!" They all giggled, in spite of Arthur's spider having taken on a slightly sinister feel in his tummy. Still, he'd always dreamed of being a secret agent, a James Bond. Maybe this was his chance to savour some secret agenting.

"Look Amanda, I was at AIL for a long time but I was hardly in any position of power," said Arthur, feeling a stirring of anxiety about what else was going to come out of his disobedient mouth, "but if there is anything you need to know that I can help you with, please do ask. As I said, I don't know any deep and dark secrets there but I might be able to steer you in the right direction. I do know how their systems work and who does what and when and all that. I probably know more than I think I do, if I think about it ..."

"Oh Arthur, I really don't want to get you into any trouble," said Amanda seriously. "Some of these people are quite without conscience, quite ... well, quite viscous, if I must be blunt. There's a lot at stake – probably a lot more than I know, actually."

"I think it's time for another cup of tea, don't you?" suggested Joan, obviously more comfortable with spirits and miracles than with criminals. She gathered up the plates and was gone before Amanda or Arthur had a chance to move. They looked at each other and smiled.

"Look Amanda, you could be right that I don't know what I'd be in for," said Arthur. "I know nothing of the criminal world and I definitely don't want to put Joan in danger. But, well, I've had some strange dreams ... or thoughts, I suppose ... about Australia, lately, and then I meet two New Zealand ladies and then I witness New Zealanders in a police scuffle on Monday. Then this young Australian man turns up. I don't know. And I don't know about all this mad spirit stuff but, well, maybe we're not as much in control of our lives as we think ..."

"Yes, Arthur, I think I know what you mean," said Amanda, smiling at his attempts to put meaning to mess. "Maybe there's a kind of destiny, a sort of inevitability, and certain things are going to happen anyway and the only choice, the only free will we have, is how we deal with them. I don't know."

"Mmm, I don't know about any of that," said Arthur, feeling the conversation turning towards those dark and creepy depths again. "But when I look at my life – and I've been shocked into doing that this week – I haven't done much of note. I haven't made much of a splash in the swimming pool of life, if you like. Now maybe, just maybe, this is my chance to do something ... oh, I don't know ... to make a difference, somehow."

They both sat looking at each other and, in the silence, they knew no words were necessary. After a moment that seemed to stretch for eternity, Amanda began to cry.

"Oh, Arthur, I wish you had been my father!" she said between sobs. "I know it's an awful thing to say but ... aah, I don't know, I can talk and you listen. I just feel a real connection with you."

After Amanda left, they both sat down, sighing to each other.

Arthur thought he was unfazed by the Australian incident, as he called it, but when the busyness stopped, that queezy, hollow feeling returned to his stomach. It just sat there mocking him while he worried about who might be watching them. He went over to the drawn curtains and peered out at the deepening gloom. 'Deepening gloom,' he thought to himself, 'it's everywhere – outside and right here inside.'

"Are you OK, Arthur?" asked Joan. "You look nervous."

"Oh, ah, yes, I'm fine dear," he said, unable to look her in the eye. "Well, stop pacing – you look like you're being stalked," she said.

"Well, if you must know, that Australian chap has me quite rattled," Arthur said. "I just can't shake the feeling of ... of ..."

"Of being followed," said Joan, finishing off.

"Yes, yes, of being followed," he said, not really wanting to say it but feeling fractionally better now that he had. "I don't know why and I don't know what it means for us. I mean, what is it, exactly, that we're not to do? I just don't understand," he said as a shudder coursed up his spine.

"Oh, Arthur, my dear," said Joan embracing him in a bear hug. "I'm worried too ... no, I'm frightened, I'm really frightened. Let's be honest about it. We're both frightened and we don't know what to do about it."

"Oh Joan," said Arthur, feeling the warmth of her body and lost for any more words. He didn't want to let her go, she felt safe and comforting ... like a little boy needing his mother's hugs. Quite pathetic, really, he surmised. He went to pull away.

"Don't go now, Arthur," said Joan quietly. "I feel like a little girl needing a really big hug from Daddy. Bit pathetic, really, but there you are."

Arthur smiled and relaxed into her again. Then an idea struck him.

"You know, Joan, I daresay the more we stay in here, the more we'll feel trapped. You know, not seeing or facing the enemy," he said, pulling back a little and looking into her tear-stained face. "Why don't we go for a walk, face the rotten sods ... I don't know, maybe just prove to ourselves we're safe and we can do normal things."

"Brilliant Arthur! Brilliant!" said Joan, brightening. "Let's do it now!" She strode off and returned with coats and keys.

# The Making of Mary Collins

*Up to 2010*

Life hadn't worked out as Mary Collins had hoped, not at all. In fact, if she'd had a plan (which she didn't) this definitely wouldn't have been it.

In a strange way, her life had gone fast and slow at the same time. In her honest moments, she would admit that most days were interminably slow, like wading through a swamp. At the same time her life had seemed to flash by so fast for her to ever to have grabbed it by the lapels or even the bloody neck, and say, "Now, look here, Life, we're going this damned way. OK!" It just passed her by too quickly.

Of course, there had been some bright spots (just enough to stop her giving up entirely), some glimpses of hope that kept her believing that elusive happiness was just around the next wee glass of wine ... glimpses of hope that usually died a sad old death that chocolate and red wine could not help her forget though, God forbid, she tried hard enough to forget that way!

She still had her dreams of long, languid, luscious Sunday mornings, rural views, sun filtering in, breakfast with a luscious chap, reading together, crosswords together, cuddling together, making love together ... all that stuff.

Somehow, that luscious chap had never materialised – well, not in any bed on any Sunday morning. There had been a few interested and quite-luscious chaps but, though there'd been dinners out, movies together and furtive snoggings in dark pub cubicles, none of them had gone the distance – any distance, really – and she now believed herself to be too old for a first marriage and children and too young for someone else's second marriage. She just seemed to fall between the cracks in everyone's life ... and her own life, too, it seemed.

She had left Dunfermline with such hope. This Scottish town, the birthplace of Andrew Carnegie, the wealthiest man of his time, had absorbed little of Carnegie's wealth and her parents had absorbed even less. Her father, a butcher who left the house at 4.30am every day (perhaps that's why she dreamed of long Sunday mornings as she'd had none), from the three-bedroom brick, terraced house they rented. Determined not to follow her family's dogged wretchedness – her brother, Angus, also worked with his hands, as a welder – she had left with high hopes of emulating Mr Carnegie. Her slim five-foot three-inch frame, topped with long, luscious, black tresses, strode from the house that day, oozing confidence while her mind struggled, in vain, to hide her fear of the big, wild world out there.

She stayed with her Uncle Hughie but his Camden flat in London was no more than a bachelor pad and she soon found a job and a flat of her own. Hughie was fun to stay with but she'd told herself that she'd never make it if she was saddled down with others – success came to those who walked the high road alone. Perhaps, she sometimes ruminated, that was why she was still single ... though where the *making it* was, she never knew.

She always loved the fuzziness of the mist over the heath, with the sun quietly filtering through but, somehow, she'd ended up in jobs without fuzziness – all sharp edges, objective, serious and very urgent. She discovered her mind was more astute than others' – she'd easily see what needed to be done, how to do it and who best to do it. Sometimes she'd get down and dirty, as Uncle Hughie would say, but she really couldn't see why she should when she could order three people to do three jobs and do triple the work she'd do alone.

It wasn't long before she was developing the hard edge of the business world she fell so effortlessly into. Her long locks were gone, replaced by a coiffure that needed little prissing and her black suits echoed those of the men she worked with.

Of course, her apartments had always been in the City, only minutes' walk from work. What a stupid waste of time, spending hours a day on some train, tube or other, when you could jolly well be at work doing something useful. Mary was always the first to work, the last to leave and the first one home. Stupid to do otherwise.

Her brusqueness enabled things to get done and, though her Scottish burr softened the long, cold English vowels she developed, she was more feared than loved, more admired than liked. Maybe, unconsciously, her quick tongue kept people at bay, avoiding connection, closeness, and disappointment. Maybe …

One psychic told her that she had put on weight to insulate herself from the harsh realities of the world. Another suggested it was an unconscious attempt to make her look less attractive and then avoid the abuse her mother had faced. Well, yes, there was a thinner woman in there, not screaming to get out but certainly hiding.

She did wonder why it was she often found herself back at Uncle Hughie's lively little flat, surrounded by his theatrical and New Agey friends – all bright colours, edges as soft as the mist, quick, inconsequential and harmless tongues and no urgency about anything. Nothing mattered and yet everything did, with great passion. So unlike the sterile, uncommitted and cynical types she worked with. Maybe she just needed balance. Maybe, deep down, this lively Scottish lass was really a romantic, an artist, in disguise. A creator not a commander. Who knows?

One of Uncle Hughie's more insightful friends had told her, sitting in his small garden on a Sunday afternoon amid a respectable collection of empty wine bottles, that she should grow her hair – that it was beautiful and it shone like the dew on heather. She had smiled, held herself in and later gone home to cry herself to sleep. As she'd lain there, she wondered, between sobs, if she'd lost something of herself or if there was another part she'd been afraid to lose.

# The Business Of Mary Collins

*Monday 7<sup>th</sup> June 2010, 8.00 a.m.*

The next day she shrugged off all those silly notions and questions and had girded herself in the warrior's black suit, along with a black tie to prove she was done with all that prissy, crying stuff.

She stormed into the office, rearranged the organisation chart and then held a ten-minute meeting to tell everyone who was promoted, demoted and moved sideways. She knew that some of the rearrangements weren't entirely logical but decided that the whole place needed a damned good shakeup anyway – keep the buggers on their toes. That afternoon she had formed two new policies without approval from Commonwealth Insurance's Swindon head office – she just wasn't in the mood for all the paperwork, justifications and two months of procrastination. It was fortuitous that her boss was on extended leave and that his deputy, the chinless wonder of an Operations Director, had a terror of ferocious women and had conceded to Mary's bizarre ideas without a whimper of objection.

The first policy was that all claims, from any client for any reason, would be rejected on first application. Certain minor claims would also be rejected on second application. It saved a lot of paperwork and money and if clients had the gumption to make a claim after being rejected twice, they probably deserved the money and so it was investigated.

The second policy was actually a protection racket, marketed under the pretence of caring for clients. It was a simple matter of creating a new type of policy to cover people who had made claims and didn't want to lose their no-claims bonus – they paid the insurance company a new premium so they wouldn't increase their premiums! The new premium was twelve percent higher than the noclaims bonus would have been so the company made more money and got more clients who, weirdly, thought the insurance company was caring and protective of them. Of course, Mary had to clear the idea with the statisticians but none of them could fault her logic or maths.

When head office found out about it they were up in arms. How dare she break protocol and go over the heads of her superiors? Of course, an example had to be made of her, a young upstart. Can't have people thinking out of line, acting like renegades and encouraging others to do the same – where would things be if chaos reigned? She was summarily dismissed and the insurance club, the British Insurance Institute, was told never to hire her for she was nothing but trouble, uncontrollable, disrespectful and the rest. Of course, everyone at the club heartily agreed with the Commonwealth Insurance representative's sentiments and commiserated on his company's misfortune in hiring her in the first place. Within days of her sacking, through the mist of her shock and depression, there appeared letters and phone calls from nearly every member of the insurance club, very healthy offers of employment. Mary chuckled at the duplicity – they held no trust of honour to their clients and here, she realised, they held none to one another.

Though strangely comical, it was also a sad moment for Mary as she realised what a greedy, faithless world she'd thrown herself into. Though she had rejected the plodding poverty of her parents, she realised what good and honest people they were and she yearned for that for herself.

Though there was pressure from the job offers to answer quickly, she decided to return to her native Scotland for a holiday. Before she did, however, something made her decide to have one interview before she went. Perhaps it was sort of insurance or a way of providing comfort, knowing that something would be organised now, for when she got back. Anyway, she called Sam Black of Allied Insurance Limited, dressed in her favourite "power" clothes and arrived like a virgin, more nervous than she could have guessed at, three hours later.

As he introduced himself, he held her hand a little longer than was usual, while looking deeply into her eyes. She was surprised – intimidated and thrilled, somehow – and felt a little unsure about how to respond. His plump white hands had never performed manual labour, she surmised, and one of them gently grazed her shoulder and she felt comforted to be steered towards a family of lounge chairs in one corner of his massive office. As she eased herself into the ample folds of the black leather chair, she wondered if it was such a good idea to have worn a short skirt. As she wondered how to extricate herself gracefully, she surveyed the oak-panelled office that looked more like a library than an office. Deep green carpet soaked up the sounds and the absence of technology suggested that the modern, outside world stayed outside. This serene and stately island amid the mayhem of the world's financial capital spoke of a guardian with taste and a determination to rule his world his way. She accepted a coffee – Columbian – that appeared almost as soon as she chose it, at the hand of Mr Black's threateningly young secretary.

He seemed to be in no hurry to talk of business or her career and he was most interested in her family and personal interests. He had a way of coaxing out her intimate details without causing discomfort and, on more than one occasion, she had the strange feeling that he already knew the answers to his questions. When he did, eventually, move on to her experience and career aspirations, she knew for sure that he had done his research thoroughly. She felt comforted by his genuine interest – and flattered, in fact – and a little trapped. She knew, without a doubt, there would be no comfort in this position, no safe place to fall as his subordinate. The soft and nurturing glove of his considerable charm, she just knew, could easily and quickly be exchanged for the sharp steel gauntlet of his anger. A far cry from the insipid niceness with which she had previously been surrounded, her spirit felt the call of the wild – a challenge she knew would test her and one she knew she couldn't walk away from.

"So, Mary, what do you think you're worth to us?" he asked, giving her the unexpected challenge of putting a value on herself.

His brazenness emboldened her. "I don't have the answer right now, Mr Black ..." "Sam. Please do call me Sam," he said, interrupting her.

"Oh, ah, Sam," said Mary, trying to recover when she was just getting under way. "You're asking a direct question that I have no answer for." He smiled patiently. "I've been totally engrossed in the insurance industry since I left school and, as you know, my world has been rocked and I have a sense that my whole perspective on anything, especially my work, is severely out of kilter."

"Such honestly and self-awareness from one so young," he mused. "What would help the return of your right perspective?"

"Time out," said Mary, blushing at the compliment and at the embarrassment of wondering if she should really be here, looking for a job. "I've decided I need to get out of the industry, out of the city, and reconnect with my roots for a while. Then I'll be ready for work." "Not for too long, I hope," said Sam, leaning forward, interested.

"I don't know," said Mary, leaning back, acting more nonchalant than she felt. "It may be a week, it may be a month. I just don't know – the last few weeks have been very trying and I want to return to work fully restored."

"Return to the work of insurance, I hope," said Sam.

"Well, it's all I've ever done and I do seem to be very good at it," said Mary, surprising herself. "But, I do find myself treading on very sensitive toes at times."

"You sure do!" said Sam laughing and clapping his hands as he settled back into his chair. "That, my dear, is just what we need here and why we're having this conversation. Things need shaking up around here, around the insurance industry in general, and I'm looking for a co-shaker. As I said, that's why we're having this conversation, Mary."

"I suppose it is," said Mary musing. "I'm just finding it hard to believe an insurance mogul, like yourself, could be a stirrer – I didn't think they existed in these large corporations. They all seem to be so ..."

"Insipid!" said Sam, finishing her sentence. "Let me just say, Mary, that when – not if – you come to work here, you'll have a lot of pleasant surprises," he said, looking meaningfully at her.

"Yes, right," said Mary, unsure if the surprises would be business or personal ones. "Let me take my mini-sabbatical and I'll call you as soon as I'm back on balance and ready to commit."

"Look, Mary, I have to be honest," said Sam, sitting forward again. "I really do want you to work with me ... with us ... and if you accepted now, we can start paying you from tomorrow. Take whatever time you need and you can slip right in when you're ready." He stood up and extended his hand. The interview was obviously over and Mary found herself heading for his door with his guiding arm round her shoulders. "Just give me the phone number where you'll be and we can stay in contact." Mary gave him her mobile number and walked off down the corridor wondering why she had done that. Through the fog of her bewilderment, she fancied she had seen the suited man with the slicked-back, black hair, greying around the edges, who exited the lift as she alighted, somewhere before. She wasn't sure. She looked at the man quickly, with a glint of recognition that was quickly spun from her mind by the other swirling thoughts there. They looked at each other, smiled, and were gone in their separate directions in an instant.

As she walked away from the interview and reviewed it from the nearby café, she was left with the faint impression that Sam could be interested in her for more than her professional ability. She felt tingly inside, anticipating the possibilities. He had made her a firm offer of employment – an attractive offer of employment – but she was determined to make her decision in the clear light of day, so to speak, away from the rush and stress of London. Her desire to go to Scotland waned but she knew she had to make the trip – to reconnect, to restore and to refocus on what she wanted her life to look like. Her parents were pleased, in their dour Scottish way, to hear she was coming home and she felt like a princess all over again.

# Homecoming

*Wednesday 21st June, 2010, 4.30 p.m.*

Out of the office, out of her work clothes, out of London and on the train to her Scottish home, she felt the excitement rising, unexpectedly. Her mind conjured up all sorts of warm family things – cosy chats, funny moments and happy tears – and she was feeling childlike anticipation as she stepped off the train onto the familiar, grimy station. The weather was surprisingly warm and she just knew that this was going to be an especially happy time of her life ... till she saw her mother, hunched shoulders, waiting unsmilingly at the far end of the platform. Of course! She forgot that the child must run to the parent. No great shows of enthusiasm or affection.

"Hmph! Hello lass," said her mother, stepping back from Mary's impending embrace. "So, ye be liking that English food, then?" she asked. Her mother stepped back and eyed Mary's girth with obvious distaste and Mary immediately regretted her trip home.

At a loss for an effective reply, Mary muttered something incoherent and they walked in silence to the bus stop. Neither was inclined to utter more words on the ten-minute bus trip and Mary followed her mother into the house feeling both familiar and strange. Nothing had changed – the frayed rug, the stained and peeling ceiling, the chipped table – and every memory of her childhood flooded back at once. Her mother reacted to her tears by throwing a tea towel at her while telling her to go and clean herself up. Mary escaped to the bathroom, sat on the shaky toilet and gave vent to the mixture of feelings that rose together. Despite her mother's grim proximity – or perhaps because of it – she howled as she'd never done before. Poignant and happy memories mixed themselves with frustration about resistance to her youthful ideas, anger at her father's abuse and her remembered dreams of freedom. The brick in her stomach made her feel physically sick.

Despite the fantasy she had built up about her home town, from distant London, and despite her desire to reconnect with her roots, she realised she just did not belong in this place. She'd been away too long to fit back in comfortably. She even wondered if she had ever loved her parents. Feelings of love and affection certainly did not make their appearance as she rocked and sobbed on that ancient toilet – a good place to let it all go. Eventually she regained some composure and told herself to be strong as she entered the old kitchen for the customary cup of tea and a piece of shortbread.

Mary tried to give her mother enthusiastic and colourful glimpses her life "way down" in London but she knew she was describing something too alien for her mother to comprehend, had her mother even wanted to comprehend it. Mary then listened to her mother's dour description of all the people who had died – and the gossip surrounding those deaths – over the past ten years. Gosh, had it only been ten years since she had last visited? Something drastic had obviously changed in that time and it hadn't been here in Dunfermline. She realised how badly she fitted into this landscape now and wondered if she ever had, really. She listened intently and looked fascinated by her mother's sordid tales of change, while her mind plotted an early escape.

While the smells of the one dinner she ever remembered here filled the kitchen, her father and brother sauntered in, dropped their lunch boxes on the bench and wandered into the lounge with a beer each to watch television. They'd each mumbled their "hellos" and "how yer been, Mary?" as they passed and were gone from the room before she could reply. She wondered if they realised she was back or if she'd even been away at all. She felt small and then the anger exploded. She strode into the room, turned off the TV and stood in front of it, defiantly. You could have heard the carpet sneeze.

"Aw, come on Da, Angus. I come all the way up here to see ya and ye can't even give me the time of day," she said, glaring at them.

"Ouch, Mary, I'm sorry. I just ..." Angus started saying.

"Turn that damned television on!" roared her father, butting in.

"No!" said Mary, starting to regret her outburst and wondering what to do next.

"I said turn that damned television on, woman," shouted her father, sitting forward, ready to pounce, "or I'll clock ye one."

"I'm not your wife, Da. I'm your daughter," said Mary, her anger rising above her indecision.

"Turn that bloody television on, you stroppy wench!"

Never being one to back down, especially when she knew she was right, Mary was tempted to stand her ground. But the memories returned, memories of her mother beaten and sobbing and nothing ever being resolved and the simmering hatred and the inability to be honest and and and ... the whole frustrating futility of it, the powerlessness and the inability to be heard, to be acknowledged, all came flooding back and she was a scared little girl again. She ran as she always had from this home – not to her mother's embrace for that could be cold and threatening too – outside, down the street to sit under the street-lamp beside the old bakery.

James Fordyce was the kindest person she had ever known and many a time he'd wiped a tear, listened to her story and given her a healing doughnut. The simplest things touch the deepest and this spot was a magnet when the world threatened – a still and quiet spot where listening always happened. The bakery had closed long ago and Mr and Mrs Fordyce had moved somewhere else. This Mary knew but the sacredness of this listening spot drew her in with its safe and loving arms. Under that old streetlamp her sobs subsided and she found a little peace, a little quietness, a little acknowledgement in the darkness. No one was there to listen but the image of the Fordyces, those many years ago, reached out with safe arms, enfolding her and dissolving the wretched pain.

She sat with her back to the street lamp, hugging her knees, looking into what was that old bakery shop and wished with all her aching heart that Mr Fordyce would come out the door, slowly smile and invite her in through that leadlight door, over the wide and uneven floorboards and he'd lift her onto a stool and ask, "So, Mary lass, your sadness comes again. What's it feeling like, young lady?" And she'd tell him. And he'd listen. She'd just talk and it would feel like she couldn't stop as the thousands of words crowding in her head were crazily pushing at each other to get out of her mouth and into Mr Fordyce's ears. He'd continue to listen and nod and listen and, eventually, all the words were out and her head was empty of them. She'd feel lighter because the words had been heavy in her brain and she'd smile a little at the relief.

"So what can we do about all that, then?" he'd ask.

By then all thoughts of running away, of burning her house down, of killing her father, of beating her mother were gone and all she wanted to do was to hug her parents and pray for peace.

As she sat there on those wet stones with tears drying on her cheeks, she wished with all her heart to have Mr Fordyce's quiet strength with her now.

"Ye're not only wise, young lass, but you're very strong ... very strong indeed," he'd have said, or words to that effect, and then given her a choice of delicious, doughy, sweet treats ... 'Oh my God!' she thought, 'maybe that's the reason for my weight problems!' She'd been inoculating herself against the pain with delicious, doughy, sweet treats. Then she laughed, realising that *stressed* spelt backwards was *desserts* – one was the antidote for the other! As she chuckled to herself, she heard a scuffle behind her.

"So, Mary lass, yer sadness comes again. What's it feeling like, young lady?" asked Mr Fordyce.

Before she knew it she was in his arms, hugging him with a lifetime's deep gratitude.

"Och aye, lass, not so hard on an old man," he said, chuckling.

"Oh, oh, sorry!" said Mary, loosening her grip on him but unable to let go completely.

"So ye've come back to the old shop for another doughnut, then?" he asked, standing back with his hands on her shoulders.

"Oh I know it's silly, really," she said. "I know the old shop's shut up and no one's here but it just seems so safe here. So calming."

"Well, we weren't here till a month ago when the house next door came up for rent and so we've moved back," he said, looking into her eyes steadily. "I do miss the shop and I do miss our chats. But life goes on, doesn't it?"

"Yes, I suppose it does," said Mary with a smile. "But why do the good things change and the bad things stay the same?"

"Do ye think it's time for a doughnut, Mary lass?" he asked, wiping his hand over his bald head.

"Oh, Mr Fordyce, no doughnuts but a cup of tea would be lovely!" she said, hugging his broad frame again.

"What! No doughnuts?" he said, chuckling. "But they fix everything!"

"No they don't," said Mary. "You do."

"Och aye lass, ye're too kind," he said. "Let's get ye inside and have a chat about that big London town and everything else – see if we can fix the world tonight!"

As she entered the small cottage, the smell of wet wool and home baking welcomed her with its familiar homeliness. The worn patterned carpet, the ugly china ornaments, the traditional embroidery and doyleys all smiled back at her with the welcome of an old friend. In the kitchen, where all good chats and cups of tea were held, she smiled to see Mrs Fordyce had not changed – this short, round, bright-eyed lady with the white curly hair, the red and white checked apron and the soft smile. The quiet, warm love of these two people eked out of the walls and the furniture and filled Mary to overflowing. Her tears started again.

"Och lass, come here," said Mrs Fordyce, taking her hand and looking into her eyes. "It's all a bit bloomin' much, sometimes, isn't it?"

"Oh Mrs Fordyce ..." said Mary, "why couldn't you have been my parents? It's all so unfair."

"Aye, it seems to be an upside down world and, for all we know, it probably is," said Mrs Fordyce smiling while her husband put cups, teapot, milk and cakes on the table. "Take a seat and tell of yer upside down world, lass."

Mary sat, wiped her tears with the back of her hand and smiled. "Actually, I feel like a lost zygote ..."

"Lost what?" asked Mr Fordyce.

"Lost zygote," said Mary. "You know, it's like God or one of his angels was flying over with the seed of me to plant in this household, your family, and they got the wrong address or got bumped or confused or lost or something and that seed ended up in the wrong family. I got the wrong parents!"

The Fordyces laughed at the picture she had painted and Mr Fordyce patted her hand. "Yes, it all seems so wrong at times but there's nothing we can't learn from everyone, lass." Mary chuckled at his confusing double negative, trying to unravel it.

"Oh, Mr Fordyce, I don't want to learn anything. I just want nice people I can love," she said. "Just some simplicity, some compassion. It shouldn't be so hard ..."

"Now, Mary lass, yer a grown woman so there'll be nae more Mr Fordyce and Mrs Fordyce – it's James and Isobel, ye ken?"

"Uh, yes," said Mary, pleased to be welcomed into the world of adults, while a little saddened to have left her childhood somewhere.

"And, t'other thing I ken is that, aye, the world does seem so unfair at times," said James. "But I ken this to be true and I dinna' ken how I know – it's that God does not make an unfair world, we do.

The unfairness, as we see it, is because we choose to look at it that way."

Mary was silenced by the longest speech she had ever heard from Mr Fordyce ... oh, James. Something resounded in her heart and she knew it was a truth she should savour for a long time.

"Ye see, Mary lass, it's ower likely yer parents, who you struggle with so much, are yer special teachers," he said.

"What?" exclaimed Mary.

"Hear me out, lass," said James, holding his hand up. "It's a possibility that yer learning a grand lesson from yer family – that ye can't win the battle by fighting back."

Mary smiled at the irony of his words and just knew, somehow, that there certainly was something in what he said.

"Well, whatever I'm learning," said Mary with a wry smile, "it's gotta' be about fighting, so you may well be right! But it's all so unfair. Why won't they talk to me, listen to me … just be reasonable?"

"Ye sound just like a young baker I once knew," said Isobel, patting her hand. Her gentle smile was calming. "Ye see, he was so enthusiastic and wanted to make a splash in the village. Ye ken, do something special, like. So he rushed into making all sorts of fancy delicacies, delicacies that hadn't been seen in those parts before. He was so proud of himself for his original creations and, day after day, there be another batch of something wondrous displayed in his window." "And the people flocked to see them?" asked Mary.

"Aye lass, they did!" said Isobel smiling at her husband. "But they only came to look. They weren't buying and of this 'foreign muck' as some called it."

"That's … that's just silly. What's wrong with people! Didn't they want to try the new things?" asked Mary.

"Aye, many did want to try them but they were afraid of what their neighbours would think, buying all this fancy new stuff," said Isobel. "Those in fear or uncertainty are always the noisy ones, the ones others have to listen to."

"So, what happened to the baker?" asked Mary. "Did he have to close his shop?"

"Aye lass, it nearly came to that," said James, smiling at Isobel. "But for the intervention of a sweet young thing who came into his shop one day and insisted on taking him out the back for a chat." "A chat?" asked Mary.

"Aye lass, a chat about baking, business and the affairs of the world!" said James, chuckling. "I was furious with the world for not buying my wonderful baking …"

"Aha, so you were the young baker!" said Mary, suddenly getting it.

"Aye, twas I!" said James. "And this young lass sat me down and asked if I wanted to make a success of this bakery and of my life. Silly question! So, between outbursts of indignation from me, she explained that I could only make a living by making what people wanted – not what I wanted to force on them."

"And so that's how you made such a success of your bakery …" said Mary.

"Ooo, not too fast there lassie!" said Isobel. "Just as James had to give people the opportunity to buy what they wanted, I had to give young James here the opportunity to buy my ideas. It took a little time, I can tell you!"

"Och aye, I wasn't very open to logic in those days as I thought I knew it all. Ye ken, like most young people," said James. "And so it took a little time for me to accept her wisdom and the shortage of money is a great thing to change a person's mind! I did catch on quite quickly, I thought." "So, that's how you two met?" asked Mary.

"Aye, so it was," said Isobel, smiling at the memory.

"And why are we telling ye this?" asked James.

"Oh, I don't know," said Mary.

"The self same lesson, lassie," said James, patting her hand. "Ye can't force folks to accept yer way o' things. If they're not ready for change, ye've got to be the one to change. Fair or not, that's just how the world works."

"So you think I should be nice and sweet and agreeable all the time, just to suit them?" asked Mary grimly.

James opened his mouth to speak when Isobel put her hand gently on Mary's and asked, "How many buns have ye sold since you've been up here this time?" "How many buns?" asked Mary.

"Yes dear, how many buns have ye sold?" asked Isobel, smiling. "How many moments of true peace and happiness? How many moments of what ye might call a breakthrough, a success, have ye had?"

"Uh, none!" said Mary, grinning sheepishly. "I don't suppose I've sold a single bun!" "And how many buns would ye like to sell on this trip?" asked Isobel.

"Well, even one sale would be an improvement!" said Mary, sighing. "But why do I have to do all the work, all the bending and compromise?"

"Because ye can, lass," said James. "Because ye can. Ye're blessed with a little willingness to make a difference; they're not. They're happy in their misery and may never change. That's how my customers were ... still are. That's how yer customers – family and everyone else ye meet – are. Some will change, some will be as you'd like them to be but most are happy in their misery."

"But it's still unfair!" said Mary sitting back running her fingers through her short, thick hair.

"Ye sound *just* like a young baker I once had a chat with!" said Isobel. "Would ye rather be them – happy in their misery, unwilling and unable to communicate nicely. And frightened." "Frightened?" asked Mary.

"Yes, frightened. I was," said James. "Anger comes from unmet expectations – the world owes me this and I'm not getting it – and then there's fear in not being able to control the world. Yes, anyone who is angry is frightened."

"Oh, I hadn't thought about it like that," said Mary, sitting forward again. She looked at her watch.

"Gosh, it's late and I'm keeping you from your dinner, aren't I?"

"Aye and ye're welcome to join us," said Isobel. "But I suspect ye'll be wantin' to go home and sell a few buns."

Outside her parent's house she stopped and listened. The only sound was the television. She wondered if they ever really talked with each other and realised, sadly, that it may never change and that it wasn't her job to try and change it. She immediately felt lighter and skipped up the steps and into the kitchen for a glass of cordial.

"Why're ye looking so happy with yeself, lass?" asked her mother, without turning as she mashed potatoes.

"Not sure really," said Mary. "I guess I'm just happy to be home."

"Ye wouldn't be so happy if ye had to do the work to feed another mouth, would ye!" said her mother gruffly.

"Would you like some help there, ma?" asked Mary.

"Aye no, I've done it on my own for all these years and I suppose I'll be doin' it this way till I die," said her mother, spooning mashed potato into a bowl.

Mary went through and watched television with the men, in silence, watching the thoughts going through her mind. Actually, there weren't many at all where, before, her mind would have been a whirl of anxiety, trying to anticipate problems and solve them before they happened.

Dinner was held in silence, upon laps in front of television. Mary actually enjoyed the silence and the company – she needed nothing of anyone. They continued their silent dance while they each got themselves dessert and then cups of tea and Mary began to see the comedy of it all – three people in one house, doing practical things around each other and actually living in their own separate worlds.

She had as much companionship living on her own!

Eventually, the television was turned off and her father, getting up from his chair, said, "Aye, Mary, this London may be a wondrous place but I ken you're needing to come back home, time to time, for a dose of sanity!"

Mary detected a wee smile and appreciated that she had, at last, been acknowledged. And, maybe, in his own way, he was seeing the insanity of his household but had not the skills to make it sane. Maybe.

Angus, who now felt he had permission to address his sister, said, "Aye Mary, it is grand to see ye lass. Will ye be stayin' a few days?"

"Yes, a few days," said Mary. "Do you want me to bring your lunch down to your work, tomorrow?"

"Och aye ... ah ... I suppose," said Angus, caught between gratitude and embarrassment of having his sister at work. "Aye, I suppose ye could if ye wanted to."

'Whoopee!' thought Mary. 'I've passed the first test – being allowed into the men's domain. I think I've sold two buns tonight ... well, one and a half anyway.' As the men left she stood up and bumped into her mother and then realised her mother had come over to hug her. 'This is a first,' thought Mary, uncertainly. But she wasn't going to miss the moment. She hugged her mother back, easing into it gently, softly. It felt so warm and good. Then she heard her mother sniffing over her shoulder. Her mother pulled back and retrieved a handkerchief from her sleeve.

"Aye it's a chill place, this. I have a wee sniffle," her mother said. "Aye lass, I ... ah ... ye used to push us away all the time but yer ... ah ... nicer this time." Her mother fled and Mary dabbed at her own tears and smiled dreamily.

'Whew!' she thought. 'Maybe I've sold three buns tonight. A world record in the Collins household!'

She sat back down while the others shuffled around upstairs, going to bed, and wondered if everyone was so lonely, so separate, as those in her family. As she pondered while the upstairs became quiet, a deep peace overcame her and she had the strong impression, somehow, of everyone in the world, desperate to feel connected, desperate not to feel alone but not knowing how to ... in fact, most not believing that they could ever feel connected and at one with anyone else. A sadness came to her and she realised that's how she'd felt all her life – alone, separate and yet yearning for the opposite – to be connected with someone, something, anything ... but knowing that it was never possible. And, as that thought of separation became more personal, more about her, she realised that she could feel connected – did feel connected, even just a little, to her family when she'd stopped grasping for it. The years of isolation, feeling like she was different, didn't belong ... all of it washed past her as debris in a swollen river. She watched the dirty water and broken logs of her discontentment flood past and the raging river eventually slowed to become a gentle brook – clear, sparkling and alive. Yes, so alive and content with itself. She had a clear sense, somehow, of being enveloped in loving arms – warm and caring – and they stayed around her as she climbed the stairs to her bed and fell into a deep dreamless sleep.

The rest of the week passed rather amicably. More amicably than she'd ever known. Mary didn't learn anything – no hidden secrets, no unfulfilled dreams, no deep wisdom – but she did feel something ... a fullness in her heart.

Of course she did pop back into her old behaviour from time to time – whining, demanding, asking questions – and, eventually, she'd catch herself asking, 'Will I sell any buns doing what I'm doing now?' That question would bring her back to surrendering to the moment, to giving up, giving in and feeling that now-familiar peace envelop her. Even when she messed up, they seemed happy that she apologised – something she'd not really done before.

Staying out of her mother's kitchen, that sacred space, she bought food and took it round to the Fordyces, several times. Amid their protests that she shouldn't, they enjoyed convivial chats and they reminded her, often, what a quick learner she was – even quicker than James had been! This pleased her immensely.

Her brother, Angus, promised to visit her sometime in "that London town". She knew he wouldn't but his attempt at connection was touching.

Her father had obviously spent some time ferreting around in the attic and gave her three photos of her childhood and two of him as a child. He'd explained the photos with obvious and badly concealed emotion. On the last evening her mother had asked Mary if she'd help with the dinner and, though much of what she did was the wrong way 'o doin' it, she knew it was an honour never bestowed on anyone else before.

She left for London with an empty head and a full heart, quite oblivious that the universe had hatched plans to test her new-found sense of deep peace.

# The Empty Nest

*Monday 12th July, 2010, 9.30 a.m.*

Sam Black settled back into one of the three deep leather chairs around the coffee table in a corner of his office. "So Mary, the position you're looking at is Assistant Manager but, really, you'll be the manager here," he said. "I've recently become Director of Government Liaison which means that I'm actually part of a head office team and I'm not here all the time."

Sam had obviously chosen the chairs to fit his large frame but, for Mary, a foot shorter, it felt like being engulfed in a leather cloud – very comfortable but she wondered how she'd lever herself out again. She was relieved that she'd remembered to wear a long skirt today, given the awkward chair and Sam's frequent, flitting looks at her legs during their previous interview, before she'd left for bonny Scotland ... bonny Scotland, it seemed a whole world away now and she'd only just returned from there two days ago.

"So that's partly why the great salary," said Sam as Mary smiled. She'd never imagined such a large income this soon in her career. "We're going to have to be gentle with each other." Sam smiled impishly.

"We are?" asked Mary, wondering what direction this conversation was taking as her knees squeezed themselves together in automatic reflex.

"In a manner of speaking!" said Sam, laughing at her coy reaction. "I'll need to show you the ropes as best I can, when I'm here, and you're going to have to learn them when I'm not. You won't always be able to get hold of me so we'll need to trust each other and you'll need to be making some decisions without me. This is all new for both of us – both with new jobs and it being a bit tenuous at times – but I know you are very capable of thinking independently. That's what you got fired for from your last job, wasn't it!"

"Yes it was," said Mary, ruefully. "So I'm being promoted here for what I was sacked for at Commonwealth Insurance?"

"Absolutely!" said Sam, laughing as he flicked back his blonde cowlick with his hand. "I ... we need someone who is not afraid to take a stand but we also need someone who understands the framework. You'll be at a higher level than you've been before and different rules apply now." Sam's smile had vanished.

"Different rules?" asked Mary as an uneasy lump formed in her stomach. She leaned forward, knowing she must not miss anything he said.

"Look, let's go through them as they arise," he said, leaning back with an uncertain smile. "Let me introduce you to a few of the chaps across town at head office, this afternoon, and, in the meantime, we'll get your office set up how you like it, make sure you have lists of who's who and how to access the system and then I'll introduce you to some of the team downstairs."

"Right, yes," said Mary, with so many questions needing answers. The foreboding lump in her stomach hadn't moved.

"Then I'll shout you to lunch so you can grill me on what you've learned this morning and I can update you on some of the head office team before you meet them," said Sam. "Does that sound like a grand plan?"

"Oh, gosh, that would be nice," said Mary, settling back while feeling a lightness enter the room. Her lump dissolved a little.

Sam really didn't seem to know his junior staff very well, or much of what they did. "Oh, they get on with what they need to do. I sign their assignments off and stay out of their way. Justin Talbot always saw to the details," he said at one point. He did, however, know the senior staff well and had left her with Stephen Lawrence, the Finance Director, a round, florid man with a fluffy, ginger moustache and little hair above it. Stephen took her round and stiffly introduced her to the staff on his, the sixth, floor. He suggested they have a guided tour of one floor a day. Very logical and systematic. Just like an accountant, she thought.

Justin Talbot, Mary assumed, was her predecessor and she determined to find out more about him and why he left.

"Ah, the silly sod," said Sam, as if reading her thoughts, after he had returned while she was rearranging her office, "had his hand in the till, so to speak ... taking backhanders from claims. Quite unsavoury."

'Unsavoury? Unsavoury!' thought Mary, 'it's illegal and bloody immoral!'

"That's why I need someone I can trust," said Sam evenly. "Been quite shaken by the twerp's underhand tactics and why I've had the research done on you."

"Oh," said Mary, knowing it was a compliment that she passed his close scrutiny but, all the same, felt queasy at the thought of an undercover team filtering through the life she held so privately.

They entered the Executors Club for lunch, and Sam knew the staff better there. He asked Andrzej, the doorman, how his son was getting on with his rugby (something he was obviously proud of) and asked Henri, the Maître d', how his wife was recovering. It turned out she had the plaster taken off her leg yesterday.

Mary felt quite special, escorted in by the two men – the swarthy, dapper Henri in front and the blonde, pink Sam behind, in pinstripe suit, pink shirt and florid, multi-coloured tie. She tried to take it all in, walking as gracefully as she could across the thick, burgundy carpet, feeling cosseted by the old oak panelling, several chandeliers and the expensive shine of silverware and glassware. Sam's hand touched her shoulder lightly, several times, giving her assurance as he exchanged restrained greetings with diners already there – mainly, it seemed, men in pinstriped suits with shirts and ties that clashed absurdly.

Their table was in an alcove in a distant corner of the dining room and, she noticed, it had a thick, red curtain to the side – able to be pulled across for private chats and trysts. Mary declined alcohol, determined to keep a clear head for the day, while Sam was served whisky and water. Obviously his 'usual'. She enjoyed the entrée of caviar – the first time she'd tried it – and Sam recommended the grouse, which was in season. Mary didn't watch television much but, as she looked around discretely, she fancied she saw some faces she'd seen on the small screen.

"Yes, you might recognise a few faces here," said Sam, as he tucked into his grouse enthusiastically.

Mary looked at him and smiled uncertainly. The blasted man just seemed to know what she was thinking!

"Let me know if there's anyone you'd like me to introduce you to," said Sam. "In their own environment, with their chums, they're generally quite friendly."

So Sam was chums with these movers and shakers – it fitted with his role as Director of Government Liaison.

"But I've put the flag up so we won't be disturbed," said Sam, obviously enjoying his meal. "And what do you want to know from this morning?"

"Put the flag up?" asked Mary, suddenly aware of a whole new set of behaviours and customs in this lavish setting.

"Ah, yes, the candle's on the front of the table; it says I'm busy," explained Sam, smiling. "If we put it back here, I'm bound to have some visitors wanting to inquire about my new guest! Now, what questions do you have?"

Mary was interrupted by a waiter taking their dishes away. As he left, Henri materialised to ask how their meal was. Mary noticed a small piece of paper pass to Sam. He unfolded it on the table to read while Henri inquired of Mary's first impressions of the club.

"Yes, that's fine, Henri," said Sam, folding the paper and putting it in his coat pocket. Henri smiled, bowed subtly and moved away. "Now, Mary, if you will indulge me a moment, I would like to help a fellow traveller on his way."

"Oh," said Mary, mystified. "Should I leave you for a moment?"

"No, no, not at all," said Sam, smiling and patting her hand. "No need for secrets here." As he said this she realised that the red velvet curtains were drawing themselves quietly together. The alcove darkened, a light came on and, suddenly, between them, a small door opened and a solid barrel of a man squeezed himself through. Mary recognised him as Andrzej the doorman, who, with his crewcut, could have passed as a bouncer at any London club. He closed the door and sat on the bench between them.

"So, Andrzej, your brother is in trouble and wants to come here and start again? Like you did?" asked Sam quietly.

"Yes sir, he is good man and was in wrong place at wrong time," said Andrzej in his thick Eastern European accent. "Bad man in Kraków want to cover his tracks and so he accuse my brother of his deeds."

"And your brother – does he have some qualifications, some trade, some expertise that would recommend him to the British authorities?" asked Sam.

"Oh, yes, Dominik be champion wrestler like me and he be good, very good plumber, too," said Andrzej, his eyes beseeching Sam's.

"Dominik? A plumber? Yes, we certainly need good plumbers here! We don't need any more English plumbers making our bad plumbing worse. A shot of new plumbing blood is just what we need, Andrzej, more hard-working and reliable Polish plumbers. I will have a chat with a friend in the immigration business. And Lord Atkinson is in need of help, he told me recently."

"Oh, dziękuję ci ... thank you, thank you, Mr Black!" said Andrzej, recovering from his Polish language.

"Shhh Andrzej, please keep it quiet," said Sam evenly. "Now, do I have your number?"

"Ah yes, I have it written on paper here, Mr Black," said Andrzej, passing a piece of paper which Sam placed in his shirt pocket.

"Thank you Andrzej. You need to get back to the door before you're missed," said Sam. "And you will hear from me very soon."

"Yes, it OK, Mr Henri look after door for me, but I go," said Andrzej, standing. "Thank you from bottom of my heart, Mr Black. Thank you so much." He disappeared back through the small door.

Sam smiled uncertainly at Mary in the dim light of the alcove.

"So you're going to bypass the government system to ship this man to England ... this Polish man who's in trouble with the law there ..." said Mary, indignantly.

"Yes I am, Mary, yes I am," said Sam firmly. "Andrzej has had a chequered and abusive past and since he's been here he's been a model citizen and an asset to us all ... in ways you don't yet understand."

"But it's illegal ..." said Mary, trying to get the information arranged neatly in her brain.

"Yes, it may well be but when the law's an ass, you've got to kick the ass in the ass and use other means to serve justice," said Sam as the curtain began to quietly slide back.

"But what do you know of this brother, this alleged innocent in trouble with the Polish law?" asked Mary, still aghast. "You might be getting yourself into great trouble too and ..."

"Yes, I might be getting myself in trouble, Mary," said Sam, interrupting quietly. "But I'm taking a chance on behalf of a good and honest friend – something no immigration bureaucrat is ever going to do. Don't judge too soon and I'm happy to tell you all when we have a little more time."

"But Sam, you can't just go ..."

"Look Mary, do you remember before the last month's election, Michael Caine's latest movie came out?" asked Sam patiently.

"No," said Mary, puzzled by the change in direction.

"It was called *Is Anybody There?*," said Sam. "Anyway, floating round the hustings with our most probable prime-minister-to-be, David Cameron, was the normally apolitical Michael Caine." "Ah, yes, I remember that. He was promoting Cameron's Youth Citizen Service Plan," said Mary.

"And did you hear what Mr Caine said about the Youth Citizen Service Plan?" asked Sam.

"No, I didn't, actually," said Mary.

"And nor did most people, actually," said Sam with a smile. "He just wandered round in front of the cameras, looking dastardly handsome and, when asked for a comment, talked mostly about his new movie. And you know what? That movie was the highest grossing British movie at that time." "Oh," said Mary, putting the pieces together.

"Now, it was probably a very good movie and maybe our Mr Caine did, indeed, have a heart for the youth of this fair land," said Sam. "And no one's done anything illegal or immoral – we're all just trying to help ourselves and help those we respect and like."

"But that's not the same," said Mary, defiantly. "You're trying to break the law."

"No I'm not, Mary," said Sam patiently. "A chap I know in immigration will sift through things and find where the law supports our case and Andrzej's brother will be free to enter England openly and legally."

"But he should apply like everybody else," said Mary, determined to be right.

"Well, maybe he should," said Sam. "But I know Andrzej and I know he wouldn't pester me if the situation wasn't both real and urgent."

"But what if everyone tried to slide round the law for their friends?"

"They always have and they always will, Mary," said Sam, leaning back with a second whisky in hand. "Cardinal Wolsey was only able to afford his massive digs at Hampton Court because he got things done for Henry VIII, 500 years ago. Then he lost it because he couldn't get the Roman Catholic church to agree to Henry marrying Anne Boleyn. We've been doing each other favours, big and small, ever since time began and we'll continue to do them."

"But it seems so unfair to some people," said Mary.

"And where is it etched in stone that life should be fair? It jolly well isn't," said Sam. "Once we recognise that life is unfair, we can look it in the eye, as it really is, and make a better world from the unfairness."

"I don't know what to say," said Mary.

"You can take heart, Mary, that you're in good hands," said Sam, leaning forward. "I may do things that seem devious but I do them to help people. There's plenty of chumps doing good works for all the wrong reasons. Look at the activities of our Empire Aid Bank – lovely government servants giving our money to dictators and swindlers, calling it foreign aid and all feeling mighty pleased with themselves."

# Sam Disappears

And so it was that Mary tripped up a step and stumbled into a room of finery and grace, nods and winks, favours and effortless action. The room she'd emerged from – the lower room of her life, her parents and everyone she knew – was one of toil and obedience to laws imposed from above; of watching the rich and famous as though through a window, unreachable and slightly unreal. Now she'd found herself on the other side of the window, in this upper room, where laws didn't restrict but provided opportunities. Here there were no application forms, uncertainty or queues – just discrete chats, snap decisions and instant action.

Mary was appalled, initially, and argued with the implacable Sam, who took on the role of a patient and wise teacher with a reluctant but quick student. Unapologetic and defenceless, he simply explained the ways of life in this upper room and allowed her objections and protestations of injustice to float past him, knowing she would eventually come to acceptance, which she did, haltingly, defiantly.

From what she saw, he wasn't involved in drugs or arms dealing or anything else unwholesome. He was simply helping those who had been dealt savage blows by life. What he got in return for his interventions she could not discern – perhaps he got his lawn mown for nothing or something – but it certainly didn't seem to be for fame or riches. Many of the people he helped had neither money nor influence (though some obviously had much of both) and she wondered if he got perverse satisfaction in finding interesting ways through the ass of the law, as he called it. She didn't have the courage to ask what he got for his efforts or how he'd come to acquire his influence and chumhood. One day she'd find out. As she observed carefully, she learned nothing of this but the mantle of indignation and injustice slowly fell from her shoulders and she grew to respect this man in her life.

She also came to realise that the people in this upper room, who seemed to glide through life with such grace and ease, also left it for the lower room, at times, to their dismay. They, like other people, had arguments with spouses, fears with health, problems with children and all the stresses of those who inhabited the lower room permanently. These people, however, were able to pop back up to their natural abode, the quieter and more plush room, for their money and influence would get them the best lawyers for their divorces, doctors for their illnesses and holidays and toys for their diversions.

Sam split his time between the central office and her branch office with frustrating irregularity. He was right – she was effectively in charge of the two hundred people on seven floors and, initially, leaned on Stephen Lawrence, Finance Director, and Ahmed Khan, Chief Assessor, an Asian with an Oxford accent and Oxford suits. Both were men of numbers and were refreshingly free of emotion. They gave her the facts and stayed above the office politics brewing below her.

Without Sam to rely on for guidance she was forced to dive in, learn things she'd never learned about insurance before and to make decisions with minimal information. It frightened and thrilled her. With Stephen's and Ahmed's help, she drew up a plan for educating herself. Chunking down the branch office functions into logical pieces, she systematically spent time with every section (every person, in fact), learning exactly what they did, why they did it and how each piece fitted into the whole. This, of course, enamoured her to the people she commanded and they came to her, more and more, for advice. This she welcomed for, as she got to know them, she was able to formulate succession and promotion plans – some were clearly unsuited to the work they were doing and some had ambitions and talents beyond their current roles. She stared shuffling and sifting and, as productivity grew, less people were needed and branch profits rose.

Sam was impressed and thanked Mary with many lunches and dinners, not always at the Executors Club but always at equally plush establishments. Out of the office she got to know him a little better.

In the office, they dealt with work. Out of the office they still talked work but she did start to penetrate the wall round his private life. She discovered he'd had a wife but didn't have one now and that he had a daughter and granddaughter he doted over. He visited them every Thursday evening. He enjoyed folk music and that was a surprise – she expected his tastes to be in classical music. He didn't explain but Mary surmised that part of the attraction was the raw, amateurish feel of it – a welcome change from his otherwise polished and perfect life.

He never invited her to his folk music escapes and she yearned, patiently, for such an invitation. At times he'd reach out and touch her shoulder, pat her hand and then, as if remembering himself, pull back. She felt (hoped?) he was feeling what she was, which was a great companionship, comfort and caring. She wasn't falling in love with this chameleon of a man (no, not really) but she hoped he was falling in love with her.

Though he came and went from the office at irregular times, he did commit, at Mary's insistence, to two regular meetings a week so they could, at least, guarantee a flow of information between them. Monday at 4.00 p.m. and Friday at 9.00 a.m. were agreed for these hourly meetings. These reliable spots in her frenetic schedule were cherished and the Monday afternoon meeting sometimes evolved into dinner and the Friday morning meeting into lunch out together. Sometimes Sam might bring her a little gift for something she'd done well – chocolates, a pen, a brooch or something else small enough to conceal in her bag, from the suspicious eyes of her staff. She was hesitant about buying him anything – perhaps it was fear of rejection – but she did, eventually and with great trepidation, buy him whisky liqueur chocolates, a tie pin and cuff links at various times. He was obviously touched by these and, rather than his enthusiastic and ebullient self, he would go quiet and seem to be on the verge of tears before he collected himself and thanked her quietly for her generosity.

*Friday, 9th March 2012, 9.13 a.m.*

And so it was that Sam failed to turn up for their regular Friday morning meeting, something he had not missed for two years now. She immediately knew something was wrong and talked to her secretary and to his. She sent them off to ask anyone and everyone if they knew where he might be, while she rang some of his colleagues at the head office. No one knew anything there. Some were surprised at his absence and two of them were dismissive of her fears, telling her not to worry. Their reaction caused her to worry more. These two also told her, most strongly, not to contact the police, while Stephen and Ahmed advised her strongly to alert the police.

Knowing the police could be either helpful or obstructive, depending on who was pulling the strings, she faltered indecisively.

Then she received a text from Sam. A terse text telling her he would contact her as soon as he could. His lack of further information caused her more worry than the previous lack of communication.

In the same way that tragedy survivors take on the blame for the tragedy, rather than accepting that life is out of their control, Mary took on the blame for Sam's disappearance. Had there been an obvious reason for his going or an indication of where he went, the guilt would have been less. However, like the survivor syndrome scenario, the more out of control things seem, the greater the guilt she chose to carry. She wondered if she would be happy inhabiting the building with Sam out of it – she wasn't sure.

With a troubled heart and heavy shoulders she was phoned by Terry Jones, CEO of City Investments Ltd, holding company of Allied Insurance Ltd., that afternoon. She was offered Sam's position, in the interim. Terry had received a similar text from Sam – brief and unhelpful, to say he would be back soon but was unavoidably detained at the moment. Mary was unable to provide any further elucidation.

She had no idea of the salary Sam had been on but, judging by his lifestyle, she was sure she was offered a whole lot less. Maybe he'd had other sources of income or maybe he was the sort of person who always looked wealthy, despite their real circumstances. Either way she felt insulted by the offer and she also felt a deep disloyalty in stepping into a missing man's shoes, the shoes of a man she admired.

The first part of her grieving emerged as anger as she stormed from Terry's office, leaving behind two bewildered-looking insurance executives. Thankfully she'd had the weekend to stew on it and cool down a little. By the Monday, her anger had subsided just enough to let a peek of logic in. Not trusting her acid tongue on the phone, she crafted a conciliatory email to Terry Jones, saying she was prepared to stay on until they had found a permanent replacement for Sam. This would, she thought, give her enough time to find another position. Last time it had been easy and she imagined the same this time.

She did, of course, feel like walking out and trusting the universe would provide her with something but that small, practical girl inside counselled against it, successfully, each time.

# The Call Back

*Friday, 9ᵗʰ March 2012, 3.20 p.m.*

Martin and the children had popped in – most unusual but lovely to see them. Martin seemed to be needing more contact with them at the moment.

The telephone cut across their conversation with its electronic insistence and the three adults looked

at each other in mute surprise, as if insulted that the outside world should interrupt them ... surprised, even, to be reminded that another world existed outside their several dramas. Timothy bounded, like a gazelle, out the door and into the dining room, to answer the phone.

"Hello, Timothy here," he said as he had been taught. He was soon back in the lounge, sipping on his drink.

"Timothy, who was that on the phone?" asked Martin.

"It was a wrong number, Dad," said Timothy, importantly, "they wanted Arthur Bayly and so I said he didn't live here."

"Ah, Timothy," said Arthur, "I'm Arthur Bayly." "But you're Grandad," said Timothy, confused.

"Timothy!" said Martin, irritated, "you don't answer other peoples' phones. Haven't I told you that before! It's not your property so leave well alone."

Timothy began to sob and Joan picked him up and held him on her knee. "Would you like another piece of cake, dear? And Katie?" Timothy hopped down and he and his sister leaped upon the sponge cake with enthusiasm.

"Hey, you two!" said Martin, his voice steadily rising, "put that down, now, you know better than to scoff it down like yobbos!"

The children stopped, stunned, with cake and cream on their faces and hands, looking guilty and confused.

"Put it down, now!" yelled Martin, going quite red. "Now go and wash yourselves up. You know better than that, don't you!"

"Come on, dears," said Joan cheerfully, "let's get your faces sparkling clean, shall we?" The children followed meekly, furtively looking back at their father.

As they walked out the phone sounded again and Timothy leaped forward, unable to resist his instinctive fight or flight reaction to the phone.

"Timothy! Stop!" yelled Martin, leaping up. "I told you to leave the phone!"

"It's alright Martin," said Arthur, getting up and striding across the room and out to the phone. He patted Timothy on the head as he passed. "You'll make someone a grand secretary one day, won't you?" he said, smiling down at the boy.

Timothy went red and smiled, embarrassment mixed with gratitude, as Arthur picked up the phone.

"Good afternoon, Arthur speaking."

"Ah, Arthur, I thought I might have a wrong number," came the unmistakable voice of Mary Collins. AIL Insurance seemed such a long way off, now, almost off the new map his life was drawing.

"No, it was my grandson, Timothy ..."

"Yes, well, good to talk to you, Arthur," said Mary. "I heard you'd had a bereavement. Are you okay?"

"Oh, yes, well, we've had a few things happen and ..."

"Yes, yes, okay, I'm sure it's been a particularly trying time, then," said Mary, bulldozing through the conversation as usual. "Now, Arthur, there has been ... ah, a new development with that Atkinson case you were working on and we'd like, ah, we wondered when you'd be ready to get back to it." "Yes, I suppose I should get back to it," said Arthur, feeling a sad lump in his tummy.

"Yes, well, when you're ready, Arthur," said Mary with unaccustomed reserve, "just to tidy it all up. With the reorganisation, there's lots of tidying up we need to do."

"Reorganisation?" asked Arthur, trying to imagine what new trauma had happened. "There wasn't any great hurry for that case, was there?"

"No, there isn't ... wasn't," said Mary. "But some new developments and, with your specialist knowledge, we thought it might be expedited with your valuable input." Arthur had never before heard so many compliments from Mary.

"So, has it become urgent, now?" asked Arthur, trying to get some facts.

"Look Arthur, we can explain it all when you get in here," said Mary, her voice rising a semitone.

"When might that be?"

"You want me back in?" he asked, surprised.

"Well, yes, if you wouldn't mind."

"Oh, I'm not sure, Mary, I'll need time to think about it – to talk about it with Joan." said Arthur, wishing he had the courage to say what was actually on his mind – 'I don't ever want to come back, Mary, thanks. Goodbye.'

"Look, Arthur, we can make a special reimbursement, a special rate for this assignment, we can put you on contract ... whatever is best for you," said Mary, sweetening the incentive.

"Yes, yes, I appreciate that, thank you," said Arthur, trying to absorb and understand the new developments. "But things are quite ... ah, quite tender here and I do need to talk to my wife about this. When would you like me to start?"

"Well, this afternoon would be great," said Mary, anticipating some progress. "We thought that seventy five pound an hour would be a fair recompense."

"Gosh, that soon!" said Arthur, remembering that she'd said *no problem at all* a minute ago and that seventy five pound an hour was treble the wage he had previously been on. "Yes, well, I'll talk to my wife and ring you back."

"Well, please do, Arthur, yes, please do," said Mary, speaking as if she was unable to breathe. "Now do you have a pen and paper there, Arthur?"

"Ah, yes ..."

"Good, then call me back on my direct number. Save you going through the reception. Much quicker," said Mary, giving him the number.

"Right, yes, I'll do that," said Arthur, surprised that direct numbers existed in his old firm.

"You'll ring me right back, yeah?" asked Mary, begging.

"Yes, yes, I will Mary," said Arthur, still trying to absorb the rising sense of urgency coming at him. "So what was that about?" asked Joan, coming up to him. "You look a little shaky." "Do I?" he said, more to himself than to her, shaking his head.

"What did she say that has you shaken, Mr Bond?" asked Joan. Arthur was momentarily stunned, wondering how she knew of his fantasies.

"Not sure," said Arthur, shaking his head. "I just have the odd feeling that something odd's going on."

"You look like you need a hug," she said, throwing her arms around him.

"That's the only thing that's normal or understandable, isn't it?" he said with a sheepish smile.

"What is?"

"Well, hugs and you and our family," he said into her shoulder. "Nothing else makes any sense any more."

"Mmm."

"I don't know, life used to be regular, stable, predictable," Arthur said as tears filled his eyes. "I keep doing what I've always done and it suddenly isn't good enough any more ... and then it is and they want to pay me treble for it! I sit on a park bench, minding my own business and become a hero. Your mother dies and we're supposed to be bereft but it's brought us closer together. And then there's

Martin's situation ... and there's all these Australians and New Zealanders popping up ..."

"Well, dear, you have to admit that every insane thing you've mentioned has brought us closer," she said, standing back a little and looking into his eyes. "Not just my mother's death but everything has reconnected us. Maybe that's what it's all about, do you think?"

"Actually, my love, I don't know what to think at all. Not at all."

As they returned to the lounge, Arthur explained to Martin what the call had been about.

"So, Dad, what's so important about this job that they want you back so quickly?" asked Martin.

"The Atkinson case?" said Arthur.

"Not the *Lord Atkinson* case, is it?" asked Martin, laughing.

"Well, he is a Black, actually ..." said Arthur, feeling a chill sliding through his bones.

"Oh my God!" said Martin, the laugh quickly falling from his face. "Not the one with the hunting lodge in Ludlow, the apartment in Kensington and the resort in Jamaica? The one with the race horses and mansion just south of here, in Wallington?"

"Exactly the one," said Arthur, incredulously. "How did you know?"

"Oh, one of my partners has been working for one of Lord Atkinson's larger claimants, the Empire Aid Bank, the EAB. You know, the development bank that used to be the government department that supplied everything for the empire, from railways to cutlery for the ambassadors."

"Yes, yes, I know the bank," said Arthur quickly. "They're claiming money for some project in Nigeria ..." He vaguely recalled that was the bank the young Australian was ousted from. 'Greg Cousins, wasn't it?' he wondered to himself.

"Absolutely, that's the one," said Martin, excitedly. "After the bank was privatised in 1998, it really got into funding in developing countries, using aid money from, mainly, the British, Japanese and Swedish governments."

"So what's the project in Nigeria?" asked Joan.

"I'm not sure but what I do know is that the EAB has been having a few slip-ups, lately," said Martin. "Well, it is over 150 years old and, after privatisation, it seemed to develop some holes, some slip-ups."

"What sort of slip-ups? Large ones?" asked Arthur.

"All sorts, really – big and small," said Martin, warming to his favourite subject, commercial intrigue. "Since the British colonies have dwindled over the last 100 years, they needed to diversify to keep all the jobs for the boys and girls there. So, they privatised the bank, sort-of, and became an agent

for many governments, besides the British one ... and the United Nations aid programme." "Sounds like a good cause to me," said Joan.

"Yes, and that's the problem," said Martin. "When people are dealing with what seems like benevolent work, others are loathe to question or audit that work. For example, the British government's aid department, Department for International Development, DfID, runs no aid

programmes but just gives EAB money to dispense as per its requirements." "But the DfID must audit or check that spending," suggested Arthur.

"Well, yes it does, but only superficially, not wanting to take away any jobs from people in the government club and afraid of interrupting these 'benevolent' acts," said Martin. "So, the two-yearly audit is simply a matter of visiting friends at the EAB's London head office, enjoying drinkies and food and listening to two or three inspiring talks on the great works of EAB and watching a video of their amazing success."

"But they must be doing a lot of good helping these poorer nations, surely?" asked Joan.

"Oh, absolutely," said Martin, "much of the money does go in the right direction but no one knows how much … not even EAB! No one in government – or from anywhere else, for that matter – traces each pound … or even a million pounds. They pay the money to EAB, see a result and assume they're linked!"

"So where does our Lord Atkinson come into this," asked Arthur.

"A good question and no one's quite sure, yet," said Martin. "But Simon Cruickshank, the partner I mentioned, knows that Atkinson is great friends with many in the current government and he has, over the years, provided large sums of money to both Labour and Conservative administrations." "You're talking about bribery! Surely not!" said Joan, astounded.

"Not sure. However, what we're very sure about is that the change to privatisation has not been entirely healthy," said Martin. "Instead of employing experts in international development, they've favoured existing staff and moving them sideways, some to their levels of incompetence, one might say. So, when they finally admit they can't do something, they do a quick-fix by bringing in short-term consultants … who never remain short-term. Because EAB know little of the function they're hiring the consultant for, they don't know whether they're getting valuable consultants or charlatans – it's a bit of a lottery, really."

"A lottery where cronies of the government, with inside connections, favours and knowledge of available contracts, can take advantage of, like our Lord Atkinson?" said Arthur, suddenly understanding much about the insurance claim that he didn't before.

"Well, yes, we need to be careful of who we're accusing of what, just yet," said Martin in solicitor mode, "but it seems there's intense competition for these contracts – hand out a million or so, with little checking how you spend it – quite a gift for someone with profit in mind!"

"And anyone giving out millions to poorer people would gain a lot of friends and favours from those poorer people!" said Arthur, grimly.

"My God, Dad, you should have been a detective!"

"Just my cynical insurance mind in overdrive," said Arthur.

"So, we have the perfect scenario for tossing around government money – many governments' money – to benefit the wrong people," said Martin, smiling at his father with unaccustomed admiration. "And the governments themselves are into it too. For example, the European Union's aid programme provides huge amounts of funds to UE governments to provide aid. But the checking at the EU is as shoddy as in here in England. Some of these governments – the Spanish and Italian ones are apparently the worst offenders – just don't get around to spending all the UE funds they receive and it's a great source of revenue for them – helps their balance of payments deficits considerably!" "But that's OUR money, Martin! Don't they care about that?" asked Joan, astounded.

"Why should they?" asked Martin. "It's not their money and it's free to them!"

"Well, you look after other peoples' money, other peoples' interests."

"Yes, Mum, most people do but when you've got access to large amounts of power and money, those thoughts of others just seem to slip out the window, somehow. When you create a house with lots of holes and lots of cheese on the floor, the rats turn up!"

"Oh dear, so what should I do about this work back at AIL then?" asked Arthur.

"Mmm, sounds like things are hotting up with your Atkinson case, somehow," said Martin.

"Yes, it all sounds a bit desperate, a bit … well, dangerous, if you ask me!" said Joan.

"It also sounds like a lot of fun!" said Martin, rubbing his hands together with glee.

"Insurance has never been exciting before, for me," said Arthur, feeling a tingle of adventure in his veins. "And, maybe, I could help get some of your money back from these scoundrels."

"Yes Darling, maybe you could, but I don't like the sound of it," said Joan, "and we were just starting to get along and we're just over mother's funeral and Martin needs help and you now want to go back to work?"

"Well, I'll be doing it at home," said Arthur, seeing opportunities everywhere. "I'll fit the work in between our family needs."

"I don't know Arthur ..."

"Look Mum, Dad needs some excitement in his life," said Martin, standing up for his father for the first time ever. "This could be his chance for that and a chance to really do some good."

"Yes dear, I would rather relish a challenge like this – you never know where it could lead to!" said Arthur, wondering why he was talking about unknown opportunities, while he took her hands and looked into her eyes earnestly.

"Oh, I don't know ..."

"Look dear, let's you and I sit down later and work out what we need to do for each other, for Martin," said Arthur. "Then I can tell Mary what I'm prepared to do. They seem keen to have me at any cost."

"Yes, but why?" asked Joan, still concerned.

"And if it doesn't work out, I can simply stop doing the work and hand it back," said Arthur.

"I don't know about the work but I do know I've never seen you so fired up about anything before," said Joan, still looking concerned. "Maybe it is your chance to do something really special ... I don't know ..."

"Look, you two," said Martin, "the world won't stop spinning if you do nothing today. Leave it till Monday and call AIL then. If they want an answer before then, just tell them they can't have one – you'll let them know Monday at, say, ten o'clock. This is your decision, not theirs."

# The Investigation

So it was that Arthur Bayly found himself back on the old map of his life, in Mary's office. She couldn't see that what she wanted she might not get. Or, as Halee, the elfin receptionist from New Zealand said, "They'll get what they need but not in the way they think they need."

Arthur grinned at that in a way he'd become rather used to lately – hearing something he didn't understand, quite, but knowing he might soon.

However, understanding was not something Mary was achieving at all. She was under some pressure, Arthur assumed, and needed the job done immediately. Arthur was most surprised – shocked, even – to hear that even Sam had gone. Mary was, effectively, in charge of the Kensington office and, though there were over a hundred thousand clients, this Atkinson one seemed to be her sole concern.

She had run out of words to convince Arthur to put his every waking moment into the case.

Arthur waited a moment for her to stop pacing and to sit down.

"Mary, I do see that you have rather a lot on your plate. It can't be easy for you," he said. "However, they say it's best to ride the horse in the direction it's going."

"What, ride a horse?"

"Oh dear," said Arthur, realising his helpful epithet went straight over her head. "Gosh, ah, what appears to me, Mary, is that you need a job done and there's no one else to do it. You're between an immovable object and an unstoppable force, as Newton might have said."

"Newton who?"

"Newton the scientist ... discovered gravity ..." said Arthur, feeling his fingers slipping from yet another cliff edge. "Look Mary, Joan and I have discussed this at length and what I can offer you is three days a week. I will put all my available time into finishing it just as soon as I can. We just have other things we also need to do."

"But three days, Arthur?" asked Mary, her voice rising with each syllable. "Can you not give us five days a week till this case is completed?"

"But you asked me what was best for us ..." said Arthur, confused.

"Yes, yes, I know I did," said Mary, going quite red. "But it's become quite urgent. With Lord Atkinson under surveillance with his Empire Aid Bank activities and now the burglary at his place ... I don't know. All we know is that they want the full details of our investigation and they want them soon."

"They?" asked Arthur.

"Aaahh," said Mary, heavily. "There's been an investigation started by the Financial Services Authority, the FSA, who are supposed to control banks and other financial institutions."

"Yes, yes, I know them," said Arthur, "but they've never been here before."

"No, they've never really been anywhere before," said Mary, brightening a little. "The reality is, of course, that they were never intended to actually *do* anything, but just make the public think they were protected from the large financial institutions. These banking institutions actually control the politicians – look how they've been able to wheedle billions from the government when no other industry has."

"Oh dear, I'd never really thought about it ..."

"Absolutely, they don't want you to think about it," said Mary, warming to one of her favourite subjects. "As we continue to believe the illusion of the FSA protecting us, we'll keep depositing our money with the banks and repaying our mortgages and credit cards – like dumb milking cows, every day."

"Oh yes," said Arthur at a loss for words but poignantly reminded of his own imagined references to cows going to work every morning.

"Just as the American treasury is owned and run by privately-run banks – not by the US government – so it is with our Bank of England," said Mary, obviously on a roll. "The Old Lady of Threadneedle Street, the B of E, was supposed to be the public's watchdog but when it failed to avert a series of scandals in the 1990s culminating in the collapse of Barings Bank[1],[2] the Financial Services Authority was created to give the public the impression that all was independent and professional, at last."

"Oh," said Arthur, wondering why he should be privy to this information. The feeling wasn't good.

"What the man in the street didn't twig to was that the people at the Bank of England who were supposed to be looking after his interests were the same people employed at the FSA," said Mary, obviously keen to tell the entire story. "You see, the government is quite happy for 1,600 honest, industrious steel workers to lose their jobs in Redcar, in the north of England, but it's unwilling to let millionaire bankers lose their luxurious lifestyles – lifestyles they put in jeopardy by their own gross negligence and greed."

"Gosh," said Arthur, feeling increasingly uneasy. He sat forward as if to rise, hoping to staunch Mary's verbal flow.

"No Arthur, it's important you know this," said Mary. "As you now know, the bank that committed the worst of these financial excesses – blind avarice at its worst – comes from my own fair Scotland. And they have their own employee in power and when Mr Cameron makes a big enough fool of himself, they'll appoint another Scot – probably a McDougal, McIntyre or some other Scottish name – to the post. God forbid that an Englishman should rule England!"

"But our politicians are voted in, not appointed!" exclaimed Arthur, appalled at Mary's story.

"OK, Arthur, which bank got the biggest payout from the British government?" asked Mary.

"Ah, the Royal Bank of Scotland, I think," said Arthur.

"And which bank had committed the greatest of the financial atrocities?" asked Mary.

"The same? The RBS?" Arthur suggested, tentatively.

"Exactly!" said Mary. "The biggest criminal, so to speak, gets the best treatment. I don't know how it works, or who works it, but the RBS executives continue to pay themselves their millions, annually, and throw away billions on bad investments, knowing they can always milk the cow that never dries up – the government coffers which they control, somehow!"

"And I thought the English beat the Scots!" said Arthur, chuckling while feeling more than a little queezy at these startling disclosures.

"Yes they did, Arthur," said Mary. "The English beat the Scots with their guns and then built their mansions and huge estates from the huge incomes they made from the land they stole from us. But we beat them with our money – our loyal British government has ensured that few of those huge, wealthy estates are now financially viable. So, do you know who now owns most of these defunct estates – who has obtained the finance from Her Majesty's Most Loyal government to finance the purchase of them at bargain prices and now make huge profits from showing them to the millions of gawping tourists?" "The National Trust?" suggested Arthur.

"And who actually owns the National trust?" asked Mary.

"Not the Scots, surely?" asked Arthur, incredulous.

"I'll leave you to do your own research on that," said Mary, smiling. "It's just the same in the US. After Pearl Harbour, the Americans beat the Japanese with their guns and now the Japanese – well, the Asians, generally – own America. They've disassembled the American car industry and taken it over and, at the moment the US owes China $900 billion and Japan $770 billion. They're the biggest lenders to the US, owning around 44% of it, and so they're

1.     http://en.wikipedia.org/wiki/Barings_Bank

2.     http://en.wikipedia.org/wiki/Barings_Bank

the pipers who call the tune, so to speak. America is insolvent and will never be able to repay the debt, just as England is insolvent and will never be able to repay Scotland's debt. The bankers are in charge! Anyway, we digress – back to our little problem with Lord Atkinson."

"But all the politicians and, well, everyone else, seem to be such good people. Such believable people. Surely this doesn't happen in our civilised society?" asked Arthur, wondering how he'd missed all this and what else was out there, lurking, waiting for him to stumble over.

"Yes, we would all like to think so," said Mary, smiling sadly. "However, when you move in the financial circles Sam Black and others do, you'll see the reality is that the banks have their silk-gloved gauntlets firmly round the throats of every senior politician – all very gentlemanly and proper but if any makes a wrong move, says the wrong thing, that steel gauntlet closes and our protective police department can be relied on to create all sorts of havoc in a man's life!" "No, Mary, not the police too!" said Arthur in disbelief.

"Look at the facts, Arthur," said Mary, leaning forward. "Every time a politician looks like stepping over that invisible line, there's a police investigation, a messy police investigation and no conclusion or resolution. No one's brought to trial. The poor man just has his property invaded, turned upside down, his name put to question and he quickly falls back into line or disappears like the homosexual magician."

"Homosexual magician?"

"He disappeared with a poof!" said Mary, chuckling, while Arthur realised it was a joke he didn't quite get. "Anyway, without going into any more detail just now, Arthur, you need to understand why we're treating this case extremely seriously."

"The Atkinson case?"

"Just so," said Mary. "Those who are supposed to be there to protect us just may not be on our side when the chips are down. I just ask that you be careful who you speak to about this."

"Oh," said Arthur, with real words failing him and a sense of foreboding descending on him like an elevator he's trapped under.

"So, anyway, enough of that!" said Mary, sitting back a little. "The fact is, Arthur, one of our politicians seems to have upset one of our banks – or maybe a few – and the FSA, doing its real job, is out to put a stop to his shenanigans." "Which politician is this?"

"We don't know yet, but it maybe Lord Atkinson – they're not saying yet," said Mary, shaking her head. "So, to the matter at hand." "They're investigating us?"

"Well, sort of. Their investigation hasn't started but we've been warned, from above, that the Atkinson case could be looked into," said Mary, returning to her harried look. "So, we've got to be very careful to have it completed before they turn up – we want to show how efficient we are to stop the investigation spreading anywhere else. We don't want any questions unanswered. You understand?"

"Yes, I think I do," said Arthur, feeling the elevator settling on him slowly. This project was supposed to be exciting but there now seemed to be a serious edge to it. Perhaps Joan was right after all.

"So, you see we need it done as quickly as possible."

"But, if I have the files at home till it's all settled, there's no possibility of the FSA seeing anything half complete," said Arthur, quietly. Mary sat, shaking her head. "You can say the matter is in the hands of your expert consultant and can delay giving them anything till I've answered all your questions. If the worst comes to the worst, you can delay till then, blame me and they can't see the job till it's all plastered, wallpapered and looking ready for sale, so to speak."

Mary sat and smiled at this undeniable logic. "Arthur Bayly," she said, eventually, "you're a bit of a dark horse, aren't you! I hadn't thought of it that way."

"I have my moments."

"Right, perfect solution," said Mary, standing again and coming round to Arthur's side of the desk, with her hand out. "If I was one of those New Agers, I'd give you a hug, but I'm not!" She shook his hand strongly and did what she was good at – giving orders: "I'll get my PA to photocopy all the files, you get two computer sticks, copy all you have in your computer onto them. You keep one stick and the original files. I'll lock all the copies away from anyone's view, in case the worst happens. I'll organise you a laptop, be on your way with the original files and computer stick and you can download a copy when you get home. Okay?"

"Uh, yes, fine, thanks Mary."

"And we'll keep in phone and email contact each day. I'll need to know what's happening all the time," said Mary, smiling. "Upstairs will want to know that good progress is being made. And don't forget to ask for any resources you need – money is no object, as they say!"

Arthur felt a little like James Bond with a rising sense of excitement – even danger – he'd never felt before. Every moment he feared an earnest band of pin-striped inspectors confronting him perverting – well, temporarily skirting – the course of justice and being hauled off for incarceration in the Tower of London ... his mind went wild with the awful consequences it created, one upon the other. What he was very sure of was that James Bond would not trip up on shadows on the carpet, drop his computer stick behind his drawer and spend five sweaty minutes extracting said drawer and said computer stick, dropping a bundle of files in the corridor and spend a few more precious minutes gathering them up. No, James Bond would be in his office for four and a half minutes and out the door before anyone noticed.

"So, Mr Bond, how are we going? Mission completed?" asked Mary as she strode back with the files.

All Arthur could offer in reply was a sort of grunty, giggly refrain as he stood staring at his computer screen, wondering whether to scream or cry.

"Is everything alright, Arthur?" asked Mary, her smile turning to concern.

"I'm afraid this Mr Bond just isn't up to it today, Mary ... ah, Miss Moneypenny," said Arthur, staring intently at the screen. "I turned it on and it just downloaded an upgrade of some sort and it's shut down and restarting – too dashed clever for itself, I'd say. I'm sure this never happens to our Mr Bond ... I say, how did you know I was thinking of him when you came in?"

"I didn't, it just came out," said Mary. "So you were thinking how James Bond would be doing this?"

"Well, yes I was, actually," said Arthur. "Dashed interesting, really." He saw the computer had finally downloading or uploading or whatever it did. He rushed to his chair, transferred his Atkinson file onto the two sticks, gave one to Mary, took the files from her and packed it all in the bag she gave him.

"Gosh, what's the rush?" asked Mary, surprised at his speed. "They won't be here today, Arthur."

"I must be nervous. I'm sorry," he said, sheepishly. "I really should be going, anyway, to help Joan with something." His eyes wouldn't stop darting to the door and the reception area – you never know with these investigation types, he thought.

"OK, well, please keep me informed each day – I know you'll have it completed in no time," said Mary as she shook his hand and disappeared up the corridor to the lift.

Arthur walked out with more speed than grace and bumped into two large men in black suits at the reception area. He immediately sensed who these two strangers were and he felt a most uncomfortable prickly heat in his face and it seemed to be spreading over his head. He supposed that he must be sweating, something he was not prone to do. These tense moments looked all very exciting on television and in the James Bond movies and he'd always wondered what it was like in real life. Now he knew and he didn't like it. His mind became strangely focussed, rather strongly, on several things at once.

He thought of Joan and how she'd like him to act – cool and decisive. This was not a natural state for him but, for her, he tried. He noticed the clock on the wall said 11.37 and that time stuck in his head. He noticed the black suits, nearly identical. He noticed that the man who stepped forward, had blonde cropped hair and and a faint scar from his left ear to his mouth. As he extended his hand a tattoo showed on his forearm, under his cuff-linked shirt cuff.

His colleague was slightly shorter and broader with a shaven head. Arthur noticed that he kept his right hand clenched and was sure the fourth finger was missing.

Then a strange thing happened – perhaps because he was focused on some things and not on others. Anyway, a shadow, a flicker – maybe it was a trick of the light or the dread in his brain – passed the left corner of his eye. It was there and gone and he felt a faint whisper of wind, a zephyr. His left hand felt lighter but he daren't look down; he needed his focus on these men who, he assumed, were Financial Services Authority auditors. Rather more rugged looking than he'd imagined, they had obviously caught the scent – as auditors are wont to do – of whatever intrigues surrounded the Atkinson case. And here he was, Arthur Bayly, walking from the crime scene with the stolen jewels on his person, so to speak.

"Arthur Bayly, I presume?" said Crewcut, a missing tooth marring his smile. "Ah, yes, correct. Arthur," said Arthur. "And you are?" "You got da Atkinson stuff?" asked the shorter man.

"The Atkinson file," said Crewcut, interrupting his friend. "We just want to ascertain the whereabouts of that information, Sir."

Arthur felt the prickly heat intensify and spread down his neck, as the man moved closer, his sickly deodorant filling Arthur's head. His legs felt a little unsteady. He was determined not to betray the precious information he carried but he couldn't help himself. He glanced down quickly ... and glanced again. The briefcase was not there! He knew he'd carried it out and now it was gone, like a phantom. He glanced around and saw Halee, the receptionist, smiling sweetly at all three gentlemen.

"Excuse me, sirs," she said in her New Zealand accent, "would you like to talk to our director about that?"

"Your director, who dat?" asked the Shorty.

"Mary Collins, sir, she's our director."

"But we were told ... we need to talk to Arthur Bayly about this," said Crewcut.

"Who should I tell her you are?" Halee asked with great efficiency as she held up her handpiece, ready to call.

"But it's the Arthur Bayly we need to see," said Crewcut, looking a little uncertain.

"Did you have an appointment with Miss Collins, sirs?" asked Halee, apparently unable to hear their wish to see Arthur.

"No, no appointment. We just here to see Arthur Bayly and get the Atkinson file, thank you miss," said Crewcut, losing his smile.

"Yes Miss Collins, they're here at reception now ... no, they don't seem to have any warrant or authority to take any client files ..." said Halee into her phone piece. Arthur was sure she had not dialled anyone. However, the two men stepped back a little. "The police? You think I should call the police, Ma'am?" said Halee into her phone.

Arthur suddenly found himself suspended and being carried towards his office.

"Yours is the second on the left, here, i'n it?" asked Shorty, the stench of his bad breath mingling discordantly with his strong deodorant.

"Ah, yes, just here," said Arthur, wondering how he knew.

"Right, so where's the Atkinson file, Sir?" demanded Crewcut.

"Ah, the Atkinson file," muttered Arthur, trying to remember his activities five minutes prior to this. He gulped as he realised the Atkinson file was in two places and neither was in his office. "The Atkinson file," he said again, deciding to act dumb. Though, as he smiled to himself, it wasn't acting at all, really. "It should be in this filing cabinet. I just need to unlock it," he said, fumbling in his pocket for the office keys. They weren't there. Mary had them. "Look, I most awfully sorry, I don't have the keys."

The shorter man dashed to the filing cabinet, knocking Arthur aside, and yanked on the handle, several times. The cabinet tipped towards him, spilling a pile of paper onto the floor. By now Arthur had noticed a growing number of people passing his office, looking in while pretending not to. The two men noticed this, too, and Arthur could tell they were not happy.

"Yes," said Arthur, "it's locked and so I'll just go up and get the keys for you."

"You're not bloody goin' nowhere, buddy," said Shorty sharply. "Just open this willya!"

"I ... I don't have the key," said Arthur, trying to sound calm and helpful. "I need to get the keys. They're not here, sir."

"Don't sir me, just open the cabinet," said Shorty, grabbing Arthur by the coat collar and pushing him towards the cabinet. "We ain't got time to piss around. Open the damned cabinet!"

"I'm very sorry, sir, I don't have the keys," said Arthur turning his pockets out, quickly, to show that he was carrying nothing but a white handkerchief and an oyster card.

"Good morning, gentleman, I'm Mary Collins, Regional Director!" said Mary breezily behind him.

She held out her right hand. "And you two gentlemen are?"

The two intruders looked around and down at Mary and then turned back to Arthur without a word. "What is it you're looking for?" asked Mary, dropping her hand.

"The bloody key ..." said Shorty.

"Ah, the Atkinson file, Ma'am," said Crewcut, frowning at his colleague and turning to Mary. He put his hand on his waist and, as his coat was pushed back, the top of a revolver could be seen. "We just need to get the Atkinson file. We don't intend to be mucked around, okay?"

"Of course," said Mary, looking alarmed. Then she quickly plastered her plastic smile back on. "However, we don't keep keys for confidential files down here on this floor. You'll have to come with me."

The two men looked at each other uncertainly. Their quarry was right there – do they risk leaving it?

"The alternative is hammers and crow bars, if you insist," said Mary, sensing their uncertainty. "But we don't have those here either and, as you say, you don't want to be mucked around. Keys are much quicker. Come this way and we'll leave Arthur to get on his way!" As she strode past him she whispered to Arthur, "Go, go now!" and she marched off up the corridor to the lift, fully expecting the two men to follow her. They fell in line and followed her obediently.

Arthur breathed a sigh of relief. He was free of them! But Mary wasn't. What should he do? As relief, fear and confusion swept over him in alternate waves, he felt a tug at his sleeve. He jumped.

"Oh, I'm sorry sir," said an antipodean accent behind him. He turned to see the cheery elfin Halee there with his briefcase. "Sir, right now, you need to take this and go home."

"But where did that come from," asked Arthur, confused. "It disappeared before ..." "Ah, that's easy, sir, I disappeared it for you!" said Halee with a grin.

"You did?"

"Yup! I did!" said Halee. "They seemed to want it and Miss Collins had warned me someone might want it and shouldn't have it. So I disappeared it for you. Now you must go and all will be well, I promise you."

"But Mary's with those ... those rough men ..."

"Miss Collins is fine, Arthur, just you go or she won't be."

"What?"

"You want me to spell it out?" asked Halee, with urgency. "That bag, in this building, is a lot of trouble for Miss Collins. So you just get going and make it safer for her. You understand?"

"Uh, I think so," said Arthur not understanding at all but knowing that he didn't have to. He just needed to go. "Thank you Halee. Thank you so much."

"That's no trouble at all, sir. Just you get yourself going and don't stop till you're home." Arthur turned and walked into two large men in police uniforms.

"Oh, gosh," said Arthur with a feeling of déjà vu.

"That's alright, sir, we're looking for a Mary Collins," said one of them.

"Come with me, gentlemen, and I'll see you later, sir," said Halee waving him away surreptitiously.

Arthur walked rather briskly from the building, down the street and onto the waiting tube, constantly alert. He then boarded the train with the dreaded feeling that someone was watching him. He didn't know which passenger it was. His mind whirred ceaselessly. Apart from the possibility of being discretely manhandled at the point of a gun at any moment, there was the delicate matter of telling Joan ... or not telling Joan. How do you keep something so ... well, so exciting, scary and potentially harmful to her – perhaps to his family and neighbours ... oh my God, where did it end? How do you bottle up such an experience and save others from worry while they should be warned?

# The Intruders

*Monday, 12<sup>th</sup> March 2012, 11.52 a.m.*

As she led the men up the corridor to the lift, Mary wondered what on God's earth possessed her to do this. What was she going to do with them? Say to them? She smiled bravely at them as she waved them into the lift. They waited for her – suspicious sods, she thought. The ride to the seventh floor took seventeen seconds but it seemed like a day. She smiled awkwardly at them and they smiled awkwardly back at her but their smiles turned to grimaces as they frowned at each other. Mary wondered if they were as confused as she was. She knew their day had not gone as planned – pop into the office, scare a clerk into handing over a file, disappear from said office, hand over file to Mr X, collect cash and be at the pub celebrating by 11.45 am – and here they were, still in the building, going in the opposite direction of the said file while being led around by the noses by a bossy woman. Mary was tempted to smile but she stifled it on the grounds of health and safety. Her health and safety.

The lift doors opened and everybody waited for everybody else to get out. Stupid English, she though, so insanely polite, it's a wonder anything gets done and the place is falling apart. Oh dear, maybe, just maybe, they're suspicious and want her in front of them so they don't fall into a trap. She almost giggled at the thought as she was, at that moment, quite unable to formulate any plan beyond the next three seconds, let alone make a trap for them! Again, on health and safety grounds, she stifled the giggle ... just.

As she strode off down the oak-panelled passage to her office, she was surprised that these two large men had trouble keeping up with her. Mind you, most people did. She also noticed her secretary, Toby McGuire, rising from his seat with a large, toothy smile.

When she'd moved into Sam's office, she decided changes needed to be made – not least to help expunge some of her memories of Sam – so she had told his clueless and probably quite beautiful (in a clueless sort of way) secretary that as she was so meticulous about constantly cleaning and preening herself, she would be perfect to work in the cleaning team, on her ridiculous salary. Strangely, the girl didn't turn up today. This morning Mary had plucked young Toby from the third floor processing team where she had noticed, for some time, that his typing skills were exceptional, that he seemed to have a functioning brain and, most importantly, the bounding enthusiasm of a young puppy. It was nice to have a bloke around. Then she discovered he was a black belt in Tae Kwon Do. She wasn't sure she'd ever need his brick-chopping skills, but it was, somehow, comforting.

"Ah, Toby, these gentlemen are looking for the Atkinson file to take away with them," she said loudly down the corridor, while trying to mouth *help* silently to him.

"Oh dear," said Toby, his lanky frame striding round his high desk. "Isn't that confidential, Ma'am?"

"Yes, yes it is, Toby," she said, mouthing *call the police* to him. "But it seems these gentlemen are insisting they take it." *Call the police* she mouthed again as the two gentlemen caught up with her.

Toby's frown turned into a welcoming smile. "Pleased to meet you," he said, extending his hand to them graciously. "I'm Toby and you're?"

"Just give us the key!" said Crewcut, curtly.

"Ah yes, um, the key," said Toby, thinking aloud. "The key ..."

"Yes, the key, Sir!" said Crewcut. "Just give it now and we'll be gone. Nothing said."

"Yes, the key," said Toby, backing towards his desk. He smacked his palm to his forehead as if a blinding flash of inspiration had hit him and he laughed. "Of course, I'll just need to phone our security desk. They'll know where the key is!" He backed around the chest-high counter, sat and phoned.

"Look, lady, you said you had the key to da file," said Shorty. "Are you pulling our tits?"

"Pulling what?" asked Mary, confused.

"Pulling our ... oh, shittin' us, lying to us," said Shorty. "We want that key now or else we'll just have to take the whole damned filing cabinet. What's it to be?"

"Ah, oh dear, I thought it was here," said Mary, stopping in an attempt to keep them as far from Toby's phone conversation as possible. "I forgot security look after all that stuff. I haven't been in this job very long ..."

"You're stalling lady ..." said Crewcut.

"Miss Collins, if you don't mind," said Mary, determined to keep up appearances of being in charge. "And I'm not stalling. But let's be clear about what's going on here. You've barged into our office, uninvited and unannounced. You've demanded, with threats, that we do something which is illegal – hand over confidential files. That will get me into a whole heap of trouble – I could lose my job and it could cost the company a whole heap of trouble with the Financial Services Authority. And you're whining that I'm a bit nervous about all this!" "Look lady ..." said Shorty.

"Miss Collins thank you!" said Mary, tartly.

"Uh, look Miss Collins, we got orders, see!" said Crewcut. "We just gotta pick up da file and deliver it. Den we get paid. See?"

"Delivered to whom? Paid by whom?" asked Mary, realising that Toby was trying to smile and nod at her without it becoming evident to the men.

"To George Sand..." said Shorty.

"Hey bozo, we don't say who we're working for! Okay?" said Crewcut tersely, grabbing Shorty's collar.

"Oh yeah, I forgot," said Shorty. "It's conden..., it's confild..., oh, secret. See?"

"I see," said Mary. "So what if the whereabouts of the key was confidential?"

"Ah, that's goin' to be a big problem," said Shorty, looking at his partner, perplexed. "Mr Sanderson is going to be mighty fierce with us."

"Ah, you dumbo!" said Crewcut. "Shut your mouth, you're spilling the beans."

"Ah, oh, yeah, guess I did," said Shorty. "Forget I said that."

"Yeah, well, if we don't deliver, we gotta be in a whole heap of trouble, you might say," said Crewcut. "And we prefer you's in trouble den us, so give us da key and we'll be gone and no trouble!"

"Right, yes," said Mary, still wondering what Toby seemed to be trying to tell her – something hopeful, she hoped, but what it could be she had no idea.

"So lady ..." said Crewcut.

"Miss Collins!"

"Oh, sorry, Miss Collins," said Crewcut, missing his place in his script.

"So Miss Collins what?" asked Mary, walking up to him. "So Miss Collins, if we break your arm or smash a hole in this wall, the key will magically turn up, you'll get your precious file and we'll all be deliriously bloody happy! Is that it?"

"Uh, no, not quite," said Crewcut, stepping back a pace. "We don't want to hurt anyone. We were told no damage to people or property. Just get the file."

"You have no idea how relieved I am about that!" said Mary, stepping forward again. "But, right now, you'd love to bust a limb, see some blood, hear a scream. Right?"

"No Ma'am, we just want the file, easy like," said Shorty, coming to his friend's rescue.

"Easy like," said Mary, turning on him and savouring his phrase. "Easy like. All just little lambs in here, these pathetic little clerical types. Say *boo* and they run. Is that what you thought?" "Well, yeah, ah no," said Crewcut, looking everywhere except at Mary.

"Yeah, well we don't just bow down to cowards like you trying to muscle in here and stuff us around!" said Mary venomously. "You think you haven't hurt anyone?"

"Well, no ..." said Shorty. "Nobody been harmed."

"You've scared the living daylights out of people, you've stuffed up our day here with your stupid antics and we're all going to have to work late, for no extra pay and we're going to have to beef up our security from now on. You think there's no cost?" "Well, y ..." said Shorty.

"Well, hell, of course there's a cost!" said Mary, turning on him. "I predict that we're going to have a lot of people calling in sick over the next week or so – your intrusion is traumatic and unwarranted and a lot of people here are going to be upset for months. I hope what you get paid is worth all the heartache, pain and cost you're causing!" "Look lady ..." said Crewcut.

"Miss Collins!" said Mary, turning back on him.

"Ah shut up! I'll call you what I like, LADY!" shouted Crewcut.

"Ah, so the big man has finally found some balls," said Mary, quietly.

# Burglars and Bungles

*Monday, 12ᵗʰ March 2012, 12.14 p.m.*

Mary knew the situation was dire, that she was in danger, that these thugs could harm her, that they could smash the place and that she had absolutely no idea what to do next – bluff was only going to work for so long, until one of these mutton-heads lost their cool. Maybe this was how ordinary people became brave people, she pondered, while frantically searching her little grey cells for a way out. Maybe situations just became too overwhelming, too surreal, for them to be fully absorbed by the rational brain and so the irrational one kicks in and the unexpected happens. However, this time, nothing else kicked in – Mary was still confronted by two knuckle-dragging pea brains, intent on taking something she didn't want them to have.

She could, of course, employ the karate-chopping skills of Toby but that would only delay the inevitable – they'd have friends (though, why anyone would want to be friends with twerps like these she could not fathom) and the next wave of rampaging Neanderthals would be worse. Violence never solved violence, it just perpetuated itself. She was intent only on transforming their aggression into something softer or, at the least, to deflecting their violence in another direction, in the way that Toby had explained the basic techniques of his martial art – not stopping their force but turning it either sideways or back on them.

In the split second these conversations with herself went on, nothing much else happened. She waited, they waited and Toby sat serenely behind his high desk, blithely doing something that looked important. As her mind was churning over these bewildering little things, she looked at Toby and his silly smile was infectious.

"This is not bloody funny!" said Crewcut.

"No, you guys in trouble here," said Shorty, reaching into his belt and pulling out a knife. He held it with the blade down as if to plunge it into something.

"You're not going to hurt anyone holding it like that," said Toby, quickly recovering from his laughing fit as he came round to the front of his desk.

"Oh yes I am ... I could," said Shorty.

"Oh no you won't," said Toby. "You see, my ribs are overlapped, like planks on the side of a ship, and if you chop down, the knife will just bounce down my ribs. Here, let me show you." He held out his hand.

"Uh ... oh, yeah, okay," said Shorty, taken aback by the surrealism of the moment. He handed his knife to Toby who held it with the blade facing up.

"See, if I go at you this way, it won't bounce down your ribs but will go up between them," said Toby lunging at Shorty and stopping millimetres from his ribcage. Shorty's elbows went up and he took a deep breath, immobilised. Crewcut immediately reached into the back of his belt, fumbled around and a pistol clattered to the floor. Toby, quick as a flash, kicked it across the floor to Mary.

"Don't pick it up, Mary - fingerprints!" said Toby. "Kick it behind my desk! Quick!"

Mary's body reacted quicker than her brain and obeyed Toby's instructions to the letter. Crewcut turned to chase after his gun.

"One move and this knife moves an inch and pierces your friend's heart!" yelled Toby, at Crewcut, who realised Toby had not moved the knife from Shorty's body. Crewcut seemed as paralysed as his friend.

"Wadda I do now?" asked Shorty in a squeaky voice.

"Drop that knife!" came a voice from nowhere and then Mary realised two policemen had come out of the lift, into the corridor.

"Not till you hand-cuff these men," said Toby calmly.

◇ *Philip J Bradbury*

Drop that knife, young man," repeated one of the policemen, advancing up the corridor. "You're trespassing and you're under arrest for assault."

"I work here, sargeant!" said Toby. "These crazies are the trespassers. Now hand-cuff them – what are you waiting for?"

"How do we know whose assaulting who, Sarge?" asked the second policeman.

"Uh, I ... I'm not sure," said number one.

"We damned well work here, you irks," said Toby. "You think invite people in here to be attacked by us? Come on, cuff them. NOW!"

"Uh, yes sir," said number one, leaping forward. "You, sir, are under arrest. Do not move!" Shorty had not moved a muscle for over a minute and remained scarecrow-like. "Get your hands down, behind your back!"

"But you said don't move ..." said Shorty plaintively.

"Well, move your hands, clever clogs!" said number one. "NOW!"

Mary wondered who had the lowest IQ – the burglars or the police – and quickly decided it was a dead-heat. She and Toby promised to come down to give their statements, within the half hour and Crewcut and Shorty were led off, still mumbling at each other.

Over a cup of very strong coffee in Mary's office, she and Toby worked out a battle plan to deal with the Atkinson file once and for all. It had started out so simply, this little insurance claim and now it was growing like a nuclear bomb on the horizon ... and the horizon was closing in fast. Decisive action was needed.

As Toby shut the door behind him, Mary sank into a quiet funk – she had to admit she wasn't always as strong as the presented to the world. Then text arrived:

*You thwarted me today and I will not give up. You have been targeted and I will get those files and you could be the collateral damage. Cooperate and you might be safe. Who knows. GS.*

The Only GS she knew was George Sanderson, Commissioner of the London Metropolitan Police. She staunched a frightened tear, stood up as if to battle and sat back down again, no longer a business woman but a little girl frightened by a violent father.

# Emily and Chloe

*Monday, 12<sup>th</sup> March 2012, 12.14 p.m.*

Having escaped his office, two heavies and two policemen, Arthur's brain was still in panic mode, conjuring up all sorts of consequences for Joan and him.

As these conflicting thoughts stampeded through his brain, battling with each other, he kept a wary eye on everyone, especially KGB agents, in the train carriage. Would James Bond have stood casually at the door, ready to leap off, or would he have sat down, mingling anonymously with the crowd? Yet another herd of thoughts charged round in his brain.

"Hello Mister," said a small voice at his knee. He looked down and remembered the tousle-haired little girl who had offered him ice cream in the park.

"Oh, hello, young lady," he said, "how are you today?"

"My mummy and me, we've just been to the shops to buy a gun," she said. Not quite panic but Arthur's heart leapt out of the carriage and back in again. He looked up and around and saw the girl's mother – Emily, was that her name? – smiling at him. She put her hand in a plastic shopping bag and pulled out a gun. Arthur flinched. It was a plastic water pistol ... well, he hoped it was. "Sorry to scare you, sir ... Arthur, wasn't it?" She asked.

Arthur nodded, recovering his composure.

"We're off to a birthday party this afternoon for Chloe's cousin," said Emily. "He loves guns and this is the most inoffensive one I could find!"

"Yes, yes," said Arthur, acting more casual then he felt. "Boys do seem to like guns, don't they."

"The last time I saw you, you were a very shaken hero," said Emily. "How have you been since then?"

"Oh good thank you," said Arthur, with his standard reply, then thought he'd try the truth. "Actually I've had quite some happenings of late – job's become, ah, strange, my mother-in-law died, my son's wife left him, I've just escaped from work, ... yes, a few things and in only seven days." He smiled at the memories as the film clip of those seven days played themselves through his mind.

"My gosh!" Emily said. "You have been having a time of it! And how are you coping with it all?"

"Remarkably well, I thought," he said. "And how have you been?"

"Well, to be honest, not very good," she said gently. "Three days ago my father disappeared and nobody knows where he's gone ..."

"Your father? Gosh!" said Arthur, not knowing what else to say.

"Yes, we usually talk on the phone two or three times a week and he visits every week," she said wistfully. "He's very busy as a director of an insurance company but he always makes time for Chloe and I."

"An insurance company?" asked Arthur quickly. "Not AIL is it?" "Yes, that's his company! Do you know it ... or him?" asked Emily.

"Yes I do indeed!" said Arthur, forcing a smile. "I've worked for the company for thirty years. Mr Black, your father, was the one who, aah, changed my job last week."

"Oh dear, that must have been very hard for both of you," said Emily, looking concerned. Arthur had not considered that it would have been hard for Mr Black.

"Do you have any idea where he could have gone?" asked Emily hopefully.

"Heavens no! No idea at all," said Arthur. "I thought he'd been sacked or made redundant or something. Seems like he just didn't turn up on Friday and I assumed he'd been asked to leave. Quite strange."

Oh dear, that makes it even worse," said Emily. "No one at all seems to know where he is. I've told the police and got what I thought was a rather cold reception there. Just made it worse, really. I don't think anyone's looking for him."

"Oh dear, oh dear," said Arthur, finding himself at a loss with this tearful woman. "Would you and your daughter like to come back to our place for a cup of tea? It's a short walk and my wife is very good with things like this."

"Oh Arthur, that's very kind ... but I couldn't ..."

"Of course you can! I insist," said Arthur feeling unusually masterful. "A cup of tea and a nice chat might be just what you need."

"Well, if that's alright with you ..."

"Well," said Arthur, feeling a sense of mission rising in him. "Perhaps if we all put our thinking caps together, we can come up with something. You're not alone," he said, wishing someone would say that to him from time to time.

"Oh Arthur! You're a sweet man!" she exclaimed, loud enough for all the carriage to hear ... or so it seemed to Arthur. His extreme embarrassment was overshadowed by the approaching station, East Croydon (although, as Arthur thought in a small part of his brain that wasn't trying to deal with his embarrassment, that station wasn't approaching at all. It wasn't going anywhere, the train was approaching it!).

As they walked up Addiscombe Road, Chloe skipped along between them and Arthur felt light. He hadn't been mugged on his way home by KGB agents and he would soon be in his familiar home with his familiar Joan and all the coziness and peace they evoked. Danger obviously added a poignancy to the people and things he cherished and, well, he might possibly help someone else. He smiled at Emily who seemed to catch his mood and looked happier than when he first saw her on the train.

Emily protested that it was all too much for Joan and Arthur and they didn't even know her and she didn't want to trouble them and they had enough with everything else that had happened to them and, well, her father would probably turn up soon anyway and and and ... However, Joan quietly got a resistant Emily to sit down, have a cup of tea and sandwiches while Arthur, under instructions, was fetching juice and toys for Chloe.

"Now, Emily, you're right," said Joan, sitting next to Emily on the couch. "We've had a little drama here, lately, with Arthur and Martin and we just buried my mother last week. Yes, it's a lot, Emily." "It's too much, I would say!" said Emily, looking tearful.

"Yes, we might look back and say that," said Joan, smiling. "But while we're in the middle of it, we just go day by day, hour by hour." "But I'm imposing ..."

"Emily, you're not, I promise!" said Joan with her hand firmly on Emily's knee. "You're actually doing us a favour."

"A favour?"

"Yes, a favour, isn't she Arthur?" said Joan.

"Ah, yes, a favour ..." said Arthur, looking up from helping Chloe get the Lego set out of the box. He couldn't hide his perplexed expression.

"You're giving us something to take our minds off our situation," said Joan. "You see, we can't do anything about my mother or Martin or Arthur. We could feel hopeless with all that. But, with your

father, there's probably something we can do. It'll help us feel helpful again." "Oh, I hadn't thought of it like that!" said Emily, brightening visibly.

"And, besides, I do love a project, don't I Arthur?" said Joan, smiling.

"Oh yes, she does love a project," said Arthur, chuckling while he tried to fit wheels onto a Lego block for Chloe.

"So, my friends, a battle plan!" said Joan, clapping her hands with glee. "What do we know?" "Well, we don't know much at all," said Emily, uncertainly.

"Mmm, we probably know more than we think," said Joan. "Now, what were his hobbies? What did he do outside work?"

"Oh, I'm not sure," said Emily. "His work was a big part of his life. He usually took it home every night. And he visited us often. I know he liked folk music."

"Folk music?" exclaimed Arthur, incredulously, trying to imagine Sam Black in his Versace suit, Gucci shoes and immaculate fingernails mixing in with bearded hippies. "Folk music? I would never have imagined it!" Seeing that Chloe was fully engrossed in her toys, he got up and took a seat, all ears on the adult conversation now.

"So, where did he go for his folk music, Emily?" asked Joan.

"Oh, I don't really know," said Emily, frowning. "He did mention different clubs, sometimes ... usually in Camden, I think."

"So, folk clubs in Camden – how do we find people there?" asked Joan. Silence. No one knew.

"Okay, so we put that question on the list for God, for The Universe. The answer will come." "Joan, dear, what's this about God ... The Universe?" asked Arthur, perplexed.

"Oh dear, I have a confession," said Joan, smiling at Arthur. "I haven't told you I have been studying *A Course in Miracles.*"

"Miracles?" asked Arthur, immediately regretting his first question, knowing this was headed somewhere he didn't want to know about.

"*A Course in Miracles,*" said Joan, patiently. "It's a book to help you change your life, for the better. I read it each day when you're at work and we have a fortnightly group meeting – five of us." "Why didn't you tell me this before?" asked Arthur, feeling left out.

"Because I thought you'd be uncomfortable with it," said Joan. "I just thought you'd find out when you were ready and, well, you must be now. You've just found out!" She smiled at Arthur and patted his knee. "I haven't turned into a werewolf, have I?"

"No, no you haven't at all," said Arthur softly. "Actually, dear, you seem different, softer, happier than you used to be. Not so, ah, brittle."

"Well you can blame the book for that. It's actually brilliant and I'd really like you to read it with me but I didn't know how you'd be with it," said Joan.

"Ah, Joan, this book mentions God. Is it Christian?" asked Emily. "I've had some bad experiences with the church ... one of the main reasons I'm separated."

"Oh dear! I'm sorry about that," said Joan. "But no, it's not Christian. In fact, many Christians would be challenged by it and many follow it." Joan laughed.

"But it mentions God ..." said Arthur, rubbing his temples.

"Yes it does love," said Joan. "It tells us that any decision that we need to make, if we hand it over to God and listen to the Voice for God, that still, quiet voice inside, the perfect answer will arise." "That sounds like Christianity!" said Emily with a forced smile.

"It sounds like every religion that has ever been!" said Joan. "And, for me, I don't care what religion it is, it works for me. It's very practical. It's how I dealt with Mum's death, with your job fears, with Martin's breakup and it's how I'm dealing with this. I know it works."

"Oh dear," said Arthur, smiling at his wife. "Just when I think I'm beginning to know you, you pull another rabbit out of the hat!"

"Poof!" said Joan laughing and slapping Arthur's knee playfully.

"So, I know nothing about this miracle book ..." said Arthur.

"*A Course in Miracles,*" corrected Joan.

Sorry, *A Course in Miracles* book," said Arthur. "I know nothing about it but it's caused a small miracle in you, my love, if you don't mind me saying so. So let's try it here. What do you think, Emily?"

"Well, nothing else is working, is it!" said Emily, sitting back and smiling sadly. "The police haven't found him and nor has anyone else. What do we have to lose?"

"So, Miracle Woman, what does the good book tell us we should do now?" asked Arthur, partly in jest, partly in dread.

"Nothing," said Joan.

"Nothing?" asked Emily, sitting up, surprised.

"Nothing," said Joan.

"Nothing?" asked Arthur.

"No, nothing at all," said Joan. "What it says is that nothing has happened." "Nothing has happened?" asked Arthur.

"Nothing has happened." said Joan.

"Nothing has happened?" asked Emily.

"Nothing has happened," said Joan. "Now, I don't really get it and, yes, it does sound illogical but what it says is that this whole world is an illusion, it's not really here."

"Not really here?" asked Arthur, trying desperately to think of something original but failing badly.

"Not really here," said Joan. "The course says you don't have to get it. You don't even have to believe it. You just have to try to get it, to show a little willingness." "Willingness for what?" asked Emily, sitting back with a frown.

"Willingness to try to get it that this world is an illusion. That it's not really here," said Joan.

"It's not really here ..." said Arthur, still failing in the originality department again.

"It's not really here," said Joan. "I know this chair is real, I know you're real, Emily, and I certainly don't want you to not be here, Arthur. You're real to me, love, and I certainly don't want you to disappear in a puff of smoke!"

"We're here but we're not?" asked Arthur, going bright red with Joan's public words of affection. He wasn't used to such things. He felt like he was drowning in a sea of illogic and really needed a life belt very soon.

"Just bear with me, love; Emily," said Joan. "All this in the world is an illusion – it's an insane illusion."

"It's certainly insane!" said Emily, laughing for the first time.

"That's a good step!" said Joan, turning to her. "You see, if you can just accept that this world, this busy, physical world, is insane – absolutely, totally insane – you'll stop trying to work it out, analyse it, make sense of it."

"Oh, I've given up trying to make sense of it with everything that's happened over the last few years!" said Emily, smiling grimly.

"Great, so you're on the way to sanity!" said Joan. "Now, so we just start by giving up trying to work anything out, just knowing it's insane ..."

"But how can it be insane if it doesn't exist?" asked Arthur, as a blinding flash of inspiration finally hit him.

"I don't know, love," said Joan, patting his knee again, smiling. "The course says we don't have to believe it. In fact, we can even actively reject it. We just need a little willingness to see things another way."

"Mmm," said Arthur, finding real words difficult to find again.

"Okay, I'm willing!" said Emily, sitting up with more vigour than she'd shown previously. "Life has been so insane for me and I just can't make sense of it. It's just not working for me, actually, so I'm ready to try another way – any other way! What do you think, Arthur?"

"What I think is that the whole thing sounds so totally mad but it has actually worked for Joan. She's different, I know she is, and I'd like to have something of the difference she's experienced. That's what I think." said Arthur, smiling, shaking his head. "If the madness works, let's try it!"

"So, we show a little willingness to try to accept that the world's insane, it's not really here," said Joan, summing up. "So, if it's not really here, what is?"

"Oh my God, now what?" asked Arthur with a strange buzzing in his stomach, a strange and uncomfortable buzzing.

"You're absolutely right, Arthur! There's your God!" said Emily, laughing. "That's all there is. God!"

"God?" asked Arthur, finding his originality with words slipping away again.

"So we just sit here and let God do it all?" asked Arthur, checking that he'd summed up correctly. He eased himself back down to the floor as he realised Chloe was having trouble fitting some pieces together. Maybe, too, he admitted to himself, it was easier fitting Lego together than fitting these new ideas into his mind – they just wouldn't go in properly. Perhaps Chloe felt just like him, struggling to fits pieces together.

"Well, yes, we give over to God but we don't actually do nothing at all," said Joan, patiently. "We just don't do anything in our own strength ..."

"Our own strength?" said Arthur, interrupting, with the dread feeling that it was becoming less comprehensible, not more, as he'd hoped.

"Yes, our own strength. And no, I don't fully get it and I don't do it all the time, I must admit," said Joan, smiling ruefully. "I keep falling back into my old way of doing things – deciding what must be done and trying to make them happen my way." Arthur smiled at the frank confession of her bossiness and his dread of her uncompromising demands. He didn't trust his mouth to say anything at this moment and kept it firmly shut.

"Well, what is this new way?" asked Emily. "If we do nothing, what do we do then?"

"What we do – and I'm still learning all this – is to ask the question and leave it at that," said Joan.

"Just ask a question and leave it at that?" asked Emily, frowning as she ran her fingers through her fine, blonde hair.

"We ask and we listen. We don't decide what to do, we listen and the still, small voice for God speaks," said Joan, uncertainly. "Oh, gosh, it all sounds rather silly when I say it like that but it works, believe me!"

"So, what question do we ask?" asked Arthur, unable to restrain himself any longer.

"Whatever's bothering you. Whatever you need an answer to," said Joan, admiring the Lego house that Chloe had just showed her, with great pride. "That's lovely, dear. You're very clever."

"So, that's why you suggested we state our question about Dad," said Emily, looking like a light bulb had just been turned on in her head. "We ask 'where do we find Samuel Black?' Then we wait for the answer. It can't be that simple, really?"

"That's the problem, we love things to be complicated and we mistrust the simple. We reject the simple answers," said Joan. "The really difficult bit is staying out of our own way, of not stopping to listen and of jumping in with our most logical actions."

"What's wrong with logic?" asked Arthur, taking his seat again, shaking his head in confusion.

"Nothing's wrong with logic, dear, if we know all the facts," said Joan. "The trouble is that we never, ever, in any circumstance, know all the facts and so we apply our logic to half the problem, not all of it."

"Mmm, I suppose you're right," said Arthur.

The Universe, God or whatever you call that which is bigger than all of us, does know all the facts and so its logic is the only reliable one," said Joan.

"So we ask 'where is Sam Black'?" asked Arthur, hoping desperately that Joan would say 'yes'.

"Not quite. My suggestion, dear, is that we ask what are we meant to do in this moment," said Joan. "We ask what action we should take, right now, and the rest will be revealed."

"So, it's quite practical, really," said Emily. "Knowing where he is doesn't help us to know what to do about it."

"Exactly!" exclaimed Joan, clapping her hands and giving everyone a fright. "Oops, sorry, I just love this stuff! Right now we don't need to know where he is or how he is – if we did, we may still not know what to do about that situation. We always ask for action in the present, what to do right now." "So we just sit here and Poppa will come in?" came a small, uncertain voice from the floor.

The adults all chuckled and two looked at the other one, expecting an answer. The answer came but it took a little time to rattle round in Joan's brain, travel down to her throat and come out of her mouth.

"Well Chloe, we do sit and listen and wait," said Joan, uncertainly, "but I don't think your Poppa will just pop through the door."

"Down the chimney like Father Christmas?" asked Chloe, excitedly.

"No dear, we probably won't see Poppa today," said Joan, patiently, as Chloe's face dropped. "You see, God talks very quietly, in our heart, and if we're rushing around doing lots of busy things, panting and stressed, we may not hear him."

"So we sit in silence and wait for God to speak?" asked Emily.

"Ah, sort of," said Joan, smiling through her embarrassment. "Look, what I'm saying is that if we stay alert, stay present to each moment, the answer may come to us – will come to us. It might not be loud and in dazzling lights. It could be – usually is – subtle, quiet, less obvious. That's what the course says, anyway ... I think."

"If I play here quietly, is that alright Mummy?" asked Chloe, obviously concerned. "I'll listen very carefully."

"Of course it is love," said Emily, smiling at Chloe. "Just ask God for help to find Poppa and keep on playing – an answer or idea might come."

"At the risk of repeating myself, what do we do now?" asked Arthur, feeling restless and the need to do something. "I really should be getting on with the work I picked up today." He was instantly reminded of the altercation at the AIL offices, a few hours ago, and wondered how Mary and everyone else was. He hadn't even told Joan about it yet. As he stood up there was a knock at the front door.

"Oh, Mummy, do you think that's God?" asked Chloe, leaping up and beating Arthur to the door.

"No, no, Chloe ..." said Emily, realising her words were in vain and unsure of whether to stand or sit.

"She's really getting into this, isn't she!" said Joan. "Let's us just sit back and see if it is God!" The women smiled to each other and then laughed, releasing the tension in the room.

# Looking for Sam

*Monday, 12<sup>th</sup> March 2012, 1.16 p.m.*

Arthur opened the door to Martin. "What are you doing here, in the middle of the day?" asked Arthur, shaking his hand and leading him in to a seat. "I thought you'd be at work."

"I had to come out here, just up the road, to mediate a property dispute ... oh, we haven't met," said Martin, suddenly seeing Emily as he sat down and stood again.

"Yes, sorry Martin. This is Emily and her daughter, Chloe," said Joan. Emily stood and they shook hands. Actually, thought Arthur, they just stood and stared at each other for the longest time, with their hands touching, not moving.

"So good to see you, Martin," said Joan.

"Uh, yes," said Martin, detaching himself from Emily and the trance he seemed to be in. "I just thought I'd see how you two are, after Nana's ... ah, you know ..."

"It's okay, Martin, you can say the word funeral," said Joan. "We were all there."

"Yes, yes of course," said Martin, blushing as he ran his hand through his thick black hair. Arthur thought Emily's pale skin had taken on a slight colour recently, too.

"Would you like a cup of tea, Martin?" asked Joan.

"I could murder one, thanks Mum!" said Martin. "It's thirsty work dealing with people who won't see plain logic." Arthur, Joan and Emily all smiled at each other. "Oh, did I say something?"

"We've just been talking about logic," said Arthur, hoping the subject would go away, somehow.

"Look, I'll go and make us all a cup of tea and we can tell you about it then," said Joan. "Would you like to give me a hand, Emily?"

"Yes, of course," said Emily, looking relieved to have something to do rather than sit there looking jittery, thought Arthur. Martin seemed to stir her up somehow. Maybe they knew each other from somewhere, he surmised. He watched the women take the crockery out and turned back to Martin, to discover he was on the floor, showing Chloe how to put pieces together to make a person. Martin playing with a child? On the floor? Arthur couldn't believe it. For the second time in a week he saw his son showing affection and having fun. He sat back and smiled in wonder.

"Yes, Dad, I know what you're thinking," said Martin, looking up, embarrassed again. "I never did this with my own kids. Well, I do now and I love it!" "What's happened?" asked Arthur.

"What's happened?" asked Martin. "What's happened is that the dragon's gone and I'm allowed to play with my children. You know what teachers are like – they think they're the last word on how to deal with kids. Ruth just never allowed me to go near them unless I did it the way she prescribed. I could never get it right in her eyes."

"Oh, Martin ..." said Arthur, sadly.

"Anyway, she's so besotted with this new bloke, I don't think she cares if they exist or not or how I treat them," said Martin, with traces of anger and sadness. "She's had them for a few hours but seems to have lost interest so I get to play with them my way and it's fun. It's really fun! It's what you used to do with me, Dad."

As the women returned, talking excitedly, trays in hand, Martin leapt as from an electric shock.

"Can I help you with these?" he asked Emily, taking the tray of tea cups from her.

"Ah, yes, thank you," said Emily, obviously surprised by this unnecessary show of help.

"We were just talking, Martin. Emily's keen on car racing," said Joan. "Family One or something, she said."

"Formula One, Mother," corrected Martin.

Oh well, whatever it is, you used to be fanatical about racing cars when you were small," said

Joan. "Remember all those cars you collected? And you knew all the drivers and everything about it!" "Yes, I did, Mum, but that was long time ago," said Martin, perhaps a little sadly.

"But Emily's mad about it too!" said Joan in her unstoppable way. "Why don't you take her to the next racing meeting or something?"

"But Mother! I hardly know her ... Emily," said Martin, shuffling backwards and going very red. "I'm not sure if it's appropriate."

"Appropriate? Of course it is! Two enthusiasts for racing cars – why wouldn't you go together?" said Joan, with logic unassailed by feelings.

"Darling, Martin has just lost his wife," suggested Arthur. "He's probably feeling a little ... ah, raw at the moment."

"Bloody overwhelmed, actually!" blurted Martin. "Oh, sorry, I didn't mean to swear but life's a bit topsy turvy right now. I just need time to collect myself, that's all." "But you'd enjoy yourself ..." said Joan.

"Darling, you might be right but just give our boy a little time," said Arthur.

"But he really does need to get out and stop moping," said Joan. "

"I understand, Martin," said Emily gently, her quietness stilling the noise. "I went through a separation five months ago and I still find myself paralysed at times. Not moping or complaining, just uncertain and unable to act or think clearly at times. Really annoying ..."

"My God!" said Martin, sitting forward, teacup in hand. "That's just like me. I feel quite useless at times – one of the kids will ask me a stupid question like where's the sugar or something, and I just can't think. My brain's in neutral. I get really annoyed with myself."

"Well, it does get better, I can assure you. 'This too will pass,' I say to myself," said Emily, reaching across to pat his knee.

"See!" said Joan. "They've got so much in common. Why don't you two ..."

"Joan, JOAN!" said Arthur, unable to contain himself any longer. "Just leave well alone and give Martin space to work himself out or whatever they say. He's a grown, intelligent man and I don't think he's about to sink into depression or alcoholism or anything ..."

"But," said Joan. "I just thought it would be so nice ..."

"It would be more nice if we stopped ordering others' lives around and let them be, darling," said Arthur, patting her hand and smiling gently.

"Thanks Dad, thanks," said Martin, wiping tears from his cheek. Emily had not taken her hand from his knee and he looked at her, smiling softly.

"I suppose you're right, Arthur," said Joan sighing. "But you used to be such a dynamo, Martin, a bossy britches and now you've gone all gooey and soft. It's just not the Martin I know."

"Well, if it's goo he needs to be right now, then goo's fine," said Emily. "The goo will set in its own sweet time."

"Thanks Emily," said Martin, his hand now on hers. "Thanks for that. I keep thinking I'm losing it. I really don't like myself at the moment but I can't seem to stop it. My mind just wanders off and doesn't come back and I'm so moody, up and down and roundabout. I'd hate to know what the kids think." He put his cup on the coffee table and sighed.

"What they think, Martin, is that you're there – with them, feeding them, putting them to bed, taking them to school," said Emily. "Yes, they may have a cranky father, at times, but at the moment you're there and they know that."

Martin collapsed back into the chair with both hands over his eyes.

"Oh Martin ..." said Joan, leaping up to comfort him.

"No Joan, let him cry," said Emily with quiet authority.

"But, he needs a hug," said Joan, standing there indecisively.

"No Joan, you need a hug as you feel uncomfortable," said Emily. "But your hug will stop his tears and he needs to let it all out. Wait till he stops."

"Right, okay," said Joan sitting quietly, obviously caught between seeing her son's pain and thinking about this new idea of Emily's.

"Oh, Emily, you do understand!" said Martin. "I feel such a fool, such a failure, but I can't make it stop. But you say it will pass?"

"Yes Martin, it will if you don't try to stop all the sadness and anger and everything else bubbling up when they want to," said Emily. "It probably doesn't feel like it's getting better and then, one day, you realise that you've been quite coherent and normal for hours on end – maybe a whole day – and you start to feel like there's progress at last."

"Ah, Martin, I know where you got your bossy britches from – me!" said Joan. "Sorry to be so pushy. I just want to see you happy …"

"Yes, I know, Mum," said Martin, wiping his eyes with a smile. "But if our resident psychologist here is right, you might have to see me not-happy for a while yet. It's such a relief to know it's okay that I can be like this. Thank you Emily, thank you so much." His hands went to his face as another sob came up.

"Are you alright Mister?" asked Chloe, standing beside him. Arthur wondered how she had just materialised beside his son.

"Yes thanks, young lady," said Martin, also surprised at her presence. "I'm going mad but your mummy said it's okay to do that." He chuckled and it infected the rest of the room. Smiles floated round the room from one person to another.

"Can I sit on your knee, Mister?" asked Chloe.

"What? With this blubbering old man?" asked Martin, his humour returning. "Of course you can and before you get up can you get me one of those biscuits, please? This is all very draining."

Chloe fetched a biscuit and then snuggled up into Martin's solid frame and everyone settled back with a sigh.

"Well," said Arthur, after a minute of peaceful silence. "We were saying that the right thing or person always turns up when we ask for it. You remember saying that, dear?"

"Oh yes I did," said Joan. "That feels like hours ago!"

"Well, we thought Martin was going to be the answer for Emily but it was the other way round, wasn't it!" said Arthur, smiling at his wisdom.

"You know what, Arthur? You're right!" said Joan. "We knew a solution was at hand but we were looking for the wrong one!"

"What's this all about questions and answers and solutions?" asked Martin, looking strangely peaceful, snuggled up with Chloe.

"Well, before you arrived … actually the reason Emily is here, I think, is that her father has gone missing and no one knows where," said Arthur. "Not the police, not his work, not Emily. Quite a mystery."

"And I miss my poppa," said Chloe.

"Of course you do," said Martin, gently.

"So, we were trying to work out what to do next," said Joan. "We asked the universe for an answer and you turned up!"

"You asked the universe?" asked Martin.

"Don't worry about that," said Arthur, a little embarrassed. "Some silly new theory, I think. Anyway, Emily's father, Sam Black, was just not at work last Friday, didn't turn up and hasn't been seen since."

"Not the Sam Black … your boss?" asked Martin.

Yes, my boss," said Martin.

"And the answer's not staring you in the face, Dad?" asked Martin, surprised.

"Well no, Martin, it isn't," said Arthur.

"Look Dad, what do you do when clients make a claim for missing property – cars, furniture or whatever ... even people?" asked Martin.

"Uh, we have search agents ... oh, my gosh, of course!" exclaimed Arthur. "It's what I've done for the past thirty years! How stupid of me! Why didn't I think of it before?"

"Because you needed your highly intelligent son to do it for you," said Martin, smiling. "Must be something in the air – we're all losing it! But that's okay, isn't it. Emily?"

"Absolutely," said Emily, looking relieved, Arthur thought. Maybe the possible solution Martin proposed has given her hope. Maybe Martin, the person, had given her hope, somehow. Whatever the reason, Martin felt grateful for his son and sweetly happy for Emily. The poignancy seemed to touch everyone as a gentle silence filled the room – no one seemed to want to disturb it.

"Look, I've got some contacts who might be able to help," said Martin, eventually, his usual restlessness reasserting itself. "And you must have some, Dad. So why don't we get together in a few days' time to see where we're at and take it from there?"

"Excuse me, Mister, but could I go to the car races with you?" asked Chloe.

"Oh my God, I'm not going to get away with this am I!" said Martin. "Look, it's now Monday and they're racing at the Castle Combs Circuit this Saturday. I think my mate, Stuart the steward, could wangle some tickets for us. Why don't we all go for the day on Saturday – kids and all – and we can see what we've turned up about Chloe's grandad then." "Emily, do you want to join us?" asked Joan.

"Oh, ah," said Emily as if rising from a trance. "Yes, that would be lovely. Absolutely lovely!"

"Look, I've got to go and pick up the kids from school, so let's swap cell phone numbers, Emily, and you can give me all the details I need later on tonight," said Martin, picking Chloe up and dumping her playfully back into his chair. She giggled and leapt up to grab his leg. "Sorry, kiddo, but the silly crying man has to go now."

Joan stood up to give Martin a hug goodbye and she held him for a long time, smiling.

Arthur stood to shake Martin's hand but Martin grabbed him in a bear hug.

"Oh, oh ..." said Arthur, taken aback.

"Thank you so much, Dad," said Martin. "Just for being there. You don't know how much it means." Martin then shook Emily's hand, formally, awkwardly. He ruffled Chloe's hair and sort of skipped from the room. "I'll be in touch with you all," he called as he went out the front door.

# Sifting and Sneaking

*Tuesday, 13$^{th}$ March 2012, 9.00 a.m.*

Arthur found it difficult to concentrate on his work but he just had to get it done ... and quickly. He'd yearned, just a little, for more excitement in his life and now he had it, along with fear and confusion ... in spades, as he'd heard them say.

Joan had helped him move the bed against the wall in their third bedroom and they'd set up the desk in front of the window. It was fortunate that a builder, some forty years ago, had had the foresight to place both a power and a phone switch in that corner and he now had a lovely aspect, with his desk, computer and phone, looking over their small back yard, over to the St Mary Magdalene church, with the sun smiling in at him.

Yes, most pleasant, had it not been for the unnerving situation he now found himself. He'd spread the files out on his bed, in vaguely logical order, and tried to reconcile them all. It seemed that Lord and Lady Atkinson had both been tied up while their house was being burgled. Unfortunately, Lord Atkinson had resisted and his arm and a rib had been broken in the struggle. Having just arrived from New Zealand, their daughter and son-in-law wondered why they'd not been met at the airport and, sensing something wrong, took a taxi from Heathrow to the property near Kings Wood in Surrey. That seemed quite clear to Arthur. The rest of the information, however, wasn't so clear.

The local police reported that they had been called, along with the ambulance, by one of the servants. The office had been ransacked while the rest of the house was untouched. Lady Atkinson had difficulty breathing, with the shock and her asthma, and Lord Atkinson was in considerable pain but would not leave the house to have his arm and rib attended to at the hospital – the ambulance people treated him as best they could, with a temporary brace and sling. He insisted on helping the police inspection of his office and was looking for an item or items (undisclosed) quite frantically. Tyre marks were noticed across part of the lawn, near the office and Sergeant Tomlins felt it was most likely from a four-wheel-drive vehicle. He had had no chance to confirm this.

A half hour into their investigation, four plain clothes men from MI5 turned up and, using their higher authority, ordered the police to leave the premises. Against their wishes, Lord and Lady Atkinson were forced into the ambulance by the MI5 team and the ambulance was ordered off the property. This was most irregular and Sergeant Tomlins insisted on completing a report, on behalf of his team, and forwarding copies to both his supervisors and to the Atkinsons' insurance company, Allied Insurance Ltd.

The ambulance driver's report (confirmed by his assistant) noted property damage as well as footprints by the tyre marks on the lawn, as per the police report. Their report confirmed the Atkinsons' injuries per the police report and that they were ordered from the property by a second group of police. This, again, was most irregular and both reported their concern, in writing and verbally, to their supervisor at the hospital. Lord Atkinson's arm was put in a plaster and sling and his rib cage was bandaged. He was released and returned to his home. Lady Atkinson was suffering from lack of breath, was put on oxygen and kept overnight in hospital for observation.

A succinct report from MI5 confirmed that they were called to the house and found local police in attendance. Because of their lack of experience in these matters, these police were sent away. The Atkinsons proved to be particularly uncooperative and were dispatched to the local hospital for attendance on their injuries. The report also briefly mentioned that the daughter and son-in-law (Melinda and John Maranui) had had arrived later and had been taken to the Send office for questioning and no results of that were indicated.

What the MI5 report did not mention was that Melinda and John Maranui were questioned, separately, for four hours without a break, in a military-like establishment in Send, Surrey. They were

◊ *Philip J Bradbury*

asked about every moment of their lives for the past six years. They averred that they had nothing to hide but the relentlessness of the interrogation team suggested MI5 did not believe this.

The report also omitted to mention that a Mr Brown (later presumed to be the lead character of the MI5 team) initially refused to allow Ahmed Khan and his two assessors, from AIL, to enter the property. The insurance team was eventually allowed in on the second morning. Ahmed and his team found no smashed windows or doors, but newly-repaired ones. The lawn near the corner of the library looked like it had been run over by a hundred different vehicles and no tyre treads could be identified in the remaining slush.

Lord and Lady Atkinson made a written a statement, along with an insurance claim for property missing – none of it particularly valuable and all of it portable. Their statement confirmed that, at 10.30 p.m., they were about to leave for Heathrow airport to pick up their daughter and son-in-law when they heard a crash downstairs and, shortly after, a man in black burst into their bedroom, brandishing a pistol and tied them up, with more force than was necessary. The man could not be identified as he said nothing and his face was covered by a balaclava. Lady Atkinson was sure she heard glass being broken – the office, she surmised, at the time – while they were being tied up, suggesting at least two burglars. Their attacker then left the building and a vehicle was heard, leaving. One of the servants (who called the police and ambulance) was adamant that it was a four-wheel-drive, by the sound of it.

Arthur felt that it was all quite clear but for the dissenting report from MI5, which could not be ignored. And, what were they doing at the scene, ordering everybody about? Lord Atkinson may have been a politician but a break-in was hardly cause for such tactics or such high-level investigation ... unless they knew something no one else did. Surely such a high profile person as the Minister of Immigration wouldn't risk his reputation and position with silly misdeeds.

The discomfort was that Arthur knew or sensed there was something behind the facts, the bland objectivity of a list of items missing and actions taken. Arthur knew he needed to get behind the data to the reasons for the incident. In order to accept or reject part or whole of any claim, there had to be clear evidence (or lack of it) to substantiate his decision. With the FSA breathing down his neck, he could not take any chances or have any ambiguity. Somehow, he needed to talk to Lord Atkinson and/or his wife, and hear their story. As these unwelcome thoughts crowded his mind, his phone rang.

"Arthur, how are you? How is it all going? Any progress?" asked a breathless Mary.

"Yes, yes, making progress ..."

"Good, good, Arthur," said Mary, interrupting. "Now, I have a favour to ask and I know it would help speed up your investigation."

"Oh?" said Arthur, thinking this was beginning to sound like a request he couldn't refuse.

"Now, I hope you don't mind, but Lord Atkinson wanted to know who was dealing with the case," said Mary, in full flight. "I gave him your name and he wants a meeting with you."

"Oh! Mary!" said Arthur. "That's just what I was thinking!"

"You were? How strange ... Now, Arthur, the touchy bit, I'm afraid," said Mary, obviously faltering while she phrased the next bit. "Your situation is a little ... a, interesting. There is a possibility, just a small one, that you could be followed at some time."

"I already am, Mary, by an Australian and his gang," said Arthur, smiling. That bit sounded quite exotic, quite ... well, 007ish.

"You are?" asked Mary with evident surprise. "And we thought they ... oh, he, was from New Zealand? Gosh ... so you know you could be followed again?"

"Yes, I suppose I do," said Arthur, with the exotic label quickly fading while the fearsome one lit up bright neon lights. He wiped his brow.

"So, Arthur, we have a plan," said Mary, who loved plans, Arthur knew. "You're not planning on going anywhere today, are you?"

"No, no, I wasn't ..."

"Good, so the plan is this," said Mary. "A tradesman's van will pull up outside your house at ten o'clock this morning. He will knock on your door and you're to let him in. Understand?" "Yes. Is that it?" asked Arthur.

"No, Arthur, I just want to make sure you understand every bit of the procedure," said Mary. "Now, you and the tradesman will exchange overalls and boots and you can then go out and hop into his van. There will be a passenger who will give you driving directions. You can drive, can't you?"

"Uh, yes, I can drive though it has been a long time," said Arthur, wondering if it was all that much fun being James Bond.

"Now, the tradesman will be Toby McGuire, my secretary. He's younger but about your size," said Mary, obviously ticking things off a list as she conveyed them to him. "You'll be away for an hour or so, if your wife wouldn't mind plying him with cups of tea for that time ... and please don't take your cell phone. It can be traced. Then, when you come back, you and Toby can exchange clothes and boots again. Do you follow all that?"

"Ah, yes, I think so," said Arthur.

"Good," said Mary. "And good luck."

As Arthur put the phone down he realised his apprehension over meeting the Lord and Lady was not his only problem. He had another problem – Joan. How was he going to explain this strange turn of events, especially when she wasn't keen on him starting the project, anyway? As well as that, she'd asked little about the project and he'd told her little. And now, in fifty minutes' time, a stranger was going to come through the door, exchange clothes with Arthur and stay in the house while Arthur drove off in his van to destination unknown, with a passenger unknown. How much to tell and where to start?

What a conundrum ... and one that wasn't going away!

Oh well, gird the loins, take a deep breath (a very deep breath) and wing it – just say whatever comes to mind. His brain froze, his body rose and he wondered how he'd got himself in this pickle – life was so regular, ordered and predictable two weeks ago and he'd disliked it. Now, well, yes, it was anything but regular and predictable and, yes, he had to admit, it was just the tiniest bit exciting. And fearful.

Putting on his sternest face, he strode up the short hallway, turned down the stairs and called for Joan before he reached the bottom.

"Yes dear," said Joan, from the kitchen. "Can it just wait a minute? I was just about to ring Dottie and thank her for her help over the funeral."

"No Joan," said Arthur, frowning rather seriously. "That will have to wait. I'd like to talk to you now, please."

"Oh Arthur, you do sound masterful!" said Joan appearing in the doorway of the lounge where he was standing. She was wiping her hands on her floral apron. "What has come over you? You're diff ..."

"Joan, I'm sorry, but I don't have a lot of time," said Arthur, indicating her chair.

"Right, yes, if you insist ..." said Joan, unused to such direction from Arthur.

"Now, at ten o'clock a young man I don't know will come to the door," he said, discovering his mouth (or was it his brain that was in charge?) was diving straight in. No preamble. "I will let him in, we'll exchange clothes, I will drive off in his van and he will stay here with you until I return. Probably about an hour."

"Right, yes," said Joan. "This stranger – he's quite safe, is he? He won't be torturing me or anything will he?"

"No, of course he won't!" said Arthur, not sure if she was joking or being very logical. "He's Mary's secretary, a nice young man by all accounts."

"That's good," said Joan, smiling. "What else did you want to tell me, dear?"

"I ... ah, well, that's what's going to happen," said Arthur, expecting objections that didn't eventuate. "I can tell you more if you want to know more."

"Not really, if you don't have enough time, Arthur," said Joan. "I'll have a whole hour with this charming young man so I can drill him, can't I?"

"Yes, yes, I suppose you can," said Arthur, now wishing she did want to know more so he could tell her. "It's about this Atkinson case, actually."

"Yes, I had guessed that," said Joan. "I'd like to know more about it some time but there's probably not the time now, is there?"

"Well, I could make a start," said Arthur, wondering where that bossy and demanding Joan had gone. A quite pleasant one had stepped into her body somehow, recently.

And so Arthur spent the next half hour explaining everything.

"Oh my gosh, Arthur, I didn't realise it was *that* Atkinson," said Joan, clapping her hands gleefully. "You certainly do move in exalted circles." Any previous apprehension seemed to have been dissolved by immersion in excitement and intrigue. Arthur went upstairs and assembled all his papers – again and again – while Joan spoke to Dottie on the phone.

"Come on, Arthur!" called Joan from downstairs, "I've made you a nice cup of tea to calm your nerves."

"Okay, okay," said Arthur, who felt he had done so well concealing his nerves.

As they were drinking their tea, with Joan assuring him he would be fine and safe, there was a knock at the door. Toby, in very efficient and assertive manner, had their clothes changed, Arthur's papers in his tool box and ready to go before Arthur could draw breath. There was nothing else to do but get into the van but Toby held him back.

"Let's wait a few minutes before you go out," suggested Toby.

Arthur agreed that no normal tradesman would just walk straight in and out of someone's house so they sat while Joan made Toby a cup of tea. Arthur sensed Toby looked quite nervous. Very nervous, actually. He was sure, however, that Joan would put him at his ease soon. When Joan returned with the tea and biscuits, Arthur bade them good bye, walked out to the van and opened the door ... well, he tried but it was locked. Confused, he looked back at his house and saw Toby's hand, in front of the net curtain, waving frantically at him, pointing up the street. The penny dropped. Wrong van. He wandered nonchalantly up the street, in the direction of Toby's finger and tentatively tried the door of the next van. There was an older man, with a black woollen hat pulled low and overalls, in the passenger seat.

"Welcome Arthur, and I'm terribly sorry I can't help you with your bag – this arm's a bit useless at the moment," said the man, chuckling. Arthur noticed his right arm was in a sling. "Bit embarrassing but you're in the right van now!"

"Uh, yes," said Arthur, feeling quite stupid and knowing full well James Bond would never make such an error. Maybe he was not cut out for this kind of stuff. Though he didn't believe in omens, if he did he would have recognised it as a bad one.

"Right, my man, let's get this show on the road, as they say," said the man. "Dashed exciting, really, isn't it, my man. I've never done this sort of thing before – usually have my chauffeur drive me around. However, we should be able to find ourselves out of this place, eh what! Belt up and let's get moving, shall we?"

"Yes, yes, of course," said Arthur, thankful for some direction, since his brain had none at that moment. He belted up, started up and indicated that he was pulling out ... except that the wipers went instead of the indicators.

"Oh!" said Arthur, his brain unable to formulate any more coherent words. They were soon underway with the man directing from a map on his lap. They managed to find themselves at the same point on the Croydon overpass three times and they chuckled together, a brotherhood of errors. Eventually, they were headed south to Kings Wood.

"Right, Arthur Bayly, I should introduce myself properly, now we've negotiated the tricky part," said the man, taking off his hat. "I'm Lord Atkinson. Pleased to meet you, old chap and we'll have to dispense with the hand-shaking, obviously. Let's just take it that we've shaken, shall we?" He raised his plastered arm a little and Arthur nodded and smiled. Arthur had vaguely suspected it was the Black but was afraid to confirm by asking. Arthur noted that he had been promoted from *my good man* to *old chap*.

"Now, old chap, our estate is just round the corner here," said Lord Atkinson after a ten-minute drive. They turned left off the main road and were soon passing beneath a massive stone archway as the gates opened for them. The hundred-yard, gravel driveway wandered through manicured gardens and curved in front of a three-storey Georgian mansion. Arthur noticed two gardeners working away and other assorted people walking around. A butler opened the van door for Lord Atkinson and then came around to Arthur's side to suggest that he could park the vehicle for him, if he preferred.

"Oh, yes, of course," said Arthur, as if this happened every day of his life.

Arthur took his boots off at the door and a second butler ushered them through ten-foot-high, oak doors, through a marble and oak reception area at the bottom of a curved stairway that led, it seemed to Arthur, to heaven. He had little chance for further inspection as he was whisked into a cavernous drawing room that, despite its size, had been filled to overflowing with furniture, statues, ornaments, paintings, books and all manner of collectible things, leaving little room for the lady who was sitting on one of several chairs around the stone fireplace. The fire crackled happily and she stood and smiled warmly as Lord Atkinson introduced Lady Atkinson to Arthur.

The Black suggested a cup of tea, to which Arthur assented, despite the three he had already had that morning. He really needed a toilet stop but was hesitant to ask. The Black then excused himself to change his clothes and asked Arthur if he would like to refresh himself. With a flood of relief, Arthur was led by the butler into a bathroom the size of Arthur's dining room, all tiles and gold and with plumbing worse than he'd ever experienced before. He did manage to get the toilet to flush, after much pumping, and found his way back to the drawing room.

Soon they were all settled round the friendly fire, with tea and cakes before them and with a small desk for Arthur's papers, at his side. He spread his papers out but, despite his lengthy preparation at home, was uncertain where to start. He kept shuffling his papers, hoping his brain would start.

"Now, Arthur, old chap, we have you here, ostensibly, for an insurance claim but, for us, that's incidental," said Lord Atkinson. Now that he was in his accustomed clothes, Arthur could see better that he was a tall, spare man with a good head of silver hair – a man who obviously took great care of his body and clothes, as did his wife. She was slightly shorter than his six foot, wore minimal makeup and looked immaculate. They were dressed in what might be called the casual estate collection – both were in checked shirts (hers with the collar pulled up and his with a school tie), fawn slacks and sturdy leather brogues. "We did lose some items in the burglary and some had a reasonable value, but we'll be far from upset if we're turned down for the lot, old chap."

"Oh, you will?" said Arthur, with relief and puzzlement. He wondered, in the split second that you can wonder something really big, why he'd had to spend so much time on this claim, considering it had so little import to the claimant. Squeezed into the same split second was a question mark, bigger than the drawing room in which they sat, over his real reason for being here – obviously not the reason he was led to believe.

"Of course, you'll probably want to approve a substantial portion of it so the FSA fellows don't become too suspicious," said Lord Atkinson.

"Look, let's not skirt around the woods," said Lady Atkinson. "We know your Sam Black better than you think we might and he recommended that you're to be trusted in this matter."

"Yes, absolutely, dear," said Lord Atkinson. "You see, the police and the FSA are not necessarily on our side and I'm not sure which of my political colleagues can be relied on so it always comes back to Sam Black. He's been a brick over the years, such ..."

"Anyway, the crux of the matter, Arthur," said Lady Atkinson, interrupting again, "is that a particularly important item was not taken but we suspect it was the reason for the burglary. And now

Sam has disappeared, only a few weeks later. We think they might be related."

"Oh dear," said Arthur. "You think Mr Black was behind the burglary?"

"Oh no, oh dear no," said Lady Atkinson, leaning forward earnestly. "It may be because Sam was close to completing a contract, on our behalf, and that information may have leaked. We aren't looking for stolen items – we really want to know who's behind all this nasty business."

"Oh?" said Arthur, sensing that sensible questions were less embarrassing than sensible statements.

"We're sure there's a link – initially we were concerned about the plans but now we're more concerned about the safety of Sam," said Lord Atkinson. "They're serious, these people, absolutely ruthless rotters ..."

"So, the plans my husband mentioned," interrupted Lady Atkinson, returning to the crux again, "could mean the end of the petroleum and all other energy industries and that would be catastrophic for hundreds of thousands of workers and for the billions in profits of these companies."

"Oh?" said Arthur, finding it the only one of the two million words in the English language that he had any use for, right now.

"Yes, oh!" said Lord Atkinson, smiling grimly. "That's what we thought when all this was presented to us. You see, our son-in-law, John Maranui, is a publisher in New Zealand and, though his interests are a little ... shall we say, off to the side, he's a jolly good man to our daughter and, as we've got to know him, full of integrity."

"Because of his ... shall we say, interesting interests, as my husband said, he's been drawn into something we now feel as passionate about as him," said Lady Atkinson. "He met a man who wanted him to publish his book and it started from there. This Bruce Cathie, who had written his controversial story, had been a pilot for NAC, New Zealand's national airline, now called Air New Zealand. This Captain Cathie had first seen a flying saucer over the Manukau Harbour[1],[2] in Auckland,[3] and, in discussions with other airline pilots, discovered this wasn't uncommon. However, his bosses were not impressed that he publicised his discoveries."

"There's nothing so motivates a chap to do something as to tell him not to do it!" said Lord Atkinson, chuckling.

Arthur smiled and nodded, remembering how, a few hours earlier, he had almost wished Joan had objected to him coming on this trip – then he would have had cause to stand up for himself. Maybe there was a belligerent side to his nature, unrecognised till now.

"So, our Captain Cathie felt impelled to know more about those flying saucers – how they moved and powered themselves," said Lady Atkinson quickly, warming to the subject. "In the course of his investigations, he met a Robert Adams, a scientist with New Zealand's Department of Scientific Research. Robert had started working on a free-energy motor and was impelled, by Bruce's enthusiasm, to carry on."

"Robert called his invention a ... now, let me get this right ... an *Adams Switched Reluctance Pulsed DC Permanent Magnet Motor Generator* and, after many attempts, developed a motor that was 137% efficient. That means that it produced more energy than it used," said Lord Atkinson

interrupting, his enthusiasm bubbling over. "And that's where Robert's problems started." "Problems?" asked Arthur, feeling a knot beginning to form in his stomach.

"Yes, problems," said Lord Atkinson. "You see, in New Zealand, as in many other countries, the patent office can classify any patent application under a *Military Use Clause*, meaning that inventors are prohibited from publishing details of their devices or promoting them in any manner. In other words, their devices automatically become the sole property of the government and the inventors lose all rights to their inventions."

"But they invented the device ..." said Arthur, astonished.

---

1.      http://en.wikipedia.org/wiki/Manukau_Harbour

2.      http://en.wikipedia.org/wiki/Manukau_Harbour

3.      http://en.wikipedia.org/wiki/Auckland

"Absolutely!" said Lady Atkinson. "But the state has the last say – you either take the risk to get your invention patented (and lose it) or don't get a patent at all."

"And that's what our Mr Adams did, in his naivety – he applied for a patent for his free energy machine and lost it to the state," said Lord Atkinson. "Mr Adams survived an attempt on his life by an individual affiliated with the New Zealand Secret Intelligence Service, the SIS. He believed that the former Prime Minister of New Zealand, Robert Muldoon, suppressed his invention, with pressure from unknown but powerful sources."

"Oh, my God …" said Arthur, wondering how he'd got himself involved in such matters and where it all could lead.

"Yes, my God alright!" said Lord Atkinson. "Just not cricket, by jove, no!"

"However, the government or whoever was involved, did not reckon on the persistence of people like Mr Cathie and Mr Adams," said Lady Atkinson. "Though his invention was suppressed, under the *Military Use Clause*, for 20 years, Mr Adams, with help and encouragement from his friend Mr Cathie, continued to develop his motor and eventually decided that his life would be safer if he published his findings – publish and be damned, if you like! If the public knew about it, then attempts on his life (and his wife's) would be pointless – the information's still out there. So, he published his findings in New Zealand's *Nexus* magazine and the death threats and constant surveillance stopped, much to his relief."

"My gosh!" said Arthur, enthralled. Then, he quickly realised, he was in a large drawing room in England, not in New Zealand, to investigate an insurance claim. "But, please excuse me, but what does this have to do with the burglary or your claim?"

"Ah, yes, good question," said Lord Atkinson. "This is where our son-in-law, John, comes in."

"By this time, Arthur, Mr Cathie had written several books on flying saucers and other related things and he wanted his friend Mr Adams to write a book about his invention," said Lady Atkinson. "However, Mr Adams did not feel confident about such a project and so Mr Cathie sent our John along, in the hope that he could facilitate a book somehow … perhaps ghost-write it or something."

"The problem was, however, Mr Adams' health," said Lord Atkinson. "The attempts on his life, the constant surveillance from New Zealand's SIS and his advanced years – he was over seventy by then – meant that he was becoming more frail. He wanted to have his book written but didn't feel up to it at that time. He promised to keep in contact with John and the next thing John knew, Robert Adams died."

"And so did his invention and all his writings," said Lady Atkinson dramatically. "Till they unexpectedly turned up with us."

"And so, Arthur old chap, you might see why you're here," said Lord Atkinson, smiling and leaning back in his chair as if everything was perfectly clear. "Would you like another cup of tea?"

"Uh, oh, yes … no …" said Arthur, unsure which to answer first.

"You probably mean you'd like another cup of tea and you don't have the faintest idea why you're here," suggested Lady Atkinson, ringing her little bell for the butler, who arrived and poured Arthur another cup of tea.

"Ah, thank you and, yes, Lady Atkinson," said Arthur. "I'm afraid you were rather reading my mind."

"She does that, you know," said Lord Atkinson, smiling at his wife. "It's all rather uncanny."

"Now, to cut a very long story short, Robert Adams' plans, and one of his motors, was couriered to John shortly after Mr Adams' death and John still has no idea who sent them," said Lady Atkinson. "John, in his … shall we say, interesting philosophy, puts it down to some sort of destiny he must fulfil and so he kept them firmly hidden, under lock and key, and told no one, believing he would be given a sign of some kind of sign when it was time for him to do something with them."

"Then he fell in love with this English girl, visiting New Zealand, married her and, in the process, discovered her father was a member of the House of Lords and has a passion for the environment," said

Lord Atkinson, smiling. "As soon as he met us, he felt he knew what to do with the plans." "Right," said Arthur, determined to use a different word.

"He knew it was too dangerous to do anything with them in New Zealand, given the trouble Mr Adams had," said Lord Atkinson, "and when he found about my ... er, our interest in stopping all this dashed pollution, and I'm in a position of some influence here, he approached me about them, eventually, wondering if there was anything I could do to get these devices, these motors, manufactured for developing countries."

"But I would have thought New Zealand would be safe from all kinds of interference, being so remote," said Arthur.

"Absolutely, Arthur, that's what we thought," said Lord Atkinson. "But a few years ago a chap from Hamilton, in New Zealand, invented a car battery that never went flat. He needed money to manufacture them, couldn't find any investors and eventually sold his patent to Mitsubishi for a tidy sum. And we've never heard of the *Never Flat Battery* again – Mitsubishi had no intention of manufacturing them for who can make money from a product that never wears out?" "Oh yes, obviously," said Arthur.

"So, what we're saying, old chap, is that nowhere is safe but, in a large place like Europe, it may be easier to be a little more anonymous," said Lady Atkinson.

"Ah, I've just got it!" said Arthur, as a light went on in his brain. "You had the plans, or the motor, and someone tried to find them, using a common burglary as a diversion, somehow?"

"Absolutely, Arthur, we're not sure if we should go ahead with our plans until we know who is behind all this and if it's safe," said Lord Atkinson.

"But I still don't see where I come into all of this," said Arthur, "if you don't mind me asking."

"Yes, a perfectly reasonable question and the truth of it is that you're just a pawn in the whole game, as are we all," said Lord Atkinson. "Initially, I didn't let on to Sam, or anyone else, that the real reason we submitted an insurance claim was to help us find the culprits. I suppose I thought you insurance chaps, with the resources you have to hand, might turn up something, even if it was just a lead to something else."

"And so I got the job and, later, Mr Black found out the full implications of it," suggested Arthur, as pieces began to fall into place.

"Absolutely, old chap!" said Lord Atkinson, suddenly smiling. "They did say you were good at puzzles ... you know, piecing things together."

"Anyway, we had to tell Sam, eventually, 'fess up' as the Americans would say," said Lady Atkinson, smiling. "There was nowhere or no one else to turn to so we entrusted Sam with the information."

"And then things really started to go haywire," said Lord Atkinson. "The word got out ..."

"You think Mr Black leaked the information?" asked Arthur, thinking that the explanation didn't go with his gut feelings.

"Good heavens no!" said Lord Atkinson. "We don't know who but the chief suspect is Sam's rather dotty ... pretty but dotty secretary who may not be as dotty as we all suspected. We're not sure ..."

"So, Sam had you on the case, feared for your safety and rearranged your job while the investigation continued," said Lady Atkinson.

Oh gosh!" said Arthur. His mind went blank after thoughts of the enormity of the situation and thoughts of gratitude to Mr Black flashed through. His brain was now full and it was all a bit much. "So, the plans are safe, the culprits are still skulking out there and could return, Sam disappeared and we were desperate for the investigation – any investigation – to continue," said Lord Atkinson.

"Sam had appraised us of your loyalty, discretion and ability with puzzles, as he put it."

"Oh gosh!" said Arthur. This phrase was becoming an automatic response and all he could mutter right now.

"So we prevailed upon Mary, Sam's deputy, to talk with you directly," said Lady Atkinson.

"Mmm, prevailed might be an understatement," said Lord Atkinson. "She was most insistent that you not be put in any danger so we put rather a lot of pressure on her and, being in the House of Lords,

I can do that. I exercised my royal prerogative, if you like, for what we considered the common good." "Oh gosh!" said Arthur, wishing he could form new words.

"So, Arthur, old chap, you now know why you're here – it's a conspiracy to keep you out of trouble!" said Lady Atkinson, happily. "A nice conspiracy."

"A nice conspiracy," Arthur mused, not feeling totally comfortable quite yet.

"Mmm, a nicely intentioned conspiracy that may have somehow backfired, dear," said Lord Atkinson gravely.

"Yes, dear, I daresay you're right," said Lady Atkinson, blushing a little as she looked at her husband. "We all volunteered for this mission, so to speak, but you, Arthur, seem to have been volunteered by accident. Oh dear, we are sorry we've somehow got you into this mess."

"Yes, hmm," was all Arthur could manage, knowing he should really say something gracious but not sure what it was.

"Anyway, here we are, all probably being followed, Sam gone and the sods still at large ... oh, my gosh!" said Lady Atkinson, with a stark realisation. "What a time for Belinda and John to be here! I do hope they'll be safe ..."

"I daresay they'll be safe, dear, they're holidaying in Scotland and it's unlikely anyone knows it was he who brought the plans to England a few years ago ... I hope," said Lord Atkinson, with the conviction in his voice fading noticeably.

"Look, what you don't know ..." said Arthur.

"Oh Arthur dear, please tell us," said Lady Atkinson interrupting. She started to look very tired.

"Well, it's nothing much but my son and Mr Black's daughter are both on the lookout for Mr Black as well," said Arthur, "and I've got two of my best repo agents ... repossession agents, looking for him too. The agents have their ears in all sorts of devious places we'd never know about ..." "But can we rely on them?" asked Lord Atkinson, interrupting.

"Oh yes, I've used them for years and, of course, Martin, Emily and the agents know nothing of the burglary or of Sam's connection to it," said Arthur. "They're just looking for a man who has disappeared."

"So, Arthur, can you piece together any of this?" asked Lady Atkinson.

"No, I have no idea who these people are or where Sam is or why he has disappeared," said Arthur, clearing his brain of all the drama and clutter. "But it does seem to me we have two alternative courses of action open."

"See dear, just what Sam said," said Lord Atkinson. "Decisive thinking, cuts through the butter with a hot knife."

"Darling, let Arthur continue," said Lady Atkinson.

"Oh yes, yes, just so," said Lord Atkinson with the thought of action and clarity obviously energising him. "Do go on, Arthur, please do."

"Well, we can either carry on being secretive, as we're now doing, everybody sneaking about in disguises and having whispered conversations in safe places," said Arthur, "or we can follow Mr Adams' example and go public. It seems, for him, that secrecy played into his aggressors' hands and his disclosure, his article, reduced any danger to him altogether."

"Hmm, right, so what do you propose we do?" asked Lord Atkinson.

"Me? We do?" asked Arthur shocked, realising that a Black of the realm was asking for his advice – advice that could save or endanger a number of people. "Oh dear, I have to say I have no clear plan of action but, as I speak, I do keep having a picture of you standing up in the House of Lords where, I understand, you have a measure of legal immunity, and telling your complete story."

"By jove, that sounds very cavalier and dashing" said Lord Atkinson, laughing. Then he became serious. "But might it not endanger us in some way

?"

"Well, they tried to endanger you when this was in a cone of silence, so to speak," said Arthur. "I daresay they could have shot you in your own home, here, if they'd wanted to but they didn't, by choice."

"Yes, yes, I suppose you're right, old chap," said Lord Atkinson. "It all sounds a mite dangerous ... though, I must admit, it does get the blood boiling. A little bit of excitement, dear!"

"Mmm, yes dear, it might be fun but I really do think we'd need to plan it properly, cover all our bases as they say," said Lady Atkinson. "I'd hate it to go off half-cocked and it just ends in a fizzer."

"Absolutely, Lady Atkinson," said Arthur. "Now, my son's a lawyer in the law firm, Shaftsbury Burton ..."

"By gosh, that's our law firm," said Lord Atkinson, interrupting, his palms on the arms of his chair, his elbows up as if he was about to launch himself somewhere. "Dashed good chaps, they are."

"Yes, I believe they're quite a prestigious law firm," said Arthur, "and I feel we need someone good at advertising or public relations ... I'm not sure, but someone who can organise the publicity with the newspaper and television people properly."

"Oh Charles, how about Lord Blunt?" asked Lady Atkinson. "Doesn't he own the *Herald* or the *Mirror* or something ... and that television station?"

"Yes, you're right my dear!" said Lord Atkinson, still in launch position, eyes wide. "He's quite busy at the moment. He's buying up some American magazine or newspaper chain or something, but I'll certainly ask him. He may be a mite cynical about all this environmental, free-energy stuff, but he does love a good scrap, a good controversy, to spice up his papers."

"Hmm," said Arthur, his mind seeing all sorts of possibilities. "So, what else do we need? We should start amassing some evidence – we could get copies of that, ah, what was it, *Next* magazine?" "*Nexus* magazine," corrected Lady Atkinson, helpfully.

"Oh, *Nexus*, thank you," said Arthur. "And can we contact this Mr Bruce Cathie – would your sonin-law be able to organise these things?"

"Why, yes Arthur, I'm sure he could," said Lord Atkinson.

"In fact I know he could and, what's more, he'll be at it like a rat up a drain pipe, as he's wont to say!" said Lady Atkinson. "Oh, my gosh, of course, he's a publisher and will know others in the publishing world down under. This could spread like wildfire."

"Oh whew!" said Arthur, feeling like he'd grabbed at a small branch and found it was the tail of a snake. What was he getting into, he wondered with dread. "So, we have the start of a battle plan – you talk to your people, as they say, I'll talk to mine and we could perhaps get together somewhere as soon as we can."

"Right, Arthur, that's absolutely spiffing," said Lord Atkinson, leaping up with more vigour than his age would indicate. "Gosh dear, I suddenly feel like a teenager again!"

"Ah, one thing we should mention, though it's probably quite obvious by now," said Lady Atkinson. "Given that we don't know who we're dealing with we must ask you not to talk to the police or any government agencies about this, till we're quite certain who we're dealing with." "Yes, yes, of course," said Arthur.

◇ *Philip J Bradbury*

"Probably best for all of us, we feel," said Lord Atkinson.

"Yes, I understand completely," said Arthur, feeling as if they were children, keeping secrets from the adults. He stood up and had his hand shaken ruggedly and then Lady Atkinson had a turn with a strong and lengthy hug. She seemed to have tears in her eyes. She stood back a little with her hands on Arthur's shoulders as if she had something to say. He waited uncertainly, awkwardly.

"Oh Arthur, oh Arthur," said Lady Atkinson as tears rolled down her cheeks. "I feel all choked up ..."

"Yes, it's alright dear," said Lord Atkinson, obviously embarrassed by her tears.

"Let me say this, please," said Lady Atkinson, not taking her eyes from Arthur's. "This probably sounds a bit weak or something ... I don't know what you've done here today, Arthur, but I feel so released, so clean, somehow. We've let the cat out of the bag, told a complete stranger, one we can trust, and it feels better, having it out. And now, at last, we have a plan of action, as you said, something to do."

"Oh but ..." said Arthur, finding this all a little confronting.

"No Arthur, I must say this," said Lady Atkinson, wiping her tears and smiling. "I'm not one to beat about the bush and what must be said must be said – by me here, by Lord Atkinson in the House, by all of us. We must have our secrets out, cleanse our souls, if you will, and with this battle plan ... I don't know, I've felt paralysed, helpless ever since we got those plans from John, three years ago, and more so since the burglary. I felt impotent, so useless and angry at that. Now, we all have something to do, a ray of hope."

"Absolutely dear!" said Lord Atkinson, thumping Arthur on the back. "It's so dashed annoying to have the hope for a better world, of helping people, but no way to get it done ..."

"And, most important of all, Arthur, Charles, is that none of this matters," said Lady Atkinson. An unexpected still fell on them. "It doesn't matter if this all ends in some stupid tragedy or just a whole lot of nothing or in some amazing success. We don't know how this will end up but, in the end, we're actually doing something that fires us all up. We're trying to make a difference and our hearts are on fire!"

"Yes darling, you're so right," said Lord Atkinson, quietly, as if recalling something long forgotten. "I used to have such plans for this place, for my career, when I took over the title from my father. And then, somehow, the dreams faded. I hadn't realised how many of them I'd forgotten, till now. Ah Arthur, you have done more than you can imagine."

"Oh, thank you, both of you. I don't quite know what to say," said Arthur. "I feel as if I've done so little ..."

"And maybe you have done so little," said Lady Atkinson, interrupting. "Big or little, you've got us back to where we belong, back to a sense of ... I don't know ... a sense of the warrior rising, as if we can actually make a difference and see a better world through us being here. I don't know the words but I certainly have the feeling. I know I'm not just here to attend endless cocktail parties and fill in the space between my birth and death with cups of tea and nice chats. I now have a reason! I'm sorry, Arthur, I could go on! Let's get you back to your family and we'll all keep in contact and have a meeting with all our knights at the round table soon."

"Yes, absolutely!" said Arthur, relieved that the emotional moment was over. He gathered his papers, put on his tradesman disguise and drove off with the butler, this time, beside him. His heart felt like popping and he couldn't get the silly smile off his face.

"Oh Arthur, sir, you think you be going quite fast?" asked the butler solicitously.

"Oh, oh dear," said Arthur, "just a bit excited, I daresay."

"I understand sir, with today decisions," said the butler, "and if you like, I have idea." "You have?" asked Arthur and then remembered himself. "Look, I'm Arthur. And you are?" "My name Dominik, sir," said the butler.

"Yes, pleased to meet you, Dominik," said Arthur, extending his hand awkwardly in the small van. "Yes, sir, I have idea. We just scare these people a little. Just a little."

"Oh dear, what people are these?" asked Arthur, his concentration on the road wavering as he imagined bodily harm to someone, somewhere. He brought the van back on track and tried to focus on driving.

"The ones who come here. They tell others, the good police, to go away," said Dominik.

"Oh, you mean the MI5 chaps?" asked Arthur. "Why them?"

"Well sir, we know there be lots of people doing this ... ah, how you say, um, involved?" "Yes, involved," said Arthur.

"So lots involved but only these we know about, yet," said Dominik, with unshakeable logic.

"Right, so we scare these particular MI5 men?" asked Arthur. "What exactly do you mean by scare?"

"Ah, you leave that to me. That is my speciality!" said Dominik, smiling broadly.

"Oh dear, I don't think we need to have any violence," said Arthur, shivering a little, trying to focus on the road as he imagined this bear of a man breaking necks and doing other dreadful things to people. "But how do we find these particular people?"

"Ah, that easy!" said Dominik, winking at Arthur. "They come to my brother's club and Andrzej he check the list and know where they live. Easy!"

"Oh dear, I'm not sure all this is necessary at all, Dominik," said Arthur, with the feeling he was trying to stop a steam roller by lying in front of it.

"It safe too!" said Dominik, trying to twist in his seat towards Arthur, with little success. "We be, ah, how you say ... discrete. Nobody know we do scare thing and nobody connect to anybody else."

"But, if they don't know who is scaring them, as you put it, they won't know why they're being scared and they won't know who to stop harassing," said Arthur, desperate to intervene with unassailable logic.

"Mmm, yes, that problem, yes," said Dominik, looking out at the surrounding mist.

"And, if they do know it's us scaring them, then they might go after us more determinedly," said Arthur, ramming his point home.

"Yes, you right, Mr Arthur," said Dominik, thumping his fist on his knee with a grimace.

All was quiet as Arthur negotiated his way through Croydon and he could tell, by the facial contortions and knee thumping, that Dominik was not letting his idea go. As Arthur manoeuvred into a parking space near his home, he really wanted to ease the pressure Dominik seemed to be putting on himself – diffuse the smoking cordite, so to speak.

"Well Dominik, it has been a pleasure to meet you and thank you for your great idea of scaring people," said Arthur, offering his hand, which disappeared into Dominik's massive paw. "Leave it with me and I'm sure I will come up with a way round it – a way to make them listen."

"Oh Mr Arthur, that be good if you think for it too," said Dominik, his face relaxing into a smile. "There many bad men out there and they should be stopped. I know these things."

Arthur had the impression that Dominik had dealt with many "bad men" in his life and he knew, from the frowns and lip-chewing, that Dominik had not totally delegated the solution to him. He stepped out of the van as casually as he could, while his mind wanted him to flee as quickly as he could, from this maniacal bear beside him.

"Mr Arthur, your bag!" said the grinning Dominik.

"Oh, yes, of course," said Arthur, reaching to grab the proffered bag.

His heart wanted him to dash across the twenty yards to his door, to escape the rather unnerving Dominik, and to fall into the welcome arms of his familiar home again. He sauntered, as best he could, and turned the handle to his own front door. It didn't move. Joan never locked it. He knocked, uncertainly. He knocked again, harder. Still no answer. He knew, from the bite in his stomach, that there's something wrong. Something very wrong.

# The Scottish Connection

Without Toby there to answer and filter her calls, Mary was in a less-than-generous mood when her phone screamed at her for the hundredth time that morning.

"Mary Collins speaking," she said gruffly, while trying to complete yet another useless report to tell the chinless wonders at head office the most obvious things like the world was still going round, it's still ruled by idiots and her branch was still making a profit and should not be shut down. She was absorbed in trying to report enough fascinating hogwash to save her having to mention the fact that the Atkinson case had a bit of a lean to it and she didn't yet know how to straighten it up. And she missed Sam.

"Hello Mary, how yer be?" came a Scottish brogue over the phone. "Are ye there ... Mary, are ye there?"

"Oh my God, is that you Angus?" asked Mary, astonished. She had never heard her brother's voice on the phone before. Then she wondered why he was ringing. "What's happened? Is it Da or Ma?"

"No, no, Mary, they're all fine. Well, as fine as they're ever goin' ta be," said Angus, chuckling. "It's about someone else ye don't know. They're from ..." The phone went quiet and she could hear muffled conversation. "They're from New Zealand, they say."

"What the hell are you doing in New Zealand?" asked Mary, her brain still at half-mast, still trying to construct the stupid report in front of her.

"I'm not, I'm at home, in Dunfermline, at the Fordyce's place," he said. "They called me over thinkin' I might know yer number and I remembered ye left yer card, yer business card, with me when I promised to call ye. And here I am!"

"Right ... so, well, amazing to hear your voice, Angus," said Mary, giving the conversation her full attention now. "Actually, it's lovely to hear your voice, Angus. So what do these people want?"

"Well, Mr Fordyce wants to have a word but I'll put these people on first. They're in some bother."

"Hello Mary, it's John Maranui here and you probably don't have a clue who I am but Mr Black at your firm has been very helpful to us over the last few years," said John.

"Sam Black? Do you know where he is?" asked Mary, her heart in her mouth at the mention of Sam's name.

"You don't know where he is? Damn!" said John. "We were hoping he could help us out a bit here. We've tried but we just can't get through to Belinda's parents, the Atkinsons."

"The Atkinsons ... Lord Atkinson?" asked Mary, feeling like a herd of coincidences was charging down on her.

"Yes, he's Belinda's, my wife's father. His phone seems to be off the hook or something," said John. "We're holidaying here from New Zealand and our car's been nicked. We're not sure what to do next and somehow ended up talking to this Mr Fordyce here ..."

"Right, the first thing is you can count on my family and the Fordyces for help and hospitality. I'll see to that," said Mary, interrupting and in strategic mode, her most enjoyable state. "My parents are grumpy old farts but they'd love to have a couple of Kiwis to stay. So, that's your immediate food and accommodation settled. Now, how about money – do you have any on you?"

"Yeah, we have that and a few clothes. The buggers didn't get the lot!" said John, sounding lighter with Mary's organisation. "The main concern ... oh, thank you so much for your brilliant hospitality, really appreciated, Mary ... there were some things in the car, connected to the Atkinson's burglary that we're really worried about."

"Stuff to do with the burglary?" asked Mary as the herd of coincidences thundered closer.

"Look, I don't have the time to tell you everything here but my gut feeling is that's why the car was stolen," said John, his Kiwi voice rising in passion. "The sods have been following us here, we know that but, as you might know, the police aren't much help. Sam was our last hope."

As John was talking, Mary buzzed Halee, the receptionist, on the internal line. With a phone in each ear, she asked Halee to send up Malcolm Schriever, the new Claims Manager, and to hold any further calls.

"Yes, sorry John, I'm listening and I'm also organising a few things for you here," said Mary, after thanking Halee for understanding so quickly. "Now John, what are the vehicle details - make, registration, colour, distinguishing marks – and your mobile number?"

"Though you might need that stuff so here it is," said John, giving her the details.

"Right John, I now know where your in-laws live and all your vital statistics," said Mary with a laugh. "Let me get our tracers on to it. They're quicker and more efficient than the police for they're on commission and have a reason to succeed!"

"Oh yea, tracers, they're who you use to find lost cars?" asked John.

"Lost cars, people, lovers, jewellery … everything, really," said Mary. "Now, if anyone tries to question or interrogate you, say nothing unless they can give you the password which is Fordyce doughnuts. Got it?"

"Fordyce doughnuts? Yep, got that Mary and Mr Fordyce seems to think that's funny," said John. "Shall I put him on now?"

"Not yet. Here's the number for my direct line and also my mobile. If anyone presses you for information, tell them to ring your lawyer – me – at either number," said Mary, giving John the numbers. "Now, you'll hear from someone very soon, by phone or in person, with the password.

Without it they or you ring your lawyer. Got it, John?" "Yep, got it Mary and thanks," said John.

"Hello Mary," boomed a familiar Scottish brogue down the line. "How yer be, lass?"

"Ah, James, I won't lie to you," said Mary, feeling suddenly free to unburden her soul. "I've got a flash job, a good income, a nice apartment but my boss has ruddy well disappeared and this whole

Atkinson case has got messier by the day …"

"Ah, Mary, are ye still selling buns, though?" asked James, chuckling. "It sounds from John's conversation with ye that you just might be."

"Gosh yes, James, it's the one thing that's kept me sane and keeps me going," said Mary. "When I get bogged down with my own misery, I feel picked up when I can make someone else's day. My gripes evaporate a little each time."

"Ay ye're a bonny lass and lovely to hear from ye," said James. "And if I find some bonny lad up here, pining for ye, I'll send him down to yer."

"Ah, James, it's so nice to hear your happy and … loving voice," said Mary as a deep sadness and a flood of tears threatened to erupt. She kept them at bay, thankfully, as she heard a knock on her door. "Please give Isobel a big hug from me and have yourself one from me too. Ah, James, I don't want to hang up but I really must go. Love to you both."

"Just know, Mary, that we both love ye and are always here if ye need us, while we're above the earth," said James, chuckling.

He hung up. Mary sat with the phone still to her ear and gave in to the tears and a deep wishing for more gentle people in her life, like the Fordyces. There was another knock at the door and she quickly slammed the phone down, wiped her eyes, stood up, took off the face of a sad, little girl and put on the face of a successful, dynamic insurance executive.

"Yes Malcolm, come in," said Mary, sure she looked a mess but beyond caring. She had a job to do and action was better than the meaningless reports she had to complete. Malcolm was a tall, skinny chap with a suit two sizes too big for him. Mary gave him all the details she'd got from John, with instructions to find the car.

"Yes Miss Collins, we will look into it presently," said Malcolm.

"No you will not look into it presently," said Mary, heartily sick of the corporate-speak. "In fact, I do not want to hear 'look into it' ever again. You will do it and by the end of the day you will be back here telling me what you have done and what results you have. Understand?"

"But we have procedures ..."

"But no, you have a car to find and there is no *we* in this!" said Mary, running her hand through her thick black hair in despair. She had thought this was going to be so simple and straightforward. She waved Malcolm to sit. "Firstly, Malcolm, there is no *we*. You will do it. You will pick up the phone. You will talk to the trackers. You will follow up their progress. They will ring you back on their progress before I see you at the end of the day. Have you got that?"

"But that's the job for my staff. I'm the manager," protested Malcolm.

"Look Malcolm, this is your first job since you took over from Arthur. I want to know you can do it. And, if you can't, how the hell are you going to instruct others to do it?"

"Yes, but ..."

"And, if you'd done your research instead of trying to chat up Halee, you'd know the sensitivity of the case," said Mary, elbows on her desk, looking directly at him. Malcolm went bright red. "The Director here, Sam Black, has gone missing. He may be dead. We don't know. The FSA are breathing down our necks. The police are breathing down our necks. Ape-like burglars are invading our building. This, young chump, is not just another case. You will do it and you will not tell anyone else what you're doing or that you're doing it. Got that?"

"But we have procedures for these things and we must audit our progress ..."

"Listen Malcolm. Listen very well," said Mary, not taking her eyes from his. His redness was now supplemented by sweat behind his spectacles and a licking of his lips. "We are not a government department. We *do* care about our customers. In fact, young man, we care about our customers more than we care about our little rules. Understand?"

"Well, yes, but ..."

"But nothing. We have two customers in a foreign country. They're scared. They're confused. Their lives have been thrown into turmoil by some twerps who think it's fun to take other peoples' property," said Mary, sitting back, her eyes never leaving his.

"Yes, I understand that but these procedures are in place for good reason," said Malcolm. "We can't just go grabbing cars back without due process."

"OK Malcolm, take your coat off. Now!" shouted Mary.

He stood and took his coat off, looking confused.

"Now take your trousers off. Now!" shouted Mary. He started to undo his belt and stopped.

"But I can't just do that here ..."

"You will do as I say!" said Mary.

"But, Miss Collins, this is most irregular," said Malcolm, unsure what to do next.

"Absolutely! Most irregular. It's most bloody irregular for two foreigners to be in the predicament they're in," said Mary, firmly. "Now, imagine that you were standing in this office, stark bolloking naked, and I said that I had to follow due processes and involve an audit team before you could get dressed again. Would you appreciate my love of rules then?"

"Ah, no," said Malcolm, smiling sheepishly. "I ... I do see what you mean. Appropriate rules for appropriate circumstances?"

"You're a quick learner, Malcolm," said Mary, clapping her hands. "So, shall we do it my way and, God knows, we may save a lot of unnecessary misery and, if we're really lucky and/or diligent, we could find our Mr Black again. I'm sure he'd appreciate your part in helping him out of the mess he's in."

As Malcolm left Mary's office – quicker and more unsteadily than he entered – her phone rang.

"Miss Collins, you said to hold your calls but you'll want to take this one, I know," said Halee, in her refreshingly direct way.

"Uh, yes," said Mary. Halee's efficiency and judgement, along with her ability to cut through stupid bureaucracy, were so refreshing and she wondered for a second why she had not considered the girl for Toby's or Malcolm's jobs. She trusted Halee's judgement implicitly and told her to put the call through.

"Hello Mary, how are you?" came an all-too-familiar voice.

"Oh, Sam, are you alright? You sound ... oh, I don't know, rugged," said Mary, desperately trying to staunch the thousand other words she needed to say.

"Well, yes, it has been a trying time and the end's not in sight but I'm okay ... I think," said Sam who sounded hoarse and weary. "Now, I was wondering if you could do something ..." "Oh yes, anything Sam," said Mary, interrupting. "Just tell me what it is." "Please Mary, let me talk. I don't have much time," said Sam.

"Oops, sorry," said Mary. "I'm listening."

"Can you meet me in Charing Cross Road at nine o'clock this evening? There's a blue door, opposite Pizza Express. I don't know the street number but it's just up from Trafalgar Square. You'll find it," said Sam, speaking quickly. "Can you dress like you're not you? Say, like a man with trenchcoat and hat or something? And bring my spare briefcase which is at the top of Ahmed's coat cupboard – that's most important. He doesn't know that but it's there – you know what it looks like?"

"Yes Sam, the black one with the gold fittings."

"Right, I have to go now, Mary, and you do realise it could be dangerous, don't you?" asked Sam quietly. "You don't have to do this ..."

"Oh, Sam, you know I wouldn't miss the excitement!" said Mary with mock bravado. "Yes I know it's dangerous, Sam, and I'll make sure I'm not followed." She found her excitement was rising, despite the apprehension for what could be ahead.

"Bye my dear, I must go!" said Sam and the phone clicked off.

My dear? My dear! He called her *my dear*! Her tears started to flow all over again – tears of happiness, tears of excitement and, most of all, tears of relief. She sat and let them flow, knowing she was safe as no one was permitted in without an appointment or knocking.

Her door burst open and was slammed shut and Mary realised Halee was hugging her.

Malcolm returned an hour later, flushed with success. The car had been found two streets over from the Fordyce's, locked in the police yard. He acted as if he had driven up to Dunfermline and found the vehicle himself. Mary allowed him to savour his pride.

"These people have no regard for the rules," he said.

"Yes, you'd expect the police to act ..." Mary started to say.

"No, not the police, these New Zealanders, these foreigners," said Malcolm, correcting her as the colour rose up his pink face. "When my tracker told them, they just went down there and demanded the car back ... and made a terrible to-do about it. You can't just badger the police like that. They have a job to do and there are procedures ..."

"My God, you and your bloody procedures, Malcolm!" thundered Mary, immediately wondering how quickly she could have him replaced with someone with a brain. "Before you is the evidence that the police have acted illegally, have stolen a car without due process and yet you would support these crooks because they're in a pretty uniform. I don't believe it!"

"But they're the police, Miss Collins. We can't just go ..."

"Oh yes we can, Malcolm, and we will," said Mary firmly. "Uniforms or no uniforms, I will not stand by and have people being abused. They want to act above the law and so we'll get the media in there and let the people decide on what's right and what's not."

"But you can't just do that, it's not proper ... it's ... it's, well, what would head office think," stammered Malcolm, taking off his glasses to wipe his forehead and eyes.

"Look, Malcolm, if you're more interested in looking good than in doing good, you have no place in this company," said Mary, before she realised the import or her words but realising she had little time to waste with such ineptitude. "You're off the case and back at your old job and you'd better find another company to work for within the month!"

"But ... but you can't do that! It's ... it's unfair dismissal!" stammered Malcolm, outraged, his thin body quivering.

"Oh yes I can! You are actively supporting an illegal act and so you're an accessory to the crime. We do not employ criminals here, young man, and you'd better decide, very quickly, whether you're on the side of the law or that of injustice. Give me your decision by ten tomorrow morning and, until then, I'm taking over. Now go home and ponder your options."

"But it's not time to go home yet!"

"It is for you, Malcolm," said Mary quietly. "You're no use to us in this state and you have a lifechanging decision to make. Go and make it. Now!"

As Malcolm left the office, spluttering and protesting, Mary rang two connections – one at the *Daily Telegraph* and one at the *Dunfermline Press*[1] – and gave them the scoop, along with the password so they could interview John and Belinda. Then she prayed to God she had done the right thing.

"Sam is a mysterious character, Mary, but one cannot but like him," said Ahmed, the Chief Assessor, in his perfect Oxford English. "Besides, I cannot close my eyes to this and not be there to help you if you need it. You're brusque and rude but you're also efficient and motivating to all the staff and you've done a lot of good to this branch. I do not want to see you or Halee hurt and so I will be there. I will not hear otherwise."

Mary felt flushed at this unsolicited compliment and his support and she knew he would not be dissuaded. She smiled, a little misty-eyed, at Halee who, like Ahmed, would not be put off joining her as well. They decided not to tell Stephen, the Financial Director, who would have disapproved of the whole thing. Ahmed gave Mary his coat and trilby hat – both too large – and Halee made quick adjustments with needle and thread that she had procured, magically, from somewhere, for Mary's smaller frame. Because of his beard, Ahmed could not pass for a woman so he said he'd wear his traditional Pakistani *salwar kameez* clothes, under which it would be easy to conceal several guns.

"Guns? Ahmed, you're not carrying guns are you?" asked Mary, shocked.

"Of course not, just joking!" said Ahmed, laughing, more jolly than she'd ever seen him. He seemed to be enjoying himself immensely. "I'll be strolling by and loitering in and out of Pizza Express, so I'll keep an eye on you both."

Mary was touched by his gallantry and felt like giving him a hug – she felt much less alone with this large, dark man with her, along with Halee the pixie.

---

# The Turncoat

*Tuesday, 13th March 2012, 11.46 p.m.*

The front door wasn't locked, thankfully, and he took the five paces up the passage with a thumping heart. All was quiet. Eerily quiet. He peered round the door and saw Joan, in the lounge, on a kitchen chair, hands tied behind her back, ankles tied together and with a mouth-gag. Her grey-tinged blonde curls looked as if someone had grabbed hanks of it and her eyes were wide and frightened. She nodded to her left and Arthur looked further round the door to see Mollie, their neighbour, trussed up similarly. Joan was then indicating to him furiously and he determined that she was trying to tell him about something upstairs. He listened and could hear rustling, probably in his office. He dropped the bag and rushed to Joan, untying her gag as the phone rang.

"Get it!" she whispered urgently and he fled with the wings of Pegasus into the dining room and picked up the phone.

"Help! hel ..." he yelled, then the phone went dead. There was a curse from upstairs and then the sound of someone running along the passage and clattering down the stairs. Had there been time for Arthur to panic or react, he would have done the former. As it was, Toby burst into the dining room, wrenched the phone from his hand and twisted him around in an arm lock before he had time to do either. He was then pushed, rather rudely, into the lounge and onto the couch.

"Don't you move an inch!" commanded Toby as he disappeared and reappeared with another dining room chair. "Sit!"

Arthur got up and sat in the appointed chair.

"Now, where do you keep rope?" asked Toby, looking around quickly as if it might be stored in the lounge.

"Oh dear, rope ..." said Arthur, pondering. "It's not something we usually carry here ..." "And where's the stuff for the Atkinson case?" interrupted Toby.

"Ah, I took it with me ..." said Arthur, instantly regretting his helpfulness. He made a mental note to tell more lies.

"I know that, Arthur!" said Toby. "You must have stuff in your computer ..."

"Not much, really, it's all in the files, I'm afraid," said Arthur, thankful he'd taken the precaution of regularly downloading all the Atkinson files onto computer sticks, now hidden in Joan's underwear drawer.

"My god, you old codgers, just not computer savvy are you!" said Toby, obviously impatient.

"No, I suppose not ..." said Arthur.

"So, where's your rope then?" demanded Toby, returning to his initial problem.

"Ah, it should be in the back shed, behind the mattress and freezer against the back wall," said Arthur, thinking of the most inaccessible place he could imagine. "Right. So, move a muscle and you're dead. Got it?" "Oh, yes, dead," said Arthur, trying to look submissive.

Toby fled out the back and Arthur leapt up. Joan had acted suitably statue-like for Toby not to notice her gag was loose. Arthur untied her hands and, when done, bent down to untie her ankles.

"No, no, I can do that," whispered Joan. "Get Dottie's."

"Yes, just a minute," said Arthur, rushing from the room. He quietly opened the front door and motioned frantically to Dominik, who was watching, with great intent, two young girls walking past. Arthur didn't want to be seen out of his seat or to make any noise before Dominik arrived. He continued to wave frantically and, just as he was about to give up, Dominik looked his way and then burst from the van like fireworks.

"Yes Mr Arthur, trouble?" asked Dominik, obviously relishing some action.

"Yes, aah, bad man out the back," said Arthur, pointing down the passage.

"Right suh! Me deal with bad man then," said Dominik, squaring his massive shoulders and walking purposefully, though cautiously, into the dining room. Arthur returned to the lounge to see the two ladies fully untied but sitting as if they weren't.

"So Arthur, what now?" asked Joan, constantly peering out the door.

"Hmm, I'm not sure," said Arthur, knowing that was what the two ladies did not want to hear. "Perhaps I should help Dominik and you two could rush up the road and get help ..." He was interrupted by yells, thuds, crashes and bangs. Then there was an "Umph!" in a distinctly Polish accent. Arthur felt sick and immobilised. He looked at Joan who shrugged with a quiet resignation. Dottie, on the other hand, looked stricken and Arthur was about to go over and comfort her when Toby appeared in the doorway, panting.

"So, where did you get that oaf, Arthur Bayly?" demanded Toby. "Any other tricks up your sleeve I should know about?"

"Aah, no, not ..."

"And, mysteriously, there's no rope in your wee shed, Mr Bayly," said Toby, his frustration giving way to anger.

"But what about Dominik? Have you killed him?" asked Arthur, relieved to have the thought of a diversion from his previous diversion.

"Killed him? Goodness no!" said Toby, laughing. "Just a wee prod in the kidneys. He'll be awake in five minutes or so. Just enough time for me to get the files and finish here." He opened the tool bag and Arthur felt sick all over again – all the work he'd put into the case and all the details he'd amassed ... to be taken by Karate Kid here.

"Where's the damned files, Bayly?" demanded Toby, tossing tools out of the box with increasing ferocity. "Another of your diversions, huh?"

"Uh, oh, they were there ... should be there ... I promise you," said Arthur, confused. He knew he'd put the files back in the bag at Lord Atkinson's house, he was sure of it. He stood up to help looking in the bag.

"Get back!" yelled Toby. "Stay there! Don't move!" Then he stopped and looked at the two ladies whose ropes were off. He had the look of a parachutist who realises there is a rip in his parachute that's growing wider with alarming speed. This was obviously not going the way Toby had planned.

Arthur felt a small surge of pleasure, despite Toby's ability to inflict pain. Toby now had, Arthur realised, three unruly children, a sleeping monster about to wake any minute and no files ... something that still mystified Arthur. He *knew* he had put them in the bag. Then, through the net curtains, he saw something flash past the window. It was gone in an instant but it gave him hope. In his fear and panic he had forgotten that there was another world out there – neighbours, passers-by – and he was not as alone as he had imagined.

"You're so clever, untying everyone, Arthur, I guess you need to be trussed up first," said Toby wearily. "Now, get your hands behind your back and your feet together."

Arthur did as he was commanded, while Toby looked in vain for the ropes he'd used on the ladies. Arthur could see, out the corner of his eye, Dottie was trying very hard to suppress a smile. It infected Arthur who felt at huge giggle rising up, knowing Toby could not find the ropes.

"This is not funny at all!" said Toby in frustration. "Now, where did you put those ropes, Mr Clever Clogs?"

"Uh, I'm not sure now," said Arthur, hoping Toby would not look at the floor behind the curtain.

"Not sure? Not sure!" said Toby looming over him angrily. "You were very sure where you put them a few minutes ago."

"Uh, yes ..." said Arthur.

"Look Arthur, there are two ways to do this – the easy way or the painful way," said Toby, obviously working hard to calm his troubled nerves. "Whatever you choose, I'm going to get those files out of here and so you'd better decide which way; that way of pain or the way of gain."

Arthur knew he should have felt threatened but, somehow, he didn't feel Toby really had his heart in the job. He just didn't seem to be a bad or evil kind of person. However, as Arthur reasoned, in the split second it takes to reason anything, he didn't actually know any evil people and how would he know what they were like. Dominik, for example, looked tremendously ferocious and evil but he used his force to combat bad men. It was a conundrum – should he stand for good or should he take the easy way out?

"Under the couch. The ropes are under the couch," said Joan quickly. He looked at her and she smiled and winked at him as Toby dived to the floor and fished around for the ropes which weren't there. Arthur's eye was taken by a flash of movement in the doorway and it was gone. He wondered, with all the stress, if he was losing his grip on life, if he was seeing things that weren't there. He didn't have time to wonder long as Martin's head appeared around the door, cautiously.

Arthur stared, unbelieving, then Martin's vigorous waving reminded him to act a little more moderately, even nonchalantly, which, given the tense circumstances, was a challenge for Arthur.

Toby stopped his frenetic activity and just stood there. Arthur looked at his face and he seemed about to cry or something.

"Bugger damn bugger, Mr Bayly. I'm just not cut out for this," said Toby wearily, walking over to Arthur. "This is just not working and I'm sorry, so very sorry, Arthur … Joan … all of you. I can't do this … Please forgive me …"

To Toby's side, Arthur saw Martin gesturing, again, but Arthur wasn't sure of the message, momentarily, then realised Martin wanted him to stand up. Unsure of why this was a good idea Arthur nevertheless did as bid, prompting Toby to take a step back. At the same time Martin had dived to the floor, on hands and knees, right behind Toby, who toppled over backwards and crashed to the floor on the other side of Martin. Martin leapt upon the prone and stunned Toby and Arthur wondered what to do.

"Get something to tie him up with, Dad?" yelled Martin, trying to tame four lively limbs below him. Arthur faltered, as well he might, considering his lack of fighting and tying-up-criminal skills. "Sit on his knees, Dad, and tie his feet," yelled Martin as he struggled with the tossing sea of limbs below him.

"Uh, oh, of course," said Arthur, obeying his son. He grabbed the ropes from behind the curtain and leapt upon Toby's flailing knees with considerable panache, got kneed in the testicles, felt an unaccustomed anger arise and fought back with the ferocity of a man with his back to the wall. He received a boot in the face, a twisted and painful finger and his determination (or was it his panic?) lent him the force and agility to have, in double-quick time, the young man's legs trussed up in rather a pleasing combination of ropes and knots. Meanwhile, he was aware that the top half of Toby was faring better than the bottom as Martin let out several *oomphs* and *ows*. Flushed with success, Arthur got up to help Martin with Toby's more dangerous zone, just as a shadow filled the doorway.

"I get bad man", said Dominik, quietly, determinedly. His eyes looked black and threatening. He fell to his knees with his shins crashing over Toby's upper arms. Arthur fancied he heard a *crack* and he definitely heard Toby scream in pain. "You bad man. I give you punish."

"No Dominik! No!" said Arthur, realising what could be in store for Toby. "Just tie his hands behind his back. No need to hit him, Dominik!"

"He bad man. I punish," said Dominik flatly.

"No punishment, Dominik, just restrain him," said Arthur, with growing trepidation.

"Here Dominik, help me turn him over," said Martin, quickly deflecting Dominik's offensive to something more gentle. There was a shuffling of bodies, screams from Toby and he was quickly on his front with his arms behind his back.

"Martin! Martin!" came Joan's voice through the small cocoon of maleness. "Stop Martin. I think he's badly injured."

"And what was he about to do to you, Mum?" Martin shot back angrily.

"Martin, he can't do us any harm now," said Joan standing up. "Have a little compassion, Martin."

"But he's ..."

"But he's in a lot of pain, he's tied by the feet and his arms probably don't work," said Joan, pointing out the logic of the situation. "Help him on to this chair, tie his feet to it and we can see what's next."

Martin and Dominik were obviously ready to inflict more pain on this bad man. They looked at each other in brotherly connection, shook their heads sadly and lifted Toby to a sitting position on the chair with less gentleness than they could have managed. Toby's legs were tied to the chair and when Dominik grabbed his left arm, Toby let out another ceiling-rattling scream.

"Stop! Stop!" yelled Joan, pushing Dominik aside. "We've gone far enough. Here, Dottie, you were a nurse. Can you look at Toby's arm, please?"

"It's my shoulder," whispered Toby, looking ashen and pained.

"You be careful, lady, he bad man," said Dominik, hovering helpfully behind her.

"No Dominik ... is that your name, Dominik?" asked Joan. "I'm Joan, this is Dottie and my son Martin." As Dottie gently manoeuvred Toby's arm on to his lap, Dominik and Martin shook hands.

"Please meet you," said Dominik, his ferocity softening a little.

"Now Dominik, he's not a bad man. He just did a bad thing and he won't do it again," said Joan with obvious conviction.

"Not bad man, just bad things," said Dominik as if chewing the new idea over. "So I stay if another bad thing he do."

"Yes, it's great to have your protection," said Martin, alternatively rubbing his sore cheek and tenderly checking his painful fingers.

"Ah, Mr Arthur, I have paper for you in van," said Dominik.

"Paper?" asked Arthur.

"Yes, paper on Lord Atkinson," said Dominik. "You know, paper in bag."

"Ah, the Atkinson file!" said Arthur as the realisation hit him. "You took it out of the bag?"

"Yes, I think bad thing to happen so I take from bag when you no look," said Dominik. "For your protection, Mr Arthur."

"Ah Dominik, you're a genius!" said Arthur.

"Me genius ... genius, what is this word?" asked Dominik.

"Oh, ah, you're brilliant, big brain, Dominik!" said Arthur, tapping his head.

"Ah, me genius, big brain!" said Dominik beaming as he gave Arthur a bear hug.

"Oh Dominik," said Arthur, his words muffled by Dominik's chest, "can you get the file now, please, now that Toby is disabled?"

"Yes Mr Arthur, I go now," said Dominik as he strode out to get the papers.

"Whew!" said Arthur as he collected himself and got his breath back. He could hear faint sobbing and turned to see Toby looking distressed.

"Dad, I think he's in more pain than we thought," said Martin, sounding worried.

"I think it's a dislocated shoulder – painful but not fatal," said Dottie efficiently. "I'll put him in a sling and we'll get him down to the walk-in medical centre. Do you have material for a sling, Joan?" "Mmm, probably," said Joan as she led Dottie off to find something suitable.

"I'm really sorry ..." came a murmur from Toby's direction.

"What?" asked Arthur and Martin in unison.

"I'm really sorry, guys," said Toby, weakly. Joan and Dottie returned with a table cloth and Dottie had it quickly folded and tied up to hold Toby's arm, with accompanying grimaces from Toby.

"Thank you Dottie," said Toby, falteringly. "Thank you all for being so kind. I was not so kind to you at all."

"It was nothing. In fact, it didn't happen, if we're to believe *A Course in Miracles*," said Joan, smiling.

"Oh it happened alright! Look at Dominik's eyes – both black," said Toby as Dominik returned with Arthur's file. "That's what a punch in the kidneys does. It happened alright!"

"So you little man punch big man and I go down?" asked Dominik with obvious admiration as he handed Arthur the file. "So you teach me that trick or I break your face!" Dominik burst out laughing.

Arthur was shocked but realised it must be Dominik's rough good humour. He was still wary of the big man and so were the others, judging by the way they obediently laughed along with him.

"No problem, Dominik mate, when I get my arm working again," said Toby smiling uncertainly.

"But ... but I feel so stupid, embarrassed, causing all this, thinking I could take advantage of you folk for a quick buck."

"A quick buck?" asked Arthur.

"Yes, after we had those two chaps apprehended at work, the word must have got around and a chap with a rough, gravely voice phoned me, asking if I would like three thousand pound for a morning's work."

"And you have no idea who this was?" asked Martin.

"Not sure ... ow! But he put half the money into my account immediately as a show of faith," said Toby shifting on the chair as the others sat down round him. "He paid two thugs to get the files from the office ... oh, of course, Arthur, you were there and escaped!"

"Ah, those two," said Arthur as a tremble up his spine accompanied the memory's return.

"Yes, those two," said Toby. "Well, they didn't get the files and I guess this Mr Gravelly Voice thought I had inside knowledge, coupled with discovering I disarmed his two bovver boys with knife and gun."

"You disarmed two armed men?" asked Martin with surprise.

"Well, sort of," said Toby, smiling. "Actually, they kinda' handed the gun and knife over and I took advantage of their clumsiness."

"Right, enough talk!" said Dottie, interrupting authoritatively. "The sooner we get this shoulder looked at the easier it will be to get it back into place. The swelling will not wait for our fascinating discussions."

"Yes Matron!" said Joan, saluting and laughing. "Arthur, untie your brilliant knots and let's get this silly boy to the doctor to be rearmed!"

"So, Martin, that was a clever trick, getting Toby to trip over you," said Arthur as they all settled back in the lounge with a cup of tea and with pastries that Toby had insisted on buying.

"Mmm, just a silly thing we did at school – amazing how inspiration hits when desperation bowls, as they say in cricket," said Martin, chuckling. "I just happened to be back here in Croydon with that conciliation work and thought I'd ring to see how you were. And you were yelling for help! And Dad,

I've never seen you so ferocious! I'm glad you were on my side, you quite frightened me!" "Yes, rather surprised myself, I must say," said Arthur, laughing.

"The fearsome four! Quite a team," said Joan, smiling at Arthur. "Now, Toby, this Mr Gravelly Voice, he seems to be a crucial figure. We need to find out more about him – who he is and who he's working with."

"I wish I could help," said Toby, juggling a cup of tea and food with the one hand not in a sling.

"He called on my mobile and the rest of the money was supposed to be transferred when I had the files.

I know no more than that ... well, I strongly suspect I'm in a pile of poo now that I've failed." He shuddered visibly.

# The Chase

*Tuesday, 13<sup>th</sup> March 2012, 8.32 p.m.*

Mary was shocked to see Halee as they met, as agreed, outside Starbucks, in Orange Street at eight thirty in the evening "My gosh, is that really you, Halee?" she asked. "You're usually dressed so, um, demurely at work."

"I thought if I drew attention to myself, you'd be noticed less," said Halee, adjusting her top which revealed a large acreage of ample and hitherto undisclosed cleavage. She was obviously not used to wearing such revealing attire.

"You've done us proud, Halee, and I feel quite odd in Ahmed's suit," said Mary. "I must try to act like a man and, to be brutally honest, I'm actually quite nervous. Would you like a drink; a wine or something, beforehand?"

"That would be nice George ... I suppose you have a man's name?" suggested Halee.

"Uh, I hadn't thought of that," said Mary. "Right, how about a drink, Mavis?"

"Mavis? Thanks a lot!" said Halee chuckling. "I'd rather keep my head clear so perhaps a coffee now and wine afterwards?"

As they sat in the café, looking out at the busy night life of the city, Mary imagined an Indian man nodding to her as he passed. She felt slightly uncomfortable. Actually, she felt quite uncomfortable about a number of things – the mysterious Indian, her in men's clothes, how to behave with a junior staff member in these strange circumstances, what was about to happen, what had happened to Sam. In fact, as she thought about it, there was little she felt comfortable about; like her whole life, really – the missing zygote feeling that never left her, the sense of feeling different, not feeling connected to her parents ...

"Good, Ahmed's on the case," said Halee, breaking into Mary's thoughts.

"Oh, that was Ahmed? I didn't recognise him out of his pinstripe suit," said Mary as the confusion evaporated and she tried to focus on what she had to do – talk like a man, walk like a man, act casual with Halee, hand over the case at nine o'clock ... and then what?

"What's in the case?" asked Halee. "It must be valuable."

"I don't know. I didn't dare look inside," said Mary, about to reach into her bag for lipstick and then realising she didn't have her handbag with her. What to do with her hands now, she wondered. "I just don't want to know."

"Maybe I'm just too nosey." said Halee. "I'd want to find out straight away!"

"Yes, part of me wants to know and part of me doesn't want to know what could go wrong," said Mary, stirring in her sugar.

"Do you normally have four spoons of sugar in your coffee?" asked Halee.

"No, of course I don't! It would be vile," said Mary, confused by the question.

"Well, your coffee now has four teaspoons of sugar in it. It's official!" said Halee with a smile. "You must be nervous!"

"Ugh!" said Mary, testing her coffee. "You're right! I wonder how that happened." She wondered if she was losing control of herself and shuddered.

"Miss Collins, may I suggest something to you?" asked Halee.

"Yes, I suppose so," said Mary as a worried lump of something rose in her stomach.

"I think – I may be wrong – but I think you're in love," said Halee, tentatively, perhaps fearing Mary's reaction.

"No I'm not!"

"I suspect you are."

"No I'm not!" said Mary defiantly. "Yes, I do respect Sam but I'm not in love with him. That's silly."

"How did you know I meant Mr Black?" asked Halee, smiling mischievously.

"Oh!" said Mary, momentarily nonplussed.

"You. Are. In. Love. With. Sam. Black," said Halee, slowly and deliberately. "And, believe me, when that happens, all logic and control fly out the window." "Oh," said Mary, unable to summon up any more words.

"Look, if you admit it, accept it, you have an excuse to be as weird as you like," said Halee, laughing. She sipped her coffee and held Mary's eyes with her own. Mary was stumped. She'd sort-of admitted it to herself in moments of weakness but now it was out in the open and, like a new-born baby, impossible to put back.

"Being in love, Miss Collins, can be unnerving, scary, illogical, badly-timed and everything else that's skew whiff but if it's there, it's there." said Halee, smiling gently. "Think about it and see if it fits with what's going on in your mind,"

"See if it fits ..." said Mary, considering the phrase.

"You see, Miss Collins, love knows no age, race, gender or anything else logical – it just moves in where it does and denial only makes it painful. Acceptance allows it and us to flourish. Let it grow. Let yourself grow and watch the magic happen."

"Oh," said Mary, reverting to her favourite word for now. "You seem to know a lot about it?"

"Yeah, that's another reason I'm on the other side of the world, here in London," said Halee, suddenly serious. "I fell in love and we were to be married ... oh, hell, it would have been our anniversary next week, actually. Then he was diagnosed with cancer, lymphoma, and was gone two months later. I just couldn't stand to be reminded of anything about him so I ran and here I am." She wiped her eyes quickly. "Oh heck, I didn't mean to talk about this now. How's my mascara?"

"It could do with some repair, actually," said Mary, surprised and relieved by the quick return to practicalities. "Fix yourself up and we'd better get going ... oh, gosh, which toilet do I go to, the men's or the ladies'?" Both of them smiled and Halee slipped off to patch herself up while Mary nodded imperceptibly to Ahmed as he passed again, thinking that he looked very exotic and handsome in his traditional dress. She also wondered about love and, if something happened to Sam, what would she do. Would she run to forget, like Halee? Would she work harder to forget? She tried to shake off the thoughts that really didn't want to let go.

"Right, let's go, shall we?" suggested Halee perkily as she returned.

The two women marched off down the street looking, in the artificial glow of the lights, like a very happy and in-love couple – chatting, smiling and, under it all, terrified of what might happen next. They arrived at the blue door a few minutes early, saw no one there, looked at each other nervously and then nodded in assent. Without speaking, their minds agreed that they keep walking and return to the door at the exact time. Mary was bemused at how their thinking was synchronised. Slightly comforted by seeing Ahmed stopping outside Pizza Express, and then going inside, they continued their jaunty (and nervous) way down Charing Cross Road, towards Trafalgar Square.

Back at the blue door, at the stroke of nine, Mary's heart skipped a beat as she saw Sam lounging in the shadow of the doorway. He looked gaunt, unshaven but smiling bravely.

"Give me the case, keep walking and return in three minutes," he said quickly, seriously.

"Oh ... oh, yes, here it is," said Mary, her body drawn to him as a lizard to the sun.

"Go Mary, you must go now," said Sam, his hand at her shoulder, pushing her on.

"Yes, yes, we're going," she said dumbly as she felt Halee pulling on her sleeve.

"Bother!" said Mary, angry and confused as they turned the corner into Orange Street. "Why does everything turn to mush, just when it starts to come right?"

"Yeah, my thoughts entirely," said Halee, bitterly. "The stupid universe sends you this wonderful man and, just when love hits, whips him away. It's so unfair!"

"Oh, Halee, I'm so sorry, I didn't mean to upset you too. I was just thinking of myself," said Mary, her own angst dissolving in the care of another.

"That's okay, Miss Collins," said Halee, smiling through her tears. "I suppose I've got to talk about it, deal with it, let it go sometime, don't I? I've been running from it too long."

"And how long has this all been since he … passed away?" asked Mary, sensing Halee's pain.

"Oh heck, about four years now. I thought I had been coping with it all so well, till now," said Halee grinning through her tears. "It's all your fault!" They both laughed quietly.

"Okay, let's get back on the case. Our three minutes are nearly up!" said Halee, taking Mary's arm and steering her around. "Let's do the deed and do it well. No faltering this time."

"Okay for you to say," said Mary smiling grimly as the fear and longing threatened to drown her. They slowed at the door again and Sam was there with the briefcase.

"Take the case, Mary, take it home and I'll try to ring you in an hour," said Sam, quickly. "I'll do my best to call you then. Go now, my dear and, remember, you'll see all in the clear light of morning." Mary faltered again, despite her determination not to this time.

"Go, my dear, go!" whispered Sam earnestly. She felt Halee pulling on her arm. She took the case from Sam and left, determined not to think or to look back. "Yes, the clear light of morning. Now go, my dear, go!"

As they rounded the corner, back into Orange Street, Mary stopped and leaned against a shop window, relieved they'd made the exchange safely … whatever it was they'd exchanged. She realised, only then, that her heart was thudding and she was sweating like a Turkish wrestler. Her body was quivering and she found it difficult to stand upright. She had no idea of the dangers they might have expected but, now they were over, the feeling of release was overwhelming. She looked up and saw Ahmed across the street, waving to her, animatedly … angry, perhaps.

"Come on, Miss Collins, we can't stop now," said Halee. "Let's rest when we get you home." "I just need to catch up with myself now that it's over," said Mary, breathing heavily.

"It's not over yet," said Halee. "We still don't know if we were delivering something or taking something away for Mr Black."

"Oh you're right!" said Mary, her body suddenly in charge again. Ahmed was trying to cross the street, dodging the continual stream of cars, taxis and buses. "What's Ahmed want?" "I think he wants us to keep moving," said Halee, pulling on Mary's arm again.

As Ahmed reached the curb he suddenly veered off and walked right past them. This didn't make sense. Mary's apprehension grew. She looked up to see where Ahmed had disappeared to and a tall man loomed into view, in front of them.

"Excuse me, Sir, can I have a word?" asked the tall blonde man. Mary considered running and felt hot and cold all over.

"Yes, how can I help?" asked Halee quickly. "My partner is deaf and cannot speak. I can sign for him." Confusion cleared as Mary realised her voice was not a man's. She was glad of Halee's quick thinking and wanted to hug her on the spot. All she could do was smile crookedly.

"Ah, oh, can you?" asked the man, scratching his blonde hair, uncertainly. "Oh, yes, well, can you tell your friend that this dropped out of his briefcase, just back there?" He handed Halee a sealed envelope.

"Oh, thank you, that's very kind," said Halee, obviously relieved.

"No problem, mate," said the man, who patted Mary on the shoulder and trotted off.

As Mary looked at the envelope in Halee's hand, it was snatched away and Mary realised it was Ahmed, with the envelope and in full pursuit of the man. The man was either lucky or practised and had soon disappeared into the crowd. Ahmed returned a few minutes later, puffing and scowling.

"It's not over yet, ladies, let's get you out of here, now!" said Ahmed, frantically waving and looking for a taxi. "Go into this café here, mill around and I'll call you when a taxi has arrived." Nonplussed, they did as ordered and had only just got inside when Ahmed waved them back to the street.

Mary gave the taxi her address in South Kensington and Ahmed objected, saying they could be followed.

"Sam's ringing me there in an hour," said Mary, feeling her brain and all its functions returning to normal. "I want to be there when he rings."

"Right, let's do it, Mr Taxi!" said Halee.

"You know, it's impossible to tell if anyone is following us because we can only see headlights," said Ahmed, smiling, as they set out on the ten-minute ride. "The movies all tell lies!" "Thanks Ahmed, but that's not really helping," said Mary, feeling very unsafe.

"Oh, I'm sorry, I was just trying to introduce some humour," said Ahmed, looking abashed. "Perhaps we talk practicalities and I really do have to say this: I do not think your apartment is a safe place to be at all."

"But Sam's ringing me there," said Mary, determined not to let go of that ray of hope.

"And not on your mobile phone?" asked Halee.

"He didn't say, so I'm not taking any chances," said Mary.

"Leave it to the receptionist – she thinks of everything!" said Halee brightly. "Why don't we pop into your flat, divert the phone to your mobile, then scarper."

"It's not risk elimination but it's risk reduction," said Ahmed, looking slightly relieved.

"So, what's in this case, I really want to see!" said Halee, patting the briefcase.

"That's not very safe here," advised Ahmed.

"If we lock the doors, no one can jump in at the lights," said Halee, not to be put off.

"Okay, okay, we'll have a quick look, but keep a lookout for people approaching us when we slow down anywhere," said Mary, as eager as Halee and as cautious as Ahmed.

The briefcase was filled with about a dozen manila folders, each stuffed with papers. It looked very orderly. Mary pulled out the first folder and rifled quickly through the papers. Most of them concerned the accounts of one of Britain's largest companies, Power Corporation, colloquially called PoCo. There were letters from the auditors and from the director, Sir Magnus Davenport. It all looked a bit boring, really. Mary tried the second folder and there seemed to be correspondence and reports regarding the Olympic Games, due to start in four months' time in London. With details about contracts and power supply, with amendments to particular clauses, it was mainly letters between solicitors and Sir Magnus Davenport and no more interesting than the previous file.

"There's nothing about AIL, Lord Atkinson, Sam or anything else we know about," complained

Mary. "What's Sam got to do with PoCo and the Olympics anyway?" "No idea, no idea at all, Miss Collins," said Ahmed with a frown.

"Let's get creative," said Halee with undiminished enthusiasm. "The top's boring and irrelevant so let's try that yellow one at the bottom."

As they opened the yellow folder she saw drawings of machines that baffled her.

"Oh my god!" said Ahmed with surprise, his white teeth lighting up his dark face. "This ... this is alternative technology ... ah, intermediate technology." "It's what?" asked Mary, totally confused.

"Look, when I studied accounting at university ..." Ahmed began to say.

"You're an accountant?" asked Halee, obviously impressed.

"Yes, I qualified in both accounting and economics and did accounting for a while and then found a counsellor and some good pills and got over it!" said Ahmed, laughing and then, as if remembering where they were, became serious and looked outside, around the car. The two women followed suit.

"Anyway, my favourite economist was the Austrian, E. F. Schumacher ..." "His book, *Small Is Beautiful*, is amazing!" said Halee, interrupting.

"And his thoughts on intermediate technology and the *Law of the Disappearing Middle* just had me hooked," said Ahmed. "I was going to take it all back to Pakistan and help my people ... anyway, these are intermediate technology machines, machines that are not too expensive or too complex for developing nations to use and maintain; more complex than the shovel but simpler than the tractor,

shall we say ..."

"And these intermediate technologies keep disappearing, Miss Collins," said Halee, interrupting again. "So developing countries only have a choice of spades – which are not enough to expand their agriculture and feed their people – or tractors which they cannot afford and do not have the expertise or resources to repair."

"It's like accounting where we only have the most primitive, paper ledgers, or the most advanced, computers," said Ahmed, looking excitedly at Halee. "Where are all the intermediate accounting technologies like the abacus, the slide rule, the accounting machine and so on, for developing nations to do their accounting with? They've all disappeared."

"Okay! Okay you two," snapped Mary. "We're in a taxi with a case load of papers that, apparently, contain some inherent danger to us. This is all very interesting about technologies and stuff but what value has any of it to us, right here now .... with Sam, AIL or anything else?" "Oh yeah, right," said Halee, looking mollified.

"Well, let's brainstorm," suggested Ahmed, putting on his logical hat. "We haven't seen all the papers but what we've seen is Power Corporation accounts, Olympic contracts and intermediate technology. Let's keep these big headings in mind and keep looking."

"Oh, we're nearly at my apartment," said Mary, putting the last file back in the bottom of the briefcase, just as she had found it. "Halee, please come up with me, switch my phone over – it's not really my thing, this technology – and you, Ahmed, can you hold the fort here and keep a lookout for saboteurs, please?"

"Yes, absolutely, Miss Collins, and I'll keep the case here," said Ahmed. "Then you can fly on winged feet, as we say!"

The taxi driver was happy to continue the fare for an indefinite time, especially as some of it would be paid without actually having to move. He got out for a smoke while the two women dashed inside.

Ahmed was sorely tempted to delve into the case again but disciplined himself to stay alert and keep watching, which was just as well. A car soon parked behind him and two men leapt out and ran into the building. Ahmed recognised one as the tall one who had handed Mary the envelope and then ran into the crowd. The other man was shorter, solid and dark skinned. Without thinking, Ahmed leapt out and told the cabbie not to go but to be ready to take off.

"Just like in the movies, yeah!" said the taxi driver, laughing, as Ahmed dashed up the steps to find the two men in the shadows, pushing buttons, one after another, in an attempt to gain admittance to Mary's apartment.

"Oh hell, where'd you come from?" asked the taller man, obviously not British, looking confused as Ahmed drew out the pistol he told Mary he wouldn't carry.

"Get away from the door, down the steps and be gone!" ordered Ahmed.

"Okay, okay bro', no need to get heavy," said the shorter, dark skinned man. "We're just goin', we're just goin' ..."

Ahmed stepped back to keep space between himself and the men as they backed awkwardly down the steps. He kept his pistol trained on them as they turned and fled to their car. His pistol followed their car as it leapt from the parking spot, with a screech of tyres, and disappeared into the night. His eyes went to the taxi and he realised, with alarm, the driver had disappeared. He looked around and back again, to see a head tentatively appearing from below the driver's window.

"I'm sorry Sir, I won't shoot you!" said Ahmed, realising his pistol was still aimed over the taxi, in the direction the other car went. He quickly pocketed his pistol. "Please wait. We won't be a minute!"

He turned and pressed the intercom number he knew was Mary's. He waited. He pushed again. He waited. He pushed again and heard Mary's voice.

"We need to go now!" he yelled impatiently. "We've been followed so you need to get out here now!"

"Oh, right," said Mary.

"I just wanted to get some girly things," said Mary, puffing as she was bundled into the taxi. "So I could get this men's stuff off."

"Sorry ladies, no time. We must away!" said Ahmed gallantly, calmly. "I'm really sorry to have scared you, Sir. This is not something we normally do," said Ahmed, explaining inadequately to a frightened looking taxi driver, to whom he gave the address of his apartment.

"Well, at least you'll hear from Mr Black now," said Halee, as ever, looking for the bright side as they were driven to Ahmed's apartment in Kensington. "But why do I get the nagging feeling we're still being followed, somehow?"

"I don't think we'll see them again," said Ahmed, confidently.

"How did you do that? And two of them? Did you recognise either?" asked Mary, wanting to know everything immediately.

"Yes, one of them was the one who gave you the envelope, back at Trafalgar," said Ahmed, suddenly remembering the envelope. He pulled it out of his pocket and tore it open. On it were typed the words: 'We do not give up searching the taonga for anyone or anything. Give it up now and you will not be hurt. Arohanui'.

"Taonga? Arohanui?" said Ahmed, saying the strange words slowly. "What do they mean?"

"They're Māori words," said Halee. "Taonga is a gift and arohanui is love, big love, universal love. It means they will honour their promise – we won't be hurt if we give it up now."

"Well, that's too bad. I'm not giving this case this up for anyone!" said Mary grimly. "And how exactly did you scare these two men off, Ahmed?" She had distinctly uneasy feelings about Ahmed's methods.

"Oh, I just shouted 'boo' and they ran!" said Ahmed, probably hoping humour would disperse her concerns.

"Why do I get the feeling you used the gun you said you wouldn't?" asked Mary.

"Oh dear, you've caught me out," said Ahmed, smiling sheepishly.

"You have been remiss, Ahmed, but I forgive you," said Mary, smiling at him. "I dread to think where we'd be if you hadn't done what you did, whatever it was. And you might be right about our safety, Ahmed, but something tells me they're still tailing us, somehow." "Me too," said Halee, quietly.

"They can't, as I said," said Ahmed with finality.

"You might be right but my gut tells me queasy things, whatever they are," said Halee.

"Mine too ..." said Mary. Her phone interrupted her and she snapped it out of her pocket. "Yes Sam, how are you?"

"No Mary, it's Angus," said her brother, laughing. "So yer boyfriend's Sam is it?"

"Angus, what do you want?" asked Mary, confused. "You've never rung my mobile before." "And I've never been to London before and here I am, in this stupid city," said Angus. "What the hell are you doing in London, you daft bugger?" asked Mary, feeling strangely comforted by her brother's proximity.

"I want to know where this damned house of yers is," said Angus, sounding frustrated but jovial. "I said I would pop down some time and here I am. Where do I park a car in this crazy town, girl?"

"Ah, oh hell, Angus, this is so ... so unexpected. Hell, it's awkward at the moment," said Mary quickly, trying to think clearly, logically.

"Well that's a fine welcome for a long lost brother, I must say, sis," said Angus, the joy going from his voice.

"Oh Angus, I'm sorry, it will be grand to see you. Really it will but I'm not at home right now and I'm waiting for an important call ..." said Mary.

"From boyfriend Sam, I suppose," said Angus, interrupting with a chuckle.

"From Sam, yes, but he's not a boyfriend, like I told you," said Mary, feeling embarrassed in front of Halee and Ahmed while her brain failed to come up with an immediate solution to the problem, like it usually did. Losing it again! Damn!

"And, hey, it's not just me, sis, I've got some important visitors for ye," said Angus, his chuckle beginning to get right on her craw. "All the way from New Zealand to see ye and ye're out on the town, living it up!"

"Look, Angus, let me think for a moment, will you," said Mary. "I've got your number and I'll call you back in a jif."

"Okay sis, just give us an address of the closest hotel and we'll catch up tomorrow, yeah?" suggested Angus. With a huge relief, Mary gave him the address of a hotel around the corner from her apartment and told him she'd pay the bill.

"I can't let ye pay me bills, Mary. Doncha' know I'm Scottish!" said Angus with a laugh. She wondered what he'd been smoking – she'd never heard him so chipper before.

"Yeah and so am I so shut up, book in, enjoy the amenities and I'll be round in the morning to settle up and have breakfast with you," said Mary as the solution presented itself. She was curious about his visitors but needed to have the phone clear for Sam's call. "Okay?"

"Okay, we can argue about it tomorrow, you obstinate Scot!" said Angus and the phone went dead before she could reply.

As Ahmed announced their arrival at his apartment, he grabbed the briefcase to go.

"Hey Ahmed, do you mind!" snapped Mary, not letting it go. "This is my case, not yours. Okay?"

"But I am the man and I must protect you two women," said Ahmed, obviously surprised. "That is my duty."

"Oh Ahmed, that's so kind ..." said Mary, uncertain what to say next, so long used to fending for herself.

"It's my duty," said Ahmed with finality.

"Ah, your Muslim duty," said Mary, suddenly realising the man she had worked with for the last two years had a life and beliefs beyond the insurance company. "You're not used to taking orders from women and I'm not used to men doing for me."

"Well, Miss Collins is the boss so she gets the case and you get the door, Ahmed," said Halee cheerily. "Would that work?"

"I don't feel right ..." said Ahmed, uncertainly.

"Don't feel, just do," said Mary, handing the taxi his fare. Ahmed still hesitated. "Ahmed, now! They'll be here any time, I just know it!"

"But we've lost them," said Ahmed, hesitating between the modern world he worked in and the ancient world of his ancestry.

"We don't know that so get going and let us safely into your apartment, will you!" said Mary, feeling opportunities for safety slipping away. She could see him relax as he seemed to make a decision.

"Yes ma'am," he said suddenly, releasing the case and leaping from the taxi up the steps to unlock the imposing front door, with a keypad, into the spacious foyer of the Kensington apartment block. Mary and Halee followed on his heels.

"Holy moly, you could have a choice party in here!" exclaimed Halee, her voice echoing round the cavernous space. "You didn't tell us you lived in a museum, Ahmed."

"It's not a museum, it's an apartment block, Halee," said Ahmed, explaining carefully, obviously unsure whether she was joking or not.

"Wow, you live here," said Halee turning round and round, taking in the intricately patterned marble floor, the oak-panelled walls, the marble and mahogany staircase that went up five floors, the plastered ceiling sixty feet above them and the massive chandelier in the centre of it. "You could keep your pet brontosauruses here, along with a herd of elephants, Ahmed!"

"Well, yes, it is nice to have the space – a nice contrast to the rest of London," said Ahmed smiling as he walked over to the lift.

"Space? SPACE? You could keep your pet concord in here too!" exclaimed Halee, her voice rising, obviously in a trance. "We're not using a lift when there's this *Gone With The Wind* staircase here, are we?"

"Oh, well, I've always used the lift," said Ahmed. "The stairs are for tradesmen to take furniture up and things like that. It's not seemly to use them."

"Not seemly? Not blooming seemly?" exclaimed Halee, probably finding the habits of Londoners unusual. "Come on Ahmed, I'll race you. What floor are you on?"

"Oh, the fifth floor, Halee, but you cannot run around in here. It's not done," said Ahmed, his usually calm features looking decidedly lopsided as he scratched his immaculately trimmed beard.

"Not done? 'Tis now ..." said Halee.

"I am not, I repeat, I am not clambering up any steps, young lady," said Mary interrupting and feeling terrified at the thought of the exertion required to attain those giddy heights. "If I was meant to climb things I would have had crampons for toes. I don't."

"Ah you party poopers!" said Halee skipping up to the bottom of the stairs. "I'll wait till you get in your stuffy lift and then I'll race you to the fifth floor. Quick, here it is!"

The crazy young girl fled up the stairs as Ahmed and Mary took the sensible route, not wasting the technological advances brought to this century. Mary wondered if her health would be better served by a few flights of stairs, from time to time, and she rather envied Halee's energy and unconcern for appearances. Oh well, she though, she'll ponder it from the comfort of a quiet lift and a nice glass of wine at the top. Mary was thankful for Ahmed's silence as she could ponder ... well, everything, really – Sam, night-time chases, gentle and bossy Muslim manners, Sam, childish exuberance, Sam, Angus,

New Zealand visitors, Sam ... the doors started to open and Mary hadn't realised the lift had stopped – another technological marvel – and there stood a panting Halee on the threshold.

"So you beat us ..." said Ahmed, smiling.

"Shh, they're here, they're ruddy well coming," whispered Halee quickly

"Who's coming?" asked Mary, her mind still not unwinding from thoughts of Sam.

"Shhh!" whispered Halee urgently, leaping into the lift and looking around frantically. "How do we get back down in this thing?"

"But they can't be here ..." said Ahmed, his usual calm disappearing into lopsidedness again.

"Shut up will ya! They'll hear you!" whispered Halee urgently. "They're following me up. Where's the ruddy down button in this fangled thing? Now!"

Ahmed, stunned by her language and panic, pressed the button for the first floor. As the doors closed they could hear the clattering of shoes coming up the marble stairway, towards them.

"Are we headed for the bottom? We need to get out there!" said Halee, leaning back against the elevator wall, catching her breath.

"I have a friend on the first floor," said Ahmed. "We'll sneak in there."

"They found us in this building, mate, so they'll find us anywhere in it," said Halee, grabbing Ahmed by the lapels. "This is real, Ahmed, don't you get that? They're in here, now, after us."

"And so is my plan very real," said Ahmed, gently taking Halee's hands off him as the doors opened onto the first floor.

"Okay, stop a sec. Keep the doors open and see where they go now," suggested Halee quietly.

"We need to get out and into Mohammed's apartment," said Ahmed quietly, about to step out, with his guiding hand on Mary's shoulder.

"See, they're coming down again! They're like bloody homing pigeons!" whispered Halee.

"Mary, what's this?" asked Ahmed, his poise gone. He leapt back into the elevator, pulled the women in with him and pushed the button for his floor. In his hand was a black, circular plastic thing.

"This was stuck on your coat, Mary. Do you think it's a device ... I don't know, for following us?" "Oh hell!" said Mary, suddenly feeling overwhelmed and out of control.

"Well, if it is, leave it here, we get out at the fifth and we send it back to the bottom," said Halee. "They'll follow it back down."

"And pick it up and know we're still in the building," said Mary, feeling her neurons starting up again.

"Yes, good one," said Halee, smiling and scratching her head. "So we go back down, leave it in here, send it back up and we scarper ..."

"What if one of them is waiting at the bottom?" asked Ahmed, adding his chilling thought as the doors started to open again on the fifth floor. He pushed the ground floor button, threw the thing out onto the fifth floor landing as the doors closed and they descended again.

"Ahmed, we need to work this out together ..." said Mary, as she felt control slipping away again.

"I'm sorry Miss Collins, but I didn't think we had time," said Ahmed, looking embarrassed.

"Okay, no time to discuss. You're right, Ahmed," said Mary, smiling. "So we tear out of this lift, hope there's no one at the bottom, shoot him if he is and then get out of here?" "Shoot someone?" asked Ahmed, looking aghast.

"Just joking, Ahmed," said Mary, laughing to cover her dread. "Point and pretend to shoot ... I don't know ... get out of here and then what?"

"What if there's others outside?" asked Ahmed, measuring possibilities as the lift doors opened at the second floor and a couple entered, obviously dressed for a party in a smarter part of London. They giggled at each other, oblivious to the conspiring and panicking threesome. Mary was inwardly cursing the giggling couple in front of her, barring a quick getaway, but was soon thankful. As the doors opened on the ground, a brown, tattooed arm reached in and grabbed the incredulous couple.

"Got ya now, ya bastards!" said the stocky, dark, curly-headed man attached to the arm. "Get out here and give us our stuff, will ya!"

Our Terrified Three were momentarily stunned, unsure what to do next. The problem was solved by the party-going man who reacted quickly and efficiently, ramming his attacker against the wall with quiet fury.

"C'mon!" whispered Halee, leaping from the lift and towards the huge entrance doors. Mary and Ahmed reacted on instinct, as if they were chained to Halee, and fled as they heard a clatter and curses coming down the marble stairs.

"Don't bloody move! Not one inch!" yelled the taller blond man, leaping down stairs, three at a time. Halee struggled with the mechanism of the door which was designed to open with dignity and grace.

As the brown man slid to the floor with blood on his face, the blonde one hesitated between helping his friend and pursuing his quarry, now so close.

"C'mon ya bugger, open!" demanded Halee but the door continued to open slowly, quite unmoved by her threats. Within seconds, which seemed like hours, the door had opened enough for Halee to slip through and Mary and Ahmed followed her down the steps.

"Go left Halee, go left!" ordered Ahmed, and they did until they got to the first intersection.

"Which way now?" asked Mary, panting heavily, bringing up the rear.

"I don't know. Just get out of here!" said Ahmed. "Any way."

"Hey, wait up ... *ah ha ah ha ah ha* ... please," pleaded Mary, panting and clutching the briefcase while struggling to keep up. "I don't do running."

"We can't let them get us now!" said Halee, slowing down with her hand out like a relay runner ready to take the baton. "Give me the case if you like ..."

"Not on your Nellie ... *ah ha ah ha ah ha* ... Halee!" said Mary, determined to keep hold of her dignity and the case, both of which seemed to be slipping. "Can't we hide ... *ah ha ah ha ah ha* ... hide somewhere here, Ahmed ... *ah ha ah ha* ... you must know someone here ... *ah ha ah ha ah ha* ..."

"I ... I don't really know, Miss Collins," said Ahmed, stopping round the corner in a shop alcove.

"Come on Ahmed, this ... *ah ha ah ha ah ha* ... this is your territory," said Mary, following them in. "You must have a friend or café owner who'll take us in for a mo'."

"Well, yes I do but I'm not sure it's quite the right thing ..." said Ahmed, looking conflicted.

"Right thing? Right blooming thing, Ahmed?" whispered Mary hoarsely as her breathing started to return to normal. "Look, you genteel Englishman, our lives may be at risk, Sam may be at risk ... what the heck's right about that?"

# The Call Of The Black

*Tuesday, 13<sup>th</sup> March 2012, 3.06 p.m.*

The phone cut sharply through their riviere. Arthur leapt up to answer it, his nerves still a little raw from the morning's events. He lifted the receiver.

"Hello Arthur, old chap …" It went dead. He knew who it was, immediately, but his thoughts and actions failed him, momentarily. Joan came into the dining room to see him staring into space with the phone still held by his ear. James Bond, of course, would have leapt into the fray and done something dramatic and saved the world, or a part of it, in an instant. However, Arthur's batteries were flat.

"What is it dear?" asked Joan.

"It's Lord Atkinson, dear. He's in trouble," said Arthur.

"The one who …"

"Yes, the one I met this morning," said Arthur. "It was a call for help."

"Well we'd better go and help him then," said Joan, clapping her hands as a teacher would, to get her pupils into line. Arthur jumped and looked around as if seeing the room for the first time.

"Oh Arthur, you do seem to have run out of poof, don't you?" Joan said, embracing him. "It's been a hell of a day … it's been a hell of a few weeks, really. And you've mastered it all so well. You really are my hero, Arthur. My hero and my love."

"Oh Joan," was all Arthur could manage before the tears started rolling. He wanted to embrace her forever, for the world to go away and leave him in peace. Yes, he thought, he did love Joan, this lovely, admiring and supportive woman in his arms. He really must tell her some time.

"Thank you, Joan, thank you," he said. However, he thought, right now Lord Atkinson needs help of some sort and so one must rally one's forces. "That's lovely Joan. But now I must go."

"Oh no you don't, Arthur Bayly!" said Joan, standing back with her hands on his shoulders. "You don't think you're going to rush off on your charger and leave your poor damsel here, waiting and pining, do you?"

"Uh …"

"You silly man! I'm coming too!" said Joan cheerfully. "We're in this together, my lover!"

"Well, if you think …"

"Too right I think so! Let's muster our troops, shall we?" said Joan, leading him back into the lounge. "Lord Atkinson needs our help so who wants to join us?" Everyone leapt up as one with fervent cries of assent.

"But, Dottie, are you sure you want to come along?" asked Arthur. "It could be dangerous."

"Arthur dear, I've never had such fun with my clothes on!" said Dottie, laughing. "I may be an old woman but you don't get rid of me that easy!" Everyone laughed, except Dominik who seemed to be trying to make out what Dottie meant about having her clothes on.

"And you, Toby?" asked Joan.

"I'm only half-armed but most of me works and do you think I'm only here for half the action?" asked Toby. "Besides, I've done enough damage so I'd like to make amends if I can."

"Hang on, Dad," said Martin quickly. "This is a matter for the police isn't it? Shouldn't we call them first, surely?"

"No Martin and I'm sorry but I don't have time to explain, right now," said Arthur. "However, Lord Atkinson specifically asked me not to involve the police if at all possible. It seems there's a leak, an informer, there who is not after our best interests."

"Right, if you say so, Dad," said Martin, uncertainly.

"Now, first, Arthur, that file seems to be awfully valuable," said Dottie. "Shall I hide it in my house in case yours gets raided?"

"Mmm, I hadn't thought of that. Good idea, Dottie," said Arthur.

"I'd take my car, Dad, but I have to pick the kids up from the child minder in a few hours and we don't know how long we're going to be, do we?" said Martin.

"You're right, Martin, but why don't you ring Emily and see if she can pick them up," said Joan.

"Oh hardly, Mother, I don't really even know her," said Martin, looking a little flushed.

"Well, this is one way you could get to know her," said Joan, smiling impishly. "Look Martin, she wants to help with finding her father and this little excursion could unearth him for her."

"Look, Mum, I know you only want the best for me but don't push it. I'm not ready for anyone else yet," said Martin, his politeness obviously being stretched.

"So, what are you going to do – wander on home, wishing you'd come and helped us out in a sticky situation?" asked Joan.

"Oh, okay, I'll see if she can help," said Martin, knowing his mother would not be deterred by obvious obstacles. He called Emily and was surprised that she jumped at the chance to help him out.

"Perhaps you take Dottie when she returns, Martin, along with Toby, who knows the way," suggested Arthur.

"And I'll ring Amanda to see if she can help," said Joan.

"Gosh, yes, grand idea," said Arthur. "And you, Dominik and I will go in the van." Dominik visibly brightened at the mention of his name, perhaps fearing being left out. "No Dominik, we're not going without you!"

"Me good for punish new bad man!" said Dominik, smiling and patting Toby on his good shoulder. Arthur was relieved that Dominik had made friends with Toby and had no lingering hatred or 'bad man' thoughts about him.

# The Turkish Connection

*Tuesday, 13<sup>th</sup> March 2012, 11.36 p.m.*

Ahmed's conflicted look did not disappear to any perceptible extent "Ah, yes, I see what you mean," he said. "Perhaps I could ask Safak ..."

"Don't talk about it, man, do it!" said Mary in frustration.

"Uh, right, yes," said Ahmed peering out, left and right, along the street. "Follow me!"

"Oh God, not more running!" said Mary as she hitched the case up under her arms and forced her legs to move at an unnaturally rapid pace.

"Come on, our lives could be at stake, Miss Collins!" said Ahmed, looking back and smiling.

My God, thought Mary, the sod hasn't even broken out in a sweat, as she had, and he wasn't even panting. Such an infuriating man – so resistant when action is needed, so jovial when it's serious and like a blasted robot on steroids. How do these people do this exercise thing, she wondered, it can't be good for them, surely!

"Oh, Miss Collins, I thought you were with us," said Halee, popping out of a Turkish restaurant in front of her. "Come in here."

"How the hell did you get... *ah ha ah ha ah ha* ... get here so quickly?" asked Mary, genuinely perplexed, between her heavy breathing.

"We did what they call running," said Halee, chuckling. Up at the counter Ahmed was talking rapidly to a young, dark man – obviously not in English. Another older, dark man was summoned and the foreign language discussion started all over again, accompanied by much hand-flapping and headnodding. So that's how they keep fit, thought Mary, *conversation aerobics*.

After some haggling and uncertainty, they were hustled into a small, darkish room through the back of the restaurant and told to sit. It was obvious they weren't to move from there. Mary detected a strange smell wafting through from an adjacent room. There seemed to be low murmurings coming from the room, as if men were quietly talking amongst themselves. Mary looked at Ahmed quizzically as Safak returned to the restaurant. Ahmed seemed to be looking everywhere except at Mary.

"Ahmed, what's that smell? What's that room there?" asked Mary quietly, holding Sam's briefcase to her chest.

"Oh, it's ... ah, a den, a smoking room," said Ahmed, smiling uncertainly.

"So, are they smoking drugs in there, Ahmed?" asked Mary, feeling quite queezy inside.

"Yes, I think they might be," said Ahmed. "But please keep the noise down, Miss Collins. We're only here because they know me and because I promised we'd be quiet." "Oh, sorry," said Mary, looking around uncertainly.

"Perhaps we just relax a bit, open our minds and let the angels in with an answer," suggested Halee tentatively.

"The angels? The answer?" asked Mary, now totally confused by the turn of conversation.

"An answer about what to do next," said Halee.

"Yes, just as we do, ask Allah for help," said Ahmed. "You ask angels. Perhaps it's similar."

"You two are bonkers, blooming mad," said Mary sitting back on the wooden chair, hugging the briefcase. "We're being stalked by a bunch of foreigners ..." "Kiwis," said Halee.

"Whoever. We're being stalked and they could be after our lives or Sam's life or something," said Mary, bringing the conversation back to reality. "Look, Ahmed, I don't want to say anything against your religion but this is hardly the time to be talking to God."

"So, Miss Collins, when do we talk to God? When we don't need Him?" asked Ahmed gently. He looked at Halee and they smiled to each other.

"Look Miss Collins, we're stuck in this Turkish restaurant and we need to get out and we don't know how or where to go next, safely," said Halee, looking steadily into Mary's eyes. Safak brought a pitcher of water and three glasses and then disappeared as quickly as he'd arrived. "Maybe if we just sit and pray, in our own different ways, something might happen. I don't know ... it costs nothing and, well, what else can we do here?"

"Praying? You think Allah or God or angels will just lift us out of here or something?" asked Mary, her voice rising as she fought to keep the other two idiots on the ground.

"Praying does not change Allah, Miss Collins. It changes us," said Ahmed quietly.

"Oh I give up!" said Mary, exasperated but without an immediate alternative to sitting and wishing on angels. She just wanted to cry. Nothing, absolutely nothing, was working out as it should. She thought of saying the Black's Prayer to herself and immediately felt embarrassed for some reason. The other two were silent, holding hands with their eyes closed. She put her hands over each of theirs, across the table and remembered all the times she'd asked for God's help and He hadn't delivered.

"Hey, I know!" said Mary, a little too loudly as the simplest of ideas struck. She wondered why she hadn't thought of it before. "I could call my brother to pick us up and we could stay in the hotel he's at with his two visitors!"

"Sshhh, Miss Collins, and yes, great idea. Phone him," said Ahmed. "But do try to be quiet. They don't want restaurant patrons to know others are out here. It arouses suspicions as to what else could be going on."

"Right. I'll call him from the toilet," said Mary.

Ahmed went through to the restaurant and explained what they wanted to do and that it would help get them out of there. Mary was allowed to go back through the restaurant and into the toilet to call Angus.

Half an hour later Angus sat in the back, between the two women while Ahmed drove and John Maranui sat in the passenger seat for insurance purposes – he had hired the car but Ahmed knew the London streets better. Two dark men in front and three white people in the back.

"Och aye, it's so good to see ye though I never thought it would be at midnight on a secret mission of yers!" said Angus with a huge grin.

"Angus, I've never seen you so excited," said Mary, seeing her brother behaving like a Mexican jumping bean.

"Oh aye, seems like we fit like ball bearings into whatever groove we find ourselves," said Angus. "Home's a quiet groove, work's a noisy, swearing groove and here ... hey, I don't know. I don't have a groove; it's all new and strange." He chuckled and watched the lights excitedly as they drove by.

"Aye and it's good to see you too, little brother," said Mary, smiling.

"Aye, and ye know the technology's amazing here," said Angus. "John let me drive from home, some of the way – gave him a break – and this nat sav ..."

"Sat nav, Angus," said John, smiling from the front seat.

"Oh aye, like I said, this nat sav thing here tells you where to go, what side to drive on, when you've stuffed up and what to do when you do ... everything!" said Angus. "It's amazin', just amazin'."

"Aye, Angus, you're like a kid with a room full of toys," said Mary, grabbing his hand affectionately.

"So what's with this get-up, Sis?" asked Angus. "Ye've not turned butch on us have ye?"

"Butch? No of course I haven't!" said Mary, offended. The feelings of losing her femininity – her hair, her dresses, her playfulness – to the world of insurance resurfaced immediately. She had though they had been banished forever, in her busyness and her gruffness but, damn it, they were still there. "Ouch, sorry Sis! I didn't mean to offend ye ... just jokin'," said Angus, obviously sensing her discomfort.

"Ah, it's just this business world – a girl's got to act like a man to make it and, here I am, wearing a bloody suit ... aah, sorry Ahmed, it's a nice suit but I'm not a man," said Mary as Angus held her hand uncharacteristically. "I suppose I just get sick of being in a man's world, in men's clothes, fighting for my life all the time ... or so it seems." She forced a smile between the tears that had started. "I do miss being a girl, doing girly things, being treated like a girl. But then, what's others to do if I ponce around in men's suits?"

"So what's the suit for?" asked Angus, softly, uncertainly.

"Ah, well, it's a long story, oh brother of mine, but the short version is that we had to pick up this briefcase from a chap and he didn't want anyone to know who was taking it and so I'm ... Halee and I are in disguise," said Mary, feeling a little calmer. "You see, she doesn't usually dress like a tramp!" "A tramp? Miss Collins, more decorum, please!" said Halee, laughing.

# The Mansion Attack

*Tuesday, 13th March 2012, 3.51 p.m.*

Arthur wasn't sure why he felt the need to stop so strongly. "I think we need to stop here, Dominik," he said.

"But we not there now, Mr Arthur," said Dominik, not slowing down. "Long drive to go yet." "Dominik, stop, please Dominik, stop, just here," said Arthur, his anxiety rising.

"But we not there ..."

"Dominik, I insist! Stop! Now!" ordered Arthur, unsure how to get through to this large, determined man. "Oh yes, thanks!" he said as the van skidded to a halt on the gravel driveway. Arthur thanked his lucky stars for seatbelts as he was thrown forward.

"Are you alright back there, love?" asked Arthur as his consciousness expanded from his own little world of survival to that of others.

"Uh, yes, I think so," said Joan, shuffling and groaning a little in the back. Then he realised someone was rapping on Dominik's window. Dominik lowered the window.

"What the hell do you think you're doing, stopping like that?" demanded Martin.

"Martin, sshhh, keep the noise down," whispered Arthur urgently.

"But you've dented my car. That's just bloody irresponsible ..." said Martin as Dominik grabbed his collar and yanked his head in the car window.

"Mr Arthur said me to stop. Mr Arthur said you to shut up," said Dominik as if speaking to a child.

"We in emergency so you shut up and we fix up car at later time. You understand?" "Orghhh," said Martin, trying to speak with a restricted neck.

"Good! You be quiet and alert and listen to Mr Arthur, hey?" inquired Dominik.

"Uh, yeah, sorry but ..." said Martin, as Dominik let him go.

"But sshhh, Martin!" whispered Arthur. "Be quiet and listen ... and look." There were two cars at the mansion as well as two men parading back and forwards. "Can we hide these vehicles here, Dominik?"

"Yes, behind hedge. Follow me, Martin," said Dominik.

Martin dashed back to his car and both vehicles were soon concealed from the mansion, behind a hedge just off the driveway. Arthur checked that everyone was ready and, just as they were to move off, another car appeared.

"That's Amanda!" said Joan, leaping out in front of Amanda's car, waving her to where their cars were parked. Amanda was wearing civilian clothes under a heavy jacket. Arthur wondered whether she had any police equipment under the jacket as Joan explained to Amanda why the police had not been called.

As Dominik led them on a winding path and behind immaculately trimmed hedges, the maze and from tree to tree, it seemed eerily different, quieter than it had been that morning. Then he realised there were no gardeners around and no machinery noises. They must have stopped work early for some reason. The only sound, apart from his drumming heart and the panting around him, was the crunching of gravel as the two men sauntered to and fro in front of the colonnaded steps in front of the mansion.

"I think we need to go round the back, Dominik," whispered Arthur as he tapped Dominik on the back.

"I think this too, Mr Arthur," said Dominik, stopping to confer. Arthur bumped into him and then heard two more *oofs* as more bumping-into-others occurred down the line.

"Damn! My glasses!" said Martin, two people behind Arthur.

"Martin, do be quiet!" whispered Arthur urgently.

"But they're my Bolé glasses, bloody squashed!" said Martin, quieter now. "Sorry ..." "Amanda, can you please come up the front," whispered Arthur, waving her forward.

"Yes?" she asked as she crept forward.

"Perhaps you stay just behind Dominik; it might be important for you to identify those chaps over there," whispered Arthur, pointing to the two men in front of the mansion, apparently guarding it. He wondered why he suddenly thought of this. "They may relate to your investigation."

"Mmm, good thinking, Arthur," whispered Amanda, smiling. Arthur noticed her right hand went to her belt, under the left side of her jacket. He wondered even more about what she might have under that heavy jacket. He shuddered in the warm afternoon sunlight.

"Everyone else alright?" whispered Arthur, looking back down the line of the smiling, nodding people. Joan seemed to be a little out of breath, wiping sweat from her brow, but he knew about her determination when pushed into a corner. Toby was looking remarkably calm, almost meditative, seemingly untroubled by his trussed-up shoulder. What an interesting bunch of saboteurs, Arthur thought ... The Magnificent Seven came to mind as a name. So did the Seven Swashbucklers.

"Right, Dominik, let's go," whispered Arthur with unaccustomed authority.

They started off and, just as quickly, stopped and Arthur realised they'd come to the end of the hedge and they were about to step into the open, with occasional trees dotting the expansive lawn.

"We need make running to side of house," whispered Dominik. "How we not be seen?"

"Everyone find stones," whispered Amanda to everyone. "The bigger the better."

Everyone looked puzzled but Toby and Martin set to picking out flint stones from the perfectlyweeded soil. They came up to her with a handful each.

"You keep your stones, Martin, and I'll take yours, aah ..." whispered Amanda.

"I'm Toby," said Toby.

"Thanks Toby, I'm Amanda," whispered Amanda, smiling and taking his stones. "When I give the word, we'll throw them over there, past those guys, Martin, and then we'll make a dash for the side of the house. Right?"

Everyone nodded. Martin, a happy, glazed look in his eyes and Amanda, serious and composed, braced themselves.

"One at a time, quickly, and as far as you can," she whispered to Martin. "One, two, three!" A volley of stones flew over the other side of the park grounds and thudded to the ground. The two guards turned suddenly and rushed towards the sound as the Seven Swashbucklers dashed across the open space and crashed, one by one, against the tall plastered wall of the west side, bumping into each other, smiling and panting like a group of naughty school children.

Given that anyone with a modicum of common sense will realise that stones landing must have arrived from somewhere not in the sky, the guards quickly surmised which direction these mystery stones flew from. As this realisation took effect, fractionally slower for them than the average toddler, they turned, looked at each other quizzically, pointed in various directions, grunted intelligently and then ran back in the approximate direction from which said stones may have originated. They stopped at the front steps, like returning homing pigeons, uncertain whether to leave their accustomed nest or to venture on. This second option seemed like a good one so they took off again in the same approximate direction they were headed.

Thankfully, the Seven Swashbucklers had departed this particular spot, thirty seconds before, and they were now dashing along the west wall, trying not to bump into each other, not always with success. They all attempted to follow Dominik's lead, crouching below windows and dodging around topiary trees – again, not always with success as sharp shrubbery impacted with soft skin, bringing forth *oomphs* and *aahs*. Soon an alcove presented itself and they followed Dominik into its small, shaded sanctuary, just as the two guards reached the corner of the house. Difficult though it is to pant madly with no sound at all, they all managed it with moderate success as Dominik struggled with the solid oak door with its rusty, medieval ironmongery. Opening the door was relatively easy for a man of Dominik's strength. Opening it quietly was another matter as rust, unaccustomed to moving, screamed its discordance into the sunlit gardens.

The guards heard the graunch of metal and looked at each other as if to say, with one accord, "Well, do we run after that sound or, like the stones, realise it's a ruse and run the other way?" No immediate answer emanated from God, the gardens or any other source and so they faltered, unable, it seems, to consider the possibility of one remaining and the other investigating the sudden sound. Siamese twins had nothing on these two for synchronised movement.

These precious moments of indecision gave the alcove-huddlers just the time they needed to squeeze through the small opening Dominik was able to effect and to allow the door to be slammed shut and the inner bolt secured, barring further entry from outside.

This second creaky slam and lock-sliding confirmed to the sweating security guards that they should investigate quickly. As one, their legs took them across the lawn to the source of the sound, their fine paunches wobbling gracefully ahead of them while, in some remote corner of their brains, arose the possibility that they were too late and would be in trouble. Footprints – many footprints – scarred the mossy floor of the alcove and the door would not budge.

Of course, as we all know, there is nothing in this world to fear except that which passes through our minds, kindly termed *imagination*. Had the guards known what a motley crew (and the small number of said motley crew) they were pursuing, they would have felt quite confident in themselves. However, since said motley crew existed only in their minds, they were very scared and very uncertain. Conjuring up a large group of savage killers, the guards then had to guess whether the consequences of confronting these viscious foes would be worse than the consequences would be from their guv'nor (as they called him) if he discovered their dereliction of duty and let intruders slip through their tight security ... not that big words like *dereliction* and *consequences* actually entered the frantic minds of these two men with growing fear and shrieking brains. Their thought processes probably went more along the lines of, "Oh bugger, do we scarper, save getting' our heads busted or do we tell the guv'nor we bin rumbled and then git our heads busted?"

A further thought may well have been that three weeks in the security industry was quite enough for two long-time supporters of the bar of South Norwood's *Hogs Head* pub. They weren't men of action but they needed to do something ... anything. So, like homing pigeons in a quandary, they headed home to the front of the building, considerably slower than they had left said building frontage. They were, of course, possessed of mobile phones but were loathe to use them till they had fully weighed up the pros and cons of getting their heads busted as against scarpering to the nearest pub and then looking for a job with more certainty and safety. They finally plumped for sticking to their current job and, after a brief conversation in human terms (but long in Cro-Magnon terms) they decided to continue walking backwards and forwards in front of the big house as if they had not stopped doing it – flying stones and creaking doors had never happened and when (or if) the intruders were found inside, they'd fake surprise with such style they'd be forgiven ... or even promoted. Hope is a wonderful thing.

Meanwhile, in the green, carpeted hall, with an intricately carved, plaster ceiling eighteen feet above, seven uncertain individuals took stock and wondered, in unison, just what drew them to be in such a position. With some different decisions made (or not made) only hours before, they could all be comfortably and safely doing what they'd always done, whatever that was. But, as we know, life turns on a tuppenny piece (or a dime if you're American, which none of them were) and here they were, about to attempt the saving of someone none of them knew well (some not at all) for a cause uncertain in a situation unimaginable from people with unknown intentions, abilities and armaments. The guards were probably outside the door and, by now, their employers inside would presumably know of the seven's presence. Going back was out of the question and, considering what their imaginations were creating about the events inside the mansion, going forward was also out ... but probably less out then going back. They could rely on Dominik for knowing his way round the corridors but none of them knew which one led to the captive (they all presumed) Lord and Lady Atkinson.

All was silent; eerily silent for a house that employed a dozen serving people.

Arthur found himself the centre of attention as they huddled round him, obviously expecting an answer to their uncertainty.

"I guess the most obvious thought is that, whatever they're after, they'll imagine it's in the Black's office," whispered Arthur as everyone nodded at his sage assessment of the situation though he wondered why a wild guess should be interpreted as a sage assessment.

"I know way to office," said Dominik, quietly. "But we must go past main drawing room and foyer at front. We be seen."

"We could be seen here, too," whispered Amanda urgently. "Where can we hide for a mo while we decide?"

"Ah yes, this way," whispered Dominik, moving off and waving them on with him. He slipped around the corner to the left and motioned them into a small room filled with shelves of gardening equipment, wall hooks groaning with coats and umbrellas and a floor littered with muddy boots of all kinds. "Dis the coat room. For servants," said Dominik, ducking his head under the low doorway.

"Shut the door so no one hear us."

In their cone of silence, amid the smell of rubber, mud and wet leather, they looked at one another.

"So, the only way from here to the office is through the most public part of the house?" asked Amanda.

"Yes, that only way," said Dominik, emphatically.

"But these old places have all sorts of secret alleyways and hidden doors," said Martin. "Are you sure there's no secret way to get there?"

"Secret way ... secret way," said Dominik as if savouring the words. Arthur was sure he could see the marbles moving round in the machinery of Dominik's mind as it churned over the idea. "Yes, I hear of secret way. I forgot."

"And it will take us to the office?" asked Martin hopefully.

"Not sure, maybe," said Dominik as another marble dropped into place. "I thinking what they say."

"So there might be a way in?" asked Toby, struggling to keep his strapped-up arm from touching people or the room, with little success, considering their confinement. "Perhaps it's into the back of the office."

"Ah yes, back office," said Dominik frowning and Arthur was sure the next marble could be seen, teetering on the edge, ready to drop.

"So what room backs onto the back of the office?" asked Toby, logically.

"Ah, let me think," said Dominik, drawing an imaginary picture with one finger on the other palm, as the marble hovered closer to the edge. Suddenly his face lit up. "Ah yes! It through kitchen so Black can have affair with servant girls!"

"Good Black, not Lord Atkinson!" exclaimed Arthur, appalled.

"No, no, old Blacks, hundreds years ago," said Dominik, laughing quietly. "We go out to passage, turn left then left again and we in kitchen."

"So, how about you go first, alert the kitchen staff and make sure we're safe," suggested Joan, trying to be logical in a dangerous situation. Arthur could sense her discomfort and admired the way she was dealing with it all.

"It's okay Joan, I'll go with Dominik and clear the way," said Amanda, apparently relishing the danger more than Joan was. "You all wait one minute and then follow us." The two left and the rest waited.

"Well, that's sixty seconds and no explosive or disturbing noises," said Arthur, unable to move as fear gripped him as never before.

"Come on Arthur," said Joan in her fascinatingly decisive way. "Let's go!"

"Oh, ah, yes, I suppose we should," said Arthur, still unable to move his leaden feet and churning stomach. He felt bile rising and wiped his sweaty forehead.

"It's okay Dad," said Martin, obviously noticing his father's discomfort. "We have an old man, two old women, a cripple and me. Perhaps I go first!" Arthur sensed Martin's bravado covered a deep fear, like his, and he was thankful to be led by his son, in this instance.

"Are you alright, Dottie?" asked Arthur, realising she had said nothing for a long time.

"Oh yes Arthur, it's just like going on night duty," said Dottie, matter-of-factly. "You never know what to expect and, whatever it is, you're on your own and you have to deal with it. Only, this time, there's seven of us. 'It's a doddle, Doctor,' as we used to say." Everyone smiled and Arthur felt a little better, somehow.

They followed Martin, thankful to be out of the small, stuffy room but not thankful for where they might be heading to.

"I'll go last," said Arthur, feeling gallant and scared.

As the Fearsome Five (or is that the Fearful Five?) trundled up the corridor, going as fast as they could without bumping into antique dressers or each other, Arthur suddenly stopped. He fancied he heard a noise, somewhere. The fear was growing in his mind much faster, he knew, than it would have in the mind of Mr Bond. But knowing that didn't help one bit.

"Come on Arthur!" whispered Dottie urgently, motioning him on. "No time for wavering now!"

"Yes, yes," said Arthur, knowing her logic but, illogically, his body wanted to stay rooted to the spot to see who was coming. Was seeing the unknown person scarier than not knowing? He could not decide.

"Arthur!" demanded Dottie, grabbing his arm. "Get a grip. Come on!" "Uh, yes, yes," said Arthur, forcing his legs to move again.

"Stop right there!" someone bellowed from round a corner, twenty feet away, just as Arthur was turning into the alcove leading to the kitchen. He froze at the corner and could see the others through the kitchen doorway, frantically motioning him in. He couldn't do it. Someone had nailed his feet to the floor. He just couldn't move.

"Where do you think you're going?" demanded the angry, gravelly voice, closer this time. The voice sounded strangely like his father's and memories flooded back. He knew his father would grab him by the collar, drag him into the scullery and give him yet another beating, from which it might take days for the pain to go. He whimpered and felt helpless, humiliated.

"Arthur, love, hurry up!" whispered Joan from the kitchen.

He didn't know if it was Joan's voice or the word *love* but his mind snapped out of the Newcastle coalminer's cottage of his childhood and returned to Lord Atkinson's stately home, forty years later. His feet became unstuck and he could have dived into the kitchen but the voice, which he now dared to look at, was only ten yards from him. He couldn't escape to the kitchen without endangering the others. He straightened his body and his mind.

"I, Sir, am here to help Lord Atkinson," said Arthur, in his best Bond voice. It all felt most unreal. "And thank you for alerting me to where you are holding him." He marched towards the man of the voice – slightly shorter than Arthur but twice as wide with a paunch, grey grizzly hair and thick grey eyebrows.

"Stop right there!" said the man, not lowering his voice. "You're not going anywhere."

"I am going to see Lord Atkinson right now," said Arthur, sounding more confident than he felt. He focused on his goal and took a bold step forward.

"Stop right there, schmuck!" said the man, hesitating, wrapping his eyebrows round his nose.

"I am sorry, sir, but I am here to do what I need to do, not what you tell me," said Arthur, feeling like a robot. The man put his palm against Arthur's chest, blocking his way. "Unhand me, whoever you are, or I shall be forced to call the others in." Arthur put his hand into his pocket as if fingering a dangerous device and not the mobile phone he felt.

"What others?" asked the man, his bellow having fallen to a menacing question.

"Force me to push this button and you shall find out soon enough," said Arthur, without expression. "Now let me pass." His phone beeped as he accidentally pushed one of the phone's buttons and both of them jumped.

"No, no, mate, let's just talk about this, huh?" suggested the rock of a man, recovering quicker than Arthur. "Who the hell are you and how did you get in here?"

"I should ask you that, sir," said Arthur, attempting to take a step forward. "But I don't actually care. We're here to help Lord Atkinson and that's what we shall do."

"We? Who's this we, mate?" Asked the man, his hand still on Arthur's chest but with less force now.

"If I push this button now you will soon discover who we are," suggested Arthur with more nerve than he felt. There was a crash in the kitchen, followed by a *bugger* and the man-rock stepped back a little. "Looks like they're on their way. Now let me pass."

"Like hell you do!" said the man, obviously making a decision. "I got you and we'll get the others one by one, later, huh." He grabbed Arthur by the collar and all those shaming memories of childhood flooded back. His body became as a small boy's, in the power of his ferocious father and he stumbled along behind the man as they headed down the corridor.

In the lives of most of us there is a moment (or several moments for the particularly brave ones) when we actually dare to do what we've always dreamed of doing, but have previously held ourselves back from. This was one of Arthur's moments.

During the many unexpected and painful times Arthur's father dragged him down the hall to the scullery to take his rage out on his son, Arthur fantasised about revenge. He imagined, most often, of tripping his father up and then either pouncing on him or running away ... forever. This fantasy consumed much of his young life and, in his mind, he tried countless ways of foiling his father and, eventually, dreamed the perfect technique – one that required little strength and caused maximum mayhem. His fertile mind imagined great and simple success but he never had the nerve to try it. Till now.

As this rock of a man dragged him down the hall, stumbling to keep up, his mind flashed back to the countless times he berated himself for not getting back at his father and, as his anger rose, and his technique came to mind, he acted. As the man's right foot went forward, Arthur tapped his left foot to the right and the man fell flat on his face, taking a Grecian vase and an oak hat-stand down with him, with a noisy clatter of breaking pottery and timber. Arthur had always imagined his father letting go at this stage but the man didn't and Arthur fell too. The feelings from years of humiliation, long suppressed, now burst out and Arthur fell, purposely, heavily on top of the stone-man. He rammed his forearm into the brute's neck. The man let go to protect himself and Arthur leapt up and kicked him in the side with the strength that fifty years of pent-up rage could muster. He kicked and he kicked and he kicked till his strength ran out. He leaned back against the wall exhausted, strangely happy and quite disgusted with himself. The man lay still, with shards of pottery and furniture around him.

If Arthur had been used to such activities and exertions, he would have been alert to the approach of the other man, sneaking up beside him. But he wasn't.

# The Happy Brother

*Tuesday, 13th March 2012, 11.46 p.m.*

John had phoned ahead to Belinda and when they arrived another room had been booked. With simple efficiency John arranged that Halee and Mary take one room and Angus and Ahmed take the third. After introductions all round they took the lift and then John and Belinda excused themselves.

"Ah, young love," said Mary wistfully.

"Tired love, more like," said Belinda as John led her to their room. Ahmed pleaded fatigue and went into the adjoining room.

"Look Mary, it's been a long day but would ye be wantin' to share a wee dram a'fore bed?" asked Angus. "I've a bottle of best malted in me room."

"Oh aye, why not, Angus," said Mary, smoothing her furrowed brow. "But you'd better fetch it out of your room – Ahmed's Muslim and doesn't drink. Bring it to our room."

"Look, Miss Collins, I'm knackered," said Halee. "You two have some catching up to do so how about I sleep with Ahmed ... oh, you know what I mean, in his room and you two share the other one. They're separate beds aren't they?"

"Yes, twin rooms," said Mary. They knocked on Ahmed's door and Halee suggested she sleep in the bed next to him while Angus and Mary shared the room next door. Ahmed's mouth opened and shut and a deep redness crept out from inside his swarthy face. Mary had never seen him lost for words before, this suave, gentle, dynamic man.

"Ahmed, I'm not sure what you're thinking," said Halee with a tired smile, "but I will do my best, my very best, to resist your gorgeous body. You should be safe."

"Oh, ah, yes, of course," said Ahmed finding his voice at last, though uncertainly. "We can dress in the bathroom, I suppose, if you're alright with that."

"Actually, Ahmed, right now all I want to do is collapse into bed," said Halee. "I don't care what I'm wearing and I don't care who sees whatever it is. Angus, get your stuff and be gone will ya. Let this girl get some sleep."

Angus grabbed his few possessions and left with Mary who saw Ahmed standing there, apparently unable to move.

"So, little brother, what prompted you to come down here?" asked Mary as she sat on the bed with her whisky in hand. "First time to the big city, aye?"

"Dunno lass, it just sort of happened before I knew it was happening, if ye catch me drift," said Angus, sitting back in the only chair in the room. "John and Belinda turned up in town. Their car was gone and they had a contact at an insurance company in London and Mr Fordyce knew you were in insurance and so I was hauled in and, hell, I dunno. Those Kiwis just sorta' inspired me to do what I've never done before. And here I am."

"What did they say to you?" asked Mary, intrigued.

"Don't know if it's what they said or what they did," said Angus, smiling through his puzzled look. He took a large sip of his whiskey, closing his eyes and sighing deeply, as if it was the elixir of life. "They just seem to have no ties, no obligations. They want to do something and they just do it. No explanations, no excuses, they just do it."

"Sounds a bit irresponsible," suggested Mary.

"Not irresponsible, really. They care for people and are as honest as a die," said Angus, looking at

Mary for the first time. "But if they need to act they just do ... ah, I dunno, I can't explain it. Anyway, lass, something about them got me thinking about me life and what I've achieved."

"But I thought you were happy doing what you've always done," said Mary. "I thought you'd be welding and drinking ales and watching football for the rest of your life."

"So did I, Mary lass, so did I," said Angus, sitting back, looking at the ceiling. He quickly looked back at Mary. "John asked me what I was born for. Ye know, what me purpose is in being here. I hadn't thought of that before and I got a bit shitty with him. But it got me thinkin' and I thought .... well, I suppose I've thought about it before, a million times and kinda' pretended it didn't matter – have another drink, tell another lie, another day of work – just get on with it, getting busy ..." "But you weren't really happy?" asked Mary, feeling his rising sadness.

"No Mary, not happy at all but never wanted to admit it," said Angus, wiping his eyes and taking another sip of whiskey. "Actually, to be brutally honest, I was a bit of a sad bastard and, as John suggested, my getting shitty at him was actually me getting shitty at myself for wasting my time." He stopped talking to wipe his eyes again with his big calloused hand.

"Oh little brother," said Mary standing up. She sat on his knee and hugged him. His tears burst forth and he let the cry out – the cry so long held back from years of denial and frustration.

Mary waited till his sobs died down. "So, here you are, little brother, in this big London town, crying in the arms of your big sister. What a pair we are!"

"What? You're not happy either?" asked Angus, looking surprised as Mary got off his knee and sat back on the bed. "The big flash job, the money, the poncy flat in the middle of town – I thought you had it all."

"Well, not really unhappy, Angus, as I have my work but love keeps avoiding me," said Mary. "It sneaks up when I'm not looking and then buggers off when it gets near."

"Ye and me both, Mary lass," said Angus, smiling again, brightening up the room. "What a sad, sorry mess we've got ourselves into."

"You might be right, Angus but I suspect we're not the only dysfunctional ones," said Mary, raising her glass to him.

"Yeah, cheers to all the sad bastards of the world!" said Angus raising his glass and leaning over to clink it with hers. "Anyway, I'm here, I've broken out of me little cage, I have no idea where to now and I'm scared and excited but, in a way, I don't really care. Does that make sense?"

"Aye it does – sounds just like I felt when I first left home to come down here ... and it all worked out. It's not perfect but I'm alive and reasonably sane, I think," said Mary, cheerfully.

"Yeah, when I moaned about all the reasons not to do something different, Belinda said that the worst that could go wrong is that I could fail and what would that mean? I wouldn't get rabies, my bum wouldn't fall off and I'd still be alive and kicking," said Angus, laughing at the memory of that conversation. "I'll actually survive, no matter what I chose to do."

"Yeah, I guess we all do, don't we," said Mary, musing over the recent dangers she'd survived.

"Not guess, Mary. We absolutely *do* survive," said Angus with a determination she'd not seen before. "Whatever decision we make, as Belinda put it, we're all looked after so, really, nothing matters. So I did it – took leave from the job, left me home, left me mates and here I am. I can always go back if I want to."

"And what did Mum and Dad think of their rebel son, off on his adventures to unknown lands?" asked Mary.

"Well, Mum didn't say much, just grumbled as usual," said Angus. "Dad was dead against me going. Said I'd regret it and predicted all sorts of painful and immoral things. I actually think he'll be missing me but couldn't say so."

"You'll be right, Angus, for you've always been there," said Mary. "It'll be a wrench for them. And now I've finished me whisky, Angus, I really do need some sleep." She got up and pulled the bed clothes back. "We can talk more in the morning."

"Aye lass, lots more to talk about," said Angus, finishing his drink. "Good night, Mary."

# An Inside Job

*Tuesday, 13ᵗʰ March 2012, 4.33 p.m.*

As the shadows of late afternoon stretched their darkening fingers across the expansive lawns and solid walls, the house was quiet. Unusually quiet. Deathly quiet.

Two men were unconscious and the plump bodyguard was standing over them, as if wondering what the heck to do next. He'd never actually hit anybody before and he wondered, in panic, if he'd gone too far. He stood and gazed at the prone figures, uncertainly.

In the kitchen the six had been stopped by the yelling, crashing, grunting and thumping in the corridor through the wall. They looked at one another and seemed to have the same confused mind. Do they rush out and help Arthur and be injured themselves? Do they creep out to find a band of thugs waiting for them? Do they continue through to the office and find the thugs there? The unknown, as always, posed a greater threat than the known and they didn't know much – where they were, who they were saving, why they were saving him/her/them and who was waiting round dark corners for them all.

"Time to move!" whispered Amanda decisively, taking out her pistol.

"Amanda! You can't go shooting people!" pleaded Martin in a hoarse whisper, his eyes nearly popping out.

"And your idea is?" Amanda asked quietly.

"Oh, ah, yes, I see …" said Martin. "But we can't have guns … they kill."

"And someone's not dead already?" whispered Amanda, pushing past Martin. "And who's going to be next?"

"Oh, gosh, but we can't just … let's talk about this," pleaded Martin, going quite pale.

"Dominik, you take the rest through to the office and around," whispered Amanda. "I'll go this way."

"But you can't just go … you know … shooting people," whispered Martin, grabbing Amanda's arm.

"So, you come with me, mate," said Amanda, shaking off his grip. "You can keep me from killing someone." She continued out the door to the corner.

"I'll come with you two," said Toby, launching himself out of indecision mode.

Joan held up her hands and smiled to Dottie as if to say, 'whatever we do, it's a mess'. Dottie nodded and smiled back, grimly, and they followed Dominik to the back of the kitchen, to a door that must have remained closed for many years. Dominik grimaced as the door creaked and groaned, despite his efforts to open it quietly. He opened it enough for them to slip through, one by one. The three found themselves in the dark, but for light sneaking through the half-opened door from the kitchen. The uneven cobbles and the cobwebs impaired their progress in the shoulder-width passage. They scrambled along sideways and it was soon obvious that Dominik had no idea where to find the door into the office.

"There's got to be a torch somewhere," said Joan, awkwardly squeezing herself back into the kitchen. Dottie followed her and they rummaged through drawers and cupboards as quietly as they could. In the corridor they heard a man's shout, Amanda's yell, a thud and then silence. Joan's instinct was to rush out to help Arthur but her logical mind told her to leave it to the professionals who would help him more than she could. Her prayers went out to him as she returned to their search for light. They found candles and an old box of matches.

Back in their dark, dank passage, they fumbled with matches, lit three candles and handed one to Dominik. It was good to see a little more till Joan spied a large spider, then another, then another and she desperately tried to hold back a rising bile as she saw this space between walls was overrun by insects of all kinds. She would have leant back against the wall to steady herself but realised she'd be leaning into nests of spiders and other unmentionable critters. It was only Dominik's sigh of relief – she hoped it was relief – as he was scratching around the wall, ahead of her. There was a rattle of metal – a chain? – and bumping on wood.

"Ugh! Door is bloody locked!" said Dominik, more to himself that the two women. "Oh, sorry about swear. Sorry."

"Swear all you bloody well like!" whispered Dottie, obviously anxious to escape the wall cavity.

"I think I make like a bull," said Dominik, chuckling. "Stand back. May be splinters." He groaned and thumped and Joan braced herself for what was to come, whatever that was. The door was obviously an obstinate one and withstood many grunts and thumps from Dominik, who had little room to swing his weight in. Suddenly their cavity was flooded with light and Dominik fell out of the cavity and into a room. Dottie and Joan followed soon after, relieved to be out of their confinement. As three dirty, cobwebbed people popped out into the room, they were momentarily blinded by the light. As their eyes grew accustomed to the light, they realised the large office was filled with people – presumably the Lord and Lady and their servants, gardeners, cooks, livery staff and so on – all tied up and looking at them expectantly.

As Amanda looked around the corner she could see mayhem amid the lavishly decorated Victorian corridor. There was broken wood and ceramics piled about and, amongst that, two prone men. One was Arthur and her heart went out to that gentle man. She resisted the strong urge to rush to him for, amid the bodies and the wreckage, stood a rotund man dressed as a security guard. And that's what he did – stood. His back was to her and he wasn't moving except for his head which was nodding a little as if he was talking to himself. His lack of movement confused her and she waited till she knew how to approach him.

Martin bumped into her, knocking her into the passage.

"Oh, sorry," said Martin.

The man turned and then a blur passed by her as Toby, she realised, flew at the tubby guard, feet first. Amanda yelled but too late. Toby had felled the man and sat astride him with his good hand at the man's throat. There was a thump beside her and she saw Martin sprawled on the floor. There had been no shot and nothing of his seemed to be broken so she surmised he'd fainted. She dashed to help Toby, grabbing the man's limp hands and hand-cuffed him. The guard looked terrified and seemed unable to resist.

"Please Miss, I'm sorry, I'm sorry ..." the guard said, babbling as Toby let his throat go. "I never done this before ... I didn't mean to ... I promise ... I didn't mean to ..."

"Ah, shut up!" commanded Toby, still sitting on the man's chest as he held his strapped-up arm with the other hand, grimacing.

"You okay Toby?" whispered Amanda.

"Don't know. It might have popped out again," said Toby in obvious pain. "But I'm alive and conscious. Let's see to these chaps first."

"Ow, these handcuffs hurt!" complained the guard as Amanda hauled him to his feet.

"Hurt? You ain't seen nothing yet, mate!" said Amanda, smiling grimly. "You check the others while I tie this whining baby up." She deftly swung the guard around and had him sitting on the floor with his hand-cuffed hands over his head, hooked over the brass door handle.

"Wow! That was neat," said Toby as he leant down to feel Arthur's pulse. "Yep, he's alive."

"And so's this one," said Amanda. "Quite a loss of blood. We need to patch him up somehow."

"I need some help here," said Toby, struggling with one arm. Between them they got Arthur into the recovery position. "His breathing's faint but regular and he's got a huge gash and bruise on the side of his head."

"Yeah, really need a medic," said Amanda quietly, continuing to look around like a fox at its quarry, scanning constantly for predators.

"Oh, of course, Dottie's a nurse. She fixed me up!" said Toby quietly. "Hell, she's gone the other way."

There was a groan up the passage and they both realised they'd forgotten Martin, who was rousing himself with obvious confusion ... and perhaps embarrassment, thought Amanda.

"Aha, Martin, can you see if you can find Dottie and get her back here?" asked Toby quietly as he leapt up to help Martin stand up.

"What? Who? Ah, Dottie?" asked Martin, holding his head, looking confused.

"We need medical help and Dottie's the closest," explained Toby, steadying Martin. "And keep your voice down."

"But I need medical help. I've got a sore head ... and my knee ..." said Martin with a little more clarity this time.

"Yes, but you can stand and walk," said Toby. "Look at Arthur – he's lost some blood and the other chap's lost a lot more," Martin started to stagger as he looked at the prone bodies and saw the blood. "Look, let's get you round the corner, away from that sight," said Toby, helping him into the kitchen and leaning him against a bench.

"Yeah, just don't like blood and stuff," said Martin, his pallid face beginning to fill with colour. "I ... I just never expected this. I didn't, you know."

"No, nor did we," said Toby. "Now, Arthur, your dad, needs medical help urgently. Can you see if you can find where the others went and get Dottie back here? And your mum too."

"Dad? He's the one on the floor isn't he! Oh hell!" said Martin, suddenly joining the dots. "Where'd they go? Through here?" he asked, indicating the open door.

"Probably. You find Dottie and we'll keep your father as comfortable as possible and make sure no others get to him ... or to us," said Toby.

"Others? Oh shit, I never thought of that!" said Martin, his eyes widening. "How many others are there?"

"We don't know. Just get Dottie, will you," said Toby, waving Martin on, obviously anxious to get back to the prone men and the trussed-up guard.

"Right ... yes," said Martin and, with a sudden aliveness, he went through the door into the tiny, dirty passage, now lighter for the other door being open a little. "Ugh, oh hell, it's dirty ..."

"Shut up Martin!" whispered Toby urgently. "We don't know who else is here."

"Oh, yes," said Martin as he eased himself along the narrow passage, trying not to get dirt on his business suit.

"Bloody pansy," muttered Toby as he shook his head, adjusted his painful arm and quickly returned to help Amanda.

"I'll just get something to clean these guys up," said Amanda. "Can you just keep an eye on them ... stop them doing gymnastics and stuff!" She dashed into the kitchen, filled a large bowl with warm water, grabbed a tea towel and two towels and returned to gently wash Arthur's bloody head. He showed no signs of waking but his pulse and breathing were steady, though weak. She then covered him with the two towels to help keep his body warmth up.

"You're a nurse *and* a cop!" said Toby with obvious admiration. "Anything I can do to help?"

"You could do the same with this other bloke here, if you like," said Amanda, pleased she had willing help. "Then I'll wash this stuff up when you get back. Best to have someone here all the time – you never know what's going to happen next!"

"Always one step ahead, aren't you," said Toby as he sauntered off to the kitchen. Amanda imagined that was a compliment and smiled for the first time that day. When Toby returned with a bowl of water and a rag, she took the bloody tea towel and water into the kitchen to clean up. As she returned, Toby was kneeling behind the solid hunk of a man, gingerly dabbing at the blood on his head and hand. She squatted in front of the man and discovered that his eyes were quivering and his body was twitching a little.

"This guy might be waking up," said Amanda, as the man groaned and moved his hand a little as Toby put it back down.

"Oh God!" she said, sitting back on her haunches. She looked at him closer and shook her head, disbelieving. She put her hand under his chin and gently lifted it a little, perhaps hoping the face would transform itself into one she hadn't seen before. It didn't. She lowered his chin slowly and squatted there on her haunches, indecisively. She looked across at Arthur, hoping there was something she could do for him ... hoping to delay her decision. There was nothing she could do for Arthur, unfortunately. Yes, she'd have to do something with this solid, grizzled hunk of a man she knew – the Assistant Commissioner, Special Operations, of the London Metropolitan Police, George Sanderson. How could she arrest and detain someone many levels her senior? There was no question he had attacked Arthur, who had defended himself and been knocked unconscious … or had he? She hadn't witnessed anything and so her current story was nothing but assumption. Besides, she wasn't in uniform and couldn't arrest him, except under a citizen's arrest. Also, she was carrying a police gun and handcuffs, out of uniform, and she wasn't sure of the consequences of that.

"So, why are you here?" she demanded of the portly guard with his hands still hooked over the door handle. "Did this man get you to do this?"

"Uh, yeah," said the guard groggily and Amanda realised that, with his overweightness and the awkward position he was in, he might not be faring too well.

"Yeah what?" demanded Amanda, needing answers quickly. "Who is he to you?"

"He's the guv'nor, Ma'am," said the guard. "He paid us, like, to look after him, to look after this place while he got a few things."

"What things?"

"Dunno. Papers and stuff that this Black fella' stole off 'a him," said the guard, squirming to make himself more comfortable, without success.

"And who knocked out that man? You?" asked Amanda, pointing to Arthur.

"Well, yeah, he attacked the guv'nor and I hear a crash an' I come in an' I thought the guv'nor was dead," said the guard candidly, perhaps eager to get it off his chest. "He's just knocked out … you know, alive, isn't he?"

"So you knocked him out?" asked Amanda, ignoring his question.

"Yeah, well, I panicked, like, coz I saw the guv'nor dead an' I thought this one here, he be brutal, like," said the guard, breathing heavily with sweat breaking out on his forehead.

"So you did him good, like, as you would say," said Amanda, finishing his sentence.

"Yeah, guess so. I jus' panicked and we knew we's in trouble coz we let those others get in. I knew we's in trouble already …" said the guard.

"We? You mean there's others here, working for this guv'nor?" asked Amanda, pointing at the prone, twitching body of the Assistant Commissioner.

"Yeah, jus' the two of us," said the guard. "The guv'nor said it'd be a quick an' easy job." "Where's the other guard?" asked Amanda, looking around warily.

"Dunno. He stayed outside, I suppose," said the guard, wriggling and trying to adjust his arms.

"So this man pays you to protect him, does he?" asked Amanda.

"Ah, yeah, he said he needs extra help an' so he hires people for short-term jobs," said the guard. "Cash only. We do building security at nights so we got the uniform and he thinks that scares people … oh, hell, you won't tell my company will ya? We not allowed to do moonlighting." His pained face took on an alarmed look.

"I can't promise anything, fella," said Amanda, knowing she'd have to immobilise the other guard before the area was safe. "Maybe I keep quiet about your moonlighting if you do what I say. Okay?" "Yes ma'am," said the guard, his face lightening up a little.

"So, all you have to do is call out to your friend outside. You'll have to yell," said Amanda, standing up. "Get him in here to help us all out and I'll go get the others. Start yelling!"

The guard started yelling, "Rocky, Rocky, get in here! I need your help! Hurry up Rocky!"

Amanda touched Toby on the shoulder and nodded towards the kitchen, to which she ran. Toby followed.

"Find something to tie the next guy up with, will ya," said Amanda, rummaging through drawers and cupboards, not quite knowing what might work. She soon found muslin bags, usually used for keeping meat in. "These will do," said Amanda as an idea started to form in her mind. "Why don't you go and kneel over that guy ... not Arthur, the other one and make sure he doesn't get away. I'll nab the other guard when he comes for you."

"So I'm the decoy?" asked Toby, smiling grimly as he ran his hand through his blonde hair. "You better not miss, young lady, or I'll have to beat you with whatever limbs I still have working!"

"It's a deal – I beat him or you beat me!" said Amanda, smiling and slapping Toby's good shoulder.

"Oh, careful, that jars, you bully," said Toby, striding out, holding his sore arm gingerly. Amanda sneaked up to the corner of the corridor and waited. She heard a distant door open and shut and, soon after, someone was asking, "Where are you, mate?" "Out in the passage," yelled the guard back.

Amanda could hear no footsteps on the thick carpet and made her move, based on gut feeling and guesswork, as to when the man would be over Toby. She reached the second guard just as he was about to kick an apparently oblivious Toby, kneeling beside the prone man. Amanda slipped one bag over the man's head and, as he faltered, struggling with an unexpected impediment, she grabbed his ankles and pulled them together, as good as any All Black tackler. He toppled and fell forward just as Toby rolled away and jumped up to plant his foot heavily between the man's shoulders, like a triumphant boxer. Amanda quickly tied his ankles together with a muslin bag and leapt upon his backside to claim his now-pinioned arms. Between them they managed to get his arms behind his back and tied up with another muslin bag.

It all happened so quickly there was hardly time for a sound, save the odd *oomph* and *argh* and the carpet and solid walls absorbed most of the sounds. They rolled the second, trussed-up guard off his guv'nor and let him lie there, panting surprised and embarrassed.

The man at the bottom of the little pile was stirred to life and started groaning. His hand went to his head, perhaps to feel for cuts, and Amanda knew she had to act.

"Quick, stop him moving!" commanded Amanda as she grabbed another muslin bag and trussed his wrists together behind his back, with a little help from Toby. She then did the same with his feet. "Right, we've got three we don't want moving and they can, while we've got one we want to move and he can't."

"Well, at least they won't move till the police get here," said Toby, smiling.

"The police are already here! If only you knew," said Amanda, looking at Toby and considering whether or not to say any more. "Look, I've just got to make a phone call. Can you keep an eye on these guys for a minute, please?" She went into the kitchen for privacy, dialled the number, spoke to Superintendent Hopkins at Scotland Yard and returned to the men.

As Amanda and Toby looked at each other, wondering what to do or say next, Arthur stirred and started to mumble. Amanda rushed over to him and knelt by his face. His lips were moving from time to time as if he was conversing with someone.

"Are you okay, Arthur?" asked Amanda quietly as she placed her hand gently on his forehead. "I'm listening."

"Maybe he's delusional, just raving ..." said Toby. "Sshhh!" said Amanda. "We're listening, Arthur."

"But he's just ..." said Toby.

"Shut up will ya!" said Amanda. "Give him a chance."

"He's frightened," said Arthur faintly, with a gentle smile across his face.

"Who's frightened?" asked Amanda, not sure she heard him right.

"Toby is. Toby is frightened," said Arthur quietly. Amanda had to bend close to his face to hear him.

"Toby is frightened of what?" asked Amanda, caressing his forehead gently.

"I'm not frightened. He's just ..." said Toby, stopping mid-sentence as Amanda's withering glare stopped him. He looked perturbed but he kept his mouth shut and shuffled a little closer to Amanda and Arthur as if daring himself to hear more.

"He's frightened of the love," said Arthur quietly, taking in a deliberate breath and his smile never leaving his face.

"The love?" asked Amanda, looking quizzically at Toby.

"The love he fears," whispered Arthur. "So he uses his own strength."

"His own strength?" asked Amanda, not sure whether she should look at Toby or not. Toby shuffled closer, intrigued and a little annoyed.

"His own strength ... not letting the love through," said Arthur weakly with the steady smile still on his face.

"The love?" asked Toby, intrigued and now kneeling next to Amanda.

"The love is power, is knowledge," said Arthur, panting a little as if he was tiring but had words he needed to get out. "Listen to the love inside. Amanda can teach listening."

"Listen?" asked Toby, now more sure than ever that Arthur was raving. But something invisible pulled him into Arthur's words.

"Amanda knows the listening," said Arthur. "She listens often."

"Arthur's right, Toby," said Amanda. "I know what he means, totally."

"When she listens to the love, she's not frightened," said Arthur, panting a bit but no strain showed on his face. "When she does, the love speaks its power. Life flows."

"Yes, when I do, things do flow," said Amanda. "It's effortless but I keep forgetting."

"Not forgetting," said Arthur in his hoarse whisper. "Not forget but not believe you deserve the power."

"Oh," said Amanda, not sure what to say.

"Nothing to say, just listen," said Arthur. "Listen to each other. Much power there." Amanda and Toby looked at each other uncertainly.

"I must go inside now," said Arthur, smiling uncertainly. "There is nothing to fear and I shall return." His lids slowly closed over his eyes and a deep and abiding silence filled their space.

As they stood up looking at Arthur, his closing eyes seemed to dim the light, a light they hadn't noticed before. There seemed to be nothing and everything to say and Arthur's peaceful face gave no clues. They stood there, daring to look at each other, with empty minds and stilled tongues. No one moved, not even the overweight guard who had been constantly fighting his awkward position – he stopped and his look of embarrassed annoyance was swept away by one of smiling benevolence, as if someone had just told him a beautiful and moving story. George Sanderson, too, stopped his twitching and his attempts to rouse his body to full consciousness. A warm and gentle breeze, a zephyr, touched their cheeks and Toby and Amanda looked at each other as if wondering if the other had brushed their cheeks. Neither had and it fell to their imagination to wonder at the zephyr inside a house with so many thick walls and massive doors. This zephyr, this softest of breezes, soon passed and they blinked as if waking from a sweet dream. Arthur seemed oblivious to it all, in peaceful repose.

The other two men started their fidgeting again, though tentatively as if waiting for permission to continue.

"Did you feel that?" asked Amanda quietly.

"Yes I did," whispered Toby.

It seemed as if the mysterious and gentle zephyr had touched them as one rather than each of them individually. They both felt this, somehow, but might have found it hard to explain it to others ... even to themselves. They knew what had happened and the shared experience – though brief and simple – touched them deeply, though they knew not why. Their hands sought each other out and, as their fingers intertwined, it seemed that the massive room and corridor in which they were standing filled itself with a presence – warm and caring, somehow – and they felt a deep safety, a quiet unconcern, for what was about to unfold. All their uncertainties, fears and questions were enfolded in this presence, this sense of deep and ancient caring and they needed to do nothing but smile and wait for further guidance from within.

Toby put his arm around Amanda's shoulders and she leaned into him with a sigh.

"So, what are you two doing? Snogging?" asked Dottie in a loud and commanding voice as she strode down the corridor. Amanda and Toby separated, looking shocked and embarrassed, confirming Dottie's suspicions.

Then her phone sounded and Superintendent Hopkins quickly told her he may be unable to make it as he'd been delayed. Then his call was cut off and she suddenly felt very alone. Then her aloneness invaded her brain with the story that someone devious was holding Hopkins back ... and who else was out there, coming for her, the one responsible for all these civilians?

# A Head Job

*Arthur, Arthur*, came a sound, a whisper on a breeze, that slipped quietly through his dreams. *Arthur, Arthur* slid through gently, serenely and on those words he sat, gliding down a grassy slope in the warm afternoon sun, guided by a grace that was not his own. He was content to be led on a word that felt familiar, down a hill he'd never seen but knew intimately. As he glided on, one Arthur behind the other, he realised he could lie back if he chose. Sitting up pleased him as he could see the flitting swallows above, the parting grass before him and the sun glinting on the sea far below. He approached the sea and it seemed to come no nearer.

As he looked up he fancied he could see – or was it feel? – a thudding in the clouds behind him.

He became happily drowsy and lay back on the two *Arthurs* with no sensation of their touch. Looking up he saw not sky but a face; a face he knew well, he supposed. The face was close, blurred, and its lips were moving, saying something – saying, "Arthur, Arthur," the very words he was lying on, sliding on. His eyes saw the face but didn't look at it – he looked through it, wondering – how could that be there, not the sky.

The thudding in the sky seemed to be closing in. It was definitely a feeling now.

The face moved back and the mouth – a familiar mouth, somehow – was still moving, saying *Arthur* and other words. He could see the eyes now and, like the mouth, looked sad happy ... mmm, sad happy? Yes, that's what they looked like. The face still filled his sky as he slipped gently down the grassy slope towards the sea. There was a light now, behind the face, shining through hair and around the edges. There might be, perhaps, other sounds, human sounds and the birds had stopped chirping.

The face moved closer and seemed comforting; warmly comforting and he was pleased it was there. His forehead was touched gently, caressingly, and he smiled.

And then the smell of the grass gave way to the scent of roses ... mmm, not quite roses, but a scent he knew well, a scent he longed would remain. The scent, whatever it was, revived old chipped memories, fragments of events unconnected, parts of a life that felt familiar, parts of several lives, perhaps – child-times, adult-times, baby-times, teenage-times, all scattered about as confetti in the gentle breeze of his mind. This scent, so familiar, brought with it smiles, disappointment, sweetness, loss, fear, calm, hurrying, boredom and exquisite peace as after love-making.

As he looked at her emerging face he realised he wasn't seeing it as he usually saw faces, saw bodies, saw things. There was no distinct nose or mouth or eyes, no individual pieces, different from other pieces. It was like an unfolding picture in lights but not individual, twinkling lights ... it was a picture in light, one light, bright and subtle. He imagined he was looking at a patch of water on a still lake, into which a small pebble had been dropped, a hundred yards away. The surface of the water before him might be moving. It might not be moving. He was not sure. The light, her light, might be moving. It might not be moving. He was not sure. He knew her light to be different from the background light and the light of other beings but he wasn't sure how he was distinguishing these differences.

In the gentle light he sensed a concern, a worry about the container, the capsule, labelled as *Arthur*. Ah, yes, his small capsule – that was what she feared for. He understood her fears and was, at the same time, bemused for he knew there was nothing to fear, to worry over. The small capsules, with all their different labels, were not what was really there.

He looked in and saw ... no, not saw ... knew his capsule was open – perhaps for the first time – and a larger essence had been released to encompass ... well, everything, really. There were no boundaries, no limits, and it just sort-of flowed into other essences, slightly separate but not.

The capsule he'd known so well seemed to be closed and, inside, it held all its fears and concerns. He was touched and the formless light of his essence enfolded her capsule and she burst into tears – a flood of tears so long held back and now released with the relief of an ancient knowing that cleansed face and soul.

"Arthur, you're back, you're awake!" came her voice through the mist of his gentle perplexity.

Unused to such a way of seeing things ... of knowing things ... he relaxed, unconcerned, and enjoyed the small blissful waves of light as they caressed him.

"Arthur, can you speak, can you hear me?" came her voice as her concern washed over him. "Your eyes are open, my love. Are you there?"

"Yes, yes, I'm here ... awake," he said softly, knowing she needed reassurance in physical form.

"Oh Arthur, it's been all night and now you're back," she said as he felt a dampness on his face and then her soft face against his cheek .... her soft and very familiar face against his cheek.

His temple, his cheek, were caressed in warmth and his eyes closed at the sweetness. The caress stopped and his eyes opened. The face became less blurred, more distinct. He knew the face. It had a name. His mind reached for the name. It did not come. He looked more intently and the focus improved. Her face was still close, still saying words that were starting to straighten themselves out and become separate, nearly distinct.

The thudding continued to close in on him and a small pain crept into his head. His mind went to his body and he could sense nothing – a no-body, a no-sense, unfelt, unsensed. He tried to move a finger and was surprised to find it was there, as usual. Satisfied, he looked back at the face, now becoming more distinct, more ... mmm, more ... oh gosh, he knew that face! It spoke of love, caring and a deep history to him but no name came. It then spoke a name, its name; and he was filled. It spoke of Joan and all those shattered fragments of memories fused together in a quiet completion of a life that was his own. He tried one arm and it had a familiar weight. He tried raising it and fancied it did as he bid it do. As his arm reached for Joan's face, he felt dripping on him and she embraced him as he smiled and was complete.

The thudding had filled his head now and its intensity was growing.

"Is he alright?" asked Arthur weakly.

"Is who alright dear?" asked Joan.

"The man," said Arthur, taking another breath. "The man I hit."

"Ah him, that damned Sanderson?" asked Joan. "Yes, you rather damaged his kidneys and other bits, you savage man, you!"

"But ... is he alright?" asked Arthur, desperate for an answer as he struggled for another breath.

"Well, he was in a pretty bad way after you'd beaten him with that vase and cabinet," said Joan. "I didn't know you had it in you, darling!"

"I didn't hit him with it ..." protested Arthur weakly.

"Well, no one else was there to do it!" said Joan, laughing and interrupting him before he could get another breath. "You're quite the hero, my dear!"

"But I didn't hit him with ..." said Arthur with more to say while his strength to say it deserted him. He needed to know if the man was alright but the thudding was closing in. He just wanted to escape it, in blissful sleep, which was also closing in.

"And the others?" asked Arthur weakly.

"Yes, unfortunately Sanderson got taken off to hospital while Amanda and Toby were arrested," said Joan. "One of Martin's colleagues is working with Lord Atkinson to have them released." "Oh dear," said Arthur as words became harder to manage.

"Can I tell you what else happened?" she asked and he sensed ... knew ... her need to keep him talking, keep communicating, lest their link be broken. But only the link between capsules could be broken, he knew, somehow. The link between essences was always there.

"Yes dear, what happened?" he asked to help reassure her he was still with her. In that moment he knew all that had happened. It was not a sequence of events, one thing after another that went through his mind. It was as if the Hands of Time – the Hands of God, perhaps – held the long telescope of time before him and then had silently collapsed it so that all events and sequences came to him in one bundle of knowing. He let her tell her story, however, for the throbbing was closing in and he knew he must return to more sleep to have it soften its thudding.

He could hear her voice telling of events that he already knew as the deepness of sleep called invitingly to him. Soon Arthur wasn't aware of anything.

# The Tribe Gathers

*Wednesday, 14<sup>th</sup> March 2012, 6.48 a.m.*

As Arthur softly snored in the key of G minor and dreamed in the key of C happy, the world went by without him; living and dying, laughing and sighing, truthing and lying, selling and buying. In that other imaginary world, Mary and her cohorts, with briefcase of uncertain contents and menacing intent ... well, anything uncertain is always menacing, in our fevered minds ... woke to a different day. If it's possible to wake from a night of not sleeping, that's what they all did. All but Ahmed looked bleary-eyed and slept-in. Ahmed, of course, looked his usual dapper self, despite wearing yesterday's clothes.

Choosing not to appear in public any more than they needed, they gathered around Ahmed's and Halee's coffee table, seated on beds and chairs, as a quiet London slowly stretched and yawned. Mary and Angus tucked into a hearty English breakfast of fried eggs, sausages, bacon, mushrooms, beans, toast and tea while the others preferred fruit, muesli and coffee. With the previous night's excitement over and without the familiar office and roles around them, Mary, Ahmed and Halee looked awkwardly quiet while John and Melinda looked on, bemused. Angus, like a bouncing puppy just released from his kennel, grabbed the precious briefcase Mary had brought with her and rifled through the papers, between mouthfuls of hot, dripping food.

"Dere's gotta be somethin' here," he said, undeterred by the frowns and smiles around him. "Dere's just gotta be."

"Look, Angus, we've been through it," said Mary, pouring herself another cup of tea. "There's nothing there ..."

"Maybe it's a ruse by Sam to put someone off his scent ..." said Ahmed, interrupting.

"You mean he sent those people after you to save his skin?" asked John, incredulously. "He wouldn't do that, would he?"

"No, no, I've got a feeling ... just a feeling, mind," said Angus as he lifted out paper after paper. "There's something here we missed last night. I'm sure of it."

"I wish you were right ..." said Mary.

"Hey! I bloody am, Mary girl!" exclaimed Angus, holding a sheet up towards the window as the March sun tried faintly to shine through. "Look, look what's written ..."

"But we've read all that stuff ... well, skimmed through it, anyway," said Mary, interrupting him while peering at the upheld sheet and munching her last sausage.

"Nah, yah silly bird!" said Angus, chuckling. He shuffled closer to her, being careful not to spill the remaining breakfast from his lap. Everyone else moved closer. "Don't look at the words, the typed ones. Look at the ... aah, I don't know what you call it ... like a watermark or something."

"Yes, yes, I can see it, Angus," said Belinda. "It's faint but there's definitely words sort-of inside the paper. She grabbed more sheets from the briefcase and handed them round. "See if there's any more like it."

They all held sheets up to the light while carefully balancing plates of food and cups of tea and coffee on their knees. Then the phone screamed through their fervour and, immediately, everyone dashed into the fray, tossing breakfast remains and paper aside to plunder pockets and bags in search of mobile phones ... all except Angus who reached over and picked up the hotel phone.

"Hello? Ah, I'm Angus. Who is this? Sam, Sam who? Sam ..."

"Oh Sam, Sam!" said Mary, snatching the phone from Angus. "Where are you? I waited for your call ..."

"Yes, yes my dear, I'm sorry I wasn't able to call as promised," said Sam, interrupting her. "But here I am! Would you mind awfully if I popped in now? I'm at your apartment so where are you from there?"

"Oh Sam, it's so nice to hear your voice," chirped Mary. "And you're out, you're free ..." "Mary, Mary, please tell me where you are. I may not have much time," said Sam quickly.

"Right, yes, sorry," said Mary who then gave him the name and whereabouts of the hotel, along with their room number. Sam hung up immediately while Mary held the phone to her ear still, cherishing the sound and though of him being free and near. Then the fears moved in – would he be interested in her, would he be a changed man, would he ...

"Where's Sam, Mary?" asked Angus, interrupting her thoughts. "When will he be here?"

"Soon ..." said Mary with the silent phone in her hand while her mind floated off in some otherworldly reverie.

"Soon? God, you bloody English are hopeless, aren't you!" said John, playfully punching Mary's arm. "Ask an Englishman 'how long' and he'll tell you 'not long'. Ask an Englishman 'how big?' and he'll tell you 'quite big'. Ask an Englishman 'when?' and he'll tell you 'soon'. Getting facts out of an Englishman is like extracting teeth from a beggar's bum!"

"John, you forget you're married to an English person," said Belinda, laughing. Awkward laughter from the others.

"I can't forget that love!" said John, putting his arm around Belinda. "Charm, politeness, culture, history – you've got it all. But looking for a fact in an Englishman ... or English woman ... is like looking for courtesy in a French driver." Abandoned laughter from the others.

John's tirade was interrupted by a knock at the door. The laughter stopped while everyone looked at each other. The chances of very good news and very bad news were equal and no one was prepared to open the Pandora's Box the door represented.

"Can I come in?" asked Sam and Mary flashed to the door with unaccustomed rapidity. She opened it to a haggard, slightly untidy and thinner Sam than she'd known before. She faltered, seeing the same Sam she saw last night, now in the clear light of morning.

"Yes, Mary, my dear, the full light of morning reveals all," said Sam, smiling lopsidedly while apparently reading her mind.

"Oh, Sam, do come in," said Mary, recovering but unsure whether to give into her urge to hug him or to behave a little more correctly in front of her Regional Director and other assorted people.

Sam wrapped himself around her but her body wouldn't move. Was this really happening, she wondered, after all this time? Was this the real Sam Black, the friendly, affable, sophisticated, off-hand Sam Black she'd known, wanted, desired?

"Am I being too forward, Mary?" asked Sam, releasing his hold a little. The loosening of his hold activated her arms, somehow, and she grabbed him with a ferocity she'd not known before.

"Not too forward, Mr Sam Black, just too bloody backwards for words!" said Mary into his grimy shirt, smiling through her tears.

"I don't know why it takes a crisis for us to realise we don't live forever," said Sam, relaxing gently back into her. "There just may not be a tomorrow to do and say all those things we've always planned to ... oh, Mary, I've been through a tiny bit of hell and I'm not going through anything else, hell or heaven, without telling you how much I ... aah ..." He stood back with his hands on her shoulders, looking into her eyes. "Okay, here it is, my dear, I need to say ..."

"Watch out!" yelled Angus and John together as they dashed across the room with Ahmed in close pursuit. With a perfect All Black tackle, John felled Mary and Sam as Angus fell over the three and Ahmed's pistol boomed in the plush suite. A yell came from the corridor and a white man dropped and a tattooed, brown one, eyes wide and mouth open, faltered in indecision.

"Don't move an inch! Stop, right there!" said Ahmed, evenly, stepping over the sprawled bodies. "Hands up! Now!" The tattooed man obeyed instantly. "Now, into the room here or I blow your knees off. Understood?" The man obeyed silently and walked timidly past Ahmed and into the room.

Angus rolled off the human pile and leapt across to pounce upon a pistol he just realised was lying by the felled man.

"Dangerous place, this London town," said Angus as he stood up with the pistol in hand, gingerly pointing it towards the prone man who groaned and leaked blood into the deep carpet. "Mary, can you call for an ambulance or something!" yelled Angus, recovering his composure and senses.

"Well, don't just stand there and stare!" shouted John, helping Sam and Mary up as curious heads appeared at doorways along the corridor. "Help this man here – he's been wounded. Tell the management, someone, and is there a doctor here?" Most heads quickly disappeared behind slammed doors and one man stepped forth.

"I'm a medical officer," he said as he knelt over the prone and groaning man at Angus' feet. Two uniformed hotel staff members appeared at the end of the corridor, with a first aid kit, as Angus left the medical experts to it and returned to the room, shutting the door behind him.

"Do we need the police as well?" asked Ahmed as he motioned the tattooed man to lie on the floor, face down.

"No, no police, believe me!" said Sam, tucking his grimy shirt in. "They could well be behind this
... well, protecting those behind this."

"The police? Behind this?" asked Ahmed, alarmed, as he pulled the man's hands behind his back. "Has anyone got anything to tie these hands together, please?" Halee slipped off her tights and handed them to him. He smiled his thanks to her.

"Look, Sam," said Mary, straightening her suit, "I don't know what's going on with you and the police but we can't keep them out of it, can we?"

"Hardly!" said Belinda. "A gun's gone off, a man's lying in a pool of blood, people have been alerted and the ambulance is on its way."

"And what are they going to find when they come in here?" asked Halee. "A Kiwi tart, a Scottish woman dressed as a man, a Pakistani in costume, a scruffy pommy, a Scot and two Māori guys. Questions might be asked, don't you think?" Everyone laughed at the strange spectacle they realised they would present.

"Well, we can run and keep running or we can stop and face it all, I suppose," said Sam, plonking himself down in a chair with a weary sigh. "Don't know about you lot but I'm quite fed up with running. Quite fed up, I must say."

"Well, my Da says ye can run but ye can never get away," said Angus, kneeling beside Ahmed as he tied the man's hands. "Yer sins will always follow ye."

"Our Da said that?" asked Mary, surprised. "I never knew he said anything wise in his life! But I have to agree – we're going to be surrounded soon and I don't know about you lot but I'm sick of pretending, sick of acting like I'm coping, sick of pushing against the damned wall, sick of, aah, I don't know, everything. I'm too tired to bother, actually." Sam stood to embrace her and she gave in to Sam's embrace. "But I'm not blooming well going to cry though," she said defiantly into Sam's chest.

"I committed a crime," said Ahmed. "I shot a man. I will not run from that. Never."

"But it was in self defence," said Belinda. "He was about to shoot Mary and Sam."

"Yes, Belinda, you may be correct," said Ahmed, smiling. "But I must let the law of this land decide that. honesty and openness is peace of mind."

"You're absolutely right, Ahmed," said John. "Koia te kaupapa o te rangatiratanga, o te tika, me te maungārongo o te ao. It is the foundation of freedom, justice, and peace in the world. So, it looks like we're staying so let's get this brother into a chair, a bit more comfortably because he's not going anywhere either!" John, Angus and Ahmed helped the stocky man roll over and get up into a chair. Sam and Mary sat side by side on one bed, Halee and Belinda on the other bed, Angus sat in the other chair while the two remaining men stood beside the seated man whose scared look was soon replaced by an embarrassed one.

"So what you all looking at?" he asked defiantly.

"Maybe you just tell us who you are and what you're doing here bro'," said John.

"Why should I do that? Who the hell ...." said the man, who stopped as Ahmed took his pistol from his belt for the second time that morning.

"Perhaps you'd like to tell us exactly who you are and what you're doing here," suggested Ahmed evenly.

"Ah, yeah, I suppose it won't do no harm, pass the time of day," said the man, more nervous than defiant now. "Well, I'm Hemi Ropata and my tribe is Ngati Whakaue from Rotorua. That do?" Ahmed raised his pistol as if to examine it. "Oh yeah, you wanna' know te korero, the story, huh?" "Yes we do, bro'," said John.

"Jeez, I could do with a smoke," said Hemi.

"Talk first, smoke second," said John.

"Yeah, right, te korero," said Hemi, squirming to make himself more comfortable. "Well, you see, these pakeha, these English people, stole some of our tapu taonga, our sacred pieces – three of them – and we wanted them back, see. We tried the government and the police and all that official shit ... oh, sorry ladies, but they did nothing. Just a lot of excuses about, what they call it, official immunity or something."

"Diplomatic immunity," offered Sam.

"Yeah, that's it, diplomatic immunity," said Hemi, smiling at Sam. "So these diplomatic people took our taonga – pounamu, greenstone, from our tupuna, our ancestors – and the elders wanted to keep doing the stupid government thing but a group of us said, 'stuff that,' and so Kahu and I, we's volunteered to get the stuff."

"Why you two?" asked John, smiling knowingly.

"Ah, well, we's got experience of getting' stuff, you know," said Hemi, looking sheepish. "Yeah, did a bit of time for it, of course, but got away with a lot of it. Anyway, they put us on a plane with maps and stuff of where it probably was and who might'a had it and we got here. Cor, big bloody plane, huh! Trouble was, me mate, Kahu ... well, silly bugger thought he'd make a bit of money on the side selling his weed – Māori j'wanna we call it! Yeah, marijuana. Well, I shoulda' known he'd do something stupid but I's just so excited about a trip to Ngati Wikitoria, Queen Victoria's tribe, and to use my skills to honour my people. Anyway, he got caught. I managed to nick his stash off him before he got arrested and mighta' saved him a few years in clink. So I's on my own 'cept for this lanky blonde fella' I met in Croydon when I's running from the police after Kahu was nabbed. Yeah, the one in the corridor now. He seemed to know lot'a stuff and said the taonga was in this Black's house so we

... well he took me there and I got in and found nuttin'. Then he said there's this insurance expert, aah, Mr Bayly, who knew where it was and then I's told the boss of this insurance company, this, aah, Mr Black ... bloody Blacks everywhere an' I got confused. Anyway, this blondy – said his name was Greg Cousins – said he was after stuff, some plans stolen from someone important and we could help each other get our stuff. Actually, he said this at the start, on the big plane – sorry, getting' the story arse about face here. So, yeah, we went after this Mr Black, not the Black, Mr Black ..." "Sam Black?" asked Sam.

"Yeah, that's him, Sam Black," said Hemi. "Don't know what he looks like but he's supposed to be big in the crime world, according to this Greg fella'." "He looks like me," said Sam, smiling.

"Looks like you?" asked Hemi, frowning.

"Because he is me," said Sam. "I am Sam Black, world boss of crime, no less." Sam leant forward to shake Hemi's hand and realised it was tied behind his back. Sam sat back, looking embarrassed.

"You're a crime boss?" asked Mary, swivelling round to face Sam.

"Well that's what this Greg cove says," said Sam. "However, that's new information to me, I can tell you!" A relieved chuckle circulated the room.

"Yeah, well, I started having my doubts about this Greg fella' but I had no other leads," said Hemi.

"You never know who you can trust, do you?"

"Yeah, not even burglars, Hemi," said John, punching him playfully on the shoulder.

"Yeah, suppose so," said Hemi, smiling broadly for the first time – bright, white teeth in a brown face, lighting up the room. "Anyway, you wanna' know the story or not?"

"Yes, yes, Hemi, keep going, please," said Belinda, sitting forward on her seat, hands clasped.

"Yeah, well, where to start," said Hemi, looking up as if for inspiration. "Aah, I discovered – well, I think it's right – this Michael fella' is working for, or maybe with, a George Sanderson ..."

"George Sanderson?" asked Sam, looking shocked. "The Assistant Commissioner, Special Operations, of the London Metropolitan Police? That George Sanderson?"

"Yeah, could be," said Hemi. "He's got something to do with security and police and stuff. Seems to have a lot of strings to pull."

"You're dashed right he does!" said Sam. "And he's the sod who they were taking orders from where I was held!"

"And other things I found out," said Hemi, warming to his tale. "I went through his stuff once or twice and it could be, not really sure, but this George Sanderson could be paid – paid bloody heaps if the stuff I read was correct – aah, paid by one of the power companies here or the petrol companies.

Maybe they're all the same. Y'know, owning one another ..."

"Aha, it's coming together now," said Sam with a deep sigh. "God, why didn't I see it all before? See, they captured me with the plans in my briefcase but, because the plans cannot be seen in artificial light, they thought they were useless pieces of paper. They promised to release me if I gave them the "proper" plans, which is why I got you, Mary, to bring another set of bogus plans, like the ones John and Belinda were carrying around."

"Ours were bogus?" asked John, looking astonished.

"Sorry, John, that was for your protection and I'll explain it later," said Sam looking embarrassed. "We need to focus on our immediate situation, I'd suggest."

"Oh shit ... sorry, yes!" said John, slapping his palm to his forehead. "So, if you're right, Hemi, the corporations pay the police to do their dirty work. And if it goes wrong, the government servants' heads roll."

"Well, heads are already rolling," said Angus. "There was something in yesterday's paper, at home – someone up there tipped them off about the police holding John's car without authority. There was

even a hint the police may have actually stolen it – bit brash for the paper, really." "Oh hell, I did that!" said Mary, feeling flushed and faint.

"Hey, hey, just stop a mo', guys," said John. "We're going to have the police knocking on our door so what do we do with Hemi? I gotta' say I have a good feeling about him."

"Look, I just want to get our stolen taonga back and get out of this bloody place," said Hemi.

"Enough rain here to sink a waka!"

"I think Hemi knows enough to help us and we might be able to help him," said John, excitedly. "I vote we stick together with Hemi."

"I do too, John," said Sam. "What do you say, Hemi, old chap?"

"Old chap," said Hemi, ruminating on the phrase. "Heh, I never been called that before! Yeah, right, I just want the taonga and get back to decent kai. Bloody crap food here. Dunno' how you survive on it!"

"And you'll tell us all you know?" asked Ahmed, his gun still discretely evident.

"Don't need a gun to convince me, man!" said Hemi, shaking his head.

Ahmed slipped his gun back into the back of his belt and looked around the room to see if everyone agreed. It seemed that they all did and so he nodded to John and Angus who pushed Hemi forward on the chair to untie his hands as a knock sounded on the door.

"Thanks guys, so I can put my pants on again," said Halee disappearing into the bedroom as Sam leapt up and headed for the door, the man-in-charge once again.

"Oh, hello Hoppy," said Sam as he opened the door.

"Oh, gosh, Sam …" said an older, suited man who stopped mid-sentence when he saw the others in the room. "Aah, oh, Mr Black."

"Oh, yes, of course, Superintendent Hopkins," said Sam, remembering the form. "Do come in and we can explain."

"I am so sorry, ladies and gentlemen," said Superintendent Hopkins, smoothing back his straight, sparse hair a trifle nervously. "This must be upsetting for you all but I must ask you all to bear with me. And I know what a difficult time you've had of it, lately, Mr Black." The superintendent looked evenly at Sam for some moments as if imparting information mentally.

"Yes, Superintendent Hopkins, there have been better times," said Sam jovially, closing the door and accompanying the superintendent back to the others. "Take a seat and we can explain everything."

"Thank you Mr. Black and thank you, sir," said Superintendent Hopkins as he took the seat vacated by Angus for him. "Now, I do not know what happened, though I have some suspicions, but I'm not here to ask any questions right now …"

"But I just shot a man, sir," said Ahmed, looking surprised. "Surely you want to take me in …"

"No sir, I am not going to question or take anyone in," said Superintendent Hopkins, smiling as he held up his hand to Ahmed. "This is all very irregular and, believe me, I have been following this case closely, more closely than most of you realise. Now, bear with me, as I said, and it is imperative, most imperative, that you vacate this hotel as soon as possible."

"But, what about …" asked Ahmed with his hands clasped as if already hand cuffed.

"We do not have time for 'what ifs' and 'whys' right now," interrupted Superintendent Hopkins, evenly as he took out his notebook. "I am from Scotland Yard and, to me, your safety is foremost – a consideration you may not receive from either the Metropolitan Police Force or MI5. You must all be gone before anyone from either of those agencies or the tabloid press arrive and, after that, I will have as many explanations for you as you have for me. So, I need to take your names and contact details, one by one, and, in the meantime, you must pack and then leave with me."

Something in his quiet, factual voice sent a chill round the room and everyone immediately, quietly, packed up and was ready to leave as he wrote down the last name and details in his blue notebook. He stood and they followed him to the door, where he motioned them to stop while he went out. There he had a conversation with other people. He then reappeared and motioned the eight to follow him, which they did obediently. They were surprised there was no one around to see them leave the building by the back stairs. He led them up a back alley, behind the food scraps and rubbish of other hotels and restaurants, in the cool, still morning, and stopped before they got to a street.

"From my notes I see the closest residence is yours, Miss Collins," said Superintendent Hopkins quietly. "I suggest you all repair there and I will meet you presently, with my detective constable, where we will conduct the usual investigation procedures."

The eight followed Mary to her apartment and, once inside, stood there looking at each other like dumb mules. No one spoke and no one knew what to say.

"This is weird, isn't it," said Angus, eventually, dropping his bag and looking out the window. "What you suppose is going on?"

"Dunno mate," said John, with his arm around Belinda's shoulders. "Feels creepy, weird, somehow."

"Look, I don't know what's going on but, while we're here, we may as well make ourselves more normal," said Mary, her logical mind returning from sabbatical leave. "You need a shower first, Sam, so get cleaned up and I'll find some girly clothes for Halee and myself and then Ahmed can have his suit back. The rest of you just help yourselves to coffee, tea and food, whatever you want, huh?" Mary, Halee and Sam headed for the bedroom and bathroom.

"Yes thanks, Mary, I'd love a cup of tea," said Belinda, heading off to the kitchen. "Anyone else want one?"

"Jeez thanks but I could murder a smoke," said Hemi with a hopeful smile.

"You want one of mine?" asked Angus.

"Thanks bro' and you're Angus?" asked Hemi. Angus nodded and they shook hands.

"And you're Hemi?" asked Hemi.

"Yes," said John shaking Hemi's hand.

"So you invite a brother in and don't even introduce him to the whanau, the family," said Hemi, laughing and slapping John's back. "What kind of a Māori are you, bro'?"

"Aah, bloody Rotorua Māoris always moan, Angus!" said John, laughing. "Now get your brown bum outside for a smoke and I'll get some fresh air too."

"While the little wife stays in the kitchen!" yelled Belinda, laughing, as the men left.

"You may join us if you prefer," said Ahmed, gallantly.

"Thanks Ahmed, just joking," said Belinda. "Go and get some male bonding and I can have a peaceful cup of tea on my own. I could do with a little less drama for a minute or two."

# Escape From Certainty

*Wednesday, 15<sup>th</sup> March 2012, 4.00 p.m.*

As his eyes drew a veil over a world both thoughtless and fearful, he relaxed into the glow of a home he'd never left. Behind him he left the pale and fading footprints of a dream he knew he'd dreamed but could not remember. As he quietly smiled himself into the growing light, he wondered if there really had been a him, an Arthur Bayly, a dream, at all. His singularity grew into that ancient and massive oneness that encompassed and nurtured all.

The serenity powered through him as acceptance took his tentative hand to lead him deeper into the light of lights – the shadowless light of peace – which beckoned his heart to approach. As a long-lost son of a loving father, he was drawn to join and extend, to co-create in stillness. Where strength and gentleness met in oneness, he absorbed himself into their sweet and inviting light as his formless smile beamed its extension of acceptance and love, born in the eternal and growing light of forever.

With no doing to interrupt his creativity, he was free to be the ancient greatness he'd never not been ... just forgotten while he dreamed a dream now gone. Kindness seeped into him and showered forth in quiet beams of luminescence that warmed the soul of all he ever was.

Decisions rode gently through him and he was free to ride on them to where their creator imagined them to be. Choices were gone and, in their place, was certainty that all was done, all was deeply right and all was being done by stillness and silence. Had his soul a mouth and eyes it would have shed a smiling tear but, instead, he knew with relief, the struggleless life was upon him and it had ever been so.

Then a spark of specialness crept into his mind. A part of a dream returned; a decision to be unique and separate recalled itself and, as the decision was made it was unmade and a veil fell over that microsecond of timelessness, as he returned to the glow of the power and peace of oneness. This was where he belonged, out of time and space, out of control and fear, out of struggle and vanity.

He was in the deep sigh of unity, forever untouched and unmoved but the memory of that desire for separation and control let a small shard of ice slide through him. He tensed himself, fearing expulsion from this ancient arena of awareness and immediately regretted the desire to control ... and he was gone, back into the constricting capsule that clumsily plodded a sorry earth. The more he fought his expulsion the more tightly he was tied to the plodding body. As he struggled to remain, that endless expanse of peace was lost to his grasp and the dream of fear, loss and control was reborn.

The grasping fearful mind knows only one direction to go and it took him there – back to the pain and frustration it so feverishly fought against. He knew this. Despite his gentle, knowing strength whispering to him to let go, to let be, the screeching maw of his terror-stained dread yanked him into its ghastly, cobwebbed cavern of restriction and avarice.

He had trapped himself back into this parlous state and, despite his strong and silent knowing, the weak and flailing whimper was what he fell into step with ... and that step was a body he fell back into; a body of physical pain with mental guilts and fears.

Miserably, he knew he must open his eyes and feel the loving judgement of those around him. There must, he knew, be physical pain, many questions to be answered and many answers to be questioned. On a one-way trip to the demon of judgement, he knew he must accept his fate and, as best he could, slog through the swamp of desire, plans and affairs of the world of tangible and corruptible form.

He opened his eyes a little, anticipating a strong and stinging light to be adjusted to. It was a bright light, yes, but nowhere as bright as the light in the dream he'd just emerged from. He shut his eyes again, hoping he'd find himself back in that deep and silent light. It was not to be. Noises started up as if his opening lids had flicked a switch on a sound machine. He was trapped in this clumsy body and he knew he must return, for now, to the dream of pain and separation.

As he woke into a denseness, he felt himself a stranger, as did King Harun-al Rashid in *The Thousand and One Nights* who, as the sun went down, left his palace in beggars clothes in order to mix with the poorer people and hear what they said about him. He really didn't belong. He knew that. He'd always known that and yet, here he was in this strange and straining land again, a stranger in beggars clothes with the burden of guilt, yet again.

With a grim smile he sneaked his eyes open a little and saw a movement and smelled a whiff of familiarity – a fragrance of her, restored to memory.

"Are you awake, Arthur?" asked Joan quietly. Her concern pained him for he knew (or felt) he now had to deal with her pain as well as his. He sighed inwardly and smiled.

"Yes, yes, I'm here, love," said Arthur, trying to lift his arm to pat her hand and finding it trapped in the bed clothes on which she sat.

"Oh Arthur, I'm sorry, I was sitting on your arm!" said Joan jumping up.

He eased his arm out, with her help, and took her hand to reassure, while a jangling pain stabbed him in the head and several other unidentified places. He grimaced and gripped her more tightly than he'd meant to.

"Oh dear, did I hurt you, Arthur?" asked Joan, apparently blaming herself for everything.

"No, no dear, just my head a little ... aah, wobbly," said Arthur, wondering why his head and some of his body on one side felt either sore or oddly out of sorts. As that question arose, he wondered why

he was in a strange bed ... a single bed with starched sheets and the smell of antiseptic all around. His hand went to his head and it felt like a bandage there. "Did I hurt myself somehow?" he asked tentatively.

"You don't remember?" asked Joan, looking surprised. "You remembered this morning."

"Morning," said Arthur, savouring the thought of time, something he'd been out of for eternity. "So what day is it now?"

"It's Wednesday ... aah, four in the afternoon," said Joan. "You've been unconscious since

Tuesday, except for when you woke before, for a short while."

Joan's voice mingled with the fog of his mind, flowing over him, gentle as the morning mist. Then came another, deeper sound, sneaking through the folds of his opening awareness. He recognised the sound from somewhere.

"Are you alright, Dad?" asked the voice, tremulous and unsure, as if asking a question it dare not but must know the answer to.

*Mmm, how am I?* thought Arthur. *How do I answer that that? Do I say I am disappointed and sad to be back? Do I tell of the pain in my head and tingling left side? Do I speak of the fragments of peace and ecstasy from the other world that cling to me determinedly? How do I explain that it's both good and bad to be back? What will they understand of an experience my words cannot describe?* If he tried to explain they'd think him deranged for how can anyone wish to be dead and wish to return to ... ah, whatever it was? Only insane people, judged by this sleeping world, wish to return to the arms of God. A large part of him wanted them to know of the abiding joy and peace that was possible; not in this world, ever, but in another world. Oh dear, perhaps another time, he thought sadly. So he looked around in his mind for words they might want to hear and couldn't find many at all. Then the voice's name recalled itself to him.

"I'm fine, Martin, I'm fine," said Arthur, trying out a smile while fearing it looked like a grimace.

"My head's a bit sore and my left side feels like pins and needles. But it's good to hear your voice." And it was good to hear his son's voice. Arthur sensed – rather than saw – Martin moving closer to the bed; gingerly as if walking through a minefield.

"It's okay Martin. I won't break!" said Arthur as unaccustomed humour came to him. "Yes, you can take my left hand. A bit tingly but it's still the same old hand of your same old father." "How did you know?" asked Martin as he stepped forward to hold Arthur's hand.

"Know what?" asked Arthur.

"Well, that I wanted to hold your hand," said Martin tentatively. "You seem to know my thoughts."

"Well son, maybe your mother is right about that miracle course of hers," said Arthur. "Maybe there is only one mind after all." His vision had cleared some and he could see Joan, sitting on his bed on his right side, one hand on his and the other dabbing at tears she couldn't hold back.

"Well, would ya look at dat!" said Arthur, feigning an Irish accent. "I return from the dead and your mother holds a wake!"

"Oh Arthur, I'm just relieved you're back," said Joan. "It must have been terrible for you."

"Actually, my love, it was the most peaceful I have ever been," said Arthur, now returning the tender hold she had on his hand. "I can't really explain it but there really is nothing to fear. Nothing at all."

"The only thing we fear is the greatness we are destined to be," said Joan.

"Yeah, and my silly father returning with an Irish accent and a sense of humour," said Martin, smiling broadly. "I didn't know you had it in you, Dad!"

"Aye, dere's more where dat come from," said Arthur in his new Irish accent, an accent that came to him with surprising ease.

"You sound really funny, grandad," came a small voice from a small, brunette head beside Martin.

"Aha, Katie, so nice to see you again," said Arthur, his usual reserve falling away. "Would you like to hop up here and see the world from this royal bed?"

"But, but ..." said Martin.

"Oh yes!" said Katie, bouncing up and hugging him.

"Oh Katie, be careful of granddad's head," said Martin, looking worried.

"It's alright, Martin. Katie, just don't touch where the bandage lump is here," said Martin, turning his head to show her. "And where's that rascal brother of yours?" "Uh, I'm here," said Timothy from over by the window.

"He's scared of you," explained Katie. "Like you could be really sick or something."

"I'm not scared," said Timothy defiantly. "I'm just looking out the window."

"Well, my brave man, your granddad would like a hug, please," said Arthur, realising his usual fear of asking, of rejection, had evaporated a little.

"Me? Now?" asked Timothy, a sneaky smile creeping onto his face as he turned towards Arthur slowly.

"Aye, yes you, yes now, you little mite!" said Arthur in Irish again. "Git yerself over here and give me one of those famous Timothy hugs."

Timothy wiped his eyes with his sleeve and sauntered over. Martin hefted him up and he clung to Arthur like a limpet, crying freely.

"Did you miss me, you little warrior?" asked Arthur into Timothy's hair.

"Mmm," said Timothy, trying to control his sobs. "I thought you were gone."

"Well, yes, I was gone and now I'm back," said Arthur. "It's nice to know I've been missed." Timothy released his hold a little and looked into Arthur's eyes for a long moment. No one spoke.

"You're different aren't you, granddad?" said Timothy, a statement and a question together.

"Yes, Timothy, I'm probably a trifle different," said Arthur, not wanting to belittle the gravity of Timothy's question/statement. "I don't suppose anyone can have such a shocking experience and not be different."

"But granddad, you ... you died," said Timothy, obviously grasping for words to describe something he couldn't quite comprehend. "You died and came back. That made you different."

"Holy pyjamas, this young man speaks like Solomon!" said Arthur with the relief of knowing someone vaguely understood. With Timothy, he knew, he would not have to explain things. Or, at least, he could easily explain and Timothy would know. The older man and the younger boy looked at each other with an ageless knowing and smiled.

"Ooh, boys are weird!" said Katie sitting back a little, uncertainly.

"We're all a bit weird, Katie darling," said Joan, smiling as she patted Katie's hand.

"Did you know they want to get you, Granddad?" asked Timothy quietly, evenly.

"Timothy! There's no need to be talking about that now ..." said Martin, his face flushing red.

"Martin, Martin, my son, the beast will be unearthed," said Arthur, trying to take his left hand out from under Martin's, to pat Martin on the arm. He remembered, a little sadly, that that arm wouldn't move.

"But Dad, you're still recovering ..." said Martin, pleading.

"And we'll all be better if we know and face the truth," said Arthur, smiling. "The truth in the dark is always worse than the truth in the light."

"Hello Mister!" said a new voice as a blonde head appeared next to Martin, who embraced (or held back?) the excited girl.

"Oh Chloe, careful," said her mother from behind Martin. "Mr Bayly's been very sick."

"I understand your concern, Emily, but the joy of youth is a great antidote to a broken head. Help her up here, Martin. Let's have a bed party!" said Arthur, wondering why his usual reserve and reticence seemed to be slipping away. Martin lifted Chloe onto the bed, next to Katie, who looked a little more comfortable now.

"So, my wise young man," said Arthur looking back to Timothy, "what was it you wanted to say?"

"Well, Granddad ... aah," said Timothy, looking uncertainly at his father.

"Go on Timothy, tell us what no one else wants to say, my brave man," said Arthur.

"They want to get you. They're after you, Granddad," said Timothy, seriously, looking directly into Arthur's eyes." They won't give up till they've got you ... that's it, really."

"Oh Timothy, that's an awful thing to say," said Martin. "We don't really know that ..."

"Yes we do Dad," said Timothy, not taking his eyes from Arthur's. "That's what they said."

"And you're right, young man. They want to get someone, anyone, to cover for their misdeeds and they've chosen me as a target as good as any other," said Arthur as someone else formed words in his mouth. "And, choosing to live their lives in fear, they feel lost. There is no respite in such fevered, grasping minds and taking hostages saves them from their own insanity. Or so they think."

"What the heck d oes that mean?" asked Martin, smiling at his father and then at Emily, shaking his head.

"What it means, Martin," said Joan, "is that when we choose fear as a way to live, the only way for our twisted minds to stop the world seeming to be unsafe is to make it unsafe for others,".

"But it IS unsafe, Mum, Dad!" exclaimed Martin. "I'm not sure why I need to spell it out but, as Timothy said, they're out to get you. Whether they should or not, well, who cares! They're just out to get you, Dad! That's bl ... ah, very unsafe, don't you think?"

"Yes Martin, it might seem very unsafe but, as your mother is fond of saying, from her Miracle book, we can never be upset at a fact," said Arthur, wondering where the conversation-maker in his head was leading with this.

"Oh, right, so we should just be happy they're out to get you!" said Martin. "Whoever they are and exactly what 'get you' means to them."

"Martin, Martin, my son, there is nothing to fear. There really is nothing to fear ... but fear itself, as someone said," said Arthur.

"Yeah, nice words but the reality ..." said Martin, squeezing his father's hand tighter with each word.

"The reality, Martin, is that these men – I presume they're all men – are all frightened for some reason," said Arthur as a deep peace flooded through him and, for all he knew, out into the room. "In their fear, their self-created fear, they imagine they're jumping to the strings of a mad puppeteer. That's their world, their thoughts, their insane minds. We don't have to join them, Martin."

"Yeah, whatever Dad," said Martin, running his manicured fingers through his hair. "They're still out to get you and you could be in danger and so could we all – children, adults, the lot."

"We could be in danger, Martin, you're right. You're so right," said Arthur, seeing a frenetic fear writing its script across Martin's face. How, he wondered, can he help rewrite that script in a more peaceful and accepting way?

"We're not in danger now are we?" asked Timothy steadily.

"No we're not, Timothy," said Joan. "We're in a warm hospital with family and friends and no one's hurting anyone of us at this moment. No one except our own thoughts."

"So if we think nice thoughts, we'll be safer?" asked Katie, the startled look in her eyes from a few moments ago disappearing.

"Absolutely, love," said Joan, stroking Katie's hair. "Absolutely." "But the danger's still out there, waiting!" said Martin, unmollified.

"Martin, you've been through divorce and survived," said Emily, touching his shoulder. "Now, a few years ago you might have considered it and been aghast at the thought of the havoc it would wreck in your life. Back then, it probably seemed terrible, ghastly. But now you've done it ... doing it and it's not perfect but nowhere as bad as you previously imagined it would be. Right?" "I suppose so," said Martin uncertainly.

"So, just as the present is always better than the imagined future, why don't we stay with the safer reality of now?" suggested Emily. "It works for me ... when I remember to do it!" "But I'm still scared," said Katie quietly.

"Of course you are, dear," said Joan, patting Katie's arm. "We're all scared at times when we think of the scary past or the scary future. Only the present is safe."

"So you think I should stop planning for what's inevitable?" asked Martin, shaking his head. "We just skip through the daisies thinking happy thoughts and ignore the bull that's charging us? Is that it? Sure doesn't work for me!"

"No Martin, that works for no one," said Arthur as he felt the peaceful presence again. "As the Arabs say, 'believe in God but tie your camel up'. We get our bodies to do what's necessary – tying up camels, getting away from bulls – but we keep our minds in peace, on the present moment, knowing we can never know what's to happen. Unexpected things happen. And Katie, are you still afraid, dear?"

"Yes Granddad," said Katie moving up towards him with Chloe closely following. "It's nice with you and Grandma but when you talk of bad things I get scared again."

"So, my dear, let's do a little exercise to shoo that scary feeling away, shall we?" suggested Arthur.

Katie nodded. "Now, tell me, Katie, what colour is this scary thing?"

"Umm, it's sort of black and grey," said Katie, obviously concentrating hard.

"And what shape is it?" asked Arthur.

"I don't know ... ooh, it's round and prickly," said Katie.

"Does it make a noise or have a smell?" asked Arthur.

"It sounds sort of, like, squelchy," said Katie, smiling. "Smells a bit yucky too." "And have you had this scary feeling before?" asked Arthur.

"Um, yes, when Daddy said Mummy wasn't living with us any more. I felt really scared," said Katie, looking at Martin with tears in her eyes. Martin's eyes responded in kind as he patted her head.

"Did it feel like you were alone in a scary world, no one to protect you?" asked Arthur.

"Yes Granddad ... I didn't know who would look after me," said Katie, with a shudder.

"And now you know you'll be looked after, don't you?" asked Arthur.

"Yes, I feel a bit safer now," said Katie.

"So, perhaps we can call this scary feeling the unsafe one," suggested Arthur.

"Yes, that's what it is, exactly!" said Katie, brightening visibly.

"So shall we give it away to someone who can take care of it … have it gone forever?" asked Arthur.

"Who's that, Granddad," asked Katie, frowning.

"Aah, God, of course," said Arthur. "He takes all that nasty stuff and deals with it for us. Do you want to do that?"

"I've just done it!" said Katie cheerfully. "You gave me the idea and I did it and it's gone. God took it."

"And do you feel scared?" asked Arthur, feeling that sense of peace washing through him again. "No, I'm good, Granddad," said Katie. "Do you want to try it Chloe?"

"I just did it coz I was scared when Daddy went away and my scary thing was like yours," said Chloe, smiling at her mother. "Now I feel better."

"And that, Martin, is what you can do when you want to let the fear go," said Joan cheerfully.

"Of course I want to let the fear go, if I have any," said Martin. "But the reality is that mine is adrenalin which keeps me alert and wired for trouble. It's what I need to keep us all safe."

"Just don't confuse bodily adrenalin with mental fear," said Arthur, softly. "Fear, like love, is a magnet to its own kind. If you feel it, you'll attract more fear – not just feelings but fearful events. Do you want those sort of events for your children?"

"Aah, shit Dad … ooh, sorry, but this is all a bit much, don't you think – giving thoughts to God, not thinking of the future, stuff like that …" said Martin. "I don't know, it's just not practical, is it?"

"Okay Martin, on a practical level, look at who are the most fearful people in the world, the most judgemental, and see how their lives are," said Arthur. "The evidence doesn't lie."

"Maybe they're fearful because events happen to them," said Martin, smiling triumphantly.

"And maybe it's the other way round," said Joan. "Besides, what's it cost to experiment a little – identify your fear, see where it comes from and give it to a higher power. Can't hurt to try it, can it?"

"Well, that's fine Mum, but what if you don't believe in it?" asked Martin. "It won't work anyway."

"The strange thing is that it works whether you believe it or not," said Martin. "God exists and believes in you whether you return the favour or not. Just like that chair that exists whether you believe it or not. Just do it. Just try it."

"Yeah, yeah, okay, maybe I'll give it a try some time," said Martin, straightening himself up. "But, in the meantime, what are we going to do about this situation … dare I say it, Dad, but about your safety?"

"We've already done it, Dad," said Timothy, seriously.

There was a strong knock on the door and a security guard – a very large security guard – entered.

"Oh, excuse me for interrupting but my team has been engaged to protect this unit," said the guard, looking around and seeming to take in every detail of the room.

"This unit?" asked Martin as he sprang up as if set on fire.

"Yes sir, a Mr Bayly, Mr Arthur Bayly," said the guard, looking out the window and then stepping over to the bed. "I presume you are Mr Arthur Bayly?"

"Aah, yes, I am," said Arthur, smiling and shaking his head. "And who engaged you to look after this unit?"

"I was instructed to give you this to confirm my authenticity and authority," said the guard. He pulled a brown envelope from one of his many pockets and handed it to Arthur. Arthur held it uncertainly. "You may open it, sir, if you wish."

"Oh, oh, yes, of course," said Arthur, gently opening the brown envelope. Inside was another envelope – a white one with a wax seal on the back. The seal was of an eagle with wings outspread, looking down on a deer – strength and gentleness – that Arthur recognised from Lord Atkinson's mansion. Arthur looked at the impassive guard who nodded minimally. Arthur took this as a sign to break the seal and look inside, which he did. Lord Atkinson's letterhead, on heavy bond paper, looked noble … regal, even. Arthur hesitated, afraid of damaging the expensive paper in any way. He looked up and seven pairs of eyes were looking back at him, expectantly. He unfolded the paper and read:

*My Dear Mr Bayly,*

*I am dreadfully sorry to have got us both into this pickle and, while I do have considerable resources, few of them are of any use in saving our skins. My greatest resources are prayer and a belief that good will prevail. The next among them is enough funds to pay for your physical protection and I beseech you to take advantage of that. Please consider it my privilege and honour to help protect you as best I can. I pray you will avail yourself of this protection. I also pray you will not need it. In order to authenticate this letter, I confirm that my wife and I told you about:*

1. *Bruce Cathie,*
2. *Robert Adams,*
3. *The above's free-energy machine, and*
4. *That I was the person who drove the van to your property in Croydon.*

*No one knows all of these facts but you, my wife and I.*

*I now ask that you destroy this letter and you may, with absolute surety, trust Timon (the messenger) with any message you wish to convey to me.*

*Timon is an experienced professional in the protection field and I urge you to heed his advice on any matters pertaining to your security – any matters, great and small.*

*As ever*

*Lord Atkinson*

"For disposal, sir?" asked Timon, as Arthur handed the letter and envelopes back to him.

"Yes, Timon, yes please," said Arthur, feeling quite faint. Timon pulled out a lighter and burned the papers to a cinder. He then crushed the charred remains into powder and washed them down the sink till no trace remained.

"Thank you, Timon, now meet my family – Martin ..." said Arthur.

"Yes, Martin," said Timon, interrupting. His eyes roamed round the room, looking at each person in turn. "And Joan, Katie, Timothy, Chloe and Emily, I understand. We have done our research and be assured only those on our approved list will be allowed near you, sir."

"Ah, well, that's good," said Arthur, feeling that loss-of-words syndrome creeping up on him again.

"So Dad, do you know who arranged this ... this guard ... Timon, is it?" asked Martin. Timon nodded and smiled faintly. Arthur nodded faintly. "So you'll be happy for us to leave you in his ... ah, care, will you, Dad?"

"Yes Martin, yes," said Arthur, suddenly looking forward to the grace of sleep.

"Arthur, dear, you're looking quite drained," said Joan, standing up and placing her palm gently on his forehead. "Would you like to rest? We can come back later if you like." Another weak smile was all he could manage, though he would have loved to show his family more appreciation for their love and support. They all said their subdued goodbyes and soon the room was empty but for two men – one with no energy and one with seeming limitless energy. Arthur slipped thankfully into sleep as he dreamily observed Timon checking all the room's apparatus. When he eventually found himself satisfied, he took one of the chairs to a far corner and waited, alert and calm. Arthur nodded off.

# The Committee for Inaction

*Wednesday, 14th March 2012, 8.30 a.m.*

As the men came out, they stopped and observed the street waking up – faint sun powdering the trees and street corners, robins and sparrows chattering in the oaks and elms while shop and café owners opened their doors, swept their piece of street and put out their hoardings. A street sweeper with his cart mumbled to them as they wished him a cheery good morning while suited men and women strode past, pretending not to notice Hemi's happy greeting to them all.

"They all bloody deaf and blind round here?" asked Hemi, shaking his head.

"It's the English way, old chap," said Ahmed, exaggerating his English accent. "We don't talk to anyone we have not been formally introduced to. It worked when they took over my country 200 years ago and they think it still works now."

"Yeah, well, just bloody ignorant," said Hemi, smiling at Ahmed. "So, you giving me a smoke, Angus, or do I have to wait to be introduced to it or something?"

"Och aye, sorry Hemi," said Angus, getting his cigarettes and lighter out. "Just kinda' ... I dunno, trying to soak it all in, wondering if it's real."

"Yep, three days ago, there you were, living your usual Scottish life when a Māori and a Pom lose their car and change it all," said John, patting Angus on the shoulder.

"Yeah, life turns on a dime, as the Yanks say," said Angus, wistfully as he lit his and Hemi's cigarettes.

"So, you're Ahmed, aye?" asked Hemi, holding out his hand. "Since no one else's gonna introduce us – just damned inconsiderate, don't you think old chap!"

"Yes, Ahmed Khan at your service, sir!" said Ahmed, shaking Hemi's hand and laughing heartily.

"My gosh, a good laugh does one good, doesn't it?"

"And where do you come from, Ahmed?" asked Hemi.

"I live in Kensington," said Ahmed awkwardly.

"Yeah bro', but you weren't born here, I know that," said Hemi. "You're a mountain man."

"Actually, you are right, I was born in Skardu in West Pakistan," said Ahmed with a look of relief, somehow. "I'm not used to being asked personal questions. Please excuse me."

"Personal? Hell bro', the first thing we want to know about someone is their mountain, their river and their tribe." said Hemi. "That's the Māori way. Aye, John?"

"You're right, Hemi. My mountain is Wakapuni, my river is Awhea and my iwi, my tribe, is Ngati Kahungunu," said John with obvious pride.

"So you're from the Wairarapa, huh," said Hemi. "My mountain is Ngongotaha, my river is

Puarenga and part of me is from the tribe of Maxwell."

"Maxwell! That's Scottish!" exclaimed Angus, choking on his cigarette.

"Yeah, my tangata, my grandfather, came from some place in Scotland," said Hemi. "Dumerline or something."

"Not Dunfermline?" asked Angus, recovering from his coughing fit.

"What, Dunfermline? Yeah, sounds like it," said Hemi.

"Och aye man, that's where I come from!" said a wide-eyed Angus. "I just brought John and Belinda from there yesterday!"

"No shit bro'! Cor, so's we all mountain men!" said Hemi, his cigarette suspended in mid-air while he absorbed the thought.

"Mountain men?" asked Ahmed with a smile. "By jove, I'd never thought of it like that."

So chaps," said Hemi, attempting his English accent again, as passers by continued to pretend the four didn't exist as they walked around them in an increasing stream. "How do four mountain men, from the four corners, end up meeting in this flat, little country, hey?" "Maybe it's coincidence, maybe it's not," said John, seriously.

"Allah makes no mistakes, my friends," said Ahmed. "We are always where we're supposed to be." "And what the hell have you two been smoking?" asked Angus, flicking ash off his cigarette.

"Well, Angus, why did our car get stolen in your town and not one of the many others we passed through?" asked John. "And how did you happen to be walking past the Fordyce's when I was asking them for help? Tell me that."

"It's just coincidence," said Angus, uncertainly.

"Well, if you think it's coincidence meeting me and then meeting another Māori from your home town, then it's coincidence, I suppose," said John, smiling at Angus.

"There is no coincidence," said Ahmed seriously, looking at John meaningfully as John nodded back at him, smiling.

"But, ye ken, I do wonder about things," said Angus. "Ye see, I've tried all my life to get out of Dunfermline – ye know, see the world, do different things, but every time I tried to leave, something stopped me – met a woman, lost a woman, me da got sick, broke an arm, got a promotion, stuff like that. Then I give up, thinkin' I'm stuck there for life and whoosh! Here I am, talking to a bunch of foreigners in London town! So how's that work, aye?"

"As I said ..." said Ahmed.

"Yeah, yeah, no coincidence, right?" said Angus, interrupting as ground his cigarette butt into the pavement. "How DOES that happen, hey? Oh, you want another fag, Hemi?"

"Thought you'd never ask, mate! N'I thought I was here to get our pounamu back and look what's happened!" said Hemi, shaking his head and smiling. "Not what I had planned – bit like my whole life, really."

"So you think if we figure out what we're here for – really here for, nattering on this London town street – then we can figure it all out?" asked Angus to no one in particular as he handed Hemi another cigarette. "I mean, how do ye know what yer Allah's got planned or what any of it's for? It's got me beat."

"No one knows, Angus, is my guess," said John. "A lot of people tell me they have the answer to life and they all end up wrong and then dead." All fell silent for a moment.

"Me Aunty Whina told me, time and again, to stop trying to work it out as it will just crack my brain," said Hemi reminiscing, perhaps sadly. "She said forget all those big brain people with their big words and just do the best you can, each day. Just one day at a time."

"Och aye, that's what me sister told me when she visited last time," said Angus.

"That your sister, the one in the suit, upstairs?" asked Hemi.

"Yeah, that's her, Mary," said Angus.

"Hmm, Mary, she's a wise one when she stops worrying about herself," said Hemi. "Like the rest of us."

"So, we don't know the answers but we know the questions for today," said John as he stepped back to avoid a teenager on a skate board. "How do we find your pounamu, Hemi, and how do we get our

free-energy machines to the public and stop those against them giving us grief?" "Yes, that sums it up, John," said Ahmed. "But what do we do now?" "Nothing," said John.

"Nothing?" asked Ahmed.

"Nothing?" asked Angus.

"Nothing?" asked Hemi.

"Nothing," said John. "Look at it logically. Angus only got what he wanted when he stopped trying. I've put everything into this free-energy technology and all I've got so far is trouble. Hemi's put a lot into getting his pounamu back and all he's got is trouble and no smokes!" "So we do nothing?" asked Angus. "That's your answer?" "You tell me what else has worked, Angus," said John.

"Well, I dinna ken. It just isna' ..." said Angus, flicking at his cigarette.

"Just isn't what we usually do?" asked Ahmed, smiling indulgently at Angus, finishing his sentence for him.

"Well, no, you don't just go round doing nothing ..." said Angus frowning and scratching at his red hair.

"So it's best to go round doing something and round and round and round, despite nothing actually happening?" asked Ahmed. John and Hemi chuckled.

"Yer, well, hell, I don't bloody know!" said Angus, sucking harder and harder on his cigarette.

"Look, sorry old chap," said Ahmed, his hand on Angus' shoulder. "We're not getting at you and we have no more answers than you have."

"He's right, Angus, we're all trying to get somewhere and the more we try, the further we are away from it, whatever it is," said John. "The only thing that's worked for any of us is what worked for you – giving up."

"Well, maybe we just take a day off – stop trying for a day and do nothing," mused Angus.

"Yeah bro', maybe that's the way," said Hemi, shaking huis head. "I'm not giving up on our taonga, no way, can't give up, but maybe I just leave it for a day. Just hanging loose, full of juice."

"Look Hemi, Mary's flat is a bit small for a korero, a talk, for us all and you smokers must need refuelling," said John. "Why don't you two get some more smokes, find a café with an outside smoking area and meet us back here? Ahmed can go get changed, I'll write a note for the superintendent and we'll get the others down and meet you here and we'll go for coffee, korero, cucumber sandwiches and cancer sticks."

"Yeah bro', except for the cucumber sandwiches, Timmy!" said Hemi, laughing.

When John and Ahmed brought the others down – all looking cleaner, tidier and in more appropriate clothes – they found Hemi and Angus arguing.

"Aw bro', they won't miss one little packet of smokes," said Hemi, casually.

"Ye can't just go stealing stuff!" said Angus, astonished. "It's just not done." "Just not done?" asked Hemi. "Everything here's 'just not done'!" "You stole those cigarettes?" asked John.

"Yeah, well, they won't ..." said Hemi, less casually this time.

"So you get all up in arms about someone stealing your taonga but it's OK for you to steal from others?" fumed John. "Don't you bloody see it man?" "See what?" asked Hemi, quietly.

"You get back what you give out! That's what!" said John.

"Some call it karma," offered Ahmed.

"I call it bullshit!" said Hemi.

"And I call it stupid," said John. "And I'm not surprised if your iwi has stuff stolen from it if one of its number keeps stealing things. You never get away with it, bro', never."

"Ah well, it was only a bit of fun," said Hemi. "I'll go and pay for them then."

"And don't be surprised if you don't find your pounamu till you've changed your mind about nicking stuff, Hemi," said John, his eyes never leaving Hemi's. "You do your iwi no pono, no honour, at all." Hemi went as white as a brown man could and stood there with his mouth open, perhaps somewhere between embarrassment and anger. He dropped his arms to his sides and looked down, his foot playing with an imaginary pebble.

Yeah, shit Hemi, I suppose you're right," Hemi said quietly. "You just remind me of my grandmother – she says stuff like that."

"So you get your brown behind over there and pay for those smokes and let's go have a coffee, shall we?" suggested John as everyone relaxed a little and quiet smiles appeared.

"So, band of brothers and sisters," said John as they stirred their coffees and lit their cigarettes in the café courtyard, too small for the sun to bless but pleasant and private enough. "For your information, the Committee for Action has decided not to take any today – just be still and ponder the meaning of life."

There was a momentary silence as they cogitated on John's words and his straight face – was he serious or not?

"Look, John, I'm blessed if I know what you mean," said Sam, eventually, smiling uncertainly at John as he brushed back his thick white forelock again. "But, while I've had quite enough dashed action for a lifetime, we can't be still for long as they're relentless, you know."

"I think what Cryptic John means, Sam, is that we take this opportunity to get particularly clear about what we want," said Ahmed.

"A bloody holiday ... for the rest of my life!" said Mary with a sigh as she peeled a cupcake.

"And a Prince Charming to pay for it!" said Halee.

"And a cold beer and a wahine, a woman, for me!" said Hemi, laughing mischievously.

"But Hemi, how did ye find us at the hotel?" asked Angus, suddenly changing the subject. "Ye got some newfangled contraption to track us, huh?"

"Yeah bro' it's called a mobile," said Hemi, chuckling. "See, after that bloody Bruce Lee chap had a go at me at Ahmed's house, this Brian just phoned his friends and they told us Sam was being released and to follow him. So we did. Easy when you have contacts!"

"So they knew I was sneaking out!" said Sam quickly. "They pretended to give me an angel, someone on my side, and an opportunity to escape, when they actually wanted me to go, so I could lead them to you! God, I thought I was the clever one!"

"Sam, Sam, don't be hard on yourself," said Mary, patting his leg. "It's you against a whole lot of experts in this type of thing. You're still alive and with friends now."

"Yes, I suppose you're right, Mary," said Sam sitting back with a sigh. "I feel so dratted stupid. I thought I was the clever one and they were on to me all the time."

"Look Sam, you've been in the thick of it," said Belinda. "Do you want to tell us what's been happening with you? Your experience may have some clues for us."

"I'm not entirely sure," said Sam, staring into his tea cup. "Much of the last few days have been in the dark with persons unknown." He sat back and rubbed his eyes as if trying to recall the events. Or to rub them out. "I've been kidnapped, trapped, interrogated, left alone for interminable hours, interrogated again, abused, disbelieved, fed irregularly and, eventually, believed and taken pity on by one kind soul who, I suspect, took great a personal risk to allow me to escape. It seems they determined, quite incorrectly, that I have the plans, the power and the money to give them what they wanted. I don't."

"But Sam, Sir," said Angus, butting in. "How did you find us in the hotel?"

"That's mysterious, Angus. My saviour, if I can call him that, gave me a note and suggested I check in. I really don't know if he was helping me or leading them to you, through me. It's all so confusing but I couldn't think what else to do."

"Oh, you poor thing, Sam," said Mary, gently rubbing his arm. "So what's it all about – you know, who are they and what did they think you could provide them with? Whatever it is, it must be worth a lot to go to all this trouble."

"Yes Sam, we're all at the edges of this thing," said Belinda. "But you seem to be at the centre of it all."

"Well, Charles ... ah, Lord Atkinson, is the instigator, the man at the centre of the FSA investigation, the one with so much to lose and little to gain," said Sam.

"Hmm, I hadn't thought of the lose-win thing, Sam," said Belinda, "but John and I have been trying to have the technology accepted somewhere, anywhere really. We had no idea how you and Daddy were going to achieve or finance it."

"Ah yes, the finance," said Sam smiling and looking round as if checking for hidden cameras and microphones. "I suppose it's safe to talk here while no one else is in the courtyard. One gets dashed suspicious after a time."

"After a time of being kidnapped, interrogated, abused and starved," said Mary, rubbing his arm reassuringly. "We'll all keep a lookout for anyone poking around here, huh?" Everyone nodded and scanned the cobbles, bricks and ivy, up and down, like a family of meerkats.

"In a nutshell, then," said Sam looking up as if for inspiration, "Charles came to me with his crazy scheme. When he discovered his daughter and son-in-law – John and Belinda – had these amazing plans. He was so excited. I'd never seen him like it before. He knew lots of people and so did I and so we pooled our resources and, well, I had a pal who had worked at EAB ... aah, Empire Aid Bank ... and knew the wheezes that went on, well, you know how DfID, the Department for International Development, gives EAB the money to spend on international aid, how forty plus percent of it gets swallowed up in Britain in administration and, of the rest of it, up to seventy percent, can be swallowed up in what we might call administration – bribes, payoffs and other ways of oiling the wheels – to get the remaining twenty percent to the poor blighters who need it."

"My God, what a complete bloody waste!" said John, sitting forward, scratching at his curly black hair. "Better to spend the money here, looking after needy people at home."

"Exactly John. Charles' and my sentiments entirely," said Sam, sitting back with a smile, nodding his head. "So that hatched our plan for us, really. With my pal's help, Charles created a project in Nigeria – there's huge sums poured in there, one of Africa's wealthiest states, so they can afford education and computers to send us spam for more money! They're smarter than we are, I can tell you."

"So, the plan, Sam ..." said John, probably hoping to keep Sam on track.

"Ah yes, the plan, John," said Sam, sitting forward and pawing his white forelock back again. "Charles created this needy project, got the money, moved it back here to England – pals at Royal Bank of Scotland very helpful – and now here's the clever and tricky part ..."

"Och aye, getting aid money's pretty clever, sir," said Angus, shaking his head appreciatively.

"Yes it was ... aah, Angus, is it?" asked Sam.

"Yes, Angus, sir," said Angus reaching across to shake Sam's hand.

"Aah, it's Sam, not sir, to all of you, if you don't mind," said Sam, looking round. "Now, the Olympics were coming up in a few years and it seemed to Charles it would be the best publicity possible to have this technology showcased and then, with proper backing and awareness of it, we could take it to the poorer countries to really make a difference for them – practical aid as it's supposed to be."

"That's brilliant sir ... Sam!" said Angus.

"Yes, we thought so," said Sam, chuckling. "But there were a few stumbling blocks, the chief of them being the power and fuel companies that would suffer as a result. So Charles' bold plan was to meet the lion head on, so to speak, and give them a benefit from it. We had a few chats with a chum of mine, Sir Magnus Davenport, chairman of PoCo, who had the contract to supply gas and electricity to the Olympics and he agreed to allow us the cycling arena." "The cycling arena?" asked Mary.

Yes, we'd supply power to the cycling arena," said Sam. "The deal was that we'd pay PoCo what they'd make in profit if they did it so they got the money for nothing. Then, if it was a success, they'd have a share in the profits of all future ventures, worldwide. They stood to make a lot of money for doing nothing."

"The cheeky buggers!" said Halee.

"Well, actually, we went to them with these ideas and they simply agreed to them," said Sam, smiling at Halee. "We had to deal with the biggest players or they'd just stymie the whole thing as happened in New Zealand – the Shell-BP-Todd oil consortium pressured the then Prime Minister, Muldoon, to scuttle Robert Adams' plans. We couldn't afford that. Which is why we kept Belinda and John out of it as much as we could – reduce their risk." Everyone nodded quietly, not wanting to stop Sam's story with interjections.

"Of course we couldn't apply for a patent as we'd risk losing the whole thing through the "military use" patent provisions, which was how Muldoon scuppered Adams' plans, eventually. So it was vital the plans were kept secret for, with no patent, anyone could steal them and patent them in another country and they'd be lost to us and the developing world forever. So the plan was to launch the new technology in one grand blaze of glory by operating it successfully at the Olympics and the international media exposure would ensure that the idea could never be hidden again, by governments or private concerns, we'd be able to get a patent – worldwide, hopefully – and then go ahead, manufacture, make huge money in the developed world which would enable us to provide it free to countries with inadequate financial and energy resources."

"My God man ... Sam, that's brilliant, so brilliant!" said Angus, running his fingers through his red hair with one hand as he plucked another cigarette from his pocket with the other.

"Thank you Angus. We thought so too! Just one fly in the ointment, one dashed big fly, actually," said Sam to the accompaniment of a low groan that circled the courtyard. "We had signed a secret agreement with Sir Magnus at PoCo but, somehow, the secret got out – always a danger; the more people involved the more difficult to contain things – and, unbeknown to us, one or more of the oil companies control PoCo, somehow, and they wanted to stop it."

"Ah hell! And everyone, even them, would have benefited," said John.

"Yes, John, we thought so but it's about perception," said Sam sadly. "If you see the world as fearful, you'll see everyone as your enemy. As the oil industry is run by fear, fear of imminent scarcity, they're all at each other's throats all the time and they see their customers, their source of income, as the enemy too ... everyone is the enemy, even those who could help them. Hence most wars are based around control and ownership of this fear-based resource – oil."

"And because the new technology is free it's free of fear," said John.

"Absolutely John, absolutely!" said Sam with a big grin. "We thought if we could launch an energy system that could not be controlled, that was available to all, then there'd be less for us to fight over." "Oh well, we'd just have to go back to fighting over religion!" said Angus, chuckling.

"Or land like we do in Aotearoa," said Hemi with a sad smile.

"Yes, of course you're right, sadly," sad Sam. "But that was to be our contribution to world peace." "Do you have any idea who's behind the scuttling of the plan, Sam?" asked Belinda.

"Not sure yet, Belinda, but let us not yet rule out some members of the consortium that stymied the thing in New Zealand – they could well be a part of it here," said Sam. "However, we're still not sure and maybe we'll never find out."

"So, Sam, what's with this briefcase and the mysterious hieroglyphics on paper?" asked Halee.

"Oh yes, that's rather interesting, Halee. It came from the free energy technology, actually," said Sam, flicking his forelock back again. "You see, after PoCo's takeover of several competitors, they found themselves with several buildings in Britain, surplus to requirements. They hadn't disposed of them all, luckily for us, and so, in acknowledgement of the deal we cut with them, they gave us four small facilities, for free. We split the manufacturing into three factories that know nothing about each other. Then the final assembly was in a fourth factory where no one could know what was in the sealed units they were assembling. Kept the whole thing secret ..." "Even from me," said John, quietly.

"Just so, John, and we may have been quite wrong in this but Lord Atkinson was insistent that his family – including you, John – were to be kept safe at all times," said Sam, suddenly looking embarrassed. "Anyway, in the second factory, we had to calibrate the rotor to run at a particular speed and, when it did, the marker on the graph paper stopped writing ... or so we thought."

"It started writing in invisible ink?" asked John, as the jigsaw started coming together for him.

"Exactly, John, and it seemed an opportunity not to miss," said Sam. "One of our technicians worked on it for several months and was able to create an invisible writer, based on the earth's magnetic frequency, which is the same as the human brain's alpha state, incidentally, and we've only just created a computer program that can read this writing – photocopying and scanning don't work on it so we can keep our plans secret."

"So, as you said earlier, the plans we thought were the real ones were bogus," said John.

"Absolutely, John," said Sam with a twisted smile. "What the police took from your car in Scotland were, shall we say, slightly adjusted plans that won't ever work, like the ones Mary delivered to me last night. You insisted on wandering all over this country with no protection and so all we could do was to make the plans safe. Sorry John."

"Mmm, perhaps we were a little naïve, Sam," said John, patting his arm. "Did we make it difficult for you?"

"Let's just say you forced us to be creative ..." said Sam who suddenly stopped talking as he looked up with his mouth open. He put his finger to his mouth to indicate quietness and looked up. Everyone followed his gaze, quietly, to see Hemi scaling the ancient, pitted wall. Like a monkey he darted back and forth, climbing higher up the labyrinthine old ivy branches and stopped suddenly, just below the eaves, two storeys up. He pulled something from his boot and tossed it. There was an immediate scream and a clatter as a large camera crashed to the cobbles, narrowly missing Halee. Above, Hemi's knife slid into the gutter.

"What the hell! You can't go killing people ..." yelled an obviously shocked person on the roof-top, rolling sideways into sight, holding his bloody wrist.

"Ah, shut the hell up and piss off," said Hemi, moving sideways, closer to the indignant young man. "Unless you want more of my treatment."

"I am the free press in a public place. You can't just do that," said the lanky young man as he tried to stand on the ancient, slate roof.

"Just did mate," said Hemi, smiling and obviously enjoying himself. "Now, how fast can you run?" Hemi started to climb over the out-jutting eave and the young man realised he was in mortal danger, which gave his legs power and he scuttled up the uneven roof, his feet slipping with every step. Hemi reached up, retrieved his knife from the gutter, slipped it back into his boot and slithered back down, landing like a panther, quietly smiling his huge smile.

"That superintendent fella said we should keep a lookout for snooping reporters, didn't he?" said Hemi, obviously flushed with pride.

No one said anything for a moment. And then everyone had something to say: You can't just injure the press! What would the implications be? How did their secret meeting place get found? How much did the press know? How much did anyone know? What to do now? Do we dump the camera or leave it there? Do we take the film out? What was legal and illegal for the press to do? What was legal and illegal for citizens to do? Should they tell the authorities? Should they tell the superintendent?

Hey dudes .. SHUT UP, will ya!" yelled Hemi, standing there with his arms akimbo and feet apart. "It's done so legalities don't count. Question is, what now? I say we take the film out and bugger off. Right?"

"Just like we've all been running for all our lives," said John quietly. "And how's that working for us all?"

Another silence descended on them.

"What? We just sit here and wait for them to come again and again?" asked Hemi, his eyes wide in astonishment.

"Actually, Hemi, John's right," said Halee bending down to pick up the camera. It was heavier than she'd imagined but got it onto her lap. "What are they going to expect us to do? Run? Let's confuse them and not do that."

"And what did the Committee for Action decide?" asked Angus with a nervous giggle.

"Yeah well I broke the rules didn't I!" said Hemi glaring disbelievingly at them. "Sometimes you gotta break rules, do stuff and I saved us from those newspaper pricks. So it's time to do more stuff. Like now! Let's go!"

"Can we perhaps take a vote on it?" suggested Sam tentatively, obviously unused to such directness.

"Who votes for another coffee and cake ... actually, I'm famished so I'm having another panini. Anyone else?"

"Aw, Jeez fellas! They come for us from the roofs and you just wanna sit there stuffing yourselves ... beggin' your pardon, Sam, but we gotta go! Now!" said Hemi walking uncertainly toward the door.

"Hey Hemi, Hemi, you did a brilliant job. That was amazing. It really was. You saved us, brother," said Belinda. "But think about this – what do we know? What do we know what's waiting for us out there?"

"Yes Belinda, you're absolutely right!" said Mary, finally recovering from the shock of the Tarzan scene. "Running isn't good for anyone – I know, I've tried it! And, I don't know, maybe we should plan something before we act."

"Aw, you's all just chickens!" said Hemi. "I'm outa' here."

"And where has going it alone got you in the past, Hemi?" asked John.

Hone stopped and slowly turned, his mouth open, his head shaking a little. "That's a low blow, Hemi," he said quietly.

"But a true blow, Hemi," said John getting up, walking over and hugging him. "I know where you've been, man, the lone wolf all your life, the whole world against you and running and running and running to no blooming where in the end. Yeah?"

"Yeah mate, howja know this stuff, huh?" asked Hemi, slowly relaxing into John's hug.

"Because I've been there too, brother. I've been there too," said John softly as everyone else looked on, stilled and a little tearful. "Then I met this bloody pommy bird and I learned about true connection with another ... how much we can achieve and how deeply we can feel in true connection with others."

Hone's stout muscular body shook in the hug of a slightly taller John as muffled whimpers and howls emanated.

"It's OK bro," said John. "This is your moment, your defining moment to choose the same or to choose again, Which is it?"

"What a stupid damned question, bro'!" said Hemi standing back, wiping his eyes while trying to smile. "Course I want different. I'm sick to death of lone wolf stuff, like you said. It's just ... just ..."

"Just, just shut your big trap and choose differently," said John, his hands in Hemi's shoulders. "Choose the pack and choose doing nothing."

"It's just ... aah, I don't know, I feel like a bloody sissy, crying and all, in front of you ..." said Hemi, wiping his tears roughly again.

"Mr Hemi Ropata," said Ahmed, walking over to the standing men. "I see no sissy. I see a man who stood for his tribe, for a group of strangers in fact, and saved their missions, maybe even saved their lives. I see a true warrior who I want as my friend." Ahmed held out his hand.

"Aah, yah big bloody oaf!" said Hemi, trying to smile through another flood of tears. "Waddya wanna say stuff like that for, Koro?" Hemi pumped Ahmed's hand and then buried his head in Ahmed's chest as he wrapped his hands around him.

"Koro?" asked Ahmed, looking at John and then slowly down at Hemi's head.

"Koro means old man, Ahmed, it's a compliment," said John. "Wise old man, really."

Sam came up and shook Hemi's hand, looking awkward, as if he had something to say but didn't quite know how to put it.

"Hey mister, misters, ladies, everyone!" yelled the café owner as he burst through the door, "they out there ... they, they ..."

"OK, OK young man, it's all OK," said Sam to the alarmed man wringing his hands in his apron.

"Now take it easy, my good man, slow and easy."

"Ah, umm, you said not let people in here," said the wretched man. "You pay to keep others out."

"You did that, Sam?" asked Mary, surprised and impressed. "You didn't tell us!"

"Mmm, I though a little peace of mind might serve us well for a time," said Sam, blushing. "And now, young man, tell us: who is it who's there? Is it the police? Reporters? Maybe it's aliens?" Sam chuckled at his attempt at levity.

"Maybe they all want climbing lessons from the world expert!" said Hemi, laughing.

"No, no, not aliens. Not climbers," said the swarthy young man, now looking confused as well as worried. "They banging on door, demand be let in. No uniforms. Yes, could be newspaper people, ah, notebooks, cameras ..."

"Actually, Sam, it doesn't really matter who they are, it's not what we want, is it?" said John.

"Maybe, maybe not," said Ahmed quietly.

"And maybe we can put them to good use," said Halee jumping up as if a sharp idea had prodded her in the bum. "Is that what you mean, Ahmed?"

"Yes, Halee, exactly!" said Ahmed, looking directly into her eyes with obvious admiration.

"Look Sam, everyone, you all say you don't get what you want, that everything goes wrong and the harder you try, the wronger it gets," said Halee. "Well, sometimes we get what we want – just not in the way we expected it. Maybe this is the publicity you're looking for."

"My God, Halee, my thoughts exactly," said Ahmed, putting his arm around Halee in an unaccustomed show of affection. "Let's use this God-given moment!"

"Look, that's all very well," said Angus, nervously lighting another cigarette, "but what exactly are we going to say?"

"Absolutely, Angus," said Mary, getting up, "we need to organise our story. You know, decide what we're going to say, what we're not going to say and so on. We'll sound like a bunch of mad squirrels, all squawking at once."

"Or, Angus, Mary," said Belinda, her hand on Mary's shoulder. "We decide not to decide, per the Committee for Action ruling today. We listen and let the quiet voice within be spoken." "The Voice for God," said John.

"Te irirangi o te Atua," said Hemi.

"Look, I don't know what you're suggesting here," said Sam looking worried, "but Mary and Angus are right. We need to have a battle plan, organise our defences, agree on tactics and so on."

"It's not a battle unless we choose it be so," said Halee. "You see, we didn't deliberately, with any forethought, create this bizarre situation. It is beyond us to have imagined or created this. I suggest – and you might think I'm quite loopy here, that's OK – but it might well be that we're pawns of a greater force, a force for good, and we could allow that force to work through us, still."

Let Allah speak through us," said Ahmed, his arm still around Halee's shoulders.

"But ... but we need time to organise ..." said Angus, puffing hard on a cigarette that might have been crying out for kinder treatment.

"That we don't have, I guess," said Mary. "I have no idea how this Allah's going to speak through us, Ahmed, but I can't see another, logical choice. The sods will have the font door smashed down soon if we don't let them in."

Sam's phone trilled and he answered it: "Yes Hoppy, just come down to the café on the note we left. You've got it? Good. Ah, yes, right now is fine. Just that you'll have to lever your way through a bit of a crowd. Your sergeant? Yes, of course he can come and you can join us at the table. See you soon." Sam smiled indulgently, perhaps reflecting on the immaculate timing of it all.

With the assistance of an increasingly nervous café owner, they moved tables away from the centre of the café and set up tables and ten chairs at one end. The reporters were allowed in but not before Scotland Yard's finest was ushered through the crowd and introduced to them all. This had a magically calming effect and a sense of relative order ensued as questions were asked and answered, while numerous photos of the seated team were taken.

# Moving On

*Thursday, 14$^{th}$ March 2012, 7.30 a.m.*

Arthur opened his two eyes as the sun opened its one. He smiled to see his angel beside his bed, his hand in both of hers. Timon slipped out of the room as silently as the sun rose while clamour from a frantic hospital filtered through the double doors. Yes, he thought, the noise has started again – time to gird one's loins, brace oneself and to act strong in a weak and defensive world. Time to wake up and be brave again.

"How are you feeling, love?" asked Joan, hopefully.

Hmm, how am I feeling? Arthur wondered. Or, what's more important, what answer is she expecting?

"I'm feeling ... mmm, good to see you," said Arthur, realising he truly meant it as the words emerged.

"That's good to hear, Arthur," said Joan, now looking more relaxed. "They say the tests show no brain damage. It's just a surface wound."

"You mean there's been someone in my head, looking around while I've been away?" joked Arthur as the talking made him aware of a dull thud in his skull. "I wonder if they're still there, do you think?"

"Arthur Bayly, I do believe that sense of humour of yours is growing," said Joan, squeezing his hand. "I wonder what else has changed since you've been gone."

"Get me home and you'll find out!" said Arthur with a grin, feeling strangely brazen.

"Oh Arthur ..." said Joan, unsure what else to say as she leaned forward to kiss him. "They think another day here would be advisable, love, so hold the thought."

"I will," said Arthur, as the faint, dull, thudding moved to the right side of his head. "So, tell me, what's been happening in the world since I left it?"

Over the next few days Arthur was able to glean as much information as he didn't need to know as newspapers and people arrived at the hospital and, later, at their home. From these now-famous friends and family he was happy to receive wishes of speedy recovery and perplexed to receive the occasional offers of employment. He and Joan were plagued by reporters and publishing houses wanting to know their story and, when he was fully recovered, they escaped the furore and spent two weeks on the Camino walk – some of it walking and some of it contemplating. It was a spiritual experience that changed his life ... or was his life already changed and did the peculiar and uplifting experiences simply bear witness to a change already happened? It didn't matter and it was enough for him to know he wasn't stuck in unhappiness and drudgery – he could leave it any time he chose.

The events related to this point were reported extensively (and often inaccurately) by the clamouring press, while individuals were negotiating publishing contracts for their more intimate views of these events. It is apparent that several books are currently being ghost-written and neither Arthur nor I are at liberty to disclose the details of those books. You'll see them soon enough.

However, from the periphery, Arthur was able to discover some fascinating and/or banal facts.

Firstly, there was an eventual swapping round (a technical, legal term) whereby Amanda and Toby were released from police custody while George Sanderson, Commissioner of Police, head of the London Metropolitan Police Force, was made to appear before the Police Disciplinary Committee. To appease a salivating public, he was placed on three months suspension and much of that time was spent recovering, at Her Majesty's governmental expenses, on the island of Majorca and then, having been suitably admonished, was promoted to fill the gap left by his retiring boss, a fact probably met with great applause by many in industry.

◇ *Philip J Bradbury*

Superintendent Hopkins, working for an organisation less influenced by government, was able to quietly continue his life-long ambition of protecting innocent victims from corporate crime. His sergeant, a previously astute and upcoming detective, became quite disoriented by the affair he found himself at the fringe of and his strong and simple views on crime were shattered as he began to wonder who really were the bad guys and who were the good ones. In fact, he pondered with concern, were there no good or bad guys at all; just good people all doing their best in an imperfect world? The jury is still out but it's odds on that he will join the Israeli monastery he visited recently, in an effort to simplify (or banish) all such thoughts.

While tied to a chair in his office, Lord Atkinson had not witnessed the events in the corridor nearby. However, when he heard about it, he was incensed that a young man and woman who were trying to help him should be dragged off into custody while that dratted Sanderson, that wolf in sheep's clothing, had got away with it, again. Lord Atkinson had quickly assembled his political friends and, days later, was able to welcome Toby and Amanda back into the free world. Both men formed an immediate and easy companionship – a brothers with arms in slings camaraderie – and he insisted that Amanda and Toby recuperate at his country mansion.

Though Lord Atkinson had sustained financial and political damage in the past, he'd never been physically hurt. This recent series of events shocked him into a deep reverie about what was really important in his life. In conversations with his wife and with the two young people, he realised there was a way to fit all their changing puzzle pieces together. He and Lady Atkinson decided to keep three horses for her to ride and to sell the rest of the race horses. Half of the massive, modern stables were leased to a neighbouring trainer, one stall was kept for saddling Lady Atkinson's horses and the rest was turned into a fitness and defence training academy – a dream that both Amanda and Toby had had since their very different childhoods. They were soon ensconced in one of the cottages recently vacated by the head groom. The Atkinsons took on Toby as the son they never had and he took on the Atkinsons as the parents he never had; being raised in several orphanages, he had learned to fight for everything he needed. The Atkinsons enjoyed Amanda's Antipodean sense of humour and directness and Toby learned, from her, among other things, that defenselessness is strength.

And, yes, you guessed it – Arthur and Joan were invited to their wedding, along with others in this small saga. Toby and the Atkinsons helped Amanda's parents sneak into England and appear before Amanda three days before the wedding, much to Amanda's surprise and delight. She was able to show them some of Surrey and Kent and to enjoy their company ... well, her mother's, anyway. Her father, who had not been abroad before, grumbled about the monotony of England's landscape, the unfriendly natives and the crumbling old houses they insisted on living in. However, Toby charmed him mercilessly and Amanda was not a little tearful when she heard her father tell Toby that he and his new wife must come to New Zealand to see how real people live.

Lord Atkinson, with Sam's help, had formed the Robert Adams Free Energy Trust (RAFET) and, after the Olympics and the ensuing publicity, the enterprise really took off, free from the needs of secrecy.

No one else in this tale of intrigue was able to return to the maps of their old lives and the AIL insurance company will never be the same again. Because of its spectacular profits, it was bought by the Greenwich Bank (GB) and the chairman appointed just happened to be a nephew of one of GB's directors. He appointed Malcolm Schriever, the indecisive stickler for form, as his deputy and, between them, they managed colossal change – staff turnover increased seven-fold and profits plummeted to such an extent that GB was forced (quite happily, really) to ask for a four million pound injection of funds the following year. The government immediately and without evidence saw an immense benefit to the nation of such a transaction and that relationship was further cemented by said nephew's promotion to the House of Commons as the Member for Croydon. Malcolm Schriever took his place as chairman for GB and the world waits with baited breath on next year's published accounts.

After a respectable time, Arthur and Joan received another wedding invitation – that of Sir Samuel and Lady Mary Black. Ah, yes, they had also attended, along with Martin and Emily, Sam's investiture for his contribution to finance and peace. The bride's hair was long, glossy and thick. Her dress was feminine, her figure slimmer and her smile couldn't be chiselled off. The happy couple did not live happily ever after. No one does. They did, however, experience occasional erotic and spiritual explosions of ecstasy, petty bickering and longer and longer periods of quiet, companionable ordinariness. The requests (demands?) of his devoted wife meant Sir Samuel had to be more discerning and brief at his club and this sacrifice gradually turned itself into a choice and a joy. Lady Mary took on a new diet – instead of reaching for a plate, she reached for her mate – and though their sexual proclivity more than made up for so many years of abstinence, Mary was ever determined that no creature was ever to pass through her loins. Happily, she was able to acquire (as it were) a daughter and granddaughter in Emily and Chloe without the ghastly loin-passing event ever occurring. Mary, of course, got her wish to lie in on Sunday mornings with her Prince Charming, doing all those delicious things she'd always dreamed of. And, once in a while, their mornings were shared, in bed, with a delightful blonde granddaughter.

It surprised her how many of Uncle Hughie's friends were the same ones Sam knew in the Camden music scene and so this lonely Scottish girl soon became one of a varied and fascinating mix of friends, from political and industry leaders to creative and artistic fringe-dwellers. It should have been no surprise that she bumped into Halee from time to time. Halee had kept her Camden flat while Ahmed vacillated over how his relationship should look with a bold New Zealand pixie who quickened his spirit. Ahmed fiercely desired her and none of us will know what took place in their private moments but, to the world, he treated her with the deference of a queen to her prince ... an English one, anyway.

Ahmed laid the facts of his shooting a New Zealander at the feet of Superintendent Hopkins who conferred with others at Scotland Yard. Ahmed was allowed out on bail and, after a nervous five months, discovered he had been pardoned. No one knows who influenced and/or made that decision and few facts of the case became known to the general public. It was clear that the New Zealand government, seeking to avoid further scandal – after the disclosure of it's handling of Robert Adams and his invention was made public, worldwide – chose not to press charges on behalf of a Secret Intelligence Service employee. Full of gratitude to Allah and with a realisation that life is, indeed, precious, Ahmed immediately asked Halee to marry him. Reports are that she accepted immediately though we must keep quiet about that until he has obtained his family's consent.

Halee enjoyed her new lifestyle in London, Pakistan and New Zealand and her new position as secretary for the Legal Director of RAFET. RAFET, as you can imagine, dispenses money and freeenergy technology to poorer communities, financed by sales of said technology to wealthier communities. Halee often accompanied her boss to negotiate contracts around the world and Ahmed never tired of his secretary's presence. It also pleased him deeply to be able to help the people of his homeland, with resources, and he and Halee shared many a tearful moment for the good they were able to effect.

Our red haired Scot, Angus Collins, was pleased (ecstatic, actually) to be able to put his engineering skills to work as Deputy Engineering Supervisor for RAFET's four factories in England and this necessitates the occasional overseas trip to supervise installations. He returns regularly to his beloved Dunfermline, despite the fascinations of his now-bigger world. With his increased income, he offered to buy his Ma and Da a larger, more modern house but they gave an emphatic thumbs down, preferring to live in a council house they can complain about. So Angus bought himself a larger, more modern house which his parents dutifully 'look after' most of the time when he's in his smaller semidetached in Witney, Oxfordshire. His father has been known to smile a little more (when he thinks others aren't looking) but his mother retains the need to conceal the happiness she feels for her two children.

Of course, Mary and Angus now see more of each other, both working for RAFET and living an hour's drive from one another. We are forbidden from revealing any more details about Angus, Mary and Sam because of two separate book deals.

We can tell you that Mr and Mrs Fordyce, of Dunfermline, died within a month of each other and friends mourn their passing and miss their wise company. Mary, after a traumatic grieving period, now feels closer to them than ever before, somehow.

Lucky Pintado, owner of Lucky Café, struck it lucky. After the unexpected and well publicised press conference at Lucky Café, it quickly became the favoured haunt of journalists. Because journalists only look 'out there' for bleeding hearts and bleeding bodies and never look within (or anywhere nearby), Lucky Café has also become the favoured haunt for business negotiators and those hatching dastardly plots – right there, they go undetected by the nation's greatest sleuths. The money really started to roll in for Lucky. Unfortunately, Lucky had misheard conversations and then had a small plaque inscribed with the words, "Site of the birth of the world's first time machine," and planted it in a corner of the courtyard. Despite it being a free-energy machine and that it wasn't really born on that spot, the joke of the error spread and added to the quirky aura of Lucky Café. With Sam's business contacts and techniques, Lucky Pintado started a Lucky Café franchise and now new cafés are springing up around London and further afield at a rate of about one a month. For all we know, there could be a Lucky Café in Dunfermline by now. Sam and Lucky have installed plaques in each Lucky Café, commemorating the birthplace of yet another as-yet uninvented invention. By careful design, they have created a pilgrimage that has thousands of people following the cafés to collect their own photo of each of these quirky, nonsensical plaques. Sam also smiles broadly at Mary each time his monthly cheque for business consultancy fees arrives. Everybody lucky at Lucky Café.

After the impromptu press conference at Lucky Café, Sam received a call which he passed on to Hemi, regarding his family's stolen artefacts. Hemi was subsequently entertained at the Gloucester mansion of Sir Magnus Davenport – a man with the slicked-back, black hair, greying around the edges. Hemi was then presented with said artefacts, along with the narrative that they had recently been unearthed and presented to Sir Magnus. It seems unlikely that Sir Magnus divulged to Hemi that the artefacts were presented to him by his butler, just after taking them from the glass display cabinet in which they had resided for the past three generations of Davenports. Had Hemi known the second, omitted part of the narrative, he might not have cared a damn – he had what he came for and all he

wanted to do was return to his mates, the green hills and the blue skies or Aotearoa … and some cold beers and waihine wera – hot women. Before the beers and women, on his return to New Zealand, he had to visit his Aunty Whina, a woman of massive girth and fearsome love. She sat on her throne – a worn and squeaky lazy-boy – in her state house in Rotorua, with assembled whanau (grandchildren, children, siblings, cousins, aunts, uncles and anyone else passing through) and grilled Hemi on why it took so long to get three bloody bits of pounamu back from those whingeing poms. Hemi spun his yarn with much laughter and lyricism and, after a bear hug from aunty and everyone else they all had a big party and got totally inebriated.

Hone woke two days later and went as white as a brown man can: "Shit, where did I leave that pounamu?" he asked himself. He walked around the party-ravaged house and found his hooded jacket discarded under a chair. Luckily, the pounamu were still rattling around in the left pocket and so he had two beers and a smoke to help with the hangover and then borrowed someone's car to take them to the kaumatua, the elders, for blessing and safe storage. His grateful grandfather took them and a meeting was planned for the next week to honour Hemi and the return of the mana, the honour, to their tribe. Then Hemi went round to a mate's – several mates, actually – and they got out the beers, smokes and guitars and had a damned good time. After total immersion in his old life pattern for a week, something strange happened to Hemi and he went bush, sitting under the stars, talking to God and demanding to know the purpose of his life. The answer came on the seventh morning and he came down the mountain and started his new life. A ghost writer is writing the rest so we mustn't say any more on that.

Meanwhile, back in London, Martin has decided that Emily is the woman for him now and Emily has decided that Martin is the man for her, later. She is insisting that he get counselling, tie up loose ends and get closure on his nine-year marriage to Ruth. Martin thinks he's fine, that counsellors and shrinks are all idiots anyway and that his alternating bouts of anger and depression are normal for anyone having to live near London. However, Emily is insistent, Martin is hungry for her and so he has agreed to attend weekly (very weakly, he says) sessions of Divorcees Anonymous, a group, he explains, of scruffy, poor gits who sit about moaning about their lot because they're too scared and/or unattractive to find another partner. It's an uneasy truce between Martin and Emily but the three children get on famously, which helps them to feel that they should be together. It's a wait and see, that one.

John and Belinda continue to study *A Course in Miracles*, a course that changed their lives and their relationship. Realising that free-energy machines do not make a better world but that the intent of those working together does, John turned down an offer of managing RAFET in preference to writing, publishing and speaking, alongside Belinda, in ways and places that help people realise their true calling, their true greatness. Discovering that Joan was *A Course in Miracles* student (as is Arthur, of late) they meet regularly, when not in New Zealand, having a jolly good laugh and a deeper connection every time.

John and Belinda continue their connection with RAFET on a consultancy basis and they're often called in to mediate disputes when someone (usually a large corporation) feels threatened by freeenergy machines arriving in their patch. Knowing we are never upset for the reasons we think, John and Belinda (they're an interchangeable pair in this work) are able to quickly get to the heart of the matter, to everyone's surprise and joy.

And the tall, blonde, clumsy, mysterious Australian? Well, he might just pop up again very soon, in his very own novel. Who knows?

# Arthur Writes His Story

*16<sup>th</sup> April, 2012*

Just as their lives changed, so did their address and his occupation – now by the sea in Cornwall from where Arthur is able to conduct his part-time occupation of Insurance Director for RAFET, online mainly.

Arthur might have wished for a fairy tale ending but the quiet gnawing at his bones, in those quiet, early-morning moments, reminded him he was in no fairy tale.

He had, he realised, become accustomed to his uncomfortable, restricting life. He had to admit to himself, finally and begrudgingly, that he'd rather wallowed in his own mud. For all those years he'd sordidly revelled in the pity he'd had for himself ... in the pity others showered in his wake.

Beneath the glittering lights of his recent adventure, he imagined his life as a little car, purring along contentedly for a time and then sliding into a ditch, to move no more. The weeds and rust had grown through it and no one had done anything to rescue it. No one could. It was his rusting life – no one else's – and whatever glitter his outer experiences threw over it, there was still a rusting, immobile carcase beneath the glister of others' envy and admiration.

Despite the freedom of working from home and the expanse of the sea before him, every single day, he still felt trapped. It annoyed and shook him for nothing was logical any more. This resistant though had him asking the illogical – did his attachment to restrictive thoughts keep limitation in his life? Or, more alarmingly, would he attract it back somehow.

He'd tried to explain this in his halting, hesitant way to Joan. She smiled indulgently and he realised he should have thought it through some more, explained it to himself better before trying out his new thoughts on someone else. He couldn't quite get to grips with it so why should he expect others to?

"So, this rusting carcase, Arthur," she said. "What is it?"

"Oh, aah, it's my life," he said, really wishing he hadn't opened this uncooked can of beans, right now.

"Your life is your life, don't you see?" she asked patting his knee. "Your life, I think you mean, is the events you're plodding through."

"Yes, I suppose so," he said, slightly irritated that she was about to turn his thoughts upside down ... take his precious new realisation and rip it into unrecognisable pieces.

"The evidence doesn't lie, does it?" she said with as much care and concern that it was difficult to argue back with the irritation he felt.

"But ... but events have happened, yes," he said, desperately trying to formulate his thoughts again, to restitch the ragged pieces together again. "They've happened and things are different ..."

"We have more money, new freedom, interesting friends, yes?"

"Well, yes, exactly," he said, smiling weakly as he saw his realisation coming together again. "It's all different but something is still the same. I thought would all change."

"Are your feelings of being trapped still the same?"

"Well, yes, I suppose ..." he muttered as a faint light began to glow through the fabric of his realisation.

"Does your mind still imagine itself as bored?"

"Not during the day when I'm busy."

"No, but when you're left with nothing but your thoughts," she suggested. "In your labelless state." "Labelless state?"

"When we're asleep and dreaming, we're who we want to be," she explained. "Then, in the halflight of dawn, we're empty. Simply open vessels our deeper selves."

"Yes?" he said, his curiosity piqued.

"But we must awaken and, as we do, we must remember who we want the world to have us be. We put our masks back on. During the week you're a business man, you're Arthur, you have these tasks to do, you have these attitudes to shrug on, these people to pretend to and so on. In the weekend you're a husband, a father, a gardener and so on.

"Right?"

"But, before we don the heavy layers of all these masks, we're naked to our deeper thoughts and they arise in their purity," she said, looking at the ceiling as if for inspiration. Or the right words. "We're all the same, Arthur, believe me. We desperately rush around to avoid the persistence of our innermost thoughts, untainted by the pretence that we're coping. They're purely boring, purely bitter, purely sad, purely vengeful; whatever it is that's our prevalent though form. We can't escape from it by running."

"We can't? We are?" he asked, as words tumbled out over ill-formed thoughts. "We're all thinking dreadful, thoughts, depressing thoughts?"

"We are till we fall into them, embrace them, name them and let them go."

"We embrace them and then let them go?" he asked, wondering at the stupid contradiction. He's spent his sleep-less time trying to shove the thoughts away.

"If we don't let them go, we'll bring witnesses to them."

"Witnesses?"

"If I keep thinking I'm bored, my life will soon become boring, proving my thinking right."

"Aha, witnesses – witnesses to our thoughts."

"So your prevalent thought is *boring* and mine is *regret*," she said.

"Regret for what?"

"For nothing. Just regret," she said, quietly. "I just have this undercurrent of regret and the witnesses turn up. I regret I didn't have more time with the children. I regret we didn't travel. I regret we didn't have more money, more fun. Just regret."

"Do you still have it?" he asked, dreading her answer.

"Less than I used to. I've been working on letting it go," she said. "I realised that if I let it hold me captive, my life would become a witness to it. As I let it go, I find I have less to regret. More to appreciate. More gratitude."

"So, if I keep having this boredom thought, perhaps my former life will return, somehow," he mused out loud, "despite recent events."

"Exactly, my love. Exactly," she said brightly, her hand moving up his leg. "And I don't want to regret missing out on you." She stood up uncertainly. As if she had something to say and couldn't form the words.

"Or not being bored with our juice-less lives," he said. He stood awkwardly, trying to hide the growing bulge in his trousers.

"Darling, aah, this is very embarrassing but I'd like to ask for something," said Joan, looking round their new home with boxes scattered everywhere, some opened and some not. She held him tightly so he couldn't look her in the eyes.

"Yes, what is it?" asked Arthur.

"Well, since we're being more honest nowadays, about feelings, I'd really like to ..." said Joan, looking flushed and lost for words. "Oh, to hell with it – I'd really like you to make love to me. There. There, I've said it!"

"Gosh, yes, that sounds like a ... huh, what are we waiting for?" said Arthur, relieved that she felt as he did. "Come upstairs with me, my Lady, and let's make passionate music together." He wondered where such phrases came from but he now felt quite abandoned, fearless ... and a flow of love that he hadn't experienced for so long.

As they were skipping up the stairs the phone rang. In a reflex action, Joan stopped to go down and answer it.

"Leave it, dear, it can wait," said Arthur touching her arm.

"Of course. Of course, Arthur. Yes, it can wait," said Joan smiling childishly. "I'll race you into bed!

The phone rang several times more but they were otherwise engaged in other things more interesting.

Later, in the afterglow of their love-making, there was little to say. Lying in each other's arms – two middle-aged people who had previously grown apart – they felt the years, the recriminations, the judgements and disappointments drift away. They were together, close, warm. Any sense of difference and separation seemed like an illusion, a gossamer sheet blown aside to reveal the truth of connection that had never really left them. Neither wanted to move from the warm cocoon of love, with the fragrance of their love-making wafting around them.

"I suppose we must be going soon," said Arthur wistfully.

"Going where?" asked Joan.

"Going to … oh, golly, there's nowhere to go, is there!" said Arthur, chuckling. "It's so ingrained that I need to go to work, I just can't shake it off. Would you like a cup of tea?"

"Mmm, I suppose so … not just yet," said Joan, putting her head into his chest as tears began again. "Just be still and hold me, love."

# Return To The Red Earth

*July 15th, 2014, 5.00 am, Uluru, Australia*

Two years after their move to Cornwall, Arthur was sitting beside Joan in a van with eight other people, enjoying the passing vista of the Australian desert – bush, they called it – and he pondered about how easy it had been to get Joan to agree to a trip to this strange, parched land. He wondered what had drawn him to this place, so very different from the grey wetness of England. He gave up wondering, knowing he wouldn't find an answer and just knew he had to be here for some reason – a reason that may or may not reveal itself. He also pondered how easily the whole trip had fallen into place and how at home he felt, right now.

They'd arrived in Alice Springs in the morning, off the train – the Ghan, they called it – and were taken to a hostel. There, they had immediately agreed to a five-day guided tour of Uluru, Kata Tjuta, Mt Connor and other sights in The Centre, as they called it. As they approached Uluru, the secondlargest monolith in the world, he smiled at the rising feeling of sweet joy. He had the strange feeling of returning home, somehow, and saw – superimposed over the sand, tough spinafex grass and gnarled mulga trees – groups of people hunting, as if he was one of the hunters, many eons ago. He knew this land, somehow – intimately, lovingly and respectfully.

Then, with a quiet smile, he realised it was the same scene that had played itself through his imagination the day his world turned over, the day he was asked to leave AIL and work at home. He remembered the day – the fifth of March, 2012.

They were helped with setting up their tent, in a circle of six tents, and were then taken for a short walk to watch the orange sun slide down behind Uluru as an apricot moon came up behind them. He sighed with relief to know it had not changed and then wondered how he could remember something he'd never known. He put his arm around Joan and she leaned into him, silently. They returned to a meal cooked over the camp fire and listened to stories of stars, aborigines and white people. They went to bed, remembering to take in their boots lest the dingos take them.

Arthur woke at five o'clock, bright eyed and his head full of words. He sneaked out of the tent with pen and pad and stood to take in the dark, limitless expanse about him and that uncomfortable, familiar stab went through him again. That lightning shock of a feeling of being trapped and bored and it sat there taunting him.

*How COULD it,* he thought with anger. *Right here? Right now?* As he fought the feeling, it grew and threatened to suffocate him. Then, just in time, he remembered the process. He relaxed, accepted the irksome feeling, sat with it, rode it. *For why*, he asked for the millionth time, *can I fight what is?*

As he relaxed into it, it softened. Its fire burned lower and dissipated and he watched the blood-red sun rise over the blood-red earth, as if his fire was the one rising before him, warming the world.

"G'day mate!"

He spun round and too fast, wobbling uncertainly, his sleep-weakened senses still warming up. Strong arms grabbed him. Stood him upright.

"Struth! You okay, mate?" asked the paunchy, Akubra-hatted fellow from one of the other six tents scattered among the spinifex grass.

"Aah, yes, I think so," stammered Arthur, adjusting his spectacles. He still hadn't become used to people greeting him without being properly introduced.

"You a long way from home, by the looks."

Unsure if that was a question or a statement, he decided to blunder into conversation like others seemed to do.

"Yes, a long story, I'm afraid," he said as his legs finally took charge of themselves and he smiled weakly.

"Plenty of time for stories out here. Plenty of time for everything." The man swiped at flies on his bare legs and Arthur surmised his long trousers were out of place here.

"Look," he said, his mind finally making itself up. "I just need a little time to sit and think. And to write."

"Wow, you a writer?"

"Not yet but who knows," he said with an unaccustomed chuckle.

"Righto. See you at breakfast over tea and damper, mate." As the man strode off, Arthur wondered what damper was. In this dry heat, nothing was damp.

He sat on a log next to last night's burnt out fire. Between the rising sun and the massive shape of Uluru, he breathed in the early morning desert air, warm and still, and closed his eyes in dreaming. He looked through the bars, into the prison of his old life and wondered, with a small shudder, how he'd been able to put up with such unrelenting drudgery and sameness for so long. There were no regrets for he now knew he was free, had always been free, to create the story of his life in an y way he wished to write it. He opened his eyes in gratitude and succumbed to the voice of the story that had been calling him to write since sitting on a park bench in Croydon on the fifth of March, 2012.

He started writing ...

*The map of Arthur Bayly's life was a narrow one and, like a child in a cot of steel, can only dream of another life. He awoke from his fitful sleep at 6:30am with his usual sense of foreboding and wondered, again, how it was ever possible to feel elated about the day, about life. Apparently, some people did ...*

Arthur's phone screamed in the desert silence and he wished he'd left it off and in his tent. He quickly scrabbled for it and saw an unknown number.

"Hey, mate, I got your number from Superintendent Hopkins from Scotland Yard," said the Australian – or was it New Zealander – voice. "I hope it's okay to call you."

"Aah, yes, who is this?" asked Arthur, his mind emerging from the peace he'd previously been ensconced in.

"Oh sorry, mate, it's Greg. Greg Cousins. Remember me? The one who was shot at the hotel?"

"Aah, yes, Greg," he said, his mouth going as dry as the desert. "I remember Hemi telling us about you. We never found out what happened to you in all the fuss back then. It was all kept so quiet.

"I'm doing fine. I just wanted to catch up with you some time as we need to talk."

"We do? Aah, it will have to wait a couple of weeks though."

"Where are you?"

"Well, I'm not in England at the moment. We're actually down in Australia at Uluru."

"Well, while you're down that way, call into New Zealand, much more interesting than the red desert."

Joan

"Who was that on the phone?" asked Joan who was suddenly behind him.

"Ooh, you gave me a start, Joan!" said Arthur, his hand flying to his chest.

"Sorry, Arthur. Sorry."

"Aah, that was Greg Cousins. Remember him?"

"Yes, he attacked you in the street, stole the keys, made threats. Of course I remember him!"

"Yes, exactly. He seems very friendly, now."

"Of course. I suppose he wants something! I don't trust him."

"I don't know. He's alive and wants to meet up when we return. Well, he will just have to wait because we're here to enjoy life a little for a while. I do have to wonder what he has got to say, though ..."

*[You, Dear Reader, will find out, along with Arthur, what Greg Cousins has to say in the sequel to this book, The Last Expulsion.]*

# APPENDIX AND AFTERWORD

Since the federal government bailed out Bear Stearns in March 2008, the six largest U.S. banks and their main trade associations have paid roughly $600 million for lobbying activities, according to a report released by labour union SEIU and progressive political groups in May 2010. The financial industry spent an average of $1.4 million per day during the reform fight.

But the key to effective lobbying is getting into the upper room. Fortunately, it has a revolving door. In all, 243 lobbyists working for six big banks and their trade associations are former federal government employees, according to the report. Of these, 202 worked in Congress, mostly as aides to lawmakers, while the rest were in the White House, U.S. Treasury or another government agency. Goldman Sachs has the biggest team of "revolving door" lobbyists. Then it is Citigroup with 37 inhouse lobbyists and "outside consultants", followed by JPMorgan, Morgan Stanley, Wells Fargo and B of A.

Here, as summarized in the report, are some of the big banks' top lobbying guns:

Bank of America - B of A's in-house lobbyist team is headed by John Collingwood, formerly the FBI's congressional liaison and a top official under three different FBI directors. After retiring, he became a top lobbyist for credit card company MBNA and played a major role in passing the 2005 bankruptcy reform bill. When B of A bought MBNA, he became the bank's top lobbyist and brought other credit card lobbyists with him.

Citigroup - Head lobbyist Nick Calio was formerly a top congressional liaison for both George H.

W. Bush and George W. Bush. As the Republican arm of lobbying firm O'Brien-Calio during the Clinton administration, he was hired by big business to lead the lobbying fight over the North American Free-Trade Agreement, fast-track trade authority and expanded trade with China.

Goldman Sachs - Head lobbyist Faryar Shirzad joined the bank after serving as a top national security and international economics adviser to President Bush. He coordinated trade policy for the Bush-Cheney Transition Team in 2000 and was previously a top international trade adviser to the Senate Finance Committee.

JPMorgan Chase - The bank's top government relations executive and in-house lobbyist is William Daley, former Clinton official, brother of Chicago mayor Richard Daley and co-chair of President

Obama's inauguration. The bank's top registered lobbyist, Democratic insider Peter Scher, reports to Daley. Scher was a top Democratic staffer during the Clinton years, serving as chief of staff to Sen. Max Baucus, D-Mont., then to Secretary of Commerce Mickey Kantor.

Bruce Cathie first saw flying saucers over the Manukau harbour, NZ, in 1952. He has published several books, the first being *Harmonic 33*, which was published in New Zealand in 1968. Quentin Fogarty, an Australian TV reporter (and his cameraman, David Crockett) filmed flying saucers over New Zealand on 30th December 1978 and that was aired on Australia's Channel 10 network. New Zealand authorities refused to allow that programme to be shown in New Zealand.

### The story of the story becoming a podcast

This book has just been written as a screen-play, to be made in into a podcast and (hopefully) a film. This is how the podcast came about ...

I wrote and published this book in 2010. Then it asked for an upgrade ...

I used to work with Jeff as a business trainer and then I resigned, meaning we hadn't seen each other for eight months. In that time, he decided to give up the part-time training and move on to his greatest love. He'd worked in radio for all his life and decided to return to it with a modern twist – start a podcasting company, Brisbane Podcasting Centre ...

(http://brisbanepodcastingcentre.com.au/).

He started getting non-fiction clients – wine makers, coffee roasters, business sales, consultants – and then he heard that fiction was all the go. He knew that he knew someone who wrote fiction but his brain just couldn't lasso the name.

Two weeks later, in a café, he suddenly remembered the name – Philip Bradbury! Two minutes later, I (Philip Bradbury) walked into that self-same café!

In that happily serendipitous moment our podcast adventure began, somewhere in October 2019.

We recorded some of my short stories, with me reading them. A simple exercise and a good way to start an increasingly complex process.

Then, in another café not far away, I later met with another friend and he explained how to turn audio/podcasts into video. I had a play and four videos appeared on my brand new Youtube channel and on my website.

In the meantime, Jeff was going to podcasting conferences and doing a huge amount of research into this new (for both of us) medium. Through that he met Hollywood's top sound man, Stuart, who had just sold his massive company to his son in New York and had decided to retire in Brisbane, our city! Wow, what contacts, expertise and encouragement he lent our fledgling scheme!

Jeff was insistent that we do a full production treatment of my book's podcast – a cast of thousands, all the background sounds of London buses and trains, café noises, running feet and so on. Well, perhaps not thousands, but a group of actors to give voice to the 42 characters in the book ... I just counted them!

Because of this, I had to rewrite the book as a screen play and it was a format and skill I was out of my depth in. I pushed myself to do it but, somehow, it was just too hard. I was overwhelmed and felt like giving up. Jeff couldn't understand why I was having trouble with it. After all, I had written 18 books so what was so hard about writing the same one in a different way? Then Stuart explained to Jeff that, if I'd written the book, I'd be unlikely to be able to write the screen play – they are such different applications.

We stopped, rethought and, the next day, we fell upon a website that helps you turn your novel into a movie script. We were away again!

We've found the actors needed, we've recorded sounds in cafes, trains, roadsides, offices and have all that background sound ready.

Jeff typed the book into the screen writing program as eight episodes, with all the directions required for a movie, and I'm currently editing them all. Our big, hairy goal is to have the book taken up as a movie so, while we're doing the podcast, we're acting as if it's really a movie, while we continue to look for people and opportunities to have it made into a movie.

So that's where we're up to at the moment – editing is continuing, actors are on standby, sound technicians and website people are being engaged, opportunities are being sought for funding and sponsorship and destiny is leading us in it's sweet way, day by day.

I'll keep you updated on further progress as it presents itself. if you'd like to follow me on my Facebook page at https://bit.ly/34bzdr4

**Maori words used**
Aroha Love
Aroha mai Sorry
Atua God
Awa River

Irirangi  Voice

Iwi      Tribe

Kai      Food

Kia ora  Literally, it means *to life*. It's used for hello, goodbye, thank you and other friendly greetings.

Korero   Talk, a story

Koro     Old (wise) man

Maunga Mountain

   Ngati Wikitoria The tribe of Queen Victoria, English people

Tangata  Person - usually person at the head of a family

Taonga   Gift

Tapu     Sacred

Waihine Woman

Waka     Boat, canoe

Wera     Hot

Whanau Family

   In Maori, plural is denoted by nga at the start of a word. For example, tangata is person. Ngatangata is people.

**Aboriginal words used**

   Kata Tjuta Literally, it means *standing heads* - there are 12 standing heads, or massive rocks - and it was a men-only place for the Aborigines. The place is also called The Olgas, named after Queen Olga of the Netherlands.

   Uluru Ayers Rock, the largest lump of rusting iron in the world, the rust accounting for its reddish colour.

# Expulsion

*An excerpt from the 2^nd^ in **The Last** series*

Feeling as cold and lonely as the last bus home in the rain, I started packing my desk up. I knew I'd never see it or anything else in this familiar office again. What do I keep and what do I take? There would be no chance to come back for anything; once I was out the door, I would never be back. When one door shuts, another is supposed to open. Today, however, only the sound was of of slamming doors in my soul.

I shook my head, hoping the world would turn back into the one I was used to, but it just hurt my head and everything was still upside down. I was the only one who seemed to notice. There they were, dozens of heads on shoulders, staring at computer screens just like they always did. They controlled the world with their little buttons, and my world was out of control. I had just been deprived of my little buttons and my screen to a world concocted by Microsoft, Mozilla and Money, as well as the desk on which they sat, along with my comfortable executive chair. They had divorced me … no, I had just been told that they were leaving me because I had been unfaithful. I had proudly blogged to six followers that I had a job at Empire Bank Ltd and, since banks were all about secrecy, that was forbidden. A naïve, country boy in a suspicious city.

I shook my head again, but the vast office was still filled with ordinary people doing an ordinary job on an ordinary British day, and no one noticed my shaking head. I was not at the CIA or MI5. Nope, no badges or guns or secret agent stuff about me I confirmed as I patted myself. Just an ordinary pin-stripe suit as befits a bank's corporate trainer.

I shook my head as I couldn't think of a more useful thing to do. I smiled but the rest of my body couldn't respond to a mind that refused to start.

"You alright, mate?" asked Martin.

What do you say to a question like that? I'm fine, Martin. I've just been sacked for being thrilled to be working in this great place—the job of my dreams. And everyone else thinks it's okay, doesn't care or doesn't know. If I start thinking about it anymore, I'm going to get bloody nasty, punch your stupid pink face in and burn this lousy place down. Probably best not to say that. I could feel my anger rising as my mind went into first gear. I stopped it going into second for fear of the consequences. I quelled the revving motor inside and tried to think of an answer that had nothing to do with my twisted reality but would suit the other world in which ordinary, employed people live.

"Yeah fine, Martin. Just great," was the best lie I could dredge up.

Every year of my life was leaping into my face, demanding explanation for this sudden turn of events.

"All these years at university – wasted!" hissed my twenty-three-year-old self, vehemently.

"Yeah but I was only …"

"And all that time as an accountant and business coach," whispered my thirty-three-year-old self, sadly, interrupting my reply.

"But it wasn't all wasted …"

"Not wasted? Not bloody wasted?" demanded my thirty-nine-year-old self, menacingly.

"Well, no, and I didn't know …"

"Didn't know? Didn't know, he says!" shouted my forty-year-old self into my echoing brain as I tried to concentrate on clearing my desk and computer under Martin's watchful eye. "You always loved to break the rules!"

"But they didn't explain them properly …"

"Explain them properly? You never ruddy listened," interrupted my twelve-year-old self in my cranium, sounding suspiciously like my father.

"But it was only a family blog, easy to delete …"

"Family blog? It was a blog, dumb arse! Blog equals the whole wide world," offered my thirty sixyear-old self (from last year), helpfully.

"But ... an innocent mistake ... I just wanted to tell my friends how proud I was of this job ..."

"So proud you get turfed out," said my twenty-two-year-old self with vague strains of my mother in its voice. "Oh hell, I didn't mean to stuff it up ..."

"You okay, mate?" asked Martin hesitantly, a real voice interrupting my inner rant as I said goodbye to my desk.

"Ooh, aah, yeah ... well, not really," I said, quickly returning to the tangible world as I turned and we set off, the bank's green carpet passing beneath my black business shoes. We walked shoulder to shoulder past desk after desk after desk, all containing heads-down-pretending-to-be-working inhabitants.

"Damnably awkward," said Martin helpfully, perhaps afraid of the silence that had descended in this massive acreage of office.

"Awkward? Bloody unnecessary, actually," I said, louder than I'd meant. A bout of sniggers burst around us and was quickly quelled by Martin's withering look at the red faces.

"Just keep it civil, old chap, huh," he whispered as we neared the double doors; one of several double doors my security card opened – the card that was now safely deposited back in the HR department's custody ... the security card I would never see again.

"Look, thanks Martin, I can make my own way out from here. You go back to work if you like," I suggested as we neared the stairs and lifts.

"Thanks Greg, but I need to take you to ... aah, go with you to reception," he said as we strode past the lift doors to the stairs. Easier to be walking down stairs, doing something, than standing together in a lift, mutely and mutually embarrassed.

"To make sure I don't make off with the crown jewels, huh?" I said lightly. He smiled wanly. "Look Martin, I know it's not your fault, mate," I said as our shoes clattered down the stairs, echoing round the fourteen-storey chasm. I stopped, wanting to console him. Wanting to ... I don't know ... perhaps taking in a few last mental snapshots for the family album.

"Come on, we need to keep moving. The cameras cover the stairs too, you know."

"Cameras? What? Oh, security. Yeah," I said as my mind struggled to rise above the tide waters of embarrassment, fear and anger, to the logical things of life and take in one more useless detail. I looked round, one more quick snapshot, and started down again, looking furtively at Martin's stoic, inscrutable face. The poor sod, I thought, twenty years in the same job, his daily three-hour commute by car, bus and two trains, and the same again in the opposite order, every night because of his wife's part-time psychic/palm reading business. He might wear the pin-stripe trousers, but he didn't crack any whips in his household.

Four flights of stairs is one heck of a long way when you really don't want to go, when no one's talking, when you're pretending to the business-suited athletes going up that it's just another day, when you're on a mission to hell. Caught between the equally tempting bouts of self-pity and self-righteous anger, I kept my mouth shut and my brain in neutral.

"Hey, aah, you had breakfast?" asked Martin as we reached the double doors at the bottom. He held his plastic badge up to release them.

"What? Breakfast?" My brain struggled to find somewhere relevant to file this unexpected question. "Yeah, breakfast, you had it? You need a cup of tea?"

"Oh, right, yeah, had breakfast but could murder a coffee." I realised, with frightening slowness, he was offering friendship. I appreciated the gesture and also saw him as part of the enemy, the bastard employer that didn't care a toss about employees. I didn't know whether to hug him or slug him. I could easily have done both.

"Coffee? Aah, yes, you Kiwis prefer your coffee, don't you," said Martin. I sneaked a look – so he wouldn't see me looking – at his lopsided grin.

Poor bugger, I thought, so easy to embarrass.

"You shouting?" I asked with more bravado than I felt, not expecting him to accede and do something he'd never done before – have a chat out of the office with anyone he worked with. Twenty years in this place and neither he nor anyone else in the office knew much about anyone else's social or family life. The English way, you know.

"Shouting? Oh, you mean buying? Buying coffee? Yes, well, of course." I could feel the heat of his embarrassment from here.

"You sure it's okay?" I asked as we approached the high reception desk, the last blockade. "You know, fraternising with the enemy. Shouldn't you really go back to work?"

"Probably not okay at all, old chap," he said stopping and looking me in the eye for the first time today. "But I need ... aah, some air, a cup of tea, something. Dash it all, Greg, I'll see you off the premises and we'll have that cuppa, that coffee, what."

"Only if you're shouting," I said punching him lightly on his pin-striped shoulder.

"Ooh, perhaps you shouldn't do that. Cameras you know ..."

"Ah, yes, sacked employee apprehended for grievous bodily harm to boss." I tried to stifle a giggle but the giggle won. "Hi Penny, I've just been sacked and so I think I have to sign something on my way out."

"Yes sir, this here," said Penny, the receptionist, pointing to a form without changing her plastic welcoming expression. As I went to sign the register, I noticed a folded piece of paper there. I picked it up to hand it to Penny. She looked fleetingly at Martin and then frowned at me, her hand going in and out of her jacket pocket. "Somebody must have left ..."

"Sir," she said, her frown deepening as she shook her head imperceptibly. "If you would just sign the register, please." "But there's ..."

"Sir, the register, please," she hissed, looking quickly at Martin again. He'd wandered away a little and she mimed stuffing something into her pocket again. I smiled sheepishly, signed the register and slipped the paper into my pocket. She smiled broadly, nodding happily. Feeling the prickly heat of embarrassment – and a little curiosity – I thanked her and turned to Martin with the wildly stupid

feeling I'd lost control of my life ... or that I'd never had it. And I wondered what was on the note in my pocket.

# ABOUT THE AUTHOR

In New Zealand I experienced life as an accountant, credit manager, company director, shepherd, scrub-cutter, tree pruner, freezing worker, plastics factory worker, saxophonist, army driver, tour bus driver, stage and television actor and singer, builder, lecturer, facilitator for men's groups, reporter, columnist, magazine editor, publisher, writer ...

In South Africa as an AIDS workshop co-facilitator ...

In the Australian bush as a barman, horse and camel trekker and stock-whip teacher ...

In England as a contract accountant, corporate trainer, estate manager, lecturer, singer/songwriter, website editor/writer and freelance writer ...

Now that I'm back in Australia, house renovating, teaching and writing, I'm wondering what's next!

The constant for me is *A Course in Miracles*, a psychological life-style course in forgiveness. Through it I have found the peace I had always been searching for - the journey to where we have always been.

**Philip J Bradbury in social media**

*Website*: www.philipjbradbury.com[1]

*Website*: www.writethatbooknow.com[2]

*Wordpress blogs:*

https://pjbradbury.wordpress.com/

*Facebook*: https://www.facebook.com/AuthorPhilipJBradbury/

*Linked In* - http://bit.ly/2aTzZMS

*Smashwords*: http://bit.ly/2aNjkic

*Twitter*: https://twitter.com/PhilipJBradbury

---

1.  http://www.philipjbradbury.com

2.  http://www.writethatbooknow.com

# MORE BOOKS BY PHILIP J BRADBURY

*Non-Fiction*

Whose Life Is It Anyway?

Life Rejuvenated

Write That Book Now

Change Your Life, Change Your World

The Twelve Week Miracle (with Anna Bradbury)

*Some-Fiction*

53 SMILES

97 SMILES

Dactionary - a dictionary with attitude

*Fiction*

My Whispering Teachers

Circles of Gold

Gerald the Great of Gorokoland The Meaning of Larf

For more information on these books, see www.philipjbradbury.com

◇ *Philip J Bradbury*

Did you love *The Last Stand Down*? Then you should read *My Whispering Teachers*[1] by Philip J Bradbury!

We're a story-telling lot, us humans.

Sometimes it's an earnest actor in a white lab-coat or a black suit, trying to convince us that his toxic fluoride toothpaste is good for our health or that his party's million-dollar spend on weapons is for peace. And they do it with such a straight face!

Sometimes the story's presented with a chuckle and we know another fiction is on the way: "did you hear the one about ..."

And, sometimes, just sometimes, there's a story parading as nought but itself – a clear fiction – and you're in it. The real, non-fictional you. That's why the authentically fictional stories – fables, proverbs, legends – outlast us all and are told down the centuries ... we're in them; parading our best and worst, our most silly and most sublime. The universality of stories is the unity of humans. We're all strangely, uniquely alike and we can all see – if we so choose – our reality in the unreality we closet ourselves with round the fireside, in schools, churches and pubs and in our quiet, solo moments.

Stories are the comforters we carry in our hearts and minds and our own particular stories are the way we initiate and create friendships and relationships.

These stories, my friend, are my offering of friendship and may they provide balance, smiles, tears and insight when no other exist for you.

What do you remember from childhood? The myriad facts that become daily obsolete or the stories – prose, poetic and lyrical – you were told?

My friend, Faisal, is Somalian and he tells me there is no written Somali language. Their history, rituals and roots are written on the tongues of the elders and passed down the hundreds of generations by verbal stories. We who write facts down, forget what happened last week while those with just stories never forget. Stories are how we remember Truth for, while "truths" of scientists change by the month, the Truths of who we are and how we serve each other never change. Goodness and mercy are ever the same as are the battles of good and evil, the anguish and triumph of humans and simple fallibility and strength we have.

---

1. https://books2read.com/u/bzL1YE

2. https://books2read.com/u/bzL1YE

The stories here are the stories of old with refreshing new garb, with unique wit and insight and surprise endings.

These are the stories of you and me – what we are and what we can be – and they can be passed down to your grandchildren so they remember who they are and who you were.

Stories outlast us and are told down the centuries because we're in them, parading our best and worst. We're all strangely, uniquely alike and can see – if we choose – our reality in the unreality we closet ourselves with round the fireside, in schools, churches and pubs and in our quieter moments.

Stories are the comforters for our hearts and minds and our own particular stories are the way we initiate and create friendships and relationships.

This story is my offering of friendship and may it provide insight when no other exists for you.

Read more at https://philipjbradbury.com/.

# About the Author

In New Zealand I experienced life as an accountant, credit manager, company director, shepherd, scrub-cutter, tree pruner, freezing worker, plastics factory worker, saxophonist, army driver, tour bus driver, stage and television actor and singer, builder, lecturer, facilitator for men's groups, reporter, columnist, magazine editor, publisher, writer ...

In South Africa as an AIDS workshop co-facilitator ...

In the Australian bush as a barman, horse and camel trekker and stock-whip teacher ...

In England as a contract accountant, corporate trainer, estate manager, lecturer, singer/songwriter, website editor/writer and freelance writer ...

Back in Australia, house renovating, teaching, writing and website building.

My constant is *A Course in Miracles*, a psychological life-style course in forgiveness. Through it I have found the peace I had always been searching for – the journey to where we have always been.

Read more at https://philipjbradbury.com/store/.